Victoria Routledge worked in publishing for three years before her first novel, *Friends Like These*, was published. She was born in the Lake District and now lives in London, and writes full time as a novelist and a journalist. She is the author of *Friends Like These*, *Kiss Him Goodbye*, *. . . And For Starters* and *Swansong*.

Praise for *Constance & Faith*

'The story of a colourful town and a cast of strong women . . . deeply satisfying' *Good Book Guide*

'Tender and moving' *Eve*

'A fat, plot-rich novel . . . a diverting fable about daring to look back' *Daily Mail*

'A beautifully woven tale of tangled lives and dark family secrets. It's our book of the year so far' *Company*

Also by Victoria Routledge

Friends Like These
Kiss Him Goodbye
. . . And For Starters
Swansong

CONSTANCE
& FAITH

VICTORIA ROUTLEDGE

POCKET
BOOKS

LONDON • SYDNEY • NEW YORK • TORONTO

First published in Great Britain by Simon & Schuster UK Ltd, 2004
This edition published by Pocket Books, 2005
An imprint of Simon & Schuster
A Viacom company

1 3 5 7 9 10 8 6 4 2

Simon & Schuster UK Ltd
Africa House
64–78 Kingsway
London WC2B 6AH

www.simonsays.co.uk

Simon & Schuster Australia
Sydney

A CIP catalogue record for this book
is available from the British Library

ISBN 0-7434-1520-5
EAN 9780743415200

Printed and bound in Great Britain by
Bookmarque Ltd, Croydon, Surrey

For James Hale

Chapter One

The first thing Hannah did after she heaved her bag off the train was to walk to the dark-panelled kiosk at the station gate where, out of habit, she bought a Mars bar and a packet of Marlboro Lights. Even though she still didn't smoke, and didn't really want a Mars bar.

It was a minor transgression by most teenage standards, but was about as much as she had been able to summon up in the old days. Both items were banned in the Marshall household. It was a long time since anyone had looked askance at her for buying cigarettes, and quite a while since she'd actually smoked, but while she was standing at the kiosk on Linton station, for the first time in years, some impulse made the gesture for her. A token sacrifice to the small-town life of limits and expectations she was meant to have left behind. For ever.

'Hello, Hannah,' said Mrs Armstrong, sniffing pointedly as she handed over the change, all in small coins.

Hannah looked up and did a double-take. Mrs Armstrong had seemed on the verge of senility the first time she'd sneaked a forbidden Mars bar. That had been about twenty years ago. But then again, she conceded, a polite smile appearing automatically despite her dark mood, in a town run largely by a hierarchy of impossibly old women, it wasn't so surprising to find her still there, selling newspapers and gathering gossip as if time couldn't touch her.

Mrs Armstrong and Old Mrs Armstrong had supplied travel requisites to Linton station for about a hundred years, and would probably continue to do so until the town council closed them down for their unhygienic storage arrangements. Or until the council stopped being run by their extended family and sundry cronies.

'Hello, Mrs Armstrong,' Hannah replied, and any lingering confidence that she might have mustered up vanished as her cold fingers closed round the packet of cigarettes.

Mrs Armstrong sniffed again. 'London habit, I suppose.'

'I'm sorry?' Hannah realized too late that 'I'm sorry?' was also a London habit. What she should have said was 'What?'

'Smoking. Never had you down as a smoker, Hannah. Clever girl like you. It's a very unpleasant habit. Does your mother know you smoke?'

Hannah stared with some disbelief at the old woman, who now pursed her lips in reprimand. Talk about selective-memory syndrome. Buying cigarettes at the station kiosk had been her one and only form of underage teenage rebellion. The small matter of Mrs Armstrong's roaring trade in supplying packets of ten Bensons to the town's cash-strapped adolescents seemed conveniently to have slipped her mind.

Had Hannah been in London, she would have snapped out a sarcastic retort, but here some invisible curb stopped her saying anything, much to her dismay. Ten years of glorious independence down the drain, she thought, with a shudder; straight back to meek

Hannah Marshall, golden girl and conscientious upholder of adult expectations.

'Um, no,' she said, instead. 'Well, I don't smoke, not really. Only in times of stress.'

The plucked eyebrows rose and fell in silent challenge, taking in Hannah's bulging flight bag propped up against the wall. As was the way with local old ladies, the question was not framed verbally. It was there, though.

Oh, God, thought Hannah, trying to stuff the change into her purse. The small pleasure she'd taken in walking through the dark and Gothically crenellated station – as a non-resident, at last – ebbed away, and was replaced by the realization that although you could leave Linton it never left you.

'Waiting for your mother, are you?' Mrs Armstrong went on, pretending to rearrange the women's weekly mags. 'You'll not be getting a taxi for a while. They've all just met the other train.'

Unless there had been a taxi revolution since her last visit, Hannah knew there were three cabs in the whole town, but she didn't miss the implication that a vast cab rank had only this second dispersed, and if you were daft enough to fork out good money for one (or were an off-comer), you'd have to wait.

Mrs Armstrong was waiting for an answer, her hands poised over *Take A Break*.

'Yes, she's picking me up.' Hannah looked out to the car park but there was no sign of Fran's Saab. Three teenagers were kicking a tennis ball against a decorative cast-iron bollard in a resigned manner, and an empty Shopper Hopper bus waited opposite the supermarket for the return journey around the local villages.

'I'd say she'd be late, the amount she's got on her plate right now. That'd be why you're back, I'd say,' Mrs Armstrong probed expertly. 'Bit of family support, is it?'

'Not exactly.' Hannah – to her horror – squirmed and blushed, first at the implicit criticism that she'd come back to help her mother (when she hadn't), second that her mother was suffering from some crisis she didn't even know about (so what was new?), and third because her total inability to 'sort things out' was precisely the reason she was back here in the first place, her continuing reputation as Linton's sole over-achiever notwithstanding. 'Not . . . Well, no. It's . . .'

She could tell Mrs Armstrong was waiting for her to say something calm and confident. But she couldn't. That's what the London Hannah would have done. However, the current Hannah, despite her much-vaunted successes, had come to the end of the line of her five-year-plan and had found nothing there. Nothing to tell her who she was when no one was looking or expecting her to jump. No reassuring voice when she woke up alone, damp with panicky night sweats and paralysed with fear at the blankness stretching out in front of her. And that, in short, was why she was back in the claustrophobic little Linton world she knew only too well, where she at least knew what she was meant to do and say, even if it didn't really amount to very much.

I don't have to tell her any of this, Hannah told herself, with the last vestiges of her normal attitude. I can just walk away and eat my Mars bar in peace. *I don't live here any more.* Yet despite the ostentatious way in which Mrs Armstrong's wrinkly hands were smoothing out the local papers, Hannah could tell she was processing these flakes of information into a rich and satisfying drama. Hannah's family and its 'carryings on' had been a gossip mainstay in Linton for the past seventy-odd years, and her unexpected return with a large bag – *and on the train* – probably looked like an unexpected gift to Mrs Armstrong. It would be telegraphed around the WI circuit before the end of the evening, in lurid, if unspecific, detail:

Local Girl Made Good Goes Bad.
No Car Or Man Despite Posh Job.
Her Life Packed Into One Real Leather Overnight Bag.

Mrs Armstrong was observing her through narrowed eyes, as if she could be read like a tea cup full of leaves.

'I'll, er . . . have to get going, now,' Hannah said firmly, and picked up her bag, shoving the cigarettes into the front pocket. She couldn't decide which annoyed her more: still having the impulse to buy cigarettes she didn't want, or still feeling guilty about doing it.

Conscious of Mrs Armstrong's gaze boring into her back – probably assessing the impracticality of her fancy shoes for the puddle-ridden station – Hannah walked to the far side of the waiting room and settled herself on a black cast-iron bench, well out of conversational range. She stuffed a jumper into the small of her back, which ached from the long train journey, and put her feet up while she waited for her mother's car to appear in the station car park.

Five minutes later, she lit a cigarette and smoked it inexpertly.

The long windows of the waiting room, kept scrupulously clean by the town council maintenance quango, offered a grand view of the main quay, empty this afternoon apart from a few lone yachts and two fishing trawlers laid up for repairs.

There had always been a harbour in Linton, first for the Romans, who had mined the red iron ore out in the fells, and used the tiny settlement as a supply point for their northern defence legions. They had shivered to death at the furthest reaches of the Roman Empire, sustained only by the strong local beer and the fading dream of a place where it didn't rain continuously, day in, day out.

After the Romans had left, defeated by the weather and the truculence of the natives, little happened for centuries, until the coal seams opened their rich veins to local landowners, like the wealthy Musgraves, whose splendid villa overlooked Hannah's own family house, Rose View. Coal brought shipping, and shipping brought trade from all over the world, as Linton sent coal first to Ireland, then America and further afield; business filled the town with merchants and lawyers, smart houses and shops, ambition and aspiration, and a few fortunate local landowners grew as rich as the Manchester cotton barons on the apparently inexhaustible supply of coal beneath the town's newly laid squares and parks. Linton was a glittering jewellery casket, an anomaly of style and riches on the otherwise grey and hard-bitten north-west coast.

The only curious side-effect of Linton's wealth and success – or its price, as the harbingers of doom had it – was the unusually short lifespan of the male inhabitants. The Romans had lost more soldiers than they expected, even taking into account the terrible weather and strange food, and so it had gone on: within living memory, the First World War carried away hundreds, a pit disaster fifteen years later buried a decent rugby team and all their mates, the Second World War took their sons, and a fire in the boys' school in the fifties killed sixty young lads and forced the town council to bow to co-education after all.

The harbour on to which Hannah looked out was no different in structure from what it had been in its heyday, but the spirit was gone: now it was little more than a shell, the empty stage-set of a bustling harbour. The end had come quickly for Linton, crushed by the advent of cheaper coal from elsewhere, which in turn crippled its trade links. As roads and rail took over from shipping, its isolation became its downfall, and slowly the wealth had ebbed away, along with the cream of Linton's youth, leaving a small-to-middling market town with unusually smart architecture and an odd native chippiness, fed by indistinct folk memories of lost splendour.

Hannah's eyes ranged across the wide arms of the harbour walls, taking in its generous sweep and ambitious design. Tall street-lamps spiked up into the grey sky along the quayside like spears of lavender, topped off now and again with a seagull. In Linton they were freakishly huge, big enough to scoop up unattended toddlers, fattened on the fishing trawlers that still came in and out. Nothing in Linton was small or delicate, unless it was specifically designed that way to illustrate the sturdiness of something else – a trait that applied equally to the residents.

As Hannah watched the boats float gently up and down on the tide, while the gulls cawed and circled overhead, she was flooded by an unexpected certainty that she'd been right to come back – a certainty as sudden and absolute as the one that had told her to get out and far, far away about ten years previously.

It wasn't an altogether reassuring feeling.

While the grey clouds moved ominously across the sky, she was simultaneously depressed and soothed by the fact that the panorama stretching down the hill towards the harbour hadn't changed since she had last sat on the station platform – the day she'd moved to London. If anything, it had got cleaner. The Linton in her mind was always scruffy and sullen, with scabbing paint and a sky permanently on the verge of drizzle, but from up here the long rows of townhouses looked stately, almost elegant. They had been repainted, with lottery heritage money, in their original sugared-almond pinks and lilacs.

Hannah frowned. Surely everything was meant to feel *smaller* when you came back to your home town. And dingier. That was what most of her university friends had thought – they couldn't wait to leave their anonymous suburban dormitories and discover cities where things really happened and the shops changed their stock once a month.

At first Hannah had felt like that – or thought she did. Initially she'd been glad to escape from Linton's old-woman gossip net of information that stretched over everyone, holding you in, limiting your possibilities, but after a few years of London's blunting anonymity, she had realized she missed it. She missed the town as much, if not more than, she missed her mother and grandmother.

She missed the dilapidated Georgian squares, where window boxes of rambling geraniums disguised flaking old paint; she dreamed about the proud arms of the empty harbour where now only iron bollards were left to show where the trade ships had crowded to unload their sugar, rum and spices. There was a sort of imperious shabbiness about Linton, a sense of once having been worth something, that she couldn't find in the rushing self-regeneration of the big city. The town's own history seemed to walk through the streets for her, haunting the place where it had died, and appearing only to those who cared enough to see it.

It had never been enough to make her want to go back, though. Much as she loved the place, there were ghosts she didn't want to deal with in Linton, ghosts that made the anonymity of London seem comforting. Flying visits at Christmas, supplemented by weekly phone calls home, were as close as she'd wanted to get.

Yet here I am, she thought wryly, and unwrapped her Mars bar.

The afternoon train (southbound) arrived, and twenty or so people shuffled off with carrier-bags from the bigger chain stores further up the coast. No one took any notice of Hannah, or showed any sign of appreciating the architectural triumphs above and around them.

Hannah had done extensive school projects about the station, which had been built when Linton was still a destination rather than a backwater. Now it stood incongruously on top of the hill, between a DIY superstore and an Iceland freezer centre, looking as if a freak storm had blown Bristol Temple Meads about two hundred miles north. During the prosperous years of the 1860s, when coal and imports still fed the town's economy, canny local businesses, keen to grab the attention of the potential spenders pouring out of the carriages, had designed and built a cathedral to the town's industrial heart; no expense had been spared in impressing local industry's skills on the visitor, while dirtier goods were carted away from a branch line a mile down the road.

Mrs Armstrong's news kiosk was typical of the interior – dark, carved wood, with Tudorbethan embellishments and enamelled Lancastrian roses discreetly revealing it to be the work of Wm Lowther & Sons, the town's joiners and undertakers of choice.

The huge wrought-iron roof beams stretching across the ticket hall were pierced with decorative stars and flowers, through which the light from the huge glass domes still sent pinpricks of sunshine on to the stone flags below. Winter after winter, the boilers in the corner roared away in the waiting room, reminding the sweating passenger of the town's inexhaustible coal seams, not to mention the infallible and modern designs of Hartley's Plumbers and Structural Engineers Ltd.

Beneath the grey stone flooring, according to another plaque, there was storage for a thousand barrels of Cumberland light ale from the Linton Brewery Company. The elaborate lavatorial system was also fully sponsored – plaques screwed in at eye-level, of course – by Jos. Jordan. The modern paintwork had scuffed and blistered from the attentions of several generations of bored teenagers and many of the businesses had folded and gone, but the advertising plaques on the walls remained. The town had built its station in its own style: stout and hard-wearing.

Sadly for Tyson's Tea Importers and Traders, there was no use now for the frescoed tea-room, whose fading hand-painted murals of 'modern ladies' in cloches now looked down on nothing more convivial than a cluttered selection of municipal gardening equipment. Since the late sixties the motorway that ran like a spinal cord up the back of the county had starved the station of tourist trade, but even with the rail services up and down the coast reduced to five times a day each way, the town council (led by Mrs Armstrong's granddaughter) still tended the bright hanging baskets of hardy annuals along the platform as fiercely as a temple flame.

Hannah bit off a chunk of Mars bar and gazed into the echoing chasm of the ticket hall, hoping it would stop her looking at her mobile phone for messages. She didn't know which was worse: messages or no messages. Some time ago, she had changed Toby's details to read 'No one' when he called so she could hang up with dignity intact. So far No one hadn't called. She attempted to distract herself with her old trick of counting the destinations on the pillars, but it wasn't a distraction any more, since someone (more development money) had regilded them.

At least, the ones within reach had been regilded. The list of locations carved on the thick pillars stood out, traces of gold paint glittering vaguely in the etching higher up. Rather than suggesting them as trips a Lintonian could make out of the area, Hannah had always felt that the implication was more of those places coming *to* Linton, the solid hub around which the rest of the world revolved. Which was an incredible assumption for a relatively small northern town but somehow not out of character. Maybe this had occurred to the restorer: Manchester and London were both bullishly retouched, even though they were at the top of the pillar nearest her.

Hannah was struck by the unsettling mental image of run-down Linton coming back to life again, bursting with colour and refurbishment, just as she was slinking back, defeated.

There were no little stars of sunlight on the stone flags this afternoon, since the sky above was grey and sunless. As Hannah turned her attention back to the harbour and began to count the cars toiling up the hill towards the big Tesco, she noted that at least it wasn't raining. Most of her childhood memories involved storms, or floods, or wellington boots, or being cold and wet in some peripheral way.

Hannah smiled wryly. Maybe it was a good omen.

Then the droplets started to fleck the window.

By the time she spotted Fran's Saab edging into the car park, taking a wide line round an abandoned shopping trolley, it was pouring down: 'stair-rods', as the local phrase went.

Evidently Fran Marshall wasn't taking the risk of aqua-planing. She was a careful driver, unlike her mother and her daughter. Hannah knew she didn't believe in the car as the future of transport, and it showed in her mistrustful attitude to steering and acceleration.

She got up and waited for her mother to make her way round to the entrance. She made a point of standing where Mrs Armstrong couldn't see her, or take notes about their mother-and-child reunion. Mrs Armstrong knew as well as she did how long it had been since she'd been home. Everyone in the town probably did.

Fran stalled – or parked, it was hard to say which – and got out of the car. She was wearing her black court suit and seemed bonier than ever, like a ruffled magpie.

Hannah's mouth went dry and she swallowed. She hadn't planned how this part would go. 'Hi, Mum,' she said awkwardly, and went to put her bag in the back of the car before Fran could hug her. The Marshalls had never been a huggy family and she knew that she was a bit smelly after the long journey – which her mother would be sure to point out.

Fran muttered something Hannah didn't hear and pushed behind her ears the dark licks of hair that hung in her eyes. Maybe Mrs Armstrong had been right, Hannah thought, squinting to see her mother's face: on closer inspection, she was looking rather preoccupied. But no more so than usual. Fran's natural expression was of extreme concern – about the ozone layer or the plight of refugees or the state of the roof of her house.

As Hannah hoisted her bag into the car, she noticed, with a sinking heart, that the back seat was covered with packets of Bourbon biscuits and custard creams. That, and the preoccupied expression, had meant one of two things in the past: a coffee morning, either to discuss some action group or helpline, if run by her mother, or a gathering of old women to discuss knitting or gossip, if run by her grandmother, Dora.

'*Hello*, Mum,' she said again, with more emphasis.

'Oh, sorry. Hello, love,' said Fran.

Hannah deduced that she'd been in court all day. Her white shirt had a small coffee stain on the front, and her hair was sticking up because she had jammed her hands into it repeatedly – Fran's favourite non-verbal expression of despair with humanity.

'Have you read *Tristram Shandy*?' she asked. 'What's it about? You must have read it at college. I read in a crib that it was about the uncertainty of human memory, but it can't be all about that.' She fiddled nervously with a cameo on her lapel while Hannah tried to close the boot. Accessories didn't come easily to Fran.

'No, I haven't, actually,' said Hannah. *Really*. 'Not really. But thanks for asking. Are you well? Is Granny well? Yes, it's lovely to see you after all this time.'

Fran bit her thin lip. 'Yes, yes, it's lovely to see you. That goes without saying. Oh, damn. Are you *sure* you didn't read it at college?'

'Yes, I am. Positive.' Hannah got into the passenger seat. A small voice reminded her that she did, in fact, own a condensed classics book, which included sufficient salient details to feign casual familiarity. But she ignored it.

'Did Dominic read it for A-level?'

'How the hell would I know?' demanded Hannah. This wasn't

going the way she'd imagined it would. Most mothers would greet a long-absent daughter with tears, hugs or recriminations. Apologies, even. Not a bloody reading list.

She didn't miss, either, the implication that she should have read it. Not for her own erudition, but just because she *should* have done. Like she would know how to calculate tax liability, or what the German word for 'needlework' was.

'I can't believe you haven't read it,' said Fran, regretfully. 'I thought you would have done. You've read everything else.'

Hannah ignored the backhanded compliment. The rain had now intensified, and was coursing down the windscreen. 'Anyway, why?' she asked. 'I don't think you've missed much. It's not as good as everyone says . . .'

She stopped herself going any further, conscious that she was about to roll out the three facts she knew about *Tristram Shandy* (real-time narrative, tricksy printing effects, rude bit in the first three pages) and pretend she *had* read it. A habit she'd made every effort to kick after school, when she realized that the only time real people were impressed at your knowing things like that was at pub quizzes and they were hardly the kind of people she wanted to be in with.

Fran pulled on her seatbelt and fastened it carefully. 'Oh, well, I guessed it couldn't be up to much, or else the BBC would have had a go at it, wouldn't they, with Celia Imrie and – what's her name? Maggie Smith. It's your grandmother's turn to host the book group.'

She ground the gears trying to find reverse. 'She's having it at our house tonight. I have no idea why she picked *Tristram Shandy*. I wouldn't have thought it was her thing at all.'

'Maybe she's confusing it with *Cider with Rosie*.' Hannah realized, as she said it, that any attempt at humour, however lame, wouldn't register with her mother in this mood.

'No . . .' Fran narrowly missed backing into a large trough of begonias, sponsored by Boots the Chemist. 'It's more likely that she *has* read it and knows no one else has. And, of course, she's got all those first editions Faith Musgrave gave her. She'll want to get those shown off. The book group's very competitive like that, but in a negative way. Absolutely typical.'

She hauled the steering-wheel round. Hannah noticed that her mother's hands were looking old, crinkling at the knuckles, and that she was wearing her own father's wedding band on her middle finger; she'd always refused on principle to wear her own. After she'd divorced Hannah's father, Keith, she claimed to have hurled her ring into the harbour.

'It is hard,' conceded Hannah. 'It's not one I'd pick for light discussion.'

'Oh, maybe your grandmother wanted to reassert her mental superiority. Remind them of who grew up in the big house with the town intellectuals. I thought I could knock it off this week, between that licensing meeting and my day off, but what with one thing and another—'

'Mum,' Hannah interrupted, 'I know people who've taken *years* to read *Tristram Shandy*. It's unbelievably complicated.'

Fran looked grim. 'I know. I tried to get the *York Notes* out of the library, but Mrs Cowper said there was a waiting list for it. Hidden it for herself, more like.'

'When are they coming round, then?' It was a surreal conversation to be having, but at least Fran wasn't giving her a hard time about why she was here. For that, she and her aching heart were grateful. Hannah tried to see if there was anything in the shopping bags apart from Bourbon biscuits, since fatted calf evidently wasn't on the menu.

'Oh, about five-ish.'

Hannah looked at her watch surreptitiously. It was twenty to five already.

They coasted to a halt behind a stream of cars at Linton's roundabout, dressed with pansies in the red and blue stripes of the local rugby team. Now they'd stopped, Hannah wondered whether her mother would make any reference to the highly unusual circumstance of her coming home to stay for more than just a few nights, or if Fran could get all the way to their house pretending she'd just picked her up from school.

Somehow she couldn't bring herself to mention it either.

'Is Granny well?' she asked. 'Still writing her in-memoriam verses for the *Linton Gazette*?'

'She's fine,' her mother replied, suddenly tense. The familiar defensiveness in her voice might have been due to the beginnings of the rush-hour traffic, or maybe something else.

The Marshalls' domestic arrangements were lavish, considering there were only three of them — four if you counted Hannah's brother Dominic, who had moved ('escaped') to New York, where he was a freelance journalist and full-time hedonist. Dora, Hannah's maternal grandmother, lived in the old gardener's cottage at the bottom of the garden of her mother's bigger house, which was in turn built in what had once been the orchard of the Musgrave family villa, Hillcrest. Dora had been brought up there from babyhood as a ward of the last two remaining daughters, Faith and Constance. Both had died years ago, when Hannah was still a child, and no one ever spoke about how Dora had come to be there, whose child she was or why the two old women were so fond of her.

The rambling high-ceilinged rooms of Hillcrest were inhabited now by the wraith-like figure of their companion, Louise Graham-Potter, a woman whose advanced age Fran attributed acidly to a life devoted to self-preservation and expensive night creams.

'Is Granny still . . . um . . .' Hannah didn't know how to phrase 'able to cope on her own' without making it sound like a euphemism for 'incontinent'. She couldn't imagine Dora old, much less dependent, but because of that she seemed even more susceptible to an abrupt Dorian Gray decline.

Dora had never seemed grannyish to Hannah, largely because she comported herself like a much younger woman, trading on her charm, and the social gleam of her Musgrave connections, to get away with remarkable liberties. She had a rather movie-star style, with her red lips and vintage jackets – they stood out in an old-lady community where wearing a fancy hat got you talked about – but her behaviour had always been a little erratic. Whether this was deliberate, Hannah had never felt grown-up enough to tell.

'She's fine,' Fran repeated. '*More* than fine. She's perfectly able. In fact, she's *so* able that sometimes I think she's got some kind of oxygen tent in that greenhouse of hers. Or she's cut a deal with God to outlive me and everyone else in return for those bloody in-memoriam verses. I wouldn't put either past her.'

'And you?' Hannah asked, thinking of Mrs Armstrong and the dark hints about her mother's need for daughterly support. She hated asking direct questions, but it was easier in the car where they didn't have to look one another in the eye. 'Are you, er, doing OK?'

'As well as can be expected, what with the amount of work I've got on,' Fran replied vaguely. 'Don't say "doing OK", it's very American. Did I tell you there's a new Internet centre opening in the high street?'

Hannah felt a selfish relief at being let off the hook of concern. I'll ask her later, she promised her conscience. When I'm in a better frame of mind to help her. 'Mum,' she said, her eyes flicking instinctively to the side mirror in which she could see a stream of cars close behind them, 'this is a forty-mile-an-hour zone and you're doing twenty – and it's the rush-hour, if you can call it that.'

Fran relaxed her grip on the wheel. 'I suppose after London we must seem very bumpkinish to you, but I'm not totally incapable. I'm slowing down because there are some speed humps coming up.'

Hannah squinted into the distance in disbelief. 'Speed humps?' she asked. 'In Linton?'

'Oh, we're very cosmopolitan these days,' said Fran, drily. 'We've got joy-riding and everything. Just be grateful you've only got the speed humps to deal with – I'm dealing with the joy-riders most weeks.'

'Really? They're stealing cars round here now?' Hannah felt affronted. A bit of fighting on Friday night was about as bad as things had got when she was last home. Urinating in the street at New Year, cow tipping, that kind of thing.

'Oh, yes.' Fran paused to let her digest this startling piece of information. 'But that's just the junkies on speed. The heroin addicts break into them for the stereos but don't usually drive them away. Too much effort.'

'Oh.' Hannah was stymied, not wanting to sound naïve for imagining that her little home-town could be crime-free, or superior for suggesting that they couldn't deal with it themselves. As a local solicitor, her mother was a specialist in taking things the wrong way.

The thick silence to her right indicated that Fran was also thinking hard, and Hannah knew she would be bracing herself to ask an unaskable question.

Hannah turned up the radio. The local station was running a tea-time competition in which callers had to guess ten words with 'ball' in them to win a combined torch–key-ring.

'So, how are things with Toby, then?' asked Fran, briskly. 'You're not up here because something's gone wrong, are you?'

The question was delivered in a throwaway fashion, but Hannah could detect the weight behind it. Fran had always been squeamish about her children's relationships. Anyone's relationships, come to that. Her own included. She'd got divorced without mentioning it to her children until the night before Keith had left, and had still affected to be surprised when Hannah and Dominic were hardly taken aback by their father's retreat from domestic warfare.

'Not exactly,' Hannah replied evasively. A marked reluctance to talk about private matters ran in the family.

'Oh?'

'*No*,' said Hannah. She hoped Fran had caught the casual lack of concern she'd practised for twenty minutes in the lavatory mirror on the train. She'd practised over and over again for this very eventuality – that her mother wouldn't accept 'No' as a convincing enough answer and Hannah's feigned lack of concern might wear off under repeat questioning, like cheap silver plate, to reveal the hot pain beneath.

'There's nothing to sort out,' she said, feeling obliged to elaborate.

'That's a shame,' observed Fran, with equal, if more practised, lack of concern.

'Is it? For who?'

'For *whom*.'

Hannah gritted her teeth and concentrated on staring noncommittally at the grandiose town hall, whose elaborately finned buttresses and chimney-pots were swathed in billowing scaffolding and looked set to take off into the grey sky at any minute. It had been built by the same architect as the station, using, it was rumoured, a lot of left-over material.

'I meant, it's a shame because it's a waste, really, isn't it?' Fran went on, as if she were talking about Christmas wrapping-paper. 'When you know it's not really going anywhere. Your time, his time . . . And you're not getting any younger, are you?'

Hannah's resolve snapped. Fran's words flowed over her head as the moving landscape resurrected an older ache, whose power she'd forgotten until she saw the familiar street-lamps and colour-clotted flowerbeds. The numb fear that she couldn't go or stay, that there was no guarantee of any happiness anywhere. Sheer black panic filling her head until she couldn't even remember her name.

The feeling ran through her body so fast that she couldn't pin down the memory. Then more familiar anger replaced it as quickly as it had come, anger that now felt comforting. Anger with Toby, with herself for being such a fool, with everyone else for letting her believe that trying hard would be enough. 'No, it's bloody not a waste, Mum,' she hissed. 'It's bloody . . . nothing!'

Hannah bit her lips hard, not wanting to spoil any homecoming feelings, such as they were. She'd been wrestling with the same anger for months, but here, next to her mother, it felt wrong. Everything felt wrong. They hadn't even said hello properly. But, then, the only time her family did 'touchy-feely' was if a pulse needed taking. 'Can we leave that topic for a little while?' she said, awkwardly. 'Please?'

There was a pause. Fran indicated and turned left, with the usual flurry of frowns in all the mirrors.

There, thought Hannah. We're back to normal – rowing, refusing to discuss stuff, feeling guilty – and I haven't even got my coat off.

She checked her mother's face for signs of concern. Fran's face didn't betray any visible reaction; her features adjusted themselves automatically into 'patient reasonableness', acquired after years in Linton's magistrates' court and a lifetime of dealing with Dora's capriciousness.

They drove on in silence through the town, past the cramped rows of miners' cottages, the small windows and doors picked out in springtime colours. Out of habit Hannah noted the different shades — blue, pink, primrose, violet, cream — hopeful colours against the hard grey bricks. Each one was a tiny subliminal prick of recognition, jostling some moment nearer to her consciousness before it slipped away again.

It's just Linton, thought Hannah. Nothing changes.

Chapter Two

For a house built specifically with a family in mind, Rose View had never felt like a family home. It sat solidly in the lush garden of Hillcrest, more like a giant red-brick cat-scarer than a cottage, surrounded by the trees and positioned so as not to spoil the sea view from the Musgraves' long windows. Even the neat, neo-Gothic styling felt apologetic: it was intended to fit in with the high ornamental walls protecting the orchard from the main road, since it could never convincingly match the villa's white Italianate elegance. Fast-growing ivy had been trained to spread over the walls like a cloak, as if the best that could be hoped was that the house would be absorbed into the vegetation.

Rose View had been built with sturdy local brick and the best intentions, designed at great expense in the 1940s by Faith and Constance Musgrave, the last surviving branches of the affluent Musgrave tree, which had grown strong with its roots in rich coal seams. The sisters were given to charity works and improving deeds in the absence of husbands of their own to improve. Their single state, it was hinted to Hannah by the numerous old ladies in the town, had much to do with the fact that both Faith and Constance had been to university.

Dora hadn't, although she was undoubtedly clever enough. She had been married off when she was barely twenty-one to Arthur Marshall, the Musgraves' mine agent. The Musgraves couldn't find a house sufficiently smart or near for their adored ward, so they had built Rose View at the bottom of the orchard where Dora could bring up a respectable family in happy tranquillity. This plan, like the house, had never quite come off either: reliable, diligent Arthur might have managed the collieries with a sharp eye for detail, but he was no match for Dora's sharp brain and even sharper tongue. There had been some forward planning, after all, in making Rose View's walls so thick.

Neither Fran nor Dora cared to discuss family history. Hannah knew few details about her grandmother's marriage, apart from what she could extrapolate from muttered references and the almost complete absence of any pictures of Arthur Marshall in the house. The union had lasted as long as Arthur Marshall did, and Dora had worn him out within fifteen years: he had gone to an early grave through 'overwork' down at the mines office in Virginia Street, while she held bridge parties in her elegant drawing room, charming husbands with her wicked smile and quick wit while their wives played cross hands.

In a rare moment of intimacy, Fran had observed to Hannah that, as far as she was concerned, it had been suicide: the poor sod (her words) had chosen to spend every waking hour in the bloody office (her words), since Rose View had become a weapon in itself in Dora's war of attrition. The marriage was a disaster, but Dora didn't see why she should move out of her house; she didn't want Arthur to move out and ruin her reputation either. Maintaining an appropriate reputation, ironically, was Dora's most fiercely held priority in life.

Hannah's room was Fran's old childhood bedroom, and the sense of refuge lingered on like the faint smell of mothballs in the wardrobe. The children's bedrooms had been decorated, according to Faith's efficient instructions, at the same time as the rest of the house, which gave rise to all sorts of scandalized village rumours about Dora's condition on her wedding day. In the end, Fran had had no brothers or sisters – which did not surprise her, given the state of tension between her parents. Hannah's older brother, Dominic, was the first baby to sleep beneath the *découpage* dragons in the 'boy's' nursery, a mere fifty years after Constance had painstakingly glued them on to the bed.

The generous provision of rooms had always been rather too optimistic for Dora and Arthur's family ambitions, and the second storey became a retreat where adults weren't allowed. Other children rarely disturbed it either, since neither Fran, Hannah nor Dominic was over-burdened with playmates. Heaps of accumulated Marshall junk settled gradually upstairs over the years, and the shelves of old books, framed black-and-white prints of film stars, and endless doll paraphernalia flavoured Hannah's childhood to the point where the old school stories she read felt more familiar to her than her real school did.

Whenever Hannah smelt beeswax as an adult, it brought back a crystal-clear memory, so sharp that she could close her eyes and almost feel her plaits and gangling awkwardness. Rose View was full of heavy oak furniture, which Mrs Tyson, their cleaner, polished daily into a deep shine, muttering to herself with each circle of her powerful forearm. Most of it came from the Musgraves' apparently limitless stock of furniture – or so Hannah assumed, from the way Dora would refer to a sideboard as being 'from the London house' or 'from the villa'.

'Med her a house but didn't buy her owt new,' muttered Mrs Tyson, darkly.

The plethora of solid wood furniture in Rose View meant that until Hannah was about eight and tall enough to see round things, she had no idea what colour the wallpaper was in most rooms. The cupboards were a little kingdom in themselves: fitted with intriguing boxes and drawers, running along the walls with doors that opened in some places, but were false in others, big enough for Hannah to hide in. She liked cupboards for their darkness and their sweet beeswax smell of security.

Hannah was in her favourite cupboard at the time of her first real memory. It was in the dining room. Since neither Dora nor Fran had produced a family huge enough to require more than a six-setting dinner service, there was plenty of room in it for a child. Later she wished she could remember why she'd been there, and what had happened afterwards, but it remained stubbornly isolated in her mind like a snapshot.

She assumed she'd been hiding from Dominic – the constant rain and Fran's aversion to small children meant that they spent a good deal of time amusing themselves. Fortunately Rose View was large enough to accommodate their thundering feet without too much shouting, and Keith spent most of his time in his study anyway, smoking Silk Cut cigarettes and revising the paper that would re-establish his academic fire and catapult him out of the backwater in which he had found himself teaching.

Hannah worked out that she must have been around five because her birthday party the following week had been especially memorable, and featured no fewer than three birthday cakes: one from Fran (a wholewheat sponge butterfly), one from Dora (a sloppy chocolate gateau) and one sent from the villa (a glacial white fruit cake from the town bakery).

The rich smell of polished oak hung heavily inside the cool darkness of the cupboard; she was sitting cross-legged inside with a pile of Garibaldi biscuits, watching the pinpricks of light come through the carved edgings, blocking them out with her pudgy fingers, then letting the light sparkle in again.

In her efforts to reach an elusive speck of daylight in the top corner, Hannah's foot slipped and kicked the door. It swung forward and then, with oaken majesty, swung firmly shut, blocking out everything and sealing her safe inside like a stack of plates.

Hannah didn't panic: she had spent a lot of time sitting in the cupboard and it seemed a friendly place. Three of her dolls were in there with her, swinging their legs casually off an empty shelf. Besides, Dominic would be coming for her soon – he always knew where to look, and if he came too soon she'd have to share her biscuits.

She nibbled a Garibaldi with her sharp teeth and, to pass the time, thought about the long picture running behind her bed. The frieze was very old (no cars, and everyone wore hats), and Fran had insisted it had been painted for her when she was a little girl like Hannah. Hannah viewed this revelation with suspicion (it was hard to imagine Fran as a little girl), but was equally thrilled and repelled by the frozen figures trapped in acts of educational bad behaviour and/or permanent triumph. In a satisfying coup, all the boys were naughty, and all the girls were paragons of excellence.

The frieze had improved Hannah's nursery vocabulary to astonishing effect.

A is for Archibald who Acted Acquisitively was accompanied by a fading watercolour of a small child grabbing jam tarts and stuffing them stickily into his breeches.

B is for Belinda who Blushed Beautifully: Hannah smiled coyly and folded her hands in imitation of Belinda's charming downcast eyes and modestly displayed embroidery.

C is for Charles who Cheated Craftily: Hannah's mental picture of this scene of depravity was spoiled when she heard the dining-room door open. Her hand tightened over the remaining biscuits.

But it wasn't Dominic. It sounded like her mother.

'I don't know where she is!' Fran sounded cross.

Hannah's heart jumped. She had been told off only the previous day for hiding in cupboards. She sat on her hands to stop them knocking on the door and offering herself up. She liked to be a good girl.

'She's probably up there, with those interfering old bitches.' That was her father's voice, but his tone was unfamiliar. Hannah held her breath. He would yell if he knew where she was.

There was the sound of clattering.

D is for Daisy who Danced Delightfully, thought Hannah. She squeezed her eyes shut and pictured Daisy's neatly pointed toe and thin legs.

E is for Edward who Eavesdropped Everywhere. Naughty Edward, with his big ears sticking out on each side of his head like a big mouse, leaning towards two pretty little girls holding hands and telling secrets . . .

'I've sent him to his room!'

'Oh, for God's sake, Keith! This isn't the workhouse!'

'A few hours to think about what he's done will teach that boy a good lesson.'

The first flush of panic hit Hannah's chest. Dominic was much naughtier than she was – he was always giving cheek. If Dominic had been sent to his room, which she knew gave him nightmares, who would let her out? And the workhouse! Granny sometimes talked about the workhouse – it was where naughty children were swapped for poor children from the mines who'd eat up all their meals and not leave the bits they didn't like.

There was more shouting that she didn't understand. Neither her mother nor her father sounded like they normally did and she didn't understand half of the words.

G is for George who Gorged Greedily. More jam tarts, and cream buns, and biscuits, and crumbs everywhere – Hannah felt a guilty thrill of sympathy for Greedy George and remembered she'd missed out F.

F is for Felicity, who . . . who . . . Hannah racked her brains, and tried not to listen to the plates crashing to the floor outside the cupboard.

Who was yelling in pain? Was it her mother or her father?

Felicity who . . . Felicity who . . .

'Fuck you!'

Hannah decided to move on from F.

H is for Harriet who Helped Happily. Sometimes she changed that to Hannah. Hannah liked to help happily. Hannah liked everyone to be happy.

I is for Isambard who Interrupted Impertinently.

Tears were running down Hannah's cheeks and she put her hands up to her face to stop anyone hearing.

'I don't want her going up there, mixing with those terrible old snobs. They're nothing but a bunch of stuck-up whores!' That was her father but he was yelling so hard his voice sounded like a woman's. 'They ruined Dora, they ruined you, but I won't have them ruining my children too!'

Hannah stuck her fingers in her ears, wriggled herself into the corner of the cupboard with her face up to the comforting wood smell, and concentrated on J is for Jane who Juggled Jauntily. She could see the bright red balls that Jane threw up into the air, and the blue ribbons on her long plaits. Hannah wanted plaits like Jane.

Don't worry, said a disembodied voice, somewhere inside the cupboard. It was very close to her head, and perfectly clear. *Don't worry. You're safe here.*

Hannah felt all the fear drain out of her, exactly like the water drained out of the bath, leaving her ducks stranded on the white enamel.

There was a big crash, then silence.

Don't worry, said the voice, one last time.

Later Hannah assumed that someone must have found her and pulled her out. But three birthday cakes did not distract a clever little girl like Hannah from noticing that her daddy didn't come home in time for her birthday party. Garibaldi biscuits still made her feel violently nauseous.

In the spacious sitting room of Rose View, the book group was well under way. Or, rather, the old ladies who were meant to be there had arrived and a hot discussion was raging about the building of the new skatepark in the derelict loading yard of Eastern Quay down on the harbour. Most people were using their copies of *Tristram Shandy* as coasters for their cups of coffee.

Hannah shuffled in behind her mother, carrying the biscuits Fran had arranged hastily in decorative fan shapes on two spectacularly ugly cream-cracker dishes. They were from a low design point of the early 1960s, apparently constructed from calcified cabbage leaves and given to Fran as a wedding present by Mrs Jordan, the postmistress – who was perched on the window-seat staring glumly into her cup as if it might reveal the secrets of Laurence Sterne to her.

The only person who seemed at ease was, naturally, Hannah's grandmother, who was radiating hostess charm like a 1950s manual on home entertaining. She was sitting very upright in the most central chair, having positioned everyone else slightly lower and in the light so that they had to blink to look at her. On her knee was what looked like a very early edition of *Tristram Shandy*, with a bookmark pointedly near the end.

'Ah, Fran, there you are at last!' exclaimed Dora, her northern Received Pronunciation cutting through the hubbub like a knife. She was wearing, Hannah noted, a crimson silk kimono over a pair of black trousers and her hair was coiled at the back of her head into a thick white and grey bun, into which she had stuck two long hatpins with pearlized ends. She looked much younger than eighty-two, but had an air that suggested she'd made good use of every year.

Hannah decided to keep out of sight and leave the dramatic reception she was sure to get until there was a smaller audience. She didn't want to have a reunion with her granny in front of Linton's premier collection of gossips.

'And fresh coffee. Wonderful.' Dora picked up her copy of the novel. 'Now we can get started properly.'

The murmur of hot gossip faded away. Half the assembled women reluctantly picked up their *Tristram Shandy*s and started turning them over and over, paying particular attention to the back-cover copy. The other half held up their cups for coffee refills.

From her vantage-point just behind the door, but well out of the firing line of personal comments, Hannah inspected the assembled company with her trained eye. For the second time that day she marvelled that so many old women from her childhood were not only still kicking around the village but looked younger than she remembered. Was the brewery putting something into the water? Or was it that she was getting older too? With seven or so women, five of them senior citizens, packed into the room, most fresh from OAP day at the hairdresser's, there was a strong aroma of mints and setting lotion.

'Can we get on with the task in hand, do you think?' asked Hannah's primary-school teacher, Mrs Kelly. Green corduroy, it seemed, was still her fabric of choice. She dunked a Bourbon biscuit daintily in her coffee. 'I myself have badminton this evening, and our Scott wants running to judo. He's doing so well, you know. His instructor said only the other day that—'

'Quite,' said Dora, before Mrs Kelly could rehearse the familiar story of their Scott's prowess in pummelling other eight-year-olds.

It had been much the same with his father, who'd thumped most of Hannah's class at school. 'Who'd like to begin? Mrs Cowper? Would you do the honours and open the world of *Tristram Shandy* to us?'

Mrs Cowper, the librarian, turned pale pink around the cheekbones.

Hannah felt a rush of relief that for once she hadn't been called upon to step up to the mark. She'd dreaded it at school, not because she might be wrong but because she was nearly always right, which had only increased her reputation as a freak. She frowned and ate a custard cream.

'Are we all present?' asked Mrs Cowper (a transparent delaying tactic, scoffed Hannah). 'Where's Betty?'

'Betty Fisher? Oh, I doubt very much that she'll be coming tonight. She's not herself,' said Mrs Woodward. She dispensed medicine and gossip in equal measures at the surgery, not being bound to the same code of practice as the doctors. 'The usual. I shouldn't think she'll be up to reading for a while. Not with her leg.'

Hannah's mind boggled.

'And I doubt that she'd make much of this Tristan Shandy lad, anyway,' added Mrs Woodward, as an afterthought. 'She's not a lot about her, that one. No manners. Very rude she was at the dispensary. Very *personal* indeed.'

'When isn't she?' asked Mrs Kelly, tartly.

'Well, thank God she's not coming, or we'd not have enough biscuits to go round. Are we going to sit around gossiping all night or are we going to talk about this book?' demanded Dora. 'Mrs Cowper? Your thoughts?'

'Well,' Mrs Cowper began uncertainly, 'I'm not entirely sure I understood this very complex and challenging book . . .'

'And if she can't we're all done for, since she's had the crib notes out all week,' observed Mrs Hind, a leading light of the WI and the

Linton Amateur Dramatic Society. She said it in a jovial enough tone, but from the co-ordinated lip-pursing, Hannah guessed that her mother had been speaking the truth about Mrs Cowper's revision tactics.

Now Mrs Cowper blushed deep rose. 'Well, Judy, that's not true. I merely found it . . . very complex. As have a great many minds more literary than ours, I might add.'

'Do you mean you didn't understand a word?' asked Mrs Jordan, forthrightly. 'Because I'll tell you this for nowt – I didn't get past page four and I've been reading it while last Sunday.'

There was another murmur of unspecific assent.

Mrs Cowper's eyes flicked back and forth between the other group members as she tried to assess whether she could take this easy route out without threat to her intellectual high ground as librarian.

Hannah ate a Bourbon biscuit and sympathized. It was one of those gamesmanship rules. You were allowed to pour unqualified scorn on one classic novel – everyone was. It was like playing your joker: the more popular or revered the novel, the more points you got for refusing to bow down before it. But you could only do it once, twice at the most, before you started looking badly read and 'controversial'. And God knows what else they had coming up in the next weeks if they were tackling Sterne now. Mrs Cowper would be well advised to save hers for Martin Amis. If they ever got past genteel bitching.

'Is that your Hannah I can see?' asked Mrs Cowper, in desperation.

'Ah, look, look, look! Hannah! You're here!' Dora caught sight of her granddaughter skulking in the shadows. 'Come on in, darling! Let me see you! I thought you were coming on the later train!' She got up from her seat and held out her hands. *Tristram Shandy* fell to the grate with a clunk.

Self-consciously, Hannah passed the depleted dish of biscuits to her mother.

Fran took the biscuits with a barely repressed snarl. 'I told her,' she muttered to Hannah. 'She *knew* you were coming! I told her I was going to the station! Bloody theatricals . . .'

Dora landed a smacking kiss on Hannah and released her with a sigh of delight. 'My darling girl.' Her blue eyes crinkled in a smile that illuminated her whole face. 'Oh, I'm so happy to see you. So happy. Now, then,' she said. 'Hannah'll be able to start us off. What do you think are the main themes of *Tristram Shandy*, darling?'

All eyes turned to Hannah. Why do they expect me to know everything? she wondered helplessly. Why do I still feel I have to pretend I do? I'm nearly thirty.

'Come on, sit down,' said Dora, patting the arm of her chair invitingly. 'Make yourself comfortable. We're very informal here in the book group, you know. Not like those high-brow seminars you had at Oxford.'

Hannah smiled ruefully, but went to her grandmother's chair and perched on the arm. It creaked.

'Mind the—' said Fran.

Hannah stopped her with a glare and Fran tossed her head.

'I suppose you'd find this book very easy, would you?' said Mrs Cowper, grimly.

'Well, it's meant to be funny,' Hannah ventured, seeing there was no way out. She dredged through her mind for the bare facts, garnered from the condensed-classics book she kept in the loo. Hannah was addicted to learning, no matter how much she hated herself for being a swot. '*Tristram Shandy* is, um, a quasi-autobiographical novel set in real time with some innovative printing techniques that challenge the idea of reader participation in story-telling, and the process by which we manipulate our own histories.'

Silence.

'And, yes, they're having sex in the opening chapter,' said Hannah.

'Oh, Hannah,' said Dora, with relish, 'it's so *nice* to have you home.'

Chapter Three

The next morning when Hannah's eyes opened she reminded herself automatically not to notice that Toby's warm feet weren't next to hers. White light pooled over her face, streaming in from the curtains she'd forgotten to draw before crashing into bed. She closed her eyes and wondered what had woken her.

Often she woke in the middle of the night because she'd rolled over and encountered only cool sheets where there used to be a warm body. Not that that was a recent development: she and Toby had been on and off more often than the Blackpool illuminations. But that wasn't what had woken her this time.

She pushed back the sheets and frowned. Hannah loved being asleep, where no one could get her, and her brain didn't relinquish its sleep blanket without a good reason. Something had definitely disturbed her.

But there wasn't a sound from downstairs, her alarm wasn't set and outside it was pretty much silent, even by Linton standards. The only noise was a faint shushing from the harbour, of the waves slapping against the walls, a seagull creaking in the distance. Compared to the racket outside her flat first thing in the morning it was like waking up in an isolation tank.

Hannah rolled over, disconcerted and irritably wakeful.

It wasn't the strange bed — nothing had changed about her bedroom since she had slept there as a teenager, and her body had recognized all the lumps and bumps of the mattress. There was something else she couldn't put her finger on: an absence, not unlike the sensation of Toby's cold empty space next to her . . .

She threw back the blankets with a huff of annoyance and sat up. At the same moment, as if in answer to her question, the first morning train went clattering past, five carriages rattling over the rails in a familiar rhythm her brain hadn't forgotten from the seven years she'd used it as a default alarm clock. She'd become used to waking ten seconds before the train thundered past, creating a ten-second torture first thing every morning in which she could contemplate the inescapability of her daily routine.

And as soon as the noise of the final carriage died away, there was a gentle triplet knock on the door.

Hannah stared at her drawn face in the mirror opposite the bed. She looked shocking. There were two angry red spots starting on her chin and her hair was flattened at weird angles to her head.

'Hannah,' she mouthed at her reflection, in unison with her mother's voice, 'I've fetched you a cup of tea.'

Then she fell backwards on to her pillows, stunned by the weight of three thousand similar mornings reverberating on her all at once.

Hannah wondered if Fran, too, was so trapped by the routine that she'd been leaving cups of tea outside her room in the intervening years. Her previous visits had always been one or two-night stop-overs at Christmas, when Fran was too stressed to do anything but shout and tug at her hair, but maybe the shock of having her back in September, in the middle of the week, had brought this on.

She lay on her back, letting her eyes wander over the tracery of cracks on the ceiling, hoping that sleep might return. No one could get you when you were asleep. You didn't have to come up with any answers.

But her brain was circling impatiently, like a dog wanting to be fed.

Then the second train, going the other way, clattered past: her 'snooze button' train, the one that meant she had exactly twenty-five minutes until registration at Linton Grammar School.

Eighteen minutes until she had to leave the house.

Thirty seconds until Fran yelled up the stairs from the kitchen: her name on two notes, the first 'Haaaa' high and resigned, fading down to a quick, cross 'nah'. Hannah heard it in her head, and to prevent having to hear it in real life she swung her legs out of bed, collected the tea (white, two sugars, mug with Linton Rugby League Football Club logo on it) from outside her door and went downstairs, feeling oddly aggrieved.

'What are your plans for today, then?' asked Fran. It sounded like a question, but Hannah knew it was more than that: it was the initial innocuous stab that would make her defence unravel like a ball of wool if placed correctly.

'I'm not sure,' she said. The kitchen smelt like Monday mornings. She put a couple of pieces of brown bread into the toaster and flicked on the kettle. From the moment she had set foot in the bathroom, and smelt the faint saltiness in the water as she showered, it was as if she had never been away. Apart from the permanent throb of numbness in the pit of her stomach, which she'd almost got used to now, it was all pretty much as it used to be. As ever, she was acutely aware that her mother was dressed and ready for work while she was still in her pyjamas. Last-minute Hannah, her mother used to call her. And probably would in a few moments.

Out of habit, she looked to see if there was anything in the post for her on the Welsh dresser: there were some bills and a handwritten letter for her grandmother.

'It's a memoriam fan letter,' said Fran, before Hannah could ask. 'She gets a lot. Ghoulish beggars.'

'Oh. From the family, I assume?'

'No, not always. People *commission* her to write them. She gets *commissions*. Can you believe that?'

Hannah raised her eyebrows, although she wasn't entirely surprised. The local paper's 'court circular' column never ran for fewer than two pages, largely due to the expansive mourning poetry that filled the in-memoriam section. According to Dora, it had always been a local custom in an area where men's lifespans seemed about thirty years shorter than their wives'.

'It's getting out of control, if you ask me. There's definite shades of the last days of Imperial Rome about the whole thing,' said Fran. 'It doesn't help when you've got first wives, second wives, children by the first marriage, step-grandchildren all wanting to put their morbid little verses in. God knows who they imagine reads them. Unless Heaven gets local papers delivered.'

'Each to their own,' said Hannah mildly.

'Well, I'm in court until late.' Fran looked up from the *Guardian* and her bowl of bran, both of which she was consuming with quick precise movements. 'You might have to get your own lunch.'

'Well, that's not a problem,' said Hannah. She wanted to tell her mother to decide whether she was treating her like an unwanted guest or an irritating teenager, and then stick to it, but instead she peered into the teapot. It was very strong, almost black, with three bags. She tipped it slightly. Four bags.

A stand-off pause ensued, during which Hannah tried not to hear the eight-fifteen bus flying down the hill and then the eight-nineteen arrival of the milk. In a pathetic effort to break the spell, she got out a cafetière to make some coffee, a beverage traditionally served after one o'clock in the Marshall household. Fran carried on eating her bran, methodically circling her spoon around the bowl to chase the last bits.

The little radio on the window-sill was tuned to the local station, and while she spooned coffee into the cafetière, Hannah was relieved to note that at least they had had a change of presenter on the breakfast show since she was at school. That much at least was different.

Out of the corner of her eye, Hannah could see her mother winding herself up to ask a question.

She decided not to help her out.

'So, are you on holiday or what?' demanded Fran, finally, obviously unable to leave until she knew.

'Er . . . no.' Hannah had hoped this conversation could be postponed until she felt more normal, or at least until her grandmother was around to defend her. She put her cup on the table and examined the skin on the marmalade before she committed any to her toast.

'It's in date, if that's what you're worried about,' snapped Fran.

Hannah put it down and went for the counter-attack. She didn't necessarily want to know what was up with her mother, but two could play at the invasive-question game. 'Mum, is there something you're not telling me? I mean, are you feeling all right in—'

Fran arched an eyebrow and glared. '*Don't* try to deflect me. The truth, please. Are you on holiday or have you left your job?'

It's all about my job, isn't it? thought Hannah. As long as my *job*'s OK, then I can be going through nine rings of hell. But a row this early in the day would solve nothing. 'I've taken some holiday,' she lied. 'I had a lot owing to me and if I didn't take it I'd've lost it.'

Fran looked pleased at this unconvincing display of diligence. It seemed to reassure her. Her life's ambition had been to make sure Hannah left the backwaters of Linton to forge 'a proper career'. 'Good. You work very hard, love. We all need a break now and again. You'll be getting promoted soon, will you? Is that why you've come up?'

'Well . . .' Hannah looked at her mother, all hopeful in her court suit. It had always been hard to admit unpalatable things to her, especially just before she was about to go out and grapple with justice on behalf of Linton's criminal community. Fran, unlike Hannah, burned with the honourable need to do the right thing, even if it made her unpopular. Hannah preferred people to like her. That had been part of her problem – she was forever telling her mother what she wanted to hear, then having to go out and do it.

Look where that got you, she thought. She took a deep breath. 'Er, no, actually. That's not true. I came up because I've handed in my notice,' she admitted. 'And because—' The kettle boiled, and Hannah leapt gratefully to her feet to make the coffee.

Fran's paper rustled in her shaking hands and a corner fell into the milk. She put it down, devastated. 'And because what?'

'Because . . . I wanted to come home.' Hannah couldn't stop her voice cracking at the unexpected truth.

Fran gaped.

That much *was* true, thought Hannah. And it had come as more of a shock than the parting of the ways with her current position. She loved working at Christie's, organizing sales and being with the specialists. Until she landed the job, Hannah hadn't believed that something so perfect for her could exist: she'd got a post in the pictures department – competition was fierce (and so well spoken) – but gradually she'd made a niche for herself, and had begun to be taken seriously. Then her entire life had folded up as neatly as a collapsible chair. And when that had happened she'd come back, almost without having to think about it, dulled with a numb panic that she had no idea what else to do.

A bit like a racing pigeon.

'You *wanted* to come *home*?' Fran looked horrified.

'That's worse than me giving up my job?'

'I'm coming to that.'

'But isn't it normal to come home?' demanded Hannah. 'People do it all the time. I mean, look at half my class from school – they didn't even get round to moving out. The really adventurous ones, mind, got as far as Lancaster, decided they couldn't be doing with this Southern Nonsense, and came straight back.'

'Yes, but not you! You've been gone years!'

Yeah, and ask yourself why? thought Hannah, though she didn't say it. She put it to the back of her mind with the other unexploded-grenade comments. Instead she plunged the coffee and said, mildly, 'Some mothers might say it was about time for a visit.'

'Oh . . .' Fran shut her eyes, searching for the right tone. 'You know I'm not like that. I don't want to see you tied down here like I've been. You've your own life to lead.'

Hannah couldn't help feeling that this was all a little heavy for a breakfast-table conversation, and began to wonder if, with her hereditary gift for timing, she'd turned up in the middle of a wrangle about her grandmother's living accommodation. Was that the big problem Mrs Armstrong was on about? But then Dora seemed perfectly able to cope on her own. Or was it something more invasive? An investigation at work? Or some kind of illness? Fran was evading it expertly enough – if she wouldn't talk about it, there had to be something.

But, then, do you really *want* to know? asked a voice in her head. What if it's something terrible – some long-term illness or a big financial crisis? Do you really want her to tell you, to lean on you, to be vulnerable and wobbly, gradually turning into someone you don't know?

Hannah twitched guiltily. 'Mum,' she said. 'I've just come up . . . to recharge my batteries. Man cannot live by cappuccino alone.'

'But *why*, for God's sake? There's nothing round here for you!' Fran's face was flushed.

Hannah decided to risk the marmalade, on the off-chance that a show of confidence might act as a pacifier. She spread it lavishly on her toast and bit into it. 'For crying out loud,' she said, through a mouthful, 'I don't know why you always say that. Linton's a nice place. Pretty harbour, lovely houses, reassuringly mediocre weather—'

'Record unemployment, genetic idiocy and, our latest regional attraction for the under-tens, crack cocaine.'

'*Mother*. Anyone'd think you didn't want me to come home.'

Fran sighed. Her earrings didn't match, but Hannah decided not to mention it. 'Look, love,' she said, 'of course it's nice to see you. It's just that . . .' She frowned and drained her tea.

Hannah knew this presaged one of Fran's Better Out Than In pronouncements. Better for her, maybe, but not for those around her.

'Just that what?'

'Look,' said Fran, tightly, 'in my experience, people like you, who manage to get out, only come back here when something's gone very badly wrong. I . . .' she hesitated '. . . I speak from experience here, love. Sometimes I wonder if . . . if I've squandered all my chances. People always say they're coming back for a break, and they never leave again. You've given up a job other folk would kill for. I don't want to see you stuck.'

'Don't you mean that you don't want people to think I've failed?'

'Of course not!' Fran clattered her plate. 'How can any— Of course not!'

'But things haven't gone badly wrong, Mum,' said Hannah, aware that her brightness was goading Fran into an irritation she'd never admit to. 'I just needed a break. I didn't have a gap year, or a break after college, did I? I'm worn out. I wanted to see you and Granny.' Very good, she thought. You've almost got me convinced.

'OK, OK.' Fran frowned again and got up. Her jacket was on the back of her chair. It was almost as creased as her forehead. 'But you'll have to go back, you know. You can't ignore whatever the problem is.'

'Who said there was a problem?' asked Hannah.

'There's always a problem in this family.' Fran stuffed a pile of envelopes into her briefcase. 'We just don't talk about them.'

Hannah opened her mouth to protest at the hypocrisy of this statement, then pretended to read the marmalade jar without looking too obviously for the date stamp.

'And incidentally,' said Fran, pausing at the heavy kitchen door, 'we *have* cappuccino in Linton. There's been cappuccino here since 1951. Starbucks weren't the first, you know.'

Hannah let her mother have her moment of triumph and smiled through her toast. She waited until the front door slammed, then spat it out into a piece of kitchen roll. The date on the jar was Best Before Jan 1998 and it tasted somewhat older.

Although it looked sunny outside, Hannah knew better than to go on surface impressions. It was often bright but rarely warm in Linton. When it was, people stopped each other in the street to say, 'By, it's clement!' in the same tone that they might have said, 'My God, it's hailin' frogs!'

She stepped out of the house now, banging the door behind her. The wind lifted her hair off the back of her neck, shooting a chill through her denim jacket. On top of the hill, facing out towards the Irish Sea, Rose View rattled with the winter sea-storms when the clear skies could change to thick grey cloud in minutes. The ideal outfit was one that could be peeled off in layers, like an onion, according to the degree of inclemency.

She walked briskly down the hill, admiring the white gateposts and the curly iron railings that edged the gardens of Linton's smarter area. The houses up here were spacious villas, with porticos and the occasional iron barley-twist of steps leading up to a red front door. When they had been built in 1861 (amid rumours of a royal visit to inspect the flourishing town), they had marked the high-water line of respectability for the town's merchants and professionals. Even though Linton was booming and low rows of miners' cottages were going up like weeds round the pits, no one ever thought that it would spread so far up the hill, leaving it safe for the smarter residents to look down into the bowl of the harbour; from their high windows, the Georgian grid of streets looked elegant and modern and you couldn't smell the tannery.

A villa on the Hill Road was the high point of Victorian success, designed and angled to provide a view of the town uninterrupted by any other house. Dora was inordinately proud that it had a different postcode from the town centre. To which Fran always countered that the supermarket delivery cost an extra fiver.

Over the years, though, the town had crept up the hill and beyond. Estates had been built between Linton and the little satellite village of Etterthwaite until the green spaces had closed up and become the outer reaches of the town, the centre of most crime and all police activity. The modern planners, hoping to provide a central focus for the estate, had made a circular green in the centre, which had been used for bowls during the first three years and was now well known as the starting line for the boy-racers on their circuits of the town.

As the pits ran out after the war, with the shipping already faded, the town fell on harder times and it showed in the houses. More of the estate homes stayed boarded up and many of the villas were split into flats; the paint grew dull, while the big gardens were overrun with veronica bushes and long grass, or were tarmacked to make parking spaces. A few houses remained intact: Rose View was one, and Hillcrest, the biggest house on the row, of course, which had been there first.

Hannah was so busy peering over the walls to see what the new influx of money had done with the villas that she didn't notice Betty Fisher, with the non-reading leg, labouring up the hill until she had nearly collided with her.

'Hannah!'

'Hello, Mrs Fisher,' said Hannah, then added, 'How's your leg?'

Mrs Fisher glared at her and Hannah noticed that a thick white bandage was wrapped around her knee, like an inept attempt at partial mummification. Betty Fisher was another of the old ladies who'd already seemed ancient when Hannah was young, although she wasn't much older than Fran. Her face was weatherbeaten and creased with hardship, sloe gin and resentment. Hannah had always been a little scared of her. 'It's bad,' she said. She had a broad Linton accent, which was growing rarer in the town, not because off-comers were thinning down the natives, but because the natives watched more American television. 'I'm in agony.'

'Oh, I see, er, I'm sorry,' said Hannah. 'They, er, missed you at the book group.'

'Runnin' that now, are you?' A fleck of spit flew out with the words.

Hannah recoiled.

'And your mother?' The dark eyes glittered malevolently. Betty Fisher had the sort of timelessly aged face that Hannah could imagine wrapped in a Victorian headscarf or peering out from a bonnet. There was something witchy about her. 'She'll be needin' you now, I suppose? Back home, in your place.'

'Um, yes,' said Hannah, feeling obliged to agree. What was it with her mother that everyone else seemed to know about? Then she remembered Mrs Woodward's eagle eyes at the book group. Thanks to her sybil-like presence at the dispensary, you couldn't even get the Pill up at the surgery without the whole town speculating about your imminent moral decline.

'About time,' sniffed Mrs Fisher. 'Allus in a mess, your family. Either mekin' one of their own, or interferin' in someone else's. Not that anyone in your family'd know what the right thing to do was.'

'I beg your pardon?' said Hannah, unable to contain herself any longer. Really, old age was just a licence to be rude round here.

'I'll not go into it.' Mrs Fisher adjusted her plastic rain bonnet. 'But I suppose it's not your fault. There's hardly a decent example for you to follow in the whole family. Some might say bad will out.'

Hannah was speechless. School prizes, university degree, career outside Linton – what was a decent example meant to constitute, for God's sake? A bishopric? Deification?

As if she could read her mind, Mrs Fisher hissed, 'There's more to life than fancy university degrees, lady. Plenty of them professors you think are so clever couldn't get a jam-jar open. And that's where the rot set in with your whole family. That an' the company it keeps.'

Hannah opened her mouth to say something, but could find nothing appropriate.

'Oh, and while you're at it, you can tell your grandmother that that book were a load of nonsensical tripe, too,' said Mrs Fisher, as a triumphant parting shot. 'If I want diagrams I'll read a Haynes manual.'

With that she continued up the hill, jabbing her stick into the pavement as if it were a pickaxe.

Hannah took a deep breath and stared down the road into town. There was a cold film of sweat now under her three layers of clothes.

The high street, with its tall shopfronts and broad pavements, was much as she had left it, aside from a few new chain stores and – she was pleased to see – the demise of the pet shop on the corner. Hannah's flesh had always crawled as she scuttled past it, and her grandmother had frequently threatened to tip off the RSPCA about its cluttered pens. In its place was a Cancer Research shop, its window filled with two huge bridesmaids' dresses in lime satin, two matching satin ring cushions embroidered with 'Jason' and 'Karina', an extensive Eternal Beau tea service, the toaster still in its original box.

Hannah walked automatically towards her favourite place, the Coffee Pot Café, home of the Linton cappuccino. It was exactly the same as the last time she'd been in there. It had been exactly the same for the past fifty-odd years. She pushed open the green smoked-glass door and slid into the nearest empty booth.

The café was busy for half past ten on a Wednesday morning, but after a cursory glance Hannah was pleased to see she didn't recognize anyone and, more to the point, no one seemed to recognize her. This was the uptown branch; most of the book-group ladies favoured the downtown café, which was just a few yards from the bus-stop and boasted a larger ladies' loo and less-fancy cakes.

It was pleasantly warm in the Coffee Pot, when the wind was whipping up the main street as it was today, and Hannah had passed many Saturday afternoons with Fi, her best friend, lingering over coffee, watching the rain slide down the steamy glass window, trying to avoid the gaze of the bedraggled shoppers, pointing out the cakes in the window display and leaving little warm fingerprints on the glass.

The Coffee Pot, like the station, had not let down her memory by becoming smaller or cheaper. If anything, the place had been spruced up a bit – the stained-glass partitions in the booths were clean, and the black-and-white tiles on the floor seemed new, although the Formica tabletops still bore the territorial etchings of several generations of Lintonians. Who, like the owners of the ring cushions sitting forlornly in the charity shop, might or might not still be '4 eva 2 gether'.

Hannah didn't bother to look for her name on the table. It wasn't there. She hadn't been tempted to etch because she'd never been cool enough to lay claim to a booth. Fi, though, had scratched her name on most of the tables, using a Kirby-grip from her parents' hair salon, pin sharp where the plastic tip had come off. Hannah traced her fingers across the Formica. There it was: FR, for Fiammetta Rissini.

Hot coffee, wet raincoats, toasted fruit teacakes, the hissing Gaggia: Hannah's throat tightened with a sudden passionate longing for her teenage years. Her lank teenage years. She closed her eyes to dismiss it, and instead was overwhelmed by a choking sense of claustrophobia, which made her eyes snap open again, so hard she almost dislodged her contact lenses.

'Ready t'order?'

How ridiculous to feel homesick in your own town for an adolescence you couldn't wait to grow out of! thought Hannah. She blinked to get rid of the tears and didn't look up. Eye-contact didn't feature prominently in the town's communication style – which, at least had prepared her well for London – so for once she wasn't afraid of looking rude. Instead she stared at the spreading jam stain on the waitress's frilly pinafore, and reminded herself of how far she'd come since she'd worn the same pinny during an ill-fated summer before her A levels.

The Coffee Pot's uniform had been the height of fashion when the café opened, and was almost egalitarian in its failure to flatter even the cutest teenager – a satisfyingly Lintonian result.

'Large cappuccino, please, and a strawberry tart.' So what about the calories? thought Hannah, recklessly. No one here to see me.

'We're out,' replied the waitress. She managed to sound pleased and bored at the same time.

'Oh, OK . . . I'll have a . . .' Hannah peered more closely at the tray of cakes in the glass counter. In order to capture the very particular under-fives market as well as their coffee-morning mothers, the Coffee Pot had always gone in for luridly coloured sponge specials in the shape of cartoon characters, popular computer games and the like. The current crop was practically fluorescent, gleaming next to the more prosaic slabs of currant cake and Bakewell tart.

'What are those green ones?'

'Green's Golf Fancies, blue's Football Fondants.'

'OK, I'll have a . . . Golf Fancy, then. Thanks.'

The waitress ripped the order off her pad, slapped it on the table and slouched away in no rush. Hannah envied her. Slouching was another waitressing skill she hadn't got the hang of, along with surly banter, reckless milk-frothing and slamming down the wrong change.

The women in the next booth along were discussing Christmas with a peculiar negative relish. 'I don't know what there is to enjoy, apart from the soap specials,' said one, grimly. 'It's all just cooking, then washing up.'

Hannah found she couldn't tear her eyes away from the cake display. It glowed like Snow White's casket in the black and white tiled surroundings. Food colouring had clearly come on since she was last at home. There were some orange ones in the shape of rugby balls that looked practically radioactive.

No, she reminded herself. *This isn't a holiday.*

Hannah took out a notebook from her handbag and opened it portentously at the first page. Then she found a biro, started to write 'To Do' at the top, found it had run out of ink and stopped abruptly, feeling this was an omen of some sort.

She found a pencil at the bottom of her bag, and returned to her To Do list.

1. Get cakes for tea.

That was a good one to start with, one she could cross off almost immediately. Fran's cooking was erratic, and though currying favour with bought goods was always met with an outcry about additives and hygiene it was as well to have something edible in the house.

2. Write letter to Toby.

Hannah stopped and chewed her pencil. She changed that to: Write letter to Toby, *but don't post it*. Better.

3.

She jutted out her lower lip and pretended to be lost in thought when actually her brain was empty. What was the next thing to do?

See Fiammetta? She caught her breath.

No, thought Hannah. No, leave that one alone.

Oh, yeah. *Find new job.*

In Linton, or London?

A hot flush, tinged with unsettling *déjà vu*, spread through her body and she didn't even bother to pass it off as the energetic central heating in the café.

'Oh, Christ, what a fucking mess,' said Hannah, and realized that she'd spoken aloud, just as the waitress was arriving at her table bearing her coffee and fondant.

'Oh, um, I didn't mean you,' she amended quickly, as the glass cup and saucer was plonked down in front of her. The thick foam shifted but didn't spill over the edge, such was its impressive density. 'That's a fantastic cappuccino,' she added, truthfully, and even looked up with a smile, but the faint tinge of the south in her accent had taken the shine off the compliment – and compliments were generally treated with suspicion anyway.

The cake was slammed down next to the coffee, and Hannah noted a large thumbprint over the bunker. 'Thank you,' she said weakly, and went back to her list. Linton had a way of spoiling itself.

Chapter Four

By half past one Hannah had got no further with her list but had drunk four cappuccinos and eaten a variety of lurid cakes.

After the waitress started to make noises about getting the table back, she trawled around the shops for a few hours, in the familiar figure-of-eight, as practised by generations of teenagers at weekends, looping around the grid of shops, their original charm now partially hidden by plastic frontages and municipal litter bins.

As she trailed up the hill towards home, the drizzle began to whip itself into a sullen storm. Hannah pushed open the front door as the first fat drops of proper rain splattered down. She could tell from the briefcase and raincoat slung under the hall chair that Fran was back from work and, going by the clankings and bangings in the kitchen, had already embarked on cooking supper.

Hannah's heart sank and she thanked God she'd remembered to stock up on essential sugars. Fran's approach to food was worthily nutritious but largely taste-free. She peered round the door to see how far her mother had got, and whether there was any chance of rescuing the situation.

The large kitchen was dominated by an old red Aga, which Fran was manhandling as if it were a runaway steam loco, and from her vantage-point in the hall, Hannah could see that Dora was sitting at the kitchen table, scribbling in her notebook, a packet of chocolate digestives within easy reach. Her Schiaparelli-pink wellington boots were standing by the Aga to warm and she had brought a bunch of late sweet-peas from her glasshouse, their frilly heads poking out from the *Linton Gazette*.

In the background, the kitchen radio was listing the manifold roadworks in the county, and there was a strong smell of mince and recent argument in the air. Hannah acknowledged that, to the untutored eye, it did resemble a charming scene of pre-war domesticity. But she knew better. Rather than exchanging harmonious domestic views about the benefits of good beef, Fran was muttering darkly into the unspecific pot of mince, and Dora's beatific countenance suggested that she had recently been passing on some unwanted cookery hints, laced with feigned bewilderment at her own daughter's ignorance of such matters.

Fran prided herself on being a bad cook as a gender-political issue, although she clung determinedly to the idea of family meals and remained suspicious of microwaves. Throughout Hannah and Dominic's childhood, if challenged about the nutritional benefits of whatever was being served up, she would point out that she still had all her own teeth, as did her mother, and if they wanted anything different there was always Weetabix or baked beans in the cupboard. The only thing Dora had ever approved of in Fran's dietary regime was Hannah and Dominic's splendidly regular bowels.

'Hello, Hannah darling!' said Dora, spotting her sloping past the door with her shopping. 'Oooh, you went to the M and S food hall.

It's been a godsend, that place. I do love their little treats. What's in all those bags?'

Fran's shoulders hunched at the Aga and, feeling caught out, Hannah shoved the second bag of prepackaged food behind the boot rack by the door.

'Nothing, really. I just got some, er, bottled water and a few walnut whips. And some fruit.' But why shouldn't she go shopping? Nothing wrong with contributing to the household while she was here.

In a conciliatory gesture, she put the bag on the table for inspection, but her mother didn't turn, having reached a critical stage with both hotplates and three pans.

'Oh, my favourites! Thank you, dear,' said Dora. A beringed hand shot out to grab the eight-pack of walnut whips and moved it next to the chocolate digestives. 'You're so thoughtful.'

Fran snorted. 'We have fruit. And water. Honestly, I ask you, paying for water! Madness! You'll be getting special oxygen next!'

'Oh, well, there *are* oxygen bars now, you know. You get a little mask and just breathe it in to refresh yourself,' said Hannah, who was too distracted by Dora's neat move on her chocolate to realize she'd have been better off keeping that snippet of information to herself.

'How very modern!' exclaimed Dora, as Fran barked with derision. Hannah reckoned they cancelled each other out, in terms of the opinion and in attempting to provoke each other.

She slipped into the chair on the other side of the table and poured herself a cup of tea from the big pot on the wrought-iron trivet. Her head was already spinning from the four cappuccinos but she needed something to defrost her from the inside out. She took advantage of Dora's investigation of the walnut whips to pull the notebook to her side of the table. Dora's verses were remarkably versatile: she could do serious, baroquely mournful, humorous, acrostic, and some that verged on parody. Not that anyone really noticed. The current work in progress began, 'The angels sang a lovely hymn/St Peter called your name.'

She wondered when her mother was going to ask her if she'd seen anyone in town. She always asked, oblivious to the fact that Hannah never recognised a soul.

'Have a walnut whip, dear,' said Dora generously.

'Oh, too kind,' said Hannah.

Dora swiped the notebook back while Hannah was choosing between pecan and toffee.

'So, did you see anyone you knew in town?' asked Fran.

Hannah bit the top off her walnut whip and looked at her mother to see if she was being funny, but Fran was stirring the mince fiercely and her back was showing no signs of irony.

'Oh, yes,' she said. 'I bumped into Woody Allen in Smith's and the Coffee Pot was very busy so I had to share a table with Princess Caroline of Monaco. She had the last Rugby Fondant. And I might have seen David Beckham on the harbour but I couldn't quite tell because he was wearing a hat.'

'Don't be ridiculous.' Dora frowned across the kitchen table at her. She had sliced the top off a walnut whip and was systematically excavating the marshmallow with the end of a spoon. 'David Beckham was at the WI tabletop sale I went to. He was running the tombola.'

'Sarcasm is the lowest form of wit, Hannah,' said Fran heavily. She picked up a bottle of Worcester sauce and shook it doubtfully over the pan. 'I appreciate that Linton is pretty dull after the endless celebrity thrills of London, but you might try to humour me with a bit of conversation.'

'Oh dear. Was it a bad day in court, darling?' asked Dora. 'Or is it—'

'Yes,' said Fran. 'I've had a horrible day. Horrible, horrible, horrible. Horrible people doing horrible things to other horrible people, and not apparently ever noticing how horrible it all is. I hope you two aren't spoiling your appetite with chocolate when I've cooked you a proper supper.'

Dora gave Hannah a pointed look and intoned, '"The angels sang a lovely hymn/St Peter called your name./You were the greatest mam on earth/In Heav'n you are the same."' She smacked her lips with satisfaction, and drew a line under the verse. 'Now, let's see, Mrs Rowlands . . . Can you think of a rhyme for Charlotte, Hannah?'

'Not one that you could use in a memorial verse.'

Hannah wondered a little too late whether Fran's outburst might have something to do with the big problem her mother was facing. She reminded herself that she really ought to ask again. But something inside shied away, like a teenager, and she felt even worse. She wasn't sure she'd know what to do, even if Fran told her. She wouldn't thank me, Hannah thought, she doesn't need anyone's help. She's never wanted anyone's help.

Which was true, but it didn't make her feel better.

Fran was still in her blouse and skirt from work; her jacket hung over the chair at the head of the table, the sleeves concertinaed where she'd been pushing them up all day. Hannah felt bad, knowing that the cooking of the meal was the big deal, not the meal itself, whatever it turned out to be. 'Mum, I didn't see anyone in town even when I lived here. I just don't know as many people as you do.'

'Well, I don't know how you manage that,' sniffed Fran. 'I certainly *introduced* you to everyone.'

'Oh, that's not the issue. They all seem to know me, all right.'

'You're distinctive, darling,' said Dora. 'You have the family scowl. There's no need to be ashamed of it.' She ran a finger over her curving eyebrow. 'But you have to *make conversation* with these people when they say hello. You don't want to get a reputation for being standoffish, do you? Only the Queen can get away with the "And you are?" routine these days.'

Hannah refused to be riled, either by the implicit criticism or that Dora was talking to her as if she'd left home just the previous week. It was as disconcerting as Fran's weird formality. 'And did *you* see anyone you knew on your walk up from your front door to ours, Granny?'

'I think David Beckham was quite enough for one day,' said Dora, mildly. 'Would you be so kind as to help your mother and lay the table, please, darling?'

'Oh, wait, actually, yes,' said Hannah, suddenly remembering. 'I did see someone, sorry. I saw that old witch Betty Fisher on my way into town.'

'She's not old, she's about my age,' said Fran, mildly.

'Oh, horrors,' said Dora, taking the proffered cutlery. 'That dreadful woman! She's not really fit to be living on her own, you know. Not entirely there . . . Did she ask you if you knew who my father was? That's her normal opening conversational gambit to me.'

'No, she sort of impugned the family in general. I didn't let her get too specific. But what do you say to her when she asks?' asked Hannah, curious. 'Is it a trick question?' She looked over to her mother for further enlightenment, but Fran was now decanting grey mince into a serving dish with absolute concentration.

'Oh, I usually tell her he's the same man as hers, but that just sets her off again,' Dora replied airily. 'Did you know that Betty Fisher's mother used to tell fortunes down on the dock? She was very, very bad at it.'

'Mum!' Fran moved the salad crossly and put the dish of mince on the metal trivet. It looked a lot like curried slurry to Hannah, but she kept her mouth shut for fear of incurring another lecture about the corrosive effects of London on table manners. 'That's slanderous.'

'Well, she was. Everyone knew about it. She was always telling folk that their ship was about to come in, and they were always telling her that it just had, and that was why they were there in the first place. Mind you, you'd have to have been at sea for at least ten years to find Cath Fisher an attractive prospect.'

Fran sat down and pulled up her chair, which scraped noisily on the stone flags of the kitchen floor. 'What your grandmother means is that Betty Fisher's mother used to tell fortunes *on the pier to tourists*, not sailors down the docks, as you well know.'

Dora rolled her eyes at Hannah. 'Well, it came to much the same thing, in her case.'

'So is Betty Fisher so rude to everyone, or just us?' Hannah covered her mince with a thick layer of tomato ketchup before she got too close a look at it. 'She was pretty personal to me, I can tell you. And I don't even know who she is, really, to be saying all that stuff.'

'She's especially rude to us, I'm proud to say,' said Dora.

'But why?'

'Oh, I don't know, it goes back years,' said Fran, before Dora could speak. 'Like everything else round here. Her grandmother, Molly, used to work up at the villa for the Musgraves. Not surprising she holds a grudge, really. No one likes being in service. Why would they? It's just socialized slavery.'

'They kept a lot of people in work when there wasn't much work around,' said Dora.

'Yes, well, you would say that, wouldn't you?' snapped Fran. 'They were cleaning up after you.'

'She's related to Matthew Fisher, you know,' said Dora, ignoring her. 'Our famous local artist.'

'Matthew Fisher who painted the industrial seascapes?' asked Hannah, casting about vaguely in her mind. She wasn't very knowledgeable on modern art, but a lone detail had lodged in her head from a sale catalogue. Linton didn't often come up as a subject worth painting.

'That's the one,' said Dora. 'He used to live in my cottage.'

'I didn't know that,' said Hannah, with interest.

'Yes, you did,' muttered Fran, under her breath, but Hannah ignored her.

'How is he related to Betty Fisher?' she asked.

'She's his sister Molly's granddaughter. Rather sad none of his talent spread any further. Faith Musgrave discovered him, you know. He was just a miner, but she brought him out, supported his work. She built up quite a collection of local art.'

'Just a miner.' Fran snorted. 'If a person's talented, it's their own achievement, not the result of some rich woman's hobby.'

'Mum . . .' said Hannah, not wanting Dora to stop. It wasn't often that she spoke about the Musgraves or her childhood in their house.

'Anyway,' said Fran, 'let's not talk about capitalist exploitation at the dinner table.' She forked some salad on to her plate and changed the subject with the same grim crash as she changed gears in her car. 'Have you heard from Toby yet, Hannah? The sooner we start talking about it, the sooner you'll get it sorted out, that's what I say to my clients. No sense in hiding your head in the sand, is there?'

'Oh, yes. When *is* Toby going to come and see us, Hannah love?' asked Dora. Her eyes crinkled up with the familiar expression of grandmotherly innocence that Hannah knew was entirely artificial. 'Most people who've courted as long as you bring their intendeds up to meet the family. Or are you ashamed he'll find the coal in t'bath and la'al homing pigeons in t'pantry?'

'Yeah. I mean, no, don't be ridiculous. Um.' Hannah glanced at her mother, who refused to come to her aid. 'Did Mum not tell you?'

'Tell me what, darling?'

'I'm the soul of discretion,' said Fran, primly. 'It's not for me to reveal the state of your relationships. Besides, didn't you say you didn't want to talk about it?'

Hannah took a deep breath and loaded up another forkful of mince. She had to tell them some time. 'Well, Toby and I split up. Just after we got back from that holiday in America.' She put the mince in her mouth to render an immediate follow-up impossible.

A cloud passed across Dora's blue eyes. 'Oh dear, not the holiday you'd been saving up for? And you sent us such a nice postcard. Maureen commented on what lovely writing you still had, even though you were writing the card on the beach.'

Maureen was the postwoman, a woman of insatiable nosiness and an MI6-like ability to decipher bad, smudged or otherwise impenetrable handwriting. Hannah made a mental note not to send unsealed communications to any of her friends in London.

'I thought you said you split up after your birthday,' said Fran, calmly forking mashed potato onto her mince, 'because he wanted you to go on that language course.'

'That was last year,' said Hannah. 'We patched things up after that.' Toby's attempts to 'improve' her had been bloody annoying, but she'd suffered them in the hope of pleasing him. 'But . . . there was more to it, really.'

'Oh? In what way?' asked Dora, putting down her cutlery and steepling her fingers so she could lean her chin on them. Her expression was rapt. 'Did he not have the right kind of intentions?'

'No. Well, not towards me, at any rate.'

Fran made a show of pouring herself some water, although Hannah could tell she was just as intrigued as Dora. It was a cheap solicitor's trick, she thought, to feign disinterest at key moments.

'Was he . . . was he on the other bus?' whispered Dora. 'You can tell me, darling. I won't be shocked. I've been to see a recording of *Kilroy* with the WI, you know.'

'No! He wasn't on the other bus,' said Hannah. 'He was on the same bus as me, but it turns out that we weren't going to the same place. Or, rather, he intended to make a few changes along the route. And I thought it was a direct service.'

All three looked confused.

'Fran, dear, can you explain that one to me?' asked Dora. 'I lost her after she said he wasn't a homosexual.'

'Oh, you'll find out sooner or later.' Hannah sighed, bracing herself. 'We split up, because I found out he'd been seeing Jennifer. He'd overlapped us – to save having to work out his notice, as it were.'

Blank stares.

Fran looked freshly wounded as she remembered that, on top of being abandoned in a humiliating manner, Hannah had also packed in her fabulous job.

'Jennifer worked in nineteenth-century British pictures,' Hannah elaborated painfully. It was a position she'd hoped to be moved into. 'The one who was transferred from the New York offices? She lived with me for a few months while she looked for a flat. The one I thought I was rather good friends with.'

'The American girl?' hazarded Fran.

'Yes, she was American,' said Hannah, heavily. 'And blonde and clever and well shod and totally predictable in every way. She was a dead ringer for Gwyneth Paltrow, in fact.'

'Well,' said Dora, 'I may be an old fuddy-duddy but I've always said you can't trust those baby blondes. And I've said that for at least forty years, haven't I, Fran? It's all that peroxide – renders them utterly fixated on their hair. Can't get it wet, can't go swimming, have to have special shampoo.' She huffed. 'No better than children.'

Hannah knew that a fierce if sympathetic lecture about sticking with what you knew (i.e., short, swarthy Linton natives) was only seconds away from at least one of them. She tried to read her mother's face for a reaction, but Fran, spearing salad, had her expression safely back under control.

Another cheap lawyer trick, thought Hannah, remembering, with a bitter pang, the frustration of trying to get her mother to take sides in family rows with her brother. It wasn't like court. She wasn't *obliged* to remain diplomatically impartial in family arguments. Or even hear both sides out when one was clearly wrong. Her impassivity then had just given Dominic air time. And look where that had got him. Locked into a love affair with his own voice.

'And what are they doing now? Toby and this Jennifer?' Fran asked, without taking her eyes off the remaining shreds of icy lettuce on her plate. Even her voice was noncommittal.

'They're, um, in Long Island at the moment, I believe.'

'Best place for them,' said Dora. 'As far away from you as possible. He obviously wasn't up to your standards, darling, and he knew it. That *is* where they sent the convicts, isn't it? Or am I thinking of Rhode Island?'

'On holiday?' asked Fran delicately.

There was a pause, into which the Radio Cumbria mid-week rugby league reports blurted incongruously. Linton had lost again.

Hannah swallowed her mince with an effort. 'On honeymoon, actually.'

'No!' Dora's eyes widened.

'Yes.'

'Well!' said Dora. 'Dear me. I am surprised.'

'I'm not,' said Fran. 'He always struck me as one of those clueless public-school men who'd faff about for years then make the decision of his life within ten seconds and still get it wrong.

Plenty more where he came from, though. I'm more concerned that you think he's worth ruining your career over!'

'You never met him, Mum,' said Hannah.

'Didn't need to. I know a useless man from a hundred miles off.' Fran's expression was steely.

Hannah tried to concentrate on the on-going misery of Linton Rugby League Club but that only made her feel more hopeless, and she burst into tears.

'Oh, darling, don't ever cry about a *man*!' exclaimed Dora, and helped herself to more mash. 'We'd do nothing else in this town, just beat our breasts and launder handkerchiefs round the clock.'

'Speak for yourself, Mother,' said Fran, and put down her fork. She got up and awkwardly put her arms round Hannah. Her angular body, all bones and joints, didn't make her a natural comforter. 'I'm sorry it hasn't worked out, love. Bright, high-flying girls like you – they scare some men. It's not your fault you're a threat to their egos. And this Toby, he wasn't exactly your type, was he? I always worried that . . . But he's well out of the picture now, isn't he? I mean, look on the bright side. You needn't worry about all that splitting up and getting back together now. You've just got to pick yourself up and move on. There are still plenty of men out there, men who deserve you.'

Hannah gulped out a bigger sob. Her entire body was shaking with the effort of not wailing out loud. She felt so stupid, and they were just confirming it for her.

'Oh, hear, hear,' agreed Dora. 'Have you seen Lottie Lancaster's son? What was he called? Andrew? He's gone *very* good-looking now he's had his teeth done. And he's a solicitor.'

'For God's sake, Mother! This isn't the sixties!' said Fran, exasperated. 'Anyway, Hannah doesn't want some feckless water-treader from round here. She doesn't *need* a man at all, come to that! Sometimes I wonder if feminism ever reached Linton.'

Dora clattered her knife and fork onto her plate. 'Feminism? What could be more feminist than a town where the women are left to run everything?'

'Oh, don't be ridiculous. Half the folk here can't even pronounce "emancipation", let alone know what it is.'

'Women bringing up kids on their own with only their wage coming in? Isn't that feminism? Holding families together when the men are killed or away fighting or crippled?' Dora's blue eyes were hard, and her glare was fiercer than the lightness in her voice. 'What's that if it isn't female independence? Dear God, Fran, you say some half-baked things.'

Hannah felt her mother's arms tighten round her shoulders, but she knew she was mentally tightening them round Dora's neck. It didn't help to discover that she was now quite a bit bigger than Fran, who seemed to have shrunk about an inch since Hannah was last in a position to notice. But the creeping suspicion that she was stumbling into the middle of a long-running battle of wits took her mind off her immediate pain. They hadn't sniped at each other like this the last time she was home, surely.

'I think you've just contradicted yourself,' said Fran, tautly.

'Not at all.' Dora picked up her knife and fork again, apparently tranquil once more. 'I was just saying that most women in this town have had to deal with more on their own than any of that – that *dungarees brigade* could. Hannah doesn't need a man, but if she wants one around for her entertainment, then that is entirely her own business. Faith never married, and neither did Constance. They had perfectly fulfilled lives. I often wish *I* hadn't bothered. And if Hannah can't find some entertainment round here, even with the current sorry state of Linton menfolk, then she's no granddaughter of mine. Or a daughter of yours, for that matter.'

Hannah wondered if this 'entertainment' was what Betty Fisher had been getting at. She'd always had the unspoken impression that the family reputation was somewhat murky, but she'd never liked to enquire why that might be. It wasn't that her family was secretive, but they treated topics they didn't wish to discuss as if they simply didn't exist.

'So, is that why you're up here, then?' Dora went on, ignoring Fran's hyperventilation on the other side of the table. 'You gave him his marching orders, took some holiday, and what? You gave him back all his presents, packed your bags and left for your country retreat? Good girl. Very stylish.'

Hannah nodded – at which Fran moaned, for want of a cogent comment – then shook her head defensively. 'No, I did try to carry on at work.' She wiped under her eyelashes where she thought her mascara might have smudged. 'I loved my job, you know I did, and I didn't see why . . . a little personal problem should stop me doing it. But . . .'

That didn't really do justice to the agonizing weeks of pretending that she had throat nodules when her voice cracked on the phone, making stupid mistakes if colleagues so much as mentioned their relationship, and having to eat lunch secretly in the park ignoring her silent mobile phone and trying to convince herself that concentrating on work would sort everything else out. In fact, put like that, it seemed to have been a mature career decision, rather than the rank cowardice she now saw it had been.

'But . . .' She gulped as the ramifications of everything she'd lost leaped out at her in sharp focus. Hannah covered her mouth with her hand, and then, while she was at it, covered her eyes with the other.

'You gave up that lovely job. You idiot child,' said Dora, giving her a searching look, then returning to her mashed potato. 'Still . . .'

'No, no, no, you're absolutely right to be upset, Hannah,' insisted Fran. Her face was white and tight with controlled emotion. 'You worked hard to get there. But you don't want to sit around feeling sorry for yourself like this. There's no point getting all maudlin. I mean, this is exactly the time to be focused on yourself, and your prospects, not on some worthless Hooray Henry who thought you needed constant improvements.'

Hannah's shoulders gave a great shake.

'Oh, there, see what you've done,' chided Dora, sarcastically. 'Poor Hannah. There, there. Plenty more fish in the sea. Much better.'

Fran looked over Hannah's bowed head and glared at Dora. 'Will you please make up your mind what your point is? Or are you just disagreeing with me on principle?'

'I hardly think either of us is qualified to speak about successful relationships,' said Dora tartly. Then, as Fran was flinching in shock, she added, 'I'm just saying that she might as well get used to men being dispensable. She's a Linton lass, after all.'

'Yes, but she doesn't have to be a Linton lass *here*,' said Fran, quickly. 'She can be a Linton lass in London, doing a job she's good at and using her brain to—'

With a big effort, Hannah straightened up. For want of something to do with her hands that didn't involve crying or rubbing her eyes, she began to flatten her mince with her fork. 'Why are you so scared of me coming home?' she demanded. 'Is it because it's embarrassing to have me here when you've gone on and on to everyone about how well I've done to leave? Is it only me that's not allowed to fail round here? Is it such a terrible reflection on you as the perfect mother? Or are you worried that I'll throw myself off the railway bridge and—'

She didn't get to finish the sentence because Fran shut her eyes and flinched. 'Oh, Hannah, no!'

'Your mother doesn't want you getting to the bottom of all our family secrets,' said Dora, lightly. 'She's scared you'll want therapy, then it'll all come tumbling out.'

'Don't start that with me,' snapped Fran, her eyes still shut. 'I'm not the one who refuses to discuss anything. I'm not the one with repression issues.'

Hannah noticed that her mother didn't go through the whole 'I wasted my life in Linton and you will too' argument in front of Dora.

'I'm not the one with problems, though, am I?' said Dora.

'No, you just sit back and cause them!' snarled Fran, and stormed out of the kitchen.

On the radio, the sports reports finished and 'Concrete and Clay', by Unit 4 Plus 2, started.

Hannah stared towards the door. 'Granny, that wasn't . . . Is she going to come back?' She trailed off as the thundering sound of Fran's sensible shoes clumping up the first flight of stairs answered her question for her.

'I doubt it.' Dora helped herself to more salad and hummed vacantly.

Hannah wondered whether it was normal for middle-aged parents and children to resume adolescent battle tactics.

'Oh, Hannah, I saw someone today who wanted to see you,' said Dora, as if nothing had happened.

'Really?' Hannah tried to sound polite but evasive. Clearly she wasn't going to be allowed to have a minor breakdown in private. Careers lectures from everyone from newsagents to post-office workers seemed inevitable. All of them keen to rush her back to London to pick up the broken bits of her life and stick them together in an approved fashion.

'Yes. In fact she wants you to go over to Hillcrest in the morning.'

Hannah looked up from her plate. 'Do you mean Mrs Graham-Potter?' This was on a par with a Royal Garden Party invitation.

'Yes, Louise,' said Dora. 'She was very interested to see you were back. Spotted you from the drawing-room window. She said you still walk as if you're carrying half the school library on your back. She asked me if you had scoliosis. I said I didn't know.'

Hannah marvelled that in less than twenty-four hours her return and all its associated problems had been telegraphed round the town.

'It's my broken heart,' she said. 'It's weighing me down.'

Dora gave her a funny look. 'Your broken heart, eh?'

Hannah bit her lips. 'Yes. My broken heart.'

Dora looked as if she were about to say something, then busied herself with the salad. 'Anyway, go over and see her tomorrow for morning coffee.'

'Should I put on my suit?' Hannah wasn't sure she really wanted to go. Mrs Graham-Potter was hard work.

'Try a smile, darling.' Dora stabbed some lettuce on to her fork. 'Your mother has plenty she's not using.'

Chapter Five

As children, Dominic and Hannah had been forced to spend more time together than they'd have liked on account of being the only kids in their respective classes to live up on the hill and therefore condemned early on to the inverse social stigma that characterized much of Linton's adult society. They passed most of their time in the gardens, out of range of Fran in Rose View but not close enough to Hillcrest to spoil their ghost stories with human contact.

Rose View stood against the sea wall at the edge of Hillcrest's once prolific orchard, where Ellen, Lady Musgrave, mother of Faith and Constance, had somehow coaxed apples, pears and even hard little figs to grow in the Linton chill. That neither household really noticed the other said a lot about the size of the original orchard, and also about the state it was now in, thick with lilac bushes that had choked the apple trees many years ago.

During the day Hannah and Dominic stalked each other through the high grass; at night they camped under big trees, snoring in the stuffy, salty air. Fran made them wear cotton trousers for fear of sunburn, but their sturdy legs were tapestries of insect bites, nettle stings and thorn scratches. Only Fran seemed to notice: Dora's sole concern was that they didn't disturb Constance Musgrave's ornamental rosebushes, of which there were many, or Faith Musgrave's cats, of which there was an ever-expanding pack.

Fran had read books about bringing up children and was very concerned about their wildness. Her mother, predictably, was no help to her whatsoever: Dora was pleased that the children were making the sort of family bonds that they'd need for the trials of life, and not relying on mutable acquaintances. Fran tried not to worry that they had no real friends – but couldn't share her mother's amusement when Hannah declined a birthday party because all her best friends were at Mallory Towers. Dominic showed no interest in joining any rugby team, but merely invented a range of superhuman enemies and slaughtered them all in horribly creative ways.

'As long as they're happy,' Keith kept saying, more or less to himself, since neither his wife nor his mother-in-law ever listened to him, unless they were actively engaged in a row.

Hannah and Dominic didn't consider themselves lonely or weird, and probably wouldn't have brought friends into their garden to play even if they had had any. They wanted to keep it to themselves, in case it lost its spooky magic. Although they never discussed what it was about the garden that made it so enticing, both children sensed a creepy allure about the house, rising up in the corners of their eyes, beautifully white and flat like a wedding cake, deliberately bland to hide the lurid, Technicolor mysteries they imagined inside. Hillcrest, and its unseen inhabitants, loomed over them like a reliable, yet faintly unsuitable babysitter while they scrabbled around in the wild lilacs, just beyond its long shadows.

Dominic was an avid reader of ghost stories and Hannah took a masochistic pleasure in being scared witless, so the garden provided ample props, especially for two children who spent such an unhealthy amount of time reading. There were the remains of an old tennis net, which could easily pass for a hangman's rope in the twilight, and a dilapidated gazebo that they were too scared to walk near after dusk.

One summer evening, after a sweaty supper of French Fancies and Skips nicked from the pantry, Hannah sat in the tent with Dominic, and related a story Dora had told her in an off-hand manner while she was helping her repot her fusty geraniums.

As with all Dora's stories, it was made more thrilling by its vagueness; Dora thought that Faith Musgrave had told her it when she was a little girl. There was a ghost, she said, that appeared in the garden on summer nights, an unhappy Musgrave lady from way back in the family's twisty roots, who floated through the orchard, between the trees, eternally searching for a lover her father had forbidden her to see. According to Dora, the lover, who wasn't of an appropriate background, had been hiding in the gardener's cottage, waiting for the lady to sneak out, but when she'd gone there to meet him, so they could get horses and elope to Gretna Green, she had found him dead and her father sitting at the table with his shotgun, wiping the crimson speckles of blood off his face with a white cotton handkerchief.

Hannah waited until Dominic's face had drained beneath his sunburn then added, as a cruel afterthought, that the ghost only appeared to young men and boys, as a warning against leaving their wives.

Dominic was too aware of Hannah's own weak spots to let this go, and merely waited a few months until Hannah had forgotten she'd been told the story by an untrustworthy source, and had filed it away as gospel in her mind.

It was another clear night, so still that the waves in the harbour sounded as if they were only feet away. Dora had been shopping in Carlisle, so they were sleep-fuddled with cream buns and milk-shakes. Dominic started telling his tale just as Hannah was dozing off, in the lullaby voice she found terrifying in its gentleness. She lay motionless and didn't give any indication that the skin was creeping on her arms as if ants were running up and down them.

Hillcrest, he said, was built on the site of an ancient nunnery, settled by Irish sisters fleeing persecution, but it had been seized and demolished by the Musgrave family to sink the first coal mine directly underneath. Did she know that the little door in the garden wall that they sometimes squeezed through when the back gate wouldn't open was part of the original nunnery walls, used for confessions and deliveries, where local girls would leave their illegitimate babies for adoption? Mrs Tyson had told him that, Dominic said. Hannah believed him: Mrs Tyson was a Methodist and didn't lie about anything.

Dominic let his voice drop until it was barely audible beneath the wind rushing through the leaves above them.

It had been a nasty business, with the nuns refusing to abandon their home, and the Musgraves' agent threatening to send them all off on one of the ships bound for the Virginia plantations if they didn't leave. At the end, there was a struggle, and one of the older nuns died, clinging to her crucifix as she fell, issuing a curse against the male Musgrave line.

Hannah lay on her shaking hands and calmly pointed out that it couldn't be true, because where were the pit workings now?

Dominic suppressed a meaningful cackle, then reminded her that the coal seams burrowed like labyrinths under the town and out under the sea, which Hannah knew to be true, and when the coal had run out in that particular seam, the Musgraves had knocked down the pit-head buildings and built the villa over the top. Then they could look over the red-tiled roofs of Linton and out to the harbour where the ships transported their coal across to Ireland, sailing over the heads of the men in the mines.

In fact, he went on, encouraged by Hannah's trembling silence, wasn't it local tradition that Samson Pit had been a particularly unlucky one? There were probably dead miners under the ground they were lying on, buried alive in the numerous pit accidents – pit accidents that might, or might not, have been connected to the cloister curse.

As Dominic said this, a noticeable gust of wind rushed through the trees around them. The bright white circle of the moon shone clearly through the fabric of the tent as the gathering breeze blew the clouds across the sky. Hannah yelped and buried her head in Dominic's sleeping-bag, and they lay shivering in the close night air for some time, far too scared to leave the tent and run through the ever-shifting garden.

In the early hours of the morning, huddled in a sleeping-bag deep in the orchard, it was easy to believe that there was more to the house than they could see. Hannah didn't tell Dominic, for fear of giving him new ideas to scare her, but parts of the garden did make the skin prickle on the back of her arms. Never mind the dank gazebo, there was a trained arch of wild honeysuckle near the pond that she avoided even in the daytime. Its heavy scent seemed too sweet, too sickly, and she could never see what was at the end of the arch – if one of the cats was waiting to leap out at her. Faith's cats frightened Hannah, the way they'd appear and disappear like ghosts in the rosebushes, giving her terrible shocks in the twilight with their yellow eyes and hot red mouths.

There was another spot as well, not too far from the little gate in the wall, where Hannah often thought she could hear laughing all around her, under her feet, in the trees. Fran said it was water trapped in one of the ventilation tunnels, but Hannah didn't believe that. She knew it had something to do with the villa, and the old women inside it. There were parts of the garden she knew she'd never found, and shaded walks where she could feel unseen eyes on her.

Of course, had they wanted to go inside the fascinating house, Dominic and Hannah would have been more than welcome. Dora visited the three old ladies at eleven every day for morning coffee, and Fran went round twice a week or so, despite her critical mutterings. But becoming too familiar with the contents of the villa would only have spoiled the delicious fun of imagining the horrors within, so they squirmed and avoided visiting the Misses Musgrave and Mrs Graham-Potter, preferring to sit outside and make them up.

The next morning, Hannah's brain sprang awake at Linton rising time, but she lay in bed until she was sure Fran had gone to work, mentally ticking off the minutes against the sounds outside. As the eight twenty-five bus went past her window, she heard the front door slam right on cue. She allowed her mother time to get the car out of the drive and pointed in the direction of Martin Curwen & Co, Solicitors, then got up, showered and dressed, listening to the radio, pretending she was on holiday so that she wouldn't have to listen to the voices in her head.

Downstairs, the teapot was warm and the weekly local paper was left open on the table, folded at the jobs section. Fran had pointedly circled a couple of bar jobs, which paid roughly one Manhattan per hour. Hannah skimmed it as she made some toast and, probably as her mother had intended, realized that unless she could rustle up some fictitious teaching qualifications or some experience with metalworking, moving back to Linton permanently and adopting a cosy lifestyle wouldn't be easy.

She inspected the jobs page more closely. There seemed to be a particularly high turnover of teachers.

Oh, sod it, thought Hannah, turning the paper back to the front pages and more cheering news about Britain in Bloom meetings and major drug swoops. I've got some savings. I deserve a break without working. Something'll occur to me.

But even as she thought it, the over-achieving side of her brain twitched disapprovingly, and she found herself thinking, Better to do nothing and use up my savings than get a job and make folk think I've come back with my tail between my legs.

Disgusted with herself, Hannah picked up her tea and took it through to the sitting-room to read Dora's in-memoriam verses properly. She settled herself in Fran's chair by the window and angled the paper to catch what little light there was.

'Outhwaite, Miriam Gladys,' she read. 'An empty chair, an unread book/What God loved best/He went and took.'

That didn't sound like Dora. She was a stickler for grammar.

Outside it was mizzling, a Linton weather speciality: rain filled the air invisibly from a leaden grey sky. Three seconds after she had turned on a lamp to read better, the phone rang. Hannah picked it up hesitantly.

'Don't forget you're going over to see Louise Graham-Potter this morning,' yelled her grandmother's voice. There was a whirring noise in the background that made her sound as if she were calling from inside a tumble-dryer.

Hannah peered out of the window and, through the drizzle, could see Dora standing by the rosebushes in her shocking pink wellingtons, with a gardening trug in one hand and her cordless phone in the other. She wasn't even wearing a hat.

'Granny, I hadn't forgotten,' lied Hannah.

'Only I said you would, and I don't dare disappoint her.'

'Do you want to come with me? To check that I go?'

'Darling, do you know how much like your mother you're starting to sound?'

'I am not.'

'Oh, you are.'

'You're too far away from the base set with that phone. You sound like you're tumble-drying.' Hannah stuck two fingers up at her grandmother through the window and wiggled them to test how much Dora could see.

'No need for vulgarity, dear.' Dora's voice was crackly. She might have been laughing. 'Anyway, there might be something in it for you. She asked especially whether you were on holiday or not. I'll meet you over there in a little while. I need to get this pruning done first.'

She clipped her secateurs above her head like a Spanish revolutionary firing shots into the air. Dora loved pruning. She would prune anything, anywhere, sometimes even pulling off dying flower-heads in other people's houses. Hannah had always thought her grandmother was a thwarted hairdresser. Or executioner.

Hannah struggled through the tall grass and was struck again by how big everything was in next door's garden. She had half expected to be disappointed by its tameness and comparatively scaled-down size, but the apple trees still towered over her head and the grass was half-way up to her knees, drenching her jeans with the peculiarly wetting native water that, at her other extremity, was sending her carefully blow-dried hair back into its native frizz.

Some of the old shivers crept unexpectedly up her neck when she looked into the blank face of the villa behind the trees. The pretty side faced the road, and elegant steps wound to the front door framed with a smart architrave. The back of the house was bare, with smaller, deeper-set windows, designed to let in as little as possible of the strong sea wind. Hannah knew it couldn't be kept out completely: small ridges of red sand formed behind the window-sills in Rose View after the fiercer storms. It was like magic the way it found the tiny cracks and forced its way in, even if the windows were freshly painted and tightly shut.

As if the miners lost under the sea, their bones washed to sand by the waves, wanted to get back in.

She shuddered and ploughed on, trying to straighten her hair as she went but it coiled against her fingers and her skin tightened with salt.

The path became more obvious as Hannah approached the back door, traces of gravel and bigger stones marking out the edges. In the depths of the garden there were huge bushes of pink rosehips, with blowsy petals and a faint scent of ozone, but near the house the roses were of a proper pedigree. Hannah was pleased to see they were freshly pruned. Dora's secateurs had left their signature on each white-tipped stem.

Two cats, one black, one musky grey Persian, were stalking round a thick lavender bush, which made Hannah suspect there was a rabbit or a bird in it, since they didn't acknowledge her approach.

She took a deep breath and stared up at the higher windows. When she and Dominic were camping in the tent, looking up towards the villa, Dominic used to wait until the clock in their hall had struck midnight, then catch his breath and point soundlessly at the middle window, right at the top. Every single time it had sent her shooting to the bottom of her sleeping-bag, already imagining what wasn't there.

Today the window was dull: nothing, apart from some faded blue curtains.

Nothing there at all, thought Hannah, and smiled at what used to frighten her. It was just an old house.

A sudden frantic knocking at the nearest window made her step backwards in shock. Her heart thumped and she nearly fell over the cats, fighting an impulse to turn and run home. But something made her stick her fingernails into her palms and force her eyes to look towards the sound.

The cats yowled in protest.

A pale face had appeared at the window, indistinct behind the raindrops; it was looking straight at her. The lips moved, but before she could make herself step closer, it had vanished.

Hannah felt her own heart beating in her chest, pushing the blood through her veins. Who the hell was that?

The back door swung open, creaking on unoiled hinges.

She moaned quietly in fear.

'Oh, Hannah!' said Dora. 'Why didn't you come round to the front, darling? Your trousers are soaking.'

'Oh, my God,' Hannah breathed. She covered her eyes with her hands. 'You frightened the life out of me.'

'No, you frightened the life out of yourself. You always did like being frightened, you ridiculous child.' Dora flapped her hands at the cats, who streaked away into the bushes. 'Come on in and take those shoes off before you trail mud all over the house.'

The kitchen smelt of cabbage and Brasso. Hannah eased her boots off inside the door; Dora, she noted, had left her pink wellingtons on the boot rack and was now wearing a chic pair of Turkish slippers.

'Louise is expecting you,' said Dora, handing her a shabby pair with curling toes. 'I told her you were here on holiday, getting over an unhappy love affair. No need to go into the details, is there?'

'Granny!' protested Hannah. 'Did you have to—'

'Oh, we've all had unhappy love affairs, dear.' Dora was leading her briskly through the kitchen, past the hulking range that Dominic and Hannah had never wanted to get too close to. Everything looked like a period-film set to Hannah, and she realized that she had never been further into the house than the big kitchen, with its chilly pantry and high cupboards. There were dark corners everywhere. Her heart-rate increased again.

'Besides,' Dora went on, sweeping proprietorially past an umbrella stand, 'it does make you sound more like a human being to be licking your wounds for once, rather than celebrating another fantastic promotion.'

Hannah stopped walking and glared at her.

'I'm just saying,' said Dora, and came to a halt outside a half-closed door. 'She's in there. Smarten yourself up a bit, darling. Your hair's all cottery.'

'Thank you, Vidal Sassoon.' Hannah looked round for a mirror to uncotter her hair but couldn't see one. 'Is there a mirror, then? Or would you like me to style it by touch?'

'I was under the impression that was how you *had* styled it.' Dora stopped at the pegs and pulled aside a couple of black coats with musty astrakhan collars to reveal a heavy oak stand with a dark mirror. Hannah wondered what she might see if she looked into it. The last person to fluff up their hair? Censorious pillar-of-the-community Faith keeping an eye on proceedings from beyond the grave?

'Hurry up!' hissed Dora.

Hannah took another deep breath, peered into its spotty depths and saw only her own blotchy reflection. God, I look older than I remember, she thought ruefully, and made some token adjustments to the bird's nest on her head.

'That's better,' said Dora, and knocked on the door. She popped her head round it, and said, 'Here's Hannah now, Louise. No, no. Don't get up.'

Shyly, Hannah slipped in behind her grandmother, breathing through her mouth so as not to smell the thick orangy scent of pot pourri that lingered in the room. She knew she hadn't been received in the main drawing-room before, and yet it seemed very familiar.

Perhaps because, with all the paintings lining the walls, it looked like a saleroom.

Louise Graham-Potter was sitting in a burgundy leather armchair, looking lost between its generous wings. There were three identical chairs arranged around the marble fireplace, and she had taken the one with the best view of the sea outside and also of the door. A tea-tray with big silver pots, china cups and a plate of monster fairy cakes was within easy reach of her small hands. A matching leather pouffe had been pushed near her chair, but it was debatable whether her little legs would stretch that far. She looked as if she'd drunk the wrong cup of tea and shrunk, like Alice.

'Ah, Hannah,' said Mrs Graham-Potter, inclining her head graciously. Her silver bob fell, bell-like, round her face. 'Hello. Do come and sit down and stop that terrible draught racing through the place.'

Hannah shuffled in. There were occasional tables everywhere, all with delicate little legs and covered in what Fran called knick-knackery. One false move and she could wipe out a whole swathe of Beatrix Potter figurines, then send a table of framed photographs falling like dominoes just by turning to survey the damage.

Gingerly, she made her way round the tables to the fireside and started to lower herself on to the, thankfully sturdy, armchair.

A spasm passed across Mrs Graham-Potter's face and she said, 'Not that one!' apparently before she could stop herself. A tiny liver-spotted hand, covered with diamond rings, flew to her mouth.

Hannah sprang up, feeling her thigh muscles shriek in protest, and knocked the side table next to the chair, making the stuffed owl totter and slide off. She had no idea how she marshalled her reflexes to catch it, but she heard Dora's frightened gasp and suddenly saw the glass dome in her hands. The thought of what it would smell like if the glass broke made her feel sick.

The dead owl's yellow glass eyes stared up at her, and a solitary feather dislodged itself from the neck and floated down on to the simulated moss.

'Good catch,' said Mrs Graham-Potter drily. She sounded exactly like an old-fashioned radio announcer: her voice was elocution-modulated and bore only the faintest trace of a northern accent.

'Hannah!' Dora was next to her suddenly, shepherding her gently into the other chair with a finger in her kidneys. 'You're such a heifer. Just like your mother, poor woman. Now, shall I pour? We were rather wondering whether you'd got lost.'

Hannah sat down and looked at the delicate bone-china cups with misgivings. 'Sorry. For some reason it didn't occur to me to come in by the front door.'

'No, you'd come through the garden, wouldn't you, dear? Of course you would.' Mrs Graham-Potter accepted a cup of tea from Dora and placed the saucer carefully in the palm of her hand. It rattled delicately as her old hands trembled. 'You used to spend so much time out there when you were a little girl.'

In a town teeming with interchangeable old women, Mrs Graham-Potter stood out as rather different. She was bird-like, compared with Dora's elongated frame, but she wasn't fragile. Her chin jutted proudly, and her bone structure was still sharp beneath her clear skin. Her silvery hair was cut to perfection, and she dressed immaculately in expensive, if obviously old, clothes. According to one of Dora's rare revelations about her childhood, Mrs Graham-Potter had danced well when she was young, and the poise – and self-awareness – remained. A sheltered life, and the best of everything, had preserved her to a staggeringly advanced age, but there wasn't the faintest trace of decrepitude about her.

'Oh, we used to watch you two in that garden for hours,' Mrs Graham-Potter went on. 'In and out of the bushes, up and down the trees . . .'

Hannah blanched. For some reason, it hadn't occurred to her and Dominic that anyone might have been *watching* them. Elegant Mrs Graham-Potter watching her hanging upside down from branches . . .

'How is your brother?'

'Oh, he's fine, thank you.'

'Still abroad?' There was a trace of commiseration, as if working anywhere outside Linton was a temporary tribulation to be corrected as soon as possible.

'Yes, in New York. He's writing for quite a lot of different magazines now.'

Hannah kept her smile casual, but she missed Dominic more than she let on. It was hard to see the old ghost-story-telling Dominic in the suave, urbane journalist he was now – not that she did see him that often. They'd been so close, right up until her last summer at home, and then it had all changed. Something had changed in him. Or her. But he'd gone, left her to Linton and her mother.

'And any sign of little Marshalls on the horizon?' The plucked eyebrows lifted in query. 'Or is he . . . a bachelor still?'

Hannah couldn't tell how much satire, if any, was indicated by them. She wished the local little old ladies could be a bit less tart and a bit more Disney. 'No, he doesn't want to get married just yet. Neither of us does,' she said, before Dora could say it for her.

Mrs Graham-Potter sipped her tea. 'Yes, your grandmother mentioned your recent disappointment.'

'Oh, I'm not disappointed!' said Hannah. The teacup was burning the inside of her finger where she was holding it. 'I'm . . . relieved. I couldn't have made him happy – he couldn't have made me happy, really.'

Mrs Graham-Potter twisted her mouth sadly, as if she'd heard the same thing many times before. 'Indeed.'

Dora coughed into her hand.

There was a pregnant pause.

'Hannah's taking a little sabbatical up here,' said Dora. 'What do you call them? She's having a career mini-break. I think anyone working in London ought to have one at least once a year. Can you imagine? All that rushing around and dirt and stress.' She sipped her tea thoughtfully. 'It's no wonder none of them has any idea what they want.'

'So when are you going back to London, Hannah?' asked Mrs Graham-Potter.

Hannah flinched inside. I don't *want* to go back, she thought. 'I haven't decided yet.'

'Good.' The hulking marble clock on the mantelpiece whirred briefly, then chimed eleven. Its chimes sounded oddly fey for such a solid construction.

'Good,' Mrs Graham-Potter repeated, 'because I wonder if I could perhaps commission you to do a job up here?'

Hannah put her teacup carefully on to a Victorian papier-mâché table, decorated with lurid birds of paradise. 'Um . . .'

'What kind of a job, Louise?' asked Dora. 'Hannah doesn't really do much painting any more, but I'm sure if there was something—'

'No, I don't want her to do any painting,' Mrs Graham-Potter interrupted. 'I want her to do a valuation of the artwork in the house. Constance always meant to get it done, but I think it reminded her too much of Faith. But I know it needs doing and I don't trust that man from the auction place. I mean, I'll pay the going rate for her time and expertise, of course . . .'

'Oh, Louise, are you sure—' Dora said, with audible surprise, but Hannah's eyes were already wandering around the room, seeing it in a new light.

The ox-blood walls were barely visible beneath the gilt frames, and the room was dark with sombre fruit-bowls and lowering seascapes. Faith famously had 'good taste', and half of this must have been collected by her grandfather. Though what constituted 'good taste' round here, Hannah didn't know.

It wasn't her field of expertise, but she recognized a few good local artists: the elder Heaton Cooper, several Edward Thompsons. Classic polite-drawing-room stuff, expensive and tasteful. And there was a lot of it. Cataloguing it, let alone valuing it, could take weeks.

Weeks that would give her time to think about her next move.

Weeks in which she could come to terms with Toby having written himself out of her future.

Weeks in which her mother would almost certainly drive her insane, if only as a last resort to stop her staying in Linton.

Weeks in which she might even come to terms with the unspecific numbness spreading through her soul.

'That sounds really interesting,' she heard herself say, in an accent far posher than the one she normally used.

'Excellent,' said Mrs Graham-Potter. She took a giant fairy cake from the plate and began to divide it up with a silver cake knife. 'I have told Mrs Tyson that one doesn't need baking powder *and* self-raising. It's not all about size.' She pursed her lips with disapproval as a huge glob of buttercream shivered then fell in a snowy heap on to her plate.

The clock ticked as Dora and Hannah digested the information, and Mrs Graham-Potter redistributed the buttercream between the slices of cake. 'Oh, I suppose you'd better have a look round first, hadn't you?' she said suddenly. 'I wouldn't want to take advantage of your good nature.'

'No, no—' Dora began.

'Oh, no, I'm sure it's—' Hannah faltered and stopped. She didn't know how to finish the sentence.

Mrs Graham-Potter gave her a steady look. Her eyes were very clear, the colour of bluebells and hooded like a hawk's. 'Why don't you take a look at the pictures in the study next door? There's no need to go all over the house. The study should give you a fair idea of what's here.'

Hannah rose to her feet carefully under their anxious gaze.

'Turn left as you go out of the door, dear,' said Mrs Graham-Potter. She frowned over her cake. 'Try not to disturb Lizzie Siddall. She sleeps in there during the day.'

Hannah looked at Dora for confirmation that Lizzie Siddall was one of the cats, but Dora seemed lost in thought. Hannah was surprised by the expression she saw on her grandmother's face: Dora looked worried, desperate to say something but unsure how to say it.

'Now, then, Dora,' said Mrs Graham-Potter, 'do tell me about your reading-group afternoon at Fran's with all those awful old women. Was it a great hoot?'

Hannah hadn't taken her eyes off her grandmother. She hadn't ever thought of Mrs Graham-Potter being somehow in charge of Dora, senior to her, but now she could feel the cool breath of hierarchy between them.

'Dora?' prompted Mrs Graham-Potter, with a hint of Dora's own commanding tone.

Dora pulled herself together with a visible effort, and topped up their teacups. 'Well, it's the last time I try to inflict some culture on Mrs Cowper,' she began.

Hannah took this as her cue to leave and made her way to the door through the obstacle course of tables. She'd already spotted what she imagined was the jewel in the collection: a big Edward Thompson watercolour landscape above the fireplace. Quite a good one too, and very saleable at auction. Presumably the study would have more of the same, and she was required to identify the good stuff to prove she knew what she was talking about.

Typical, thought Hannah. My degree isn't proof enough for Linton. But her heart still speeded up with pleasure at the prospect of a test.

The hall was chilly after the warmth of the drawing room. Heavy oak panelling made it dark, and difficult to see which were doors and which were just elaborate panels. Hannah hesitated. The door directly on the left didn't look like a study door. Anything might lurk behind it.

Get a grip, she told herself. This isn't Bluebeard's Castle.

She grasped the handle and gave it a firm twist. It resisted. Hannah tightened her fingers round the brass doorknob. The doors at home were like this – swollen with the water in the air, and prone to sticking. She twisted and shoved at the same time, the door swung open and she stumbled into the room.

Lizzie Siddall, a pale gold Persian, woke up with an aggrieved yowl, leaped down from a high bookshelf, and shot out between Hannah's legs.

Hannah didn't notice. She was staring round the study in a state of hypnotized awe, taking in the huge oil paintings that dominated the panelled walls. It wasn't a big room, and was furnished with bookshelves, a large desk and an old velvet *chaise-longue*, but the paintings hanging from every wall seemed to change the dimensions entirely. Not all the artists were familiar to her – there were a couple of very nice Heaton Coopers, some lowering seascapes, and something that might be a Sheila Fell, which was very interesting indeed – but it was the family portraits that froze her to the spot, commanding her attention.

Hannah swallowed. How could anyone work in here, with all these people watching them?

There were Musgraves going back four hundred years, but they were identical, only different in their clothes: the same arrogant round-eyed expression stared out of each portrait, defying changing art fashions and possibly even the flattering intentions of the artist. In oils, watercolours, pencil sketches, photographs, men, women and children had the same gorgeous intensity, glaring out from rolling hills and woodland glades, demanding respect. Clearly some talented artists were represented in the collection, but the subjects rose above everything else: the Musgrave family, of which Louise was the last, unrelated, custodian.

Two Musgraves she recognized straight away hung over the fireplace: matching portraits of Faith and Constance, painted some time in the thirties, Hannah guessed. She examined them with interest: her mental image of Faith and Constance was of two old ladies, albeit smart ones, and her childhood memories didn't really differentiate much between one old woman and the next.

These pictures had been painted when they were in the full bloom of youth and, unlike the other family portraits, they were the true centre of the pictures, not the ostentatiously rolling landscapes or sumptuous interiors. It was obvious they were sisters – both had high intelligent foreheads, and thick blonde hair cut fashionably short, but there the resemblance stopped, almost as if their personalities defined their physical differences.

Constance was the prettier of the two, with round blue eyes and a pink flush to her cheeks. Her eyes were slightly downcast, as if the idea of having an artist look at her for hours on end was somehow embarrassing. She was posed on a garden seat, with a large white sunhat on her knee and a basket of tearoses next to her. A spaniel leaned its head protectively against her lap, and one of her long white hands trailed down to caress its ear. Hannah could imagine those hands trailing across the keys of the piano in the drawing room, or choosing flowers from the garden. Constance's portrait was exactly what she imagined when she thought of someone being a perfect lady: quiet, charming, demure.

Faith, on the other hand, stared out of her portrait with the family confidence burning in her dark eyes and a stern expression hovering at the corners of her red mouth. She might equally have been about to bestow a smile or bark a command. Her hair was a little darker than Constance's and her features less softly moulded; her mouth was strong and almost masculine in its firm line. She wore hunting pink and leaned against a gate, as if the artist had caught her a few seconds before she leaped over it. Movement and vigour vibrated from her, even across seventy years and a dusty canvas.

Hannah let the image burn into her mind. The Misses Musgrave. These were the youthful shadows of the old women she'd seen making slow progress around summer shows and charity garden parties, being driven to appointments in town in their old Bentley, opening local fêtes with golden scissors and regal waves. In Hannah's mind as a child, they'd been the nearest thing to royalty, appearing in her grandmother's stories; 'Faith decided this ... Constance donated that ...'

But here they were young women, only a little older than her. Faith's firm mouth had the beginnings of the sternness and autocracy Hannah remembered, but Constance's beauty was in her youth and delicacy, and she seemed a different woman altogether.

Automatically, she looked in the corner for the artist: Matthew Fisher, 1929. So they did have one or two Fishers in the collection. Of course they would, if Faith was his patron.

Hannah realized she'd been holding her breath for a long time and allowed herself to exhale quietly. She felt unnerved, as if she'd walked in on a room full of people only to find it fall silent, all attention on her. In the same second she decided she would stay and catalogue the collection – not just to give herself time but because it now seemed very rude to refuse. Not to Mrs Graham-Potter, but to these massed ranks of autocratic Musgraves.

Outside, the wind scraped a branch across the window. Hannah felt a shiver of unease at being alone in the study, having barged her way in so inelegantly and broken the stillness that filled the room like dust. Disapproval seemed to press down on her from each corniced corner. She turned and walked purposefully to the door, noting a couple of nice landscapes on the way, but deliberately not looking any of the portraits in the eye as she went. She knew it was ridiculous, but she couldn't stop herself. The door hadn't closed properly and she grabbed the handle, then slid out round it.

In the hall, her breath returned and she took a few gulps of air to steady herself before she went back in to make polite small-talk about the book group. God, she thought, breathing slowly to get her head to stop spinning. I must be run-down or anaemic or something.

She put a hand on the lintel of the door, which was ajar.

'Are you really sure?' Dora was saying, with more concern in her voice than Hannah was familiar with. 'Don't you think some things are best left alone? It affects so many people, you know.'

'No, I don't.' Mrs Graham-Potter's voice was light, but it carried. 'It would need a professional opinion in any case.'

'Oh, Louise, I hope you're prepared for what Hannah might . . .' Dora's voice trailed away. There was the clink of a teapot lid being removed so that the bags could be stirred.

'I did *tell* Mrs Tyson to put a hot-water jug on here,' said Mrs Graham-Potter, tersely.

So *that's* it, thought Hannah. There's some painting they think might be valuable but they don't want to be ripped off by the local auction house. She smiled to herself. Why didn't they just say so? She coughed and pushed the door open to let herself back in.

'So, what did you think?' Mrs Graham-Potter sat back in her huge chair and put her little hands together so the rings sparkled in the last rays of sunlight.

Dora was looking somewhat less pleased with herself than usual.

'It's a very interesting collection,' said Hannah, and she meant it. 'Some nice pieces, of local artwork in particular. The Sheila Fell next door is worth a lot of money. And, of course, the Thompson.'

She nodded towards the fireplace, knowing that Mrs Graham-Potter would prefer the rolling lines and gentle colours to the stark oils of the Fell landscape, even if it was worth a quarter of the money.

Mrs Graham-Potter looked relieved, as if she'd bitten into a nondescript chocolate and found it to be a champagne truffle. 'Indeed. That was always one of my favourites.'

'When are you going to start, Hannah?' asked Dora.

'Whenever's convenient for you.'

'Tomorrow, then,' said Mrs Graham-Potter.

'Tomorrow,' said Hannah.

Dora smiled with her lips pressed tightly together, and cut her fairy cake in half, so forcefully that the knife clinked on the fine china plate.

Chapter Six

Hannah sat on her bed to pull on her trainers, then got up to peer out of the window. The view didn't put her in the mood for outdoor exercise. It didn't put her in the mood for anything apart from going back to bed. Beyond Rose View's garden walls, the sea was a washed-out grey, with a few scudding white crests picking out the waves, and it faded into a sky so colourless that it was almost impossible to see where the two met. There were a couple of fishing-boats on the horizon, but even they didn't provide a splash of colour.

She sighed.

It had rained all night, hard little drops that sounded like someone tapping impatient fingernails on the roof. That had faded to a light drizzle, which was showing signs of settling in for the day. Hannah had often wondered if Linton had its own microclimate, one that recirculated rainfall like a giant garden water feature.

She sighed again and walked back to the mirror where she inspected her appearance in the old gym kit. That certainly didn't put her any more in the mood for outdoor exercise.

A strong yearning for the crossword and a cup of coffee in town swept over her, but she needed to get out and do something to stop the twitching in her leg muscles and the futile whirring of her brain. All of them were jumpy – her, Fran and Dora. That was what happened when three people all had issues they wanted to evade in order to keep things level between them.

Hannah had mentioned her new commission, as vaguely as she could, to Fran the previous evening. Her mother, predictably, hadn't been impressed. But, then, while Hannah was in Linton she could have been working for MI6 and Fran still wouldn't have been impressed. Fran was like a self-help tape on constant replay – on a loop, in fact: all of her suggestions involved going back to London, and came dressed up in a variety of despairing clichés. Hannah did not want to take the bull by the horns, or grasp the nettle. She wanted to be somewhere with no bulls or nettles in the first place.

Don't forget Granny's going to have to take some of the blame for me staying on to do this, Hannah reminded herself, as she undid her ponytail and plaited her hair, in the vain hope that it might make her look more purposeful and sporty.

She frowned mid-plait, trying to put her finger on what seemed so fishy about her grandmother's role in the arrangement. Had she suggested it to Mrs Graham-Potter as a way of getting Hannah to stay at home for a while? She hadn't made any attempt to lure her home before. Was it a way of getting back at Fran for something – maybe to do with whatever they were politely warring about? But then there had been that aghast look on her face when the paintings were mentioned, as if she had been unexpectedly outmanoeuvred.

That must have been an interesting new sensation for her, Hannah thought. She slipped a ponytail band round her hair, stood back and looked at her new reflection. The plait hadn't transformed her into Steffi Graf. But it was too late for that now: time was getting on.

Out of the house, Hannah's feet automatically set off towards the jogging loop she'd tried unsuccessfully to master while she was at school: down the hill, round the Ramble Way, climbing up to the high point above the harbour, then a final downhill stagger to the back garden. Mercifully, much of it was out of the public eye.

Hannah retuned her tiny Walkman to the first station playing upbeat music as she strode down the hill and towards the harbour. There wasn't a huge amount on offer, and the one station she could find playing pop music was sharing its wavelength with a farming broadcaster on the Isle of Man; any pop music was surreally intercut with auction prices when she turned her hip two degrees to the left.

She power-walked past the villas – gravity, and the fact that she was still visible to traffic, was a significant spur to her efforts – and at the bottom turned right, panting, on to the coastal Ramble Way, where she slowed her pace on the pretext of getting a better radio signal.

The Ramble Way, once a path for miners walking to the pits from outlying villages, was now barely used, despite the panoramic view it offered of the town. There wasn't the same dramatic beach scenery as further down the coast and, in any case, urban development meant that a long stretch of the path now ran through the rougher local housing development. Also, the residents didn't take kindly to people in bobble hats marching through their estate, looking at them. It also set off the violent barking of thirty-odd Dobermann-sheepdog crosses.

Hannah strode on to the track with some difficulty, pushing her legs through the long grasses that choked the sandy path. Her tracksuit was stiffening with rainwater and her lungs were burning.

How could five minutes of real exercise be more agonizing than half an hour at the gym?

It's important to get through this stage and into fat-burning mode, she reminded herself, without much conviction. Her stride slowed as the stitch spread up her left side.

I really don't have to do this, she thought. *There's nothing stopping me going straight home.*

But she marched on, imagining a little of her old heartaches disappearing with each new throb of her muscles, pushing out her misery with the toxins sweating into her T-shirt.

Exercise didn't give her the clear space in her head that she had hoped. It just displaced the throb of unhappiness with trivial new concerns: was I this unfit at school? Am I too old to be wearing these trainers? If old people dressed as chickens can run twenty-six miles, why can't I?

The drizzle had brought out the snails and Hannah couldn't get into a proper marching rhythm when she was trying not to crush them underfoot. If she'd thought about it too much, the sheer number of snails slithering along the track would have freaked her out. At first, she stepped over and round them, but then, as her legs got heavier and her pace slowed, she paused to pick them up and move them to the side of the path. There were two little snails right in the middle, with silvery trails meandering uncertainly behind them in the sand.

It struck her that snails would have made a much better symbol for Linton than the confused bear and staff that featured in the town's livery: like the snails, Lintonians seemed inseparable from their homes, vulnerable under the hard shell of their defensiveness, moving slowly and surely in gangs, their trembling horns ever alert for attack, their heads ever ready to be pulled in.

Hannah bent down, trying to ignore her irregular breathing, and picked one up. It was bigger than it had seemed on the ground, a little too big to be nice, with a speckled pattern like leopard-print on its shell and a sucker foot that glistened delicately in the light. Its head shot back into the sand-flecked shell as the cold air touched its slimy foot and Hannah shivered with revulsion.

'I'll just put you back in the hedge,' she said, and leaned over to drop it into the long grass.

Then she saw that the long grass was seething with masses of brown snails, some climbing up the thicker stems and bending them over with their weight. All were moving slowly but inexorably towards the path, their long antennae swaying and probing, the trails glittering stickily on the leaves. There were fifty or sixty in that patch alone, in a range of sizes from marble to golf-ball, all inching nearer like the battalion of a bigger snail army. Hannah jumped back with an involuntary squeal and a satisfying crack indicated that she had squashed one. 'Eurgh!' she said. She scuffed her sole along the path to wipe snail residue off her trainer, trying hard not to think about it, then shoved her hands into her pockets and marched on, keeping her eyes fixed on the furthest waves out to sea, thinking about nothing except her breathing, and not looking down at all.

Hannah carried on walking, and windmilling her arms for exercise, until she got to the tall ventilation chimney at the other side of the hill, where she sat down on a step and stretched her legs on to another piece of fallen masonry, pretending to do yoga stretches for the benefit of any passers-by.

This chimney-stack was the place she had come to when she'd been desperate to get out of the house for a bit of peace and quiet. During her school years that had sometimes been four or five times a week – when her mother was wrangling over the nasty divorce settlement with her father, or with the council over some mining-compensation body her firm represented, or with Dominic about his latest earring, or with Dora over something Hannah never quite heard.

The chimney had provided ventilation for one of the old pits in Linton, an unlucky seam that had closed down years before after a notoriously bad fire a couple of miles out to sea. A gas pocket had exploded in the upper shaft, sending a ball of flames racing down the seam too fast for the men to be saved. A whole shift had been killed along with nine ponies, and thirty more had died in trying to rescue them. A tiny clause of mining legislation had been passed because of it. After the tragedy the pit buildings had been abandoned, then fallen derelict over the years, but the ventilation chimney had been turned into a memorial to the lost miners. The names of the dead men and boys encircled the base on brass plaques like the ones they'd used to identify the burned bodies they'd recovered. The little tags went all the way round, three times.

Hannah stretched her arms above her head and breathed in the tangy ozone. An enjoyable sensation of weariness spread through her legs. It had stopped raining and a grey cloud was glowing with promise. Hannah felt a deep sense of contentment seep into her bones, and let her mind empty with each distant hush and fall of the tide.

It was so restful, she thought. From this distance you could admire the terraces and solid steeples while pretending there were no people in Linton – a state of affairs that, ironically, she, Fran and Dora all frequently wished for in their private moments. On the whole, Hannah felt Lintonians, with their dour, suspicious outlook on life, didn't deserve a town as pretty as this. A scruffier, smaller place would appeal to their innate need to twine while giving them less to live up to.

From high on the hill, Linton was charming, a Legoland town of red roofs and neat streets. Out of range of car noise or people yelling at each other, Hannah could look straight down into the harbour area, where the tall houses in the old heart of the town, built with the first gush of coal money, were all listed buildings, and the church spires rose above the houses like flowers reaching for the sun. From here Linton was a welcoming, elegant place. It was only when you got up close to it that you saw the peeling masonry paint and the pound shops nesting like magpies in the old department stores, and caught a whiff of a town doing everything it could to survive.

Hannah stared down at it and tried not to think about what might be happening to her flat in her absence. Or if she was jeopardizing her legal rights by allowing Mandy, her flatmate, to sublet to her boyfriend. Or whether Toby would have noticed her collapse and retreat.

But he was on honeymoon, wasn't he? She'd probably never even crossed his mind. The cunning bastard. 'Oh, Toby!' she moaned aloud, relishing the luxury of being able to talk as loudly as she wanted, and have the wind carry away her voice. 'Where did it all go wrong?' But she knew the answer to that one, really.

'For God's sake, shut up, Hannah. You sound like a *Jackie* photo-story,' snapped a familiar voice.

'Mum!' said Hannah. She retracted her legs self-consciously and sat up. 'What are you doing here?'

Fran dumped her briefcase on the step next to Hannah. She looked positively disgruntled to see her there. 'I could ask you the same thing. I was under the impression that you were meant to be going to see Mrs Graham-Potter.'

Apparently doing something she didn't approve of was better than doing nothing at all. 'I'm going round after lunch,' retorted Hannah. 'I wanted some peace and quiet to think about . . . things,' she went on defensively. 'I often used to come up here. To get a bit of space.'

It made her feel a bit awkward to have admitted to her mother that she'd frequently wanted to escape from the tension and amateur dramatics of their house. Hannah wasn't vindictive: she thought on balance she'd turned out OK, and she didn't want to make things worse for Fran, whose own memories of that time must be painful enough, without her daughter heaping on more guilt. She sat down again.

'Space!' muttered Fran. 'There isn't room in the world for all the space we need.'

Hannah looked at her mother. She seemed tired and her eyeshadow had smudged round her eyes like a bruise. On a bad day, Fran tended to look beaten up, rather than made up. 'I thought you were in court today?'

'I was. The trial collapsed.'

Fran inspected the step next to Hannah, spread out her scarf and sat down. She sighed like a deflating balloon as her weight transferred off her sensible pumps. 'Thank *God* it did. I don't know how much more of it I could have taken without standing up and banging all their heads together.'

Hannah didn't pursue it. Since she'd been old enough to understand what her mother did for a living, she'd never been sure how much she could discuss, or wanted to discuss, her court cases, especially the ones that irritated her. Fran threw up invisible barriers with her sparking eyes then folded her arms over the top. Hannah didn't try to cross them. She wasn't the kind of child who enjoyed testing boundaries, much to Fran's despair. She just slunk underneath.

They sat in silence for a few minutes, watching one of the fishing-boats come into the harbour. Some men appeared on the dockside and helped tie it up as Mrs Jordan, a tiny speck of red anorak in the distance, struggled valiantly along the quay with her basset hound Daisy, who seemed intent on sniffing every decorative bollard.

It occurred to Hannah that, away from the house and Dora's presence, this would be a good time to grasp the nettle and ask Fran if there really was a problem. It would be like plea-bargaining. Maybe she'd offer some information in exchange for a firm departure date.

'Mum,' she began uncertainly, 'I know you like to, um, deal with things yourself, but you would tell me if . . .' She stopped. 'I know I've been wrapped up in my own, um, life, but . . . You can tell me, you know.'

But Fran said nothing, and stared out to sea.

Hannah wasn't sure if this was a yes or a no. Well, I tried, she thought, and pushed away the relief that crept treacherously into her mind. 'I really love it up here,' she said, and she meant it. It annoyed her that Fran refused to believe she could find anything good about Linton, while maintaining a fiercely defensive opinion of it, so fierce that it bordered on aggression. 'It's so peaceful. So beautiful.'

'Do you think so?' Fran turned round. Real surprise was clear on her face. 'Why?'

'Well . . .' Hannah floundered. She hadn't anticipated this. A simple agreeing noise would have sufficed. 'Well, isn't it a gorgeous view of the town? It's so quiet and you can't see the estates, or the main road and . . . well, just look at the sea and everything! And smell the air! Don't you think it's peaceful? What do you want? Palm trees and leaping dolphins?'

Fran pulled her jacket tighter around her. 'Ooh dear, no, I think it's *incredibly* sad up here. Really . . . sorrowful. Eerie, sometimes. I always come here when I've got something hard to think about. It puts it all into perspective for me.'

'What do you mean by that?' asked Hannah, watching fish being hauled off the boat in blue plastic crates. She hated getting the wrong answer to things. It made her feel vulnerable. Now she wondered if she was going to get a social-conscience lecture for wanting to edit the estates out of her ideal Linton.

She stretched her hamstrings and wondered how often her mother had come up here during her adolescence. And whether they'd unknowingly been missing each other by seconds like the little people on the weather-house in the garden.

Fran huffed. 'I *mean* it might be hard for me to work out whether to have the roof inspected or whether to chance it until next year, but at least my father, husband and two brothers haven't been buried two miles under the sea by a collapsing mine shaft.'

'Oh,' said Hannah, chastened. *Durrrr.* Of course. It was so obvious. 'Oh, God, of course, yeah. Sorry.'

More silence. More crates unloaded. Mrs Jordan finally dragged Daisy back to heel and set off towards her little bungalow by the post office.

Hannah wondered whether her mother was working up to an apology for being inhospitable and not particularly supportive of her in her hour of need, but then decided it was unlikely.

'I used to come here when I was a little girl too, you know,' Fran said, out of the blue. 'I used to pray for hours for all the dead men and the dead horses underneath where I was sitting, imagining them waiting down there for Judgement Day. All warm in the dark pit. Wondering whether they could hear the sea at the end of the seam.' She pressed her lips together tightly and folded her hands in her lap.

'Really?' said Hannah. It was strange, sharing a moment like this with her mother. It was the first time since she'd been back that she felt Fran was talking to her like an adult rather than as a seventeen-year-old daughter.

'I used to read the names and ages of the men on the plaques, and try to imagine what they all looked like, and work out how old they'd be now if they'd not been down the pit that day. And I used to try to imagine all their wives and girlfriends turning into wrinkly spinsters while their partners were under the sea, still twenty-one. There were loads of old women in Linton even then, their other halves gone, leaving them to wander round the library and the shops on their own, like wallflowers at a dance.' She pulled a face. 'Morbid little thing, I was. And stupid.'

'No, not really,' said Hannah. 'Just sensitive.'

'That's not what your grandmother said when she found out where I'd been,' said Fran. She brushed off traces of sand from her skirt. 'She followed me up here one day, found me on my knees by the chimney, getting holes in my stockings and crying. She said I was behaving in a most hysterical manner and expressly forbade me to come up here again. She said if I wanted to pray for dead people, there were several million in London I could start with, not to mention the entire Jewish race in Eastern Europe. It was after the war, you see.'

'Oh,' said Hannah. 'Do you think she understood what you were doing?'

Fran's lips set in a thin line, one that lipstick couldn't ever hope to plump up into kissability. 'Yes, I think she knew exactly what I was doing.' She paused and scrabbled around in her bag. 'Polo mint?'

Hannah shook her head, and Fran popped one into her own mouth.

'So, did you stop coming up here, then?'

'No,' said Fran. The mint rattled against her teeth as she sucked it ferociously. 'I most certainly did not stop, so in the end she took me to the Spiritualist meeting-house in Spanish Lane and frightened the living daylights out of me.'

This surprised Hannah, since Fran was resolutely pragmatic about astrology, *feng shui* and most other invisible spiritual aids. 'A

Spiritualist meeting-house? Really? In Linton?' she asked. 'I thought people round here were too plain-speaking for that kind of nonsense.'

'Oh, no, there was a great big hall,' said Fran, 'round behind the church. I know, very ironic. Competition was hot for a long while. But where you have a lot of people dying suddenly and unfairly . . .' She shrugged. 'You can understand it, I suppose. They've got to have something. Mind you, Dora got into trouble herself for taking me there.'

'From who? Grandad?'

Fran snorted. 'Arthur? Good God, no. He wouldn't have dared to tell Dora her watch was wrong. Poor Arthur. No. She got a real tongue-lashing from Faith and Louise.'

Hannah considered this interesting new piece of information about her grandmother. Dora on the end of a tongue-lashing from someone else? Weird. 'Not Constance?'

Fran paused and pursed her lips. She might have been sticking her tongue through the hole in the mint, or illustrating Faith's disgust. 'Constance didn't like arguments,' she said eventually. 'Especially not where Dora was concerned. She slipped out of the room when she could feel one coming.'

She turned to her daughter. 'Very like you in that respect.'

'Oh, thank you.' Hannah felt aggrieved. 'Did they argue a lot, Faith and Dora? I mean, is it something that runs in the family?'

If Hannah had hoped to wrongfoot her mother into revealing something of Dora's childhood, she didn't succeed. She sensed the wall of discretion rising between them, like a chauffeur pressing the button to slide up the dividing glass screen.

Fran crunched her mint. 'Does anyone round here do anything else?'

'I don't.'

'No,' said Fran, thoughtfully. 'You don't.'

They sat in silence for a while. It was sort of companionable. As companionable as two people could be when they had more or less admitted to having painful problems to contemplate yet hadn't shared them.

But Hannah didn't feel alone and that was a big improvement on sitting in Green Park, going numb with ingrowing misery.

Chapter Seven

Hannah could vividly remember the day Dora had moved out of Rose View and into the cottage down by the sea wall. That week stood out in her mind because for once it hadn't been raining, and Linton was enjoying its hottest days since official town records began in 1843. Although, as the *Linton Gazette* pointed out, unofficial records had begun forty years prior to that: an eccentric couple of brothers in a farm out in Etterthwaite had developed their own barometer, as well as sundry other less practical agricultural tools.

Every day broke a new high watermark of heat, and the relentlessly climbing temperature was a source of fascination to Hannah. Mrs Kelly, her primary-school teacher, sweating in her green cord skirt, had decided to make a feature of the oppressive warmth and had rapidly adjusted the science project to include weather-forecasting. Hannah grasped the principles gleefully and took to carrying pine cones and seaweed with her in a little bag. They were both as dry as bone and smelt revolting.

Her predictions of an endless summer weren't taken well at home where the temperature, meteorological and emotional, was equally torpid. In the hall there was a presentation barometer whose spindly pointer never seemed to move off 'Dry', no matter how much Hannah tapped it.

'Give over tapping it,' Fran would say.

'Or I'll tap you,' Keith would add, from behind the education supplement of the *Guardian*.

Fran would leap on that as another reason to kick off an argument, and Hannah would go up to Dora's room to check on the state of her magical forecasting mice.

Dora's apartment in Rose View was the only cool part of the house. She kept a pair of white mice in her room in a large tank filled with cotton reels and shredded newspaper. For the sake of Winston and Clemmie's health, the curtains remained drawn and an electric fan was constantly blowing. Dora claimed the mice could tell when it was going to rain because they scurried faster in their exercise wheel. But they hadn't scurried for over a week, and lay, like the rest of the family, in a bad-tempered stupor.

Hannah spent a lot of quiet time with her grandmother, away from her moody parents, whose simmering arguments spat like little beads of hot fat, stinging bystanders. Dora hadn't moved out of her room when Arthur died, and turned his dressing room into her salon, which she filled with all the books he didn't like her to read, and invited all the friends that had irritated him for tea. Not that she'd ever refrained from inviting them before, but having them discussing Chanel and Belmondo where Arthur had tended his dentures gave her, she said, a deep sense of satisfaction.

Hannah poked Winston with her cyan colouring pencil. He was the bigger of the two mice and usually scurried the hardest. Dora hadn't been in when Hannah first knocked politely on her door. In the past few weeks, she'd been spending a lot of time up in the big house, 'talking to the old ladies', according to Fran, who hadn't wished to expand on this.

Dora was back now, and writing poetry. Not very quickly, though. She hadn't written a word yet, although her book was open in front of her.

'Why aren't they moving, Granny?' Hannah asked crossly.

'They might be dead,' said Dora.

'Really?' Hannah received this information with the same *sangfroid* as Dora had delivered it. Death was a new topic on the home curriculum, along with weather and fractions. Fran had chosen to give Dominic and Hannah their death-comes-to-everyone lecture that week. She hadn't sugared the pill with Heaven, as it was a terribly outdated Sunday School notion.

'Would they go to mouse Heaven?' Hannah asked hopefully.

There was a pause. 'Yes.' Dora's voice was higher than normal, but firm.

'Does everything go to its own Heaven?' asked Hannah, imagining a series of soul-sorting tubes like a giant waterslide, into which men, women, mice, dolls, cats and cars could be poured and despatched to the right section of eternal joy.

'You're very spiritual today.'

'What?'

'*Excuse me*. Not *what*. *What* is what the people from Etterthwaite say.'

'Excuse me.'

The electric fan whirred.

Hannah wondered if Dora was crying. She thought she could hear faint sniffling noises. 'Are you crying, Granny?' she enquired.

'No.' Dora's wobbly voice didn't sound convincing, even to Hannah, but they had an understanding about crying. If you said you weren't, you weren't. Fran couldn't grasp the importance of this and usually insisted on knowing if you were and why, which only made matters worse.

'OK,' said Hannah, in a knowing tone.

For a while they sat in silence. Hannah stopped poking Winston and read her book while Dora dipped and redipped her pen in the inkwell without writing anything. She didn't hum as she normally did.

Eventually Dora made a pot of leaf tea and solemnly offered Hannah her own cup and saucer. They both pretended not to want biscuits, then took three pink wafers each.

'Darling, would you mind awfully if I didn't live here any more?' she asked.

'Yes,' said Hannah. 'I'd mind a *lot*.'

Dora seemed pleased with this. 'What if I moved just a little way away?'

'Like where?'

Dora ignored the Etterthwaite sentence construction. 'Like into the cottage at the bottom of the garden.'

Hannah considered. Dominic said the cottage at the bottom of the garden was haunted. The last person to live there had been a grumpy old man, and all the curtains were still drawn. The roses in the beds around it had gone wild and scratchy, exactly like in her fairy-tale book, and for all she knew Snow White, Rose Red, Sleeping Beauty and a whole array of wolves might be hiding inside it.

'I'd rather you didn't,' she said bravely, 'but if you had to move, I suppose it wouldn't be too far to come and see you.'

'Why don't you want me to live there?'

Hannah gave her a serious look. She could confide this to Dora, but never to Fran. 'Granny, it's haunted.'

Dora raised her eyebrows, then looked over her shoulder, as if to make sure Fran couldn't hear. 'Darling, I know it is,' she whispered.

Later that evening, Hannah lay in bed, trying to fall asleep, but her head felt hot and full of white light behind her eyes. She tried staring at the figures on the frieze, willing them to move. Sometimes, if she concentrated hard enough, they twitched and the colours, faded a little by the sun, glowed brighter on the wall like fresh paint.

Now Dancing Daisy's eyes remained coyly fixed on her dainty little toe and refused to meet Hannah's.

Hannah tried pulling the sheets over her head to make sleep come, which sometimes worked, but didn't this time, then sighed heavily and fluffed the bad dreams out of her pillow. As she sat up in bed, her eye was caught by the strange red glow on the far wall and voices outside.

They sounded near, maybe in the garden.

She got up and padded over to the window. It wasn't easy to see much of the garden because the broad guttering of Dora's sitting-room bay window beneath obscured her view. It spread out like half of a big black umbrella, about a foot below the nursery window-ledge.

Hannah eased open the window so she could hear the voices more clearly. Fran had strict rules about opening windows above ground level – reinforced by Dora, who explained that evil spirits and bats would fly in – but this was obviously a special case.

Someone who sounded a lot like her mother was yelling incoherently, and Hannah could definitely smell smoke and an odd chemical smell. Dominic had just acquired a chemistry set, so she was familiar with chemical smells. There were other voices too (Dad? Granny?) and the crackle of burning sticks, like Bonfire Night.

Hannah wasn't a naturally curious child, but some impulse, perhaps because she was half asleep, made her determined to see more. If she went downstairs to look, they'd all stop whatever was going on. Fran was forever muttering about Little Piggies with Big Ears, which Hannah was now old enough to take personally. She put on her slippers and crawled out of the window, keeping her weight on the window-ledge and her bottom in her room, until she could see over the edge of the guttering.

Although her heart hammered with vertigo, the scene in the garden made Hannah forget to breathe, such was the oddness of what was going on. In the clearing where the old apple tree had been cut down, Dora was standing in front of a small bonfire, just like a witch in a storybook. She was enrobed in her red velvet housecoat and an odd turban, and was throwing bits of paper into the flames from a manilla envelope under one arm. The fire had obviously been going for some time, because fragments of black paper were flying around like tiny bats.

Fran, meanwhile, was running down the orchard in her big white cotton nightie, like a very solid ghost in wellington boots, closely followed by Keith in his striped pyjama bottoms.

Hannah noticed that her father had no hair on his chest, which was very pale in the moonlight.

'Stop it!' Fran was yelling, stretching out her arms wildly. 'Stop it!'

Dora responded by holding a large photograph at one corner and allowing the flames to lick up and devour it. Hannah admired the way Dora's long arms extended with as much scorn as elegance, not unlike Dancing Daisy's.

'It's mine to do with as I like!' she said, very clearly. This stood out in Hannah's mind later: it was a sentence she herself was fond of.

'What about Faith?' demanded Fran, between gasps, holding her sides. She wasn't used to exercise, unlike Dora, who skipped discreetly in the back garden, often with Hannah.

Dora replied, but Hannah couldn't catch what she said. She edged out a little more. The guttering, she was sure, would hold her weight, but the whole situation was so exactly like an odd dream that she wouldn't have been surprised if the window-ledge had turned into a magic carpet and flown off with her.

Her bravery was rewarded, because no sooner had she gained an extra sliver of viewing than Mrs Graham-Potter arrived on the scene to join the merry throng around Dora's bonfire. Unlike the others, she was very properly dressed in a green silk kaftan, but in deference to the late hour her hair was undone and hung down her back in long white curls.

Hannah had never seen Mrs Graham-Potter with her hair undone. She looked like a young woman, not the ancient old lady Hannah knew her to be. She rubbed her eyes. Was she imagining that too?

'Stop that, Dora!' Mrs Graham-Potter commanded, holding up her thin white hands.

'Why?' Dora demanded. 'I can't do as much damage as you have. Anyhow, it's all done.' She turned on her heel and marched away towards the cottage, which now had lights on inside and the door wide open.

'She's got no right!' yelled Fran impotently. 'She can't just—'

'She can do exactly as she wishes,' said Mrs Graham-Potter. 'She always has done. Alas.'

Hannah had noted that her father was taking an unusual back-seat role in the proceedings, but almost as if she were directing the whole thing from inside her head, he chose that moment – a brief one, in which none of the three women was talking – to shout, 'Oh, grow up! You're all behaving like bloody children!'

'Shut up, Keith,' snapped Fran. 'What would you know about that?'

'I'm a teacher.'

'Just in theory! Like everything else you do!'

Hannah's hand lurched forward as the moss she was leaning on gave way. For a second she thought she was going to fall. But her slippered feet scrabbled for grip against the dresser by the window and she righted herself, just in time to see Constance Musgrave hobbling rapidly down the garden path in a pair of white silk pyjamas, her hair around her shoulders.

This was such a transformation from her usual tight Medusa plaits and tweed suit that it took Hannah a moment to work out who on earth she was.

'Oh, Louise,' she gasped, grabbing Mrs Graham-Potter's arm. 'Come quick, it's Faith! I think she's having a stroke!'

Mrs Graham-Potter's expression stuck in Hannah's mind for ever, mainly because Constance's words made her think of a cat in a picture book being petted. What could be so awful about that? There were lots of cats up at the villa, none of which was strokable, but maybe it was different with grown-ups.

Mrs Graham-Potter's face, though, was full of fear, panic and some other adult emotion that Hannah didn't recognize, but knew to be scary.

'Mum! Mum!' Fran set off at high speed towards the cottage, while Constance clung weeping to Mrs Graham-Potter.

Keith stood there, shivering, his hand extending towards the old women, then withdrawing, then extending again, as if he wasn't sure how much physical comfort he could offer them.

Mrs Graham-Potter shot him a look of contempt, and said something under her breath that made him flinch, then flush with anger.

Hannah was leaning out further to see who else might appear when a gust of wind made the bedroom door slam behind her. Instinctively she whipped round to see what it was, and lost her balance, skinning her palm on the window-ledge and slipping out on to the guttering where she landed, hands down, toes still hooked over the ledge in an undignified and precarious handstand. The guttering was still warm from the day's heat and covered in fine sand. It creaked under her weight and shifted away from the wall.

In the garden, someone screamed. Maybe more than one person. Hannah was screaming herself, no longer caring who was doing what and where just as long as someone came and hauled her back to safety. She squeezed her knees together as tightly as she could to stop the desperate need to wee.

It felt like hours but within a minute a pair of strong hands were reaching round her ankles and, like a big fish, she wriggled back into the room.

Dominic had dragged her in, and now he stood looking down at her, with a sleepy look of panic on his face. Hannah slumped into his arms, her body heavy with relief. He opened his mouth to say something, to ask her something, but changed his mind.

Moments later, Fran and Keith crashed into the room, full of remonstrations, mostly with each other.

In the garden, Constance stood frozen to the spot, still staring up at the nursery window, her face a mask of horror.

Shortly afterwards, Dora moved all her belongings out of Rose View and into the old gardener's cottage, which she had made habitable in a magical amount of time. Hannah thought of *Sleeping Beauty*, which she had just seen at the Linton Picture House, where the fairy godmothers went round the house tidying and baking cakes with a twitch of their wands. Dominic had scoffed at the film, which he didn't think was scary enough, but Hannah had thought differently, and had been uncomfortably reminded throughout of the old ladies up in the big house, and the way they seemed to change into other people at night.

For a few days Fran talked about getting a lodger in, since there was now so much room and she was, nominally, in charge of it. She and Keith didn't move into her parents' quarters, but remained in the old upstairs sewing room they'd converted to a stuffy boudoir. Rose View had always been too big, even with Dora there, and without her, almost in compensation, the house seemed to echo with sounds they hadn't caused.

A few days later, when Hannah was nearly sure she'd dreamed the strange scenes in the garden, there was a great to-do up at the big house. Another ambulance arrived, this time without the sirens blaring, then a whole stream of people came and went. Hannah watched them all, from an upstairs window with a panoramic view of both the villa and the main road. Dora was summoned, and Fran, which left Keith in reluctant charge of Dominic and Hannah.

They went down to the harbour and listened to their father's lecture about how evil the men were who used to run the town for slavery, then, by way of compensation (or as an easy dig at Fran's wholefood tyranny), they went to the Coffee Pot for a cup of tea and a novelty cake. Hannah had a bright blue Mr Bump and Dominic had a lurid orange Mr Tickle.

At home, Hannah noticed the sombre atmosphere straight away, but guessed wrongly that it was to do with the forbidden cake. Consequently, she went straight to her room to read, and was trapped there when Fran came upstairs with her Very Serious Face on.

'I've got some sad news, Hannah,' she said. 'I'm afraid Faith Musgrave is dead.'

Hannah put down her book. 'Was it the Musgrave curse?' she asked, thinking of Dominic's nun story.

'Hannah!' Fran's eyes bulged. 'What— Where on earth did you hear that?'

Hannah shrugged, unwilling to expose her source. As soon as the words left her mouth, she half wished she'd not said them, since they could only lead to a lecture. But Fran seemed more startled than interrogative. Her fingers were fidgeting with the fraying yarn on her macramé belt. 'That's – that's very imaginative of you, love, but I don't think you should say anything like that around your granny, or – or anyone else right now. They'd find it upsetting.'

'OK,' said Hannah, and went back to her book, noting that her mother hadn't denied it.

Fran looked at her daughter for a moment or two, then went downstairs to consult a book she had bought surreptitiously about children and bereavement.

After her snail-bound circuit of the Ramble Way, Hannah decided she didn't need to drag herself out jogging more than twice a week, not now she had a project to work on. To underline this, she went down to WH Smith to buy a spiralbound notepad, a new fountain pen, plus cartridges, a pack of coloured felt-tips, a tape-measure and a Winnie-the-Pooh pencil case. She reapplied for a card at Linton Town Library.

Dora seemed pleased, but nervous, in a Sphinx-ish way, when Hannah informed her of this. 'You know, they had the nerve to tell me I had to pay extra to reinstate my card,' said Hannah. She was making a quick pot of breakfast coffee before heading up to the villa to start work. Dora had 'popped in' in search of some seed catalogues she thought she'd left, but Hannah knew she was checking up on her.

'Get away,' said Dora absently.

'Mmm,' said Hannah. She stirred the cafetière. 'There was a little confusion at first. Mrs Cowper recognized me, of course. She asked if I was still living at Rose View and I said I was, for the time being. Then she asked how long I'd been in London and I said seven years, and then Jodie – you know Jodie, the library assistant?'

'Mmm,' said Dora, less absently.

'Well, she was busy processing the new card and informed me that I had seven pounds to pay on overdue copies of Cher's autobiography and *Yoga For Sexual Health*. But not to worry as I was an OAP and not eligible for charges. Even she was confused by that.'

'Good heavens,' said Dora. 'Computers really are unreliable, aren't they?'

'No, Granny, they're not. Does Mum know you're doubling your library entitlements? On my card?'

Dora fished out her compact from her handbag and retouched her red lipstick. 'They keep records, you know, of what you borrow, just like at Tesco. It's very Big Brother. And there are some titles I might not necessarily want on my library record.'

'I've never heard anything so ridiculous in my life.' Hannah poured out the coffee and tried to look disapproving.

'Not at all,' replied Dora. 'And it's much worse now the book group's having to turn people away. I was in there last week when they were going through the overdue-book list. Mrs Armstrong had three Jeffrey Archers and a Jilly Cooper outstanding. That appalling snob Mrs Cowper put her right at the back of the list for the new Joanne Harris everyone was talking about. Said she wouldn't appreciate it.'

'And?'

'I got it first,' said Dora smugly. She smacked her lips. 'Hurry up with the coffee, darling. Louise will be waiting for you.'

Hannah knocked on Hillcrest's big front door feeling acutely self-conscious, and not just because at the top of the white steps she was clearly visible to the streams of traffic inching down the hill from the supermarkets. She'd never been in through the front door: it was up a curving iron-balustraded staircase, and had an imposing quality designed to put off anyone vaguely trade from ringing the bell.

An interminable time seemed to pass before she heard any sign of life behind the dark glass panes. A cold finger of panic touched the back of her neck as she wondered whether it would have been more polite to go to the back, as she had done as a little girl. It was closer to the drawing room for Mrs Graham-Potter's arthritic legs, and she hardly wanted to start off this whole thing by inflicting agony on an elderly lady for the sake of social correctness. Although that was probably the right thing to do, and doing the right thing probably counted for more than convenience in this house.

She hesitated, unwilling to move now Mrs Graham-Potter was presumably in transit.

The first of three bolts was shot back.

A small part of Hannah wanted the door to be opened by a maid in a white apron and frilly cap. She could almost hear Dominic's creepy ghost-story voice making up something to that effect.

When the door swung open, it was Mrs Graham-Potter who stood there, in a well-cut green tweed suit that made Hannah feel positively under-dressed. There was no sign of arthritis. 'Ah, Hannah,' she said. 'I was wondering where you'd got to.'

Hannah shouldered her bag and followed her into the chilly hall. She tried to walk quietly on the parquet floor, but her heels clumped after Mrs Graham-Potter, who walked silently, like her cats.

'I thought we'd start upstairs in the library,' said Mrs Graham-Potter over her shoulder. 'I say library, but it hasn't been used as that since Constance died, of course.'

'Of course,' agreed Hannah.

They made their way slowly up the dark oak staircase. Hannah followed the old lady, deliberately pausing to look at the old pictures hanging next to the stairs to allow Mrs Graham-Potter time to catch her breath between flights.

The first landing was spacious and airy, with light filtering through the stained glass to fall on the mirrors and refract like jewels on the polished wood surfaces. A tall vase of faded crêpe-paper poppies stood on a blanket chest between the doors. She could almost hear Dominic pointing out that the chest was big enough to hide two or three children in.

'There is a considerable number of paintings in the house that I'd like you to look at. Not all will be worth much, I dare say. The more valuable pictures, the ones Faith's great-grandfather acquired for the London house, are in storage. They were never hung here. Faith collected local art, you know,' explained Mrs Graham-Potter. 'Hers is really the modern section of the collection. She was keen to support local painters and writers – not that that went down very well in some quarters,' she added meaningfully.

'I see,' said Hannah, not seeing.

In an attempt to arm herself with information, she'd turned to the Internet, and a quick search had thrown up more modern local artists than she'd imagined there would be. She was particularly pleased to find a growing interest in Matthew Fisher's bold seascapes and stark pen-and-ink sketches of the coal industry; his output was limited, apparently, but his prices were climbing steadily. One or two blurred old photographs revealed that he had had a certain craggy charm of his own: thick hair falling into honest eyes, broad, working-man's shoulders filling out a plain jacket. The very vision, in fact, Hannah thought wryly, of how a Talented Working-Class Artist should look. Melvyn Bragg with a paintbrush.

Mrs Graham-Potter pulled out a small lace handkerchief from her sleeve and squeezed her nose with it. 'Constance was my best friend,' she went on. 'We were in the same form at school, the little girls' school, you know, where that ridiculous supermarket is now, down by the library. It had a wonderful tennis court behind it, in the gardens.' She tucked the hankie back up her sleeve. 'It's all car parking now. I hate to think of those cars parked on our lovely tennis court, those wonderful honeysuckle bushes just dug up and thrown away . . .'

'Oh, I thought the school was always where it is now,' said Hannah, thinking of her own solidly Victorian brick-built primary school, with its separate entrances for girls and boys. 'I didn't know it had moved.'

Mrs Graham-Potter put her hand on the curtain and smiled condescendingly. 'Oh, I don't mean St *Margaret's*, dear. No, that was where most of the children from the pit streets went, the Catholics. No, Mrs Burns ran her own private day school, just for girls. A sort of small preparatory place for, you know, the better kind of people.'

'Oh,' said Hannah, sensing instinctively that she was meant to feel included by this, yet she didn't. 'Did Dora go there?'

An unidentifiable emotion passed across the old woman's face and she turned to look out of the window. The light made her skin seem powdery, but there were no tears forming in her eyes, just the sheen of a vivid memory, playing inside her mind. 'Yes, she did. Constance wanted her to have a governess at home, but she wasn't Princess Elizabeth! Even Faith agreed with me there.'

Hannah sensed the brisk cut-off in that sentence, but didn't know how to wheedle out the little nuggets of truth that the old lady was hinting at but clutching tightly. It was most frustrating. She still didn't understand why she could talk with effortless fluency to some of the most knowledgeable art buyers in the world yet be reduced to mumbling incoherency with old ladies she'd known since before she could walk.

'Where would you like me to start?' she asked instead. 'With the pictures? Did you want it all done room by room, or some other way?'

Mrs Graham-Potter was still staring at the curtain, moving her thin lips silently as if in deep conversation.

Hannah was getting used to sudden silences from old women – Dora seemed prone to them – and took this to be a moment of private old lady-ness. She stepped away discreetly to look at the photographs hanging on the opposite wall, trying not to make the floorboards creak beneath her weight. They rewarded her by sighing gently underneath the worn patterned carpet.

Hannah liked any kind of old black-and-white photographs: they were like little bridges of proof, allowing her to make a real connection between the present and a past she couldn't always picture as real. Hannah knew she didn't have much imagination, needing to see something to believe it, so it was instructive to be reminded that once even very old women like Mrs Graham-Potter had been lithe and free-flowing.

There were few really old photos at home, much to Hannah's disappointment: it would have been nice to have more evidence of her mother and grandmother as children or young women, although it was hard to imagine either as anything other than fully grown adults with a range of arch adult attitudes. According to Fran's terse explanation, a fire after some birthday party had burned a lot of books and most of Dora's albums. Consequently, the family pictorial history officially started with Fran, and her morose adolescent fringe, grimly accepting the English prize in 1962.

'Are these schoolfriends of yours?' asked Hannah, gesturing towards a group picture.

Mrs Graham-Potter's blue eyes flickered back to life and she let go of the curtain. 'What? Yes. Yes, they are. School photographs. Not that I'm in any of them, though. Faith was terribly good at games, and Constance was so very good at organizing that they made her secretary of everything.'

Hannah peered at the photographs, trying to pick out familiar faces without being told who was who. The sepia print was framed in a cream border, with the school crest and the year 1916 painted underneath. All the girls looked exactly of their time: the faces were dark-eyed and solemn, the expressions peculiarly flat and shadowy, ranged against a brick wall that clearly wasn't there any more and the honeysuckle that had been cut down to make way for the car park. It wasn't a set-up in which personality could have flourished: a dark, static, formal record of appearance, rather than a casual snap to be brought out to show grandchildren. If there were grandchildren. Hannah wondered how many of these girls had grown up to find husbands after the war, let alone start families.

'That's the school lacrosse team,' explained Mrs Graham-Potter. 'I don't imagine they play lacrosse now, do they?' she added, with some pride.

Hannah shook her head. The lacrosse team was next to a debating team in drop-waisted uniforms, whose inability to sit still had blurred them for ever, and a huge hockey team, which either reflected a season of constant injuries or a touching refusal to leave anyone out.

Mrs Graham-Potter walked over. The floorboards didn't creak. 'That's Constance.' She stretched out a long finger: it was crooked with arthritis but the nail was painted with pale pink varnish, the colour of ballet slippers. 'She was no daredevil, not like Faith, but she was so good at encouraging everyone.'

Constance stood at the back of the group, awkwardly holding one of the lacrosse sticks arched above the back row. She looked profoundly embarrassed, as if she wasn't sure she should be there and had no desire to draw attention to herself by waving a lacrosse stick around. Her drawn face indicated how long it took to take photographs in those days.

'She had such beautiful hair,' said Mrs Graham-Potter fondly. 'Lovely blonde plaits. We all wore plaits then. It wasn't like it is now, young girls all trying to make their hair into birds' nests.'

Hannah flinched.

'And that's Faith,' she went on. 'At the front, holding the ball.'

She didn't need to point her out: Faith stood out on her own. Her dark eyes glared straight into the lens from under her heavy black fringe, and she held the ball in her lap as if it were a bomb, or an orb.

'She was the lacrosse captain,' added Mrs Graham-Potter, unnecessarily.

'I can see,' said Hannah, feeling intimidated from a distance of eighty years. The expression was fierce and Faith's plaits looked like the hair of some dangerous Roman warrior woman, rather than the gentle milkmaid look sported by Constance. Everyone else on the team faded back behind her. Hannah was glad she'd never had to play lacrosse: evidently you needed nerves of steel — not to mention thighs of iron.

'I was on the debating team,' said Mrs Graham-Potter, moving to one side. A faint trail of Shalimar floated on the air.

Hannah looked at the debating team, rapidly searching for her face before she could be told, keen to give the compliment of finding the old woman in her youthful form. It wasn't hard. There were only four girls: two were blurred, one wore hideous spectacles, and the last was immaculately turned out, her hands folded neatly in her lap and her hair parted crisply in the exact centre of her head, catching the light with a deep shine. She wore an expression of complete serenity.

'Is that you there?' asked Hannah.

There was a sigh and another waft of Shalimar. 'Oh dear, no. I wish it were. No, that's Elsie Litherdale. She and her pony were killed in a terrible riding accident that same summer. No, that's me.' A pause. 'With the glasses.'

'Really?' Hannah couldn't keep the incredulity out of her voice.

The old lady sighed again, a sound in which Hannah could hear the disappointment of seeing herself, so out of fashion, imprinted for ever on photographic paper, and unable to change it. 'Yes. It was so hard to get nice spectacles then, and my mother . . . wasn't able to take me to Carlisle or Manchester that year.'

'Oh, well, you should do what I do,' said Hannah. 'Everyone thinks I'm really photogenic but it's only because I destroy all evidence of me looking less than perfect on film. Then if they get a bad snap of me at a party, they think it's a fluke.'

Mrs Graham-Potter looked mildly scandalized. 'You rip up pictures?'

'Definitely,' said Hannah. 'How much do they cost, after all? Nothing. Much less effort than going on a diet or having a radical new hairdo.'

Mrs Graham-Potter laughed drily as if the idea had never occurred to her. 'That wasn't my generation's way, I'm afraid. We took things as they were and got on with it.'

'Then you should just have taken the photograph down and put it in a drawer if it bothered you.'

'Well, that doesn't make it go away, does it? Besides,' she stepped a little closer to the picture and brushed off the dust with her fingertips, 'it's not just me on that photograph.'

Hannah peered, not wanting to crowd the old lady. The sun had gone behind a cloud again and the landing had lost its lightness, leaving the pictures dim. 'Who are the other . . . ?'

'Faith and Constance,' said Mrs Graham-Potter, with a touch of surprise that Hannah hadn't seen for herself. 'They were having words, I regret to say, which is why they're a little blurred.'

'Oh dear,' said Hannah. 'Still, I suppose it was the debating team. Was Faith the captain of that too?'

'Yes. She was. She was a woman of strong principles and she wasn't afraid to let people know about them. She never lost a debate, and towards the end we even had challenge matches with the boys' school. Faith generally won those too.'

She certainly appeared to be making her views felt to her sister: Faith's shoulders faced the camera, but her eyes were blurred, as if her pose had been disturbed by a comment, and Constance's expression was ambiguous.

Hannah felt a shiver run through her. She'd been a debating captain herself, despite a polite tendency to agree with the opposition mid-contest, and dreaded coming up against an opponent like Faith – all cold stares and absolute conviction. There was no point being witty in the face of that sort of self-belief.

'Can I leave you to start in the library, dear?'

She turned to see Mrs Graham-Potter touching her nose with her handkerchief again. The dim light from the stained glass made her seem very frail, and Hannah was suddenly reminded of her extraordinary age. How odd it must feel to see yourself inspected as a sort of historical exhibit. Her own youth examined along with the contents of the house – and a house, of course, that hadn't belonged to her. 'Oh . . . of course,' she said, conscious of her own status, a visitor, an employee, even. 'Whatever you'd prefer.'

Mrs Graham-Potter smiled, her lips pressed close together. 'I am prone to migraines and I can feel one coming on. Twenty minutes with some camomile tea generally sees it off. Don't worry. I'll get Mrs Tyson to make it.'

Hannah heard the dismissal, and smiled politely. She wanted to look at the photographs alone anyway.

She waited until Mrs Graham-Potter had vanished into her room before she sat down on the wide staircase, took out her notebook and started to jot down some questions to chase up.

Was there a records book from the family's London house, maybe, listing all the acquisitions made by earlier Musgraves? Did they have some sort of insurance policy list? As soon as she had written this, the edges of Hannah's lips curled into a wry smile. What were the paintings in storage, and were any currently in a museum, loaning the family name and taste as well as the art?

As she wrote briskly, Hannah couldn't stop her mind wandering back to the unfamiliar young women in the photographs. It was odd to think of them here in this house, the hems of their long skirts trailing on the stairs where she was sitting. Even odder to think of them only a few years later with her grandmother as a little girl. Where had she slept, for a start, in this rabbit warren?

Hannah put down her notebook. The landing was large, with corridors leading off in three directions, down passageways to numerous unseen bedrooms, most of which she guessed hadn't been used for decades. There were more photographs along the walls, hung there sixty or seventy years ago, and not passed or looked at since.

She got up and walked softly across to the corridor opposite, with the unnerving sensation that by looking at these frozen figures now she was somehow bringing them back to life. They were large and formal, depicting the sort of casually grand lifestyle Dora's manner still hinted at: groups of big-hatted ladies at Cartmel races, sailing on Windermere in a launch, golfing in voluminous skirts. There were few men, although this didn't surprise Hannah unduly: she was unused to seeing male figures in her own family albums – Dominic excepted – so it seemed perfectly normal. One or two teenage boys, with the same blond good looks as Constance, hung around the edges and she assumed that they must have been the shadowy brothers.

Hannah walked slowly down the dusty corridor, allowing her attention to be grabbed by Faith, here in hunting gear, mounted on a large bay horse with a groom hanging nervously on to a rein. She remembered Dora showing her where the stables had been in the Hillcrest gardens, until all the Musgraves' horses were requisitioned for the Great War. Ten went, and none, of course, came back, so the stables had been turned into garages and filled with expensive cars. Hannah remembered feeling sorry for the horses being sent away without knowing where they were going; now, seeing it again through adult eyes, it occurred to her that Dora hadn't mentioned any of Faith and Constance's brothers who, she assumed, would have gone too, to ride those horses into battle.

Her eyes flicked to a previous photograph of the Musgrave ladies and Louise Graham-Potter, without the unflattering glasses and wearing a much smarter dress, picnicking by a lake, with a couple of angelic-looking lads. Lady Musgrave (Ellen?) looked drawn beneath her sunhat, and even Faith looked less vivid than normal in a dress that hung limply from her frame.

Carefully, Hannah lifted the photograph off the wall. It was heavy, and dust had settled around it, leaving a brighter patch on the William Morris wallpaper where the green and yellow of the pattern burned brightly in the dim corridor. She turned the frame over and, in faint pencil on the backing paper, were the words, 'Thirlmere, June 1916. Faith, Constance, Lady Musgrave, Louise, Alfred and Henry.'

Alfred and Henry. Faith and Constance's brothers were yet another fascinating but strictly off-limits topic; no one had ever elaborated to Hannah about how Faith and Constance had come to be the last barren branches on the Musgrave tree. With a tiny thrill of excitement, Hannah felt a concealed door open to her, like the hidden nun's door in the garden wall . . . a door into her grandmother's secret past.

She carried on her slow walk, wondering idly why these reminders of lost children and happier times had been hung far from the used part of the house. Were the memories still painful, so long afterwards?

Right at the end of the corridor was a large watercolour of an elegant London terrace; Hannah sensed it was somewhere in Knightsbridge, perhaps, from the white frontage and the big black number painted on the wedding-cake pillars. Next to it was a small photograph, taken outside the same front door, of a line of staff, ranging from a stiff butler and a regal cook all the way down to under-parlourmaids who looked about twelve. All wore starched black uniforms and none was smiling.

So, she thought, that was the famous London house, source of furniture and home of the artwork considered too good to hang in Linton. She tore her attention away from the creepy waxwork staff, and concentrated on the watercolour. It was a decent painting, conveying the splendour of the house with a certain feigned modesty. Presumably there would have been a companion piece in the high-ceilinged hall of the London house, of the picturesque seaside retreat, with the scruffiness painted out and the sun painted in, to leave no trace of the dirty mines that had paid for such high living.

Now, surely, *this* was something to have hanging where people could see it, Hannah marvelled. Why was it hidden away in a corridor of bedrooms that weren't used? She wondered whether the Musgrave family still owned the place, or if it had been sold and divided up into flats, the elegance of the house shared out into tenths.

Hannah made a little note, then tried the bedroom door next to the painting. It was locked. She tried the one opposite. It was locked too.

'Hmm,' said Hannah, aloud. Both doors were large, with brass handles and fingerplates, now green with neglect. At least one of the rooms would have a good sea view. Perhaps it was locked to save on cleaning and heating. Or for some other reason.

Somewhere deep inside the house, a door slammed, and although she knew it was probably only Mrs Tyson coming in to start cleaning, Hannah felt an urgent need to get back to the comparative safety of the downstairs rooms and the calm lakeland watercolours. She clattered down the stairs, not caring how much noise she made.

Chapter Eight

Just as mining had been the boom industry in Linton three hundred years previously, by the 1980s cosmetic self-improvement had spiralled into a major employer. With a surfeit of female school-leavers and a technical college up the road, it was inevitable that the town should offer a disproportionately liberal number of salons and beauty parlours, most named with excruciating hair-based puns and offering year-round special offers on cap highlighting, if taken with a course of sunbed sessions. The net result was that most of Linton's young women looked as if they lived in a different weather system from the rest of the town.

Dora and Fran did not visit such establishments. For years, they had patronized Rissini's, the only hairdresser's with any kind of reputation for quality, rather than speed. Stepping inside was like returning to 1959. Gentle selections from Peggy Lee rather than Radio One played over the hum of the hood dryer, and customers emerged looking coiffed, rather than shocked.

Rissini's was run by an Italian family who had emigrated with their ice-cream-making cousins at the turn of the century. The ice-cream cousins now gloried in a café and pizzeria empire, also named Rissini's, a little further up the coast. Despite their sultry Mediterranean looks, which smouldered in a sea of anaemic northerners, the Rissinis had become as local as it was possible to be, even down to their studied suspicion of off-comers. Salons like Curl Up and Dye, and Hairport offended the older generation, who still raged in Italian even if they chatted in broad Linton dialect. For them, hairdressing was a vocation, an art and a public service, and the children who weren't old enough to be learning about point-cutting at weekends were stationed at the desk with mints and hot towels, under the black-kohled eye of Nonna, surviving daughter of the original Francesca Rissini, matriarch and receptionist.

Their loyal clientele was composed largely of the discerning wives in Linton's managerial ranks, and teachers who didn't want to confront last year's classroom trouble-makers now armed with curling tongs. Dora liked it because the décor hadn't changed much since the salon opened in the 1920s, they did not offer ear-piercing and they were reassuringly expensive.

Fran liked it because Rissini's was conveniently located in the high street, opposite the Gothic church and next door to a bookshop, which were excellent places to leave her morbid, bookworm children for an hour or so.

Hannah liked it because while Dominic was ushered in through the gentlemen's door by a glowering *barberino*, she was allowed to follow her mother past the funereal urn of white lilies into the ladies' salon. And all the mysteries of womanhood were in the ladies' salon.

By the time she was eight, Hannah's reading had stretched to include the piles of *Vogue* and *Harper's* stacked up against the walls of Dora's dressing room in the cottage; through their discreet adverts, the complicated rituals of womanhood beyond the gates of Mallory Towers were beginning to speak to her. Not sex – she knew about that from the foul-mouthed, better-developed girls at school who read *Just 17* in the loos at break. Sex seemed pretty dull, and fraught with disease and humiliation, if their laborious reading aloud of the problem pages was anything to go by.

Hannah was far more interested in the little pots, magic lotions, lettuce diets and other paraphernalia 'necessary for maintaining feminine allure', and found that *Vogue* was not so very different from the books about witchcraft that she was also currently requesting from libraries all over the county. Mrs Cowper did not disguise her disapproval of this new interest.

Fran also disapproved, but more of *Vogue* than the pagan research. Hannah's mother was not mysterious in any way, but Dora was coy about her pearly skin and rigid hair, and Rissini's was clearly the place to learn more. It didn't disappoint. Hannah loved the different-coloured rollers and rainbow hair-dye charts and the women under the dryers, who looked so desiccated and grey until they emerged with glossy lilac hair set in frozen waves, like the manes of carousel ponies. Being a woman obviously entailed becoming ugly before you could emerge gorgeous and shiny.

So, like her mother and grandmother, Hannah had been a regular in Rissini's pungent salon, breathing in the secrets and rituals with the setting lotion and spray. Some years later, when she started at Linton Grammar School and met Fiammetta Rissini, the youngest, crossest and most anti-hairdressing child yet produced by the dynasty, their friendship locked as tightly as the perming rollers that criss-crossed Dora's head.

But with less universally pleasing results.

For one reason or another, it was a long time since Hannah had had her hair cut in Linton. Years of London hairdressing and the brain-washing of their Creative Style Directors and Colour Management

Specialists had left her suspicious of local salons and, more importantly, she and Fiammetta hadn't parted on the best of terms. Not that Fiammetta would be there, she reminded herself. Fiammetta would 'rather empty bins than cut hair for a living'. Even the careers teacher had laughed when she said that, but she had meant it.

Hannah wouldn't have gone at all, except she felt in need of some unconditional hairdresser-type flattery after a particularly tiring conversation with Fran, which had started off as a mild difference of opinion about how useful sabbaticals were and had ended up with another lecture about not letting the grass grow under her feet in the job market.

'Just say it, Mum!' Hannah needled. 'Say you don't want me here! Go on, say it!'

'It's not that,' protested Fran, buttering her bread too hard. 'You know it isn't! But you can't just mope around in Linton, waiting for your life to sort itself out. I don't want you to miss out on anything. No one's going to phone you up here or – or – suggest something new for you.'

'They're not doing that in London, Mum.'

'But they're not *ever* going to do it here. Unless you decide to go in for supermarket management. I just don't want you to make the mistakes I made. I know how easy it is to come back and get stuck. Besides, how much money are you wasting on rent?'

'I'm not! I've sublet my flat to someone from work.' Even as she said it, Hannah could hear what a bad idea that was.

'And your hair's looking very limp, dear,' said Dora, absently. She was having supper in their house for the third night in a row. Hannah knew this wasn't the norm because Fran had remarked on it when Dora strolled in, bearing the *Linton Gazette*, folded open at her own section.

'What?'

'You need to get your hair cut.'

'Here? Why would I get my hair cut here?'

Dora raised her eyebrow. 'Well, why ever not? I mean, are you planning to live in Linton for a while or aren't you?'

'*What?*'

Hannah stared at her grandmother in amazement. Surely Dora, of all people, hadn't forgotten why she might not want to have her hair cut at Rissini's? Fran knew nothing of Hannah and Fiammetta's parting, but Dora did.

Fran smiled archly, thinking erroneously that Dora was finally showing some solidarity on the London job front. 'What your grandmother means is that not many people round here go to London when they want their hair cut. And your hair is looking a bit—'

'Stringy,' said Dora.

'Stringy,' agreed Fran.

'Cheers.' Hannah felt thoroughly boxed in by two professionals, even if they were attacking from different angles. 'Right, then. Fine.' She swallowed. Her highlights were important to her: they cost more than council tax. Which was going some, where she lived. Then again, she wasn't living there any more.

'Is Rissini's still in business?' she asked bravely.

'Very much so, as they say in the book group,' replied Dora.

'I had my hair done there last week,' said Fran. She patted her smooth bob. The strands of silver were now thickening into broad highlights, but it was thick and glossy. 'Fiammetta did it. With a razor.'

'*Fiammetta* did it?' Hannah blurted out.

Fran's face registered surprise. 'Yes. She made a lovely job of the back.'

Hannah made an effort to recover herself. She knew Dora was looking at her out of the corner of her eye. 'Yes, well,' she said, 'but if they can't do that style after twenty-five years' practice they might as well give up.'

Fran tutted. 'Well, it was half what you'd probably pay in London and she didn't charge extra for the second coffee.'

Try a sixth of what I pay in London, thought Hannah, but said nothing. Even she had worked out that the 'limitless' coffees at her hairdressers came in at about eight pounds each.

'They're getting very fashionable now, Rissini's,' Fran went on, sounding more and more like an advertorial. 'Quite the place to go. It's very busy since it was featured on *Border News*.'

'Why was it featured on *Border News*?' asked Hannah, despite herself. Both Fran and Dora seemed to have developed a conversational style that required a series of questions from the other party; presumably it gave them the pleasant sensation of having information drawn out of them against their will.

'The staff cut hair dressed as the Mafia for Charity Week.'

'Oh, for . . . *why*?'

'*I* will make you an appointment, darling,' said Dora, before Fran could bite Hannah's head off. She speared some salad and cast a critical look at Hannah's darkening roots. 'Better not to wait.'

When Hannah opened the door to fetch the milk in the next morning, a note was stuck between the milk bottles, 'yr appt 10.30 today, don't forget to tip' written in purple felt-tip. The milkman had ignored it.

Before setting off she washed her hair, just to be on the safe side. Certain salons in Linton knocked off a fiver if you washed your own hair before you came; the ones that charged you an extra pound for mousse. Rissini's was not one of those, but by the same token they would look askance at someone turning up with a flaky scalp.

It didn't take her long to walk into town, with the wind at her back and dribbles of rain in the air. There were no new window displays to linger over, and on a rainy day Linton was truly depressing. It was easy to imagine how grim it must have been when the air was full of rain and coal dust and every shop smelt of wet crinolines and horse shit.

A bell jangled discreetly when Hannah pushed open the door to Rissini's ladies' salon. The overwhelming pungency of hot hair and setting lotion hadn't changed since Hannah's last official haircut aged sixteen, and the acrid chemical smell cut through the heavy fragrance of the lilies massed in the urn in the window.

Like the Coffee Pot Café, the interior of Rissini's had survived the seventies and eighties more through lack of spare cash than any desire to preserve the chrome-and-neon period décor. The sole jarring note in the general crescendo of the 1950s take on art-deco chic was the big laminated headshots of the styles on offer, stuck as they were in 1988. Women could choose from a mousse-crisp poodle perm, a Lisa Stansfield bob or a mad Carol Decker frizz. Next door, men could be any one of Johnny Hates Jazz.

Nonna was no longer looming over the front desk, but the current receptionist bore the expression of resentful curiosity that characterized the Rissini teenager.

'Have you *got* an appointment?' she demanded. The embroidered name patch on her green overalls said 'Marina'. She had a hole in her nose and two in each ear from which she had evidently been required to remove her rings. Rissini's still did not offer ear-piercing.

'Er, yes,' said Hannah. 'Half ten. Marshall. Hannah Marshall.' The girl traced her finger down the pencilled list a couple of times in order to stress the hectic nature of the business. The pencil smudged. Hannah had been to enough private views and guest-list parties to develop the skill of reading upside down and could see exactly where she was — booked in under Dora's name. 'Just a trim and blow dry,' she added, before she could be allotted whatever Dora's usual was.

'Fiammetta will be with you in a minute, if you'd like to take a seat.'

Hannah bit her lip thoughtfully. So it was true – Fiammetta was still here. *God.* What had *happened*? She settled herself on a wicker seat and looked round the salon mirrors to see if she could spot her, then looked back down at the tiled floor, not wanting to see Fiammetta's pretty, vivid features thickened and dulled by hundreds of perms and rote conversations about holiday plans.

Once upon a time Fiammetta's defiance in the face of the inevitable career path ahead of her had been one of the things Hannah had found so intriguing. It was exciting, next to her own bland acceptance of Fran's ambitions for her. Fiammetta had even gone as far as insisting on applying to Manchester University to read computer science, and had got a place.

Hannah's last blurred memory of Fiammetta was of her standing by her dad's flashy Alfa Romeo on their final speech day, telling everyone how much she was looking forward to becoming an international IT specialist. Her father had looked on the verge of tears, but her mother, immaculately presented as ever, had a grim look in her eye that spelled permanent wave – to everyone but Fiammetta.

Hannah had watched this display of bravado from the other side of the marquee, with Dora on one side, Fran on the other and Dominic, back from university with long hair and an unhealthy pallor, hovering protectively. She still had three exams to sit and the tension couldn't have been higher in Rose View, although no one made any reference to it. Hannah's five prizes had not made up for Keith's absence, and only underlined her meek acceptance of her destiny as the over-achieving school swot who'd jump through any hoop you held up as long as you paid her some attention.

'Hannah?'

Hannah looked up self-consciously and feigned casual surprise. Inside, though, her stomach turned over as everything came back to her in a tide of contradictory emotions and half-memories.

She was the same Fiammetta Hannah remembered from school. Her black hair still curled round her ears and neck in glossy loops, her brown eyes glittered with the same amusement. But there was something else that hadn't been there before. Resignation? A certain cynicism in her expression? Or maybe it was just the salon overall, very chic one.

'Well,' said Fiammetta, with a wide hairdresser's smile, as Hannah walked over to the chair, 'I didn't expect to see you in here.'

'Neither did I,' admitted Hannah. She wondered if her voice sounded normal, and was struck by the thought that Fiammetta hadn't heard it for more than ten years.

What is she thinking about me? she wondered. Have I changed as little as she has? 'I mean,' she added quickly, in case Fiammetta interpreted that as a slur on her salon, 'I didn't expect to see *you*. Back here. Hairdressing. I thought you were going to be the next Bill Gates but based in a Manchester penthouse.'

'Yeah, well, you know,' said Fiammetta, drily, 'I thought so too. But, then, we all had funny ideas about ourselves when we were at school, didn't we? What did you have in mind for your hair today? One second . . .'

She put a hand on Hannah's shoulder, a courtesy gesture, while she broke off to catch the eye of a passing junior. 'Stacy? Stacy! Can you fetch me a gown and a fresh towel, please?'

It felt weird, making small-talk, thought Hannah, feeling the warmth of Fiammetta's fingers through her shirt. It seemed more of an effort than talking about personal things would have been. In London with all the trappings of her new life to cheer her up, whenever she thought of their old friendship it was always with a shrug – that was the way some things went. Friendships didn't work out, people weren't meant to follow the same path. Shit happens. But back here, with all her other memories so vivid and the other landmarks of her childhood still as large as life, it stung to hear Fiammetta talk to her as if she was just another customer – the slightly false chumminess that, from the best hairdressers, sounds effortless. They used to be able to swap thoughts without speaking, laugh conspiratorially at the same things. 'Shame to let all those IT classes go to waste, though,' she said bravely.

Fiammetta slung a black gown round her neck, flicking wisps of blonde hair expertly out of the Velcro. Hannah contemplated the resultant double chin, and was reminded of why she didn't wear polo necks. But the clever lighting in Rissini's was flattering. It was that kind of salon.

Fiammetta tweaked curls from under Hannah's ears with quick, deft strokes, until she looked almost angelic and not in need of a haircut at all. 'Well, I could say the same about you. You were going to go to London and become a Magnum photographer. Still, I suppose it comes to us all eventually, eh? Are you back on holiday?'

'Er, no,' said Hannah.

'Hmm?' Fiammetta cocked a smooth eyebrow. '*Well*. I was assuming it wasn't to see the family.'

Hannah couldn't see her face to read the expression, and was startled by the sudden intimacy. She hadn't forgotten.

But the professional-hairdresser manner returned immediately, like a cloud moving over the sun. 'So, what are we having done today?' Fiammetta undid the plait and started to comb Hannah's long dirty-blonde hair. Bits broke off at the ends and stuck in the teeth.

'Just a trim, I think.' Hannah didn't like to think what her London stylist would say if she knew she was cheating on her like this – and with a local hairdresser who didn't even have a spa service in the basement.

'Oh,' said Fiammetta, doubtfully, fanning little sections against her fingers and inspecting them against the light, 'that might not be enough.'

Hannah stared at her glum reflection and remembered how Toby had enjoyed running his hands through her hair. How he'd said it was the prettiest thing about her. Hannah had always taken that as damning with faint praise, since all hair did was grow out of your head and hang there.

Once, sunbathing during break on the bank outside school, Fiammetta had said that she envied Hannah's hair; her own mane had proved too Italian to take to blonde Sun-In highlights. She had combed all Hannah's hair then, stroking it with her hands until it shone like honey. Hannah had kept her eyes shut, so the sun-bleached whiteness on her lids let the hypnotic rhythm of Fiammetta's touch fill up her head without distraction.

That was a real gift, Hannah thought, to be able to reveal beauty where no one else could see it. Maybe that was what Fiammetta's mother had spotted, the reason why she was a true beauty therapist, not to be wasted in some IT department.

Fiammetta combed Hannah's hair around her face so that even she could see what a sorry state it was in.

'And your point is?' said Hannah, from behind a curtain of split ends.

They stared at each other in the mirror. In the background, Julie London's 'Cry Me A River' moved towards a dramatic close, and Hannah's heart gave a painful nostalgic throb.

'No offence, but are you very stressed about something?' asked Fiammetta, unexpectedly.

'Sorry?' Hannah tensed and her shoulders rose in protest. Apart from having my hair done by you, she thought, but said vaguely, 'Well, work has been a bit . . .'

'I mean I can feel it in your hair. So much tension.'

Hannah glared at her from under her splintered fringe. 'Why do you think I'm tense? I'm back here, aren't I? And so are you.'

Fiammetta let the strands fall and raised her hands in a gesture that would have been Italian if she hadn't added the Lintonian eyes-rolled-to-heaven expression.

'Just a trim, please,' Hannah repeated.

Fiammetta sighed and began to massage the pressure points on Hannah's scalp with practised fingers. Just as Hannah began to tingle and melt, she stopped. 'I don't want to tell you what to do with your own hair,' she began, 'but you're going to need to chop a lot off to make it healthy again. It's like straw. There's no resistance in it.'

Hannah closed her eyes. Had Dora put her up to this? There was a time when she would have had her entire head shaved if Fiammetta had insisted it was a good idea, but now . . .

'Just a trim,' she said. 'Please.'

Fiammetta shrugged and clicked her long fingers for the trainee shampooist.

Hannah was relieved to be sent off for shampooing, and soothed by the rigorous head massage delivered in a robotic but thorough fashion by Sophia, who enquired diligently about the temperature of the water while soaping Hannah's ears. In the background she could hear three different hairdresser conversations going on but, true to the nature of the establishment, the holidays being discussed were in Cairo and New Zealand, and the other lady was hosting a small dinner party.

Back in her seat with a pile of magazines, she flicked through *Vogue* and pretended she wasn't watching Fiammetta in the mirror, finishing off blow-drying her previous lady.

She was a skilful hairdresser, no doubt about it. Her hands moved quickly and confidently, tempting curls out of flat layers and settling frizz into softness. Hannah thought about how much she'd envied Fiammetta's beautiful hands: delicate and white, with oval pink nails. They made everything she did look elegant, even the obscene gestures behind teachers' backs. Hannah put the copy of *Vogue* on the shelf in front of her and shut her eyes against another wash of memory.

When she opened them, Fiammetta was standing behind her. The little hands settled on her shoulders in an old intimate gesture. They smiled, uncertainly, at the same moment, and Hannah dropped her gaze into her lap where Gisele Bundchen smouldered up at her from the cover of *Elle*.

'So . . .?' said Fiammetta.

'Oh . . .' Hannah felt the resistance melt out of her. 'Just do what you think you need to.' She couldn't help it. 'I've never had my hair cut by an IT expert,' she added.

Fiammetta's scissors were already slicing through layers of split ends, making a satisfying crunching noise. Strands of hair slithered down the black gown. 'Don't worry about how much I'm taking off,' she said. 'Sometimes it's easier to cut off all the damaged hair at once, rather than pretend to yourself you only need a trim.'

'How you do work that out?'

'Oh, we get it a lot. People want a new look, but then say, "Don't cut any off," and in the end they just see their old selves in the mirror with a shorter version of their last hairdo, instead of the fabulous new person they could have turned into if they'd just been a bit braver.'

'Hmm,' said Hannah. The scissors were picking up speed as Fiammetta worked round the back of her head, holding up strands and chopping them off with swift brutality. She wanted to make a caustic comment about the dangers of mixing hairdressing with philosophy but was scared of what might result.

'They're disappointed,' Fiammetta went on. 'Mostly in themselves, I think.'

Chop, chop, chop.

'I'd rather look like a shorter-haired version of someone I'm already familiar with than a fat version of Anthea Turner,' said Hannah, in what she hoped were level tones. It had begun to dawn on her that she could be taking a major risk, letting Fiammetta cut her hair. Despite being born in the very same hospital as Hannah, Fiammetta definitely had more Italian fire than Lintonian lethargy running through her veins.

'Are you back for long?' Fiammetta asked.

'I don't know yet,' Hannah admitted. 'A few weeks, at least.'

'We should go out for a drink,' Fiammetta said casually.

'That would be nice,' agreed Hannah, equally casually.

'OK.'

'OK.'

Snip, snip, snip.

'Is Cinderella's still going?' asked Hannah. She watched the scissors hissing through her hair with something approaching hypnotism; more and more was coming off, but she was unable to say a thing. Even if it turned out to be the most horrible hairstyle ever, part of her wanted to let Fiammetta do as she thought fit. Whether that was to prove to Dora and Fran that her London hairdresser wasn't some charlatan after all, or whether a really grim hairdo would suit her hairshirt mood, she didn't know.

'Shut down a few years back. Too much fighting. And there's all the drugs now.'

'Mmm,' said Hannah. 'Mum said.'

'But there are some nice new places out on the harbour redevelopment,' Fiammetta went on, more cheerfully. 'We should have dinner, chat about old times.'

'Yes,' said Hannah. She fought back an impulse to get out her diary then and there. Fran might be chipping away at her illusions about her life, but there was no reason why Fiammetta shouldn't think she was a London success, at least for a little while longer.

While Fiammetta combed and flicked, they talked easily about old classmates, none of whom Hannah knew anything about, and new shops in the town. Hannah barely noticed as her hair dried while Fiammetta's fingers coaxed it into fullness.

'What do you think?' Fiammetta stepped back, flipping away the nylon bib with a flourish.

'It's – gorgeous,' stuttered Hannah.

It *was* gorgeous. Her hair, which had been as limp and straggly as she was feeling inside, now looked thick and healthy; Fiammetta had cut it so that chunks of buttery blonde streaks framed her face, somehow making her skin look better. A blunt fringe fell into her eyes, creating a sultry expression she didn't even have to work at. It was the most expensive-looking haircut she'd ever had and it had cost under twenty quid. For the first time in ages, Hannah thought she looked like a successful young woman instead of a worried student – and it had only happened because she'd bitten the bullet and risked a Linton haircut.

And, she thought, with the thrill of a decision taken out of her hands, I certainly can't go back to London now, not until the evidence of this hairdresser betrayal has grown out.

'Glad you went for a bit more than a trim?'

'*Thank* you,' said Hannah. 'Really.'

Fiammetta shrugged and glanced at her watch. 'Listen, I meant it about the drink one night,' she said. 'I'd love to chat for a bit but . . .'

'I know. You must have an appointment list a mile long.' Hannah couldn't tell if they were sliding back into the false intimacy of a hairdresser/client conversation. She didn't think so, but she didn't want to be caught out.

'I'll call you.' Fiammetta was tucking her scissors back into her belt. 'Number's still the same at home?'

A junior was approaching with Hannah's coat.

'Er, yeah.' Hannah didn't want to think about what Fran would say if she answered the phone. At least Dora wouldn't be there.

'Lovely to see you.' Fiammetta's little white hand was on her shoulder again. Their eyes met in the mirror – Hannah with her disorientating new hairstyle, Fiammetta looking as if the previous ten years hadn't passed but back in the place Hannah had never thought to see her again.

'And lovely to see you.' Hannah smiled. She was surprised to find that she meant it.

Chapter Nine

When she was a little girl, Hannah had never looked into a mirror after six o'clock at night. She avoided them earlier on cold winter afternoons, when the sun deserted Rose View at around half past two, leaving the rooms chilly and dark. Dark and very, very quiet. By half past three, when Fran brought her and Dominic back from school, they crashed through the three storeys of silence as if they were diving into a swimming-pool.

Rose View wasn't a particularly creepy house, but it was shadowy even in summer. Hannah felt there were things in the corners or hiding in wardrobes that she wasn't meant to know about. Fran was a firm believer in saving both the environment and money, and drilled her children to switch off lights as they passed from one room to another. It was a losing battle, and Fran knew that, but she had a taste for losing battles; it had resulted in her ending up with a client list including Linton's more clueless criminals.

When they weren't curled up reading somewhere, Dominic and Hannah expended the energy conserved by having no playground friends by clattering up and down the stairs, playing one of

Dominic's complicated games of capture and possession. Inevitably they were followed by Fran, yelling about light pollution and the electricity bill.

It infuriated Fran that the more she lectured, the more Dominic incorporated her into the game, as some kind of light-sensitive ogre. At which point, Dora would comment sweetly on the children's impressive knowledge of Grimm-derived folklore, and Fran would mutter about candles and mad old women. She put timer switches on the corridor lights: Dominic and Hannah liked to race from the top of the house to the bottom before darkness caught up with them. Dominic went fastest because he swung fearlessly round the acorn banister knobs, but even though she was smaller, Hannah usually beat him to the bottom because she was frightened of the big mirrors that lined the walls.

They had originally been hung there by Dora to maximize the meagre daylight in the corridors before modern rewiring had thrown electric light into all the corners. They doubled the size of the landings, reflecting it back on itself within the rococo gilded frames. After reading a particularly scary story about a doll's house occupied by doll replicas of a family, a seed planted itself in Hannah's mind that at night the mirrors reflected the parallel version of Rose View, the nicer one, in which Dora made fairy cakes and Fran didn't yell at them for leaving doors open – the illuminating version that showed the ends of all her mother's unfinished sentences and translated the semaphore of her grandmother's arched eyebrows and wry expressions into a language she could understand. The Rose View in which half-open doors weren't suddenly slammed shut as though they could stop the angry words leaking out into the rest of the house.

Despite the daily terror that lurked at the periphery of her life, Hannah didn't give up her ghost-story books, and she had a sneaking sensation that the mirrors never reflected exactly what she could see around her. They were always far darker than the hall, even when the lights were on. Whenever she walked past one, she was so scared of spotting something out of the corner of her eye that her twitching usually threw up a spooky movement in the glass and she would bolt. She might have passed her childhood in a continuous nervous state if her flight for the safety of the kitchen had not inevitably been accompanied by a shriek from downstairs about turning off the bloody lights.

Had Dora known what night-time horrors Hannah suffered as a result of the reading she encouraged, she might have supported Fran's more prosaic stance that Stephen King and M.R. James weren't going to get her into a decent university. But Hannah and Dominic read and read, and it was hard for Hannah to separate fiction from reality when she seemed to live in exactly the kind of creaking, echoing seafront house that most ghost stories selected as a prime focus point of psychic activity.

Rose View was an old house, and Hannah knew from her reading that old houses had old shadows and old echoes and ineradicable traces of previous occupants – flakes of skin and faded hair in the old dust between the floorboards, fingerprints on banisters and mites in mattresses. The old heating system carried noise in a funny way, and sometimes, in parts of the house she knew her parents weren't near, she thought she could feel arguments, as if old ones left traces of irritation in the air like the lingering smell of beans that never quite left the kitchen.

Outside, the night drizzle had returned with a vengeance and was leaking persistently between the cracks in Hannah's bedroom window, bubbling through the flaking paint with little hissing noises.

Hannah was unaware of this, clutched tight in the grip of a sweaty nightmare in which she was trapped inside the old telephone exchange next to the dentist's on Africa Street. Although it was another building she'd never been inside, the detail of the ominous interior was sharp: a huge switchboard set in dark wood panels, flashing red and yellow lights, with high windows letting white moonlight flood the tiled floor like a pool of paint. In order to escape (and no one had told her: she had somehow worked it out, clever Hannah), she had to connect all the flashing phone calls, but as soon as she'd plugged in the connections and stopped the ringing, another set of lights would start up on the other side of the room, and the conversations came splashing out of the ends like rushing water, filling up the room with sound.

When she stopped to catch her breath, she saw that an army of shiny snails, the size of tractor tyres, was moving slowly towards her, waving their antennae menacingly.

'Hannah!'

She forced open an eye.

Someone was standing over her in a tartan dressing-gown; the face was hidden in the darkness but a long plait hung down on either side of the head, which she knew didn't belong to Fran or Dora.

Hannah squeezed her eyes shut again and counted mechanically to ten. She could still see the inside of the telephone exchange; the snails had gone and it was empty apart from the menacing chatter of disembodied Linton voices swirling around her feet like noisy ribbons.

She wasn't scared by the apparition by her bedside. Since she was little she'd seen figures in her room when she first woke up, standing by her bed, sitting in the chair, lurking at the window, but they always disappeared if she shut her eyes and consciously opened them again. Either the figures were tricks of the light, or figments of her imagination, or something else, but they'd never stayed once she'd wished they weren't there.

'Hannah!'

None had ever spoken to her.

She opened both eyes.

Fran was leaning over her, looking flustered, but she was not wearing a tartan dressing-gown.

'Mum?' Hannah said, in case it wasn't.

Fran's eyes were flicking round the room in a frenzy of embarrassment, and she smelt of Pond's Night Cream. Hannah followed her gaze around the room, and realized that it was caused by her own nudity: she had pulled off her pyjamas in the middle of the night – it was too hot to wear them when all the windows were shut tight against the rain and, anyway, she was still in the decadent London habit of sleeping naked.

Sleeping naked in Linton was tantamount to *asking* for a cold on the chest.

Hannah pulled the covers up to her neck. 'Mum? What's the matter?'

'Oh, so you're awake *now*, then,' Fran snapped.

'What time is it?'

'I could ask you the same thing!' hissed Fran, somewhat rhetorically.

Clearly, thought Hannah, I have missed the first and second acts of this one.

'Wouldn't be much use, though, would it?' Hannah reached out an arm to get her alarm clock from the bedside table. It was unusual to have slept through the train *and* the bus. Maybe her slug-a-bed London personality was staging a late comeback.

She peered at the luminous dial and groaned. Maybe she hadn't woken up because there weren't many trains before two in the morning to wake her.

'Mum, why the hell are you waking me up at two in the morning?' Hannah sat up. 'Is the house on fire, or something?'

She shivered as the air touched her shoulders. Her skin was clammy from the dream panic and a delayed-reaction shimmer of fear went down her spine. It would be just like Fran to wake her like this if the house *was* on fire: much better to evacuate calmly than run around screaming and throwing antiques out of the windows.

'There was a phone call for you,' said Fran tightly.

Hannah squinted at her mother. The benefit of using little makeup was that you didn't look very different at any time of day. Despite it being the middle of the night, Fran merely looked more ruffled and less flushed than she did at peak times. Her hair, in fact, was sporting a fashionable bedhead look that she would have firmly waxed down in under five hours' time.

'A phone call?'

'A phone call, yes.'

Hannah stared at her. There was something not quite right about her mother: she seemed to be in the middle of a dream herself, sleepwalking her way through an argument going on in her head. Her eyes were glazed and moving back and forth too quickly. She seemed a little undone.

Hannah frowned, unable in her own fuzzy state of mind to put her finger on what it was.

Fran pulled her dressing-gown tighter round her narrow waist and pursed her lips until she looked impossibly camp.

Hannah wondered if she should wake her up, or whether that would make it worse. 'Um, did you say there *was* a phone call? As in, you hung up on them?'

'Whoever it was didn't speak. Are these clothes for the wash?' Fran asked, holding up a limp T-shirt.

'What do you mean, "whoever it was"? How did you know it was for me?' Hannah began to feel as if she was being dragged against her will into a surreal dream. 'And leave my clothes alone. I can do my own washing,' she added.

Fran dropped the T-shirt with a suspicious glance at the remainder of the heap. 'I mean they didn't say anything after asking for you. I answered the phone – which is right by my bed, as you may remember – they asked for you, I said I'd get you—'

'Hold on,' said Hannah. '*They* said? Male or female?'

'I couldn't tell.'

Pause.

Fran looked confused, then reverted to a simpler expression of irritation. 'I don't really ... Anyway, I don't like to make judgements.'

'Ohhh,' moaned Hannah, and swung her feet out of bed, pulling on her vest. Her mind was racing. This was exactly the kind of midnight attack of reason that she'd always prayed would strike Toby. The realization that he'd married the wrong woman, that he should never have let her go. The all-encompassing need to tell her how he felt. She had fallen asleep dreaming about this moment a hundred times.

'Ohhh, God, Mum, it could have been anyone!' She groaned. 'Did it sound like Toby?' In her haste to get to the phone, Hannah couldn't make that sound as casual as she'd have liked.

'I have no idea what Toby sounds like,' retorted Fran, picking up the T-shirt and absently putting it into Hannah's desk drawer. 'In fact, as I've never met him I don't know that you haven't just made him up.'

Hannah ignored the barb and tried to force her feet into her slippers. 'So what did you say? That I was asleep? That I'd be a moment?' She crashed out of the room and down the dark stairs, hanging on to the banister, heading towards the phone on the landing by the floor-to-ceiling picture window. I will be so cool, she thought. Or will I? Should I not be very thrilled, to convince him that he's made the right decision?

'Hannah,' came Fran's warning voice from upstairs.

The phone on the landing was one of the original black Bakelites that Dora had had installed when Fran was a little girl, always cool to the touch and with traces of old makeup ingrained on the earpiece.

Hannah picked it up with a steady hand, and said calmly, 'What the hell time do you think it is here?'

There was a strange silence at the other end. Not a dialling tone, and not the trace of someone breathing either. Just the faint sensation of something at the end of the line. Listening.

'Hello?' Hannah said, and shivered. Suddenly she understood her mother's confusion: she couldn't hear anything, but she knew someone was there, and that they wanted her. She sat down on the chair by the phone and stared out of the window, beyond her reflection into the thick depths of the garden.

The silence on the phone continued. Was someone calling from abroad, she wondered.

Then very faintly, as her eyes acclimatized themselves to the dark, Hannah's ears picked out the distant sounds of an argument, rising and falling like the waves in the harbour on a rough night.

'Hello?' she said again. It was eerie, sitting in the dark listening to nothing, and she was suddenly aware of the landing mirrors in the corner of her peripheral view. Were things moving? She couldn't look up at her reflection in case she saw something approaching from behind.

'Hello!' she snapped, more to remind herself that she was real and everything else was in her head.

As she spoke, there was a definite movement in the mirror, and Hannah gasped with shock.

'Hannah,' said Fran, appearing behind her. She looked different, more focused, more like her usual self. Hannah shuddered again, at something she couldn't define: the feeling that it hadn't quite been her mother talking to her a moment ago.

'Put the phone down. It's just one of those crank callers.'

'It isn't,' Hannah protested. She cradled the receiver against her chest to stop the sound travelling. 'It's Toby. He must have called me on his mobile or something, dropped it in his bag . . .'

Fran gently took the phone out of her hands and replaced it in its cradle. It made a muffled *ting*, which echoed round the house on the other extensions.

'Toby's not going to be calling you, Hannah. He's on his honeymoon, isn't he?'

Hannah set her lip in a mutinous expression she hadn't pulled for ten years, but which she now found surprisingly satisfying.

'Look, he's not coming back, love.' Fran paused as if she were struggling for better words. She finished, rather lamely, 'It's just one of those hard things we have to accept in life. Other people's feelings . . . they aren't ours to direct. And that's that.'

Is it? thought Hannah. She looked at her window reflection, the mirror Hannah sitting just outside in the garden, and a voice in her head said, He's not coming back, but you're safe here, at home, where it won't hurt as much.

No light from inside the house dimmed the perfectly round whiteness of the full moon, and Hannah wondered, somewhat mechanically, about the merchants who had used it and the lighthouse to steer their cargo ships into Linton harbour, whether they had found much of a welcome in the women there, with their mantras of endurance, cleanliness and gritted teeth. Six months at sea, and all they'd really want to see was how much washing you had.

Fran sighed, a gusty breath of air that felt cool on Hannah's ear. 'As your grandmother once said to me, in . . . in similar circumstances, we're not put on this earth to be happy, love. It's not something you're entitled to, it's just a bonus.'

As Fran squeezed her shoulder, Hannah had an abrupt and powerful feeling of *déjà vu*, without knowing what was going to come next. 'I've been here before,' she said, and was startled to hear her voice rising in panic as her mother's hand tightened on her shoulder. 'No. No, don't. This is just too weird!'

Fran bent over and kissed the top of her head – which triggered another violent *déjà vu* feeling and was such an uncharacteristic gesture that Hannah was unnerved, as though she had gone behind the glass into the alternative Marshall household.

'Please don't say anything, Mum,' she whimpered.

'It's just the middle of the night,' said Fran, and put her arms round Hannah, rocking her. 'Things always feel strange in the middle of the night. I haven't been sleeping well myself lately and . . .' Her voice trailed away. 'I've not been sleeping well.'

It was as close as she'd come yet to admitting there was something wrong, something she couldn't conquer with logic and determination. It silenced both of them.

Hannah submitted to Fran's bony embrace and stared out into the garden, refusing to look at their merging reflection, letting the cold fact that Toby was finally out of reach seep through her veins, followed by the sobering thought that the lovely, comforting pretending had to stop right now. He wasn't coming back.

And she had to start again. It wasn't just a case of passing time here, then going back to London, picking up the threads of her job and her life, and the imaginings of what Toby would say when he came to his senses. She really had to start again.

Hannah shut her eyes and wished she could join the long-dead traces of people between the floorboards of Rose View. 'Oh, God, what am I going to do?' she muttered.

They sat in silence for a few moments, listening to the ticking and rustling of the sleeping house.

'I'll put the kettle on, now we're up,' said Fran. Not necessarily in response to her daughter's question.

It was odd, thought Hannah, that the first time she really felt on equal adult terms with her mother hadn't been at her graduation, or in a restaurant where she'd picked up the bill, but sitting on the cold stairs of the family home, sharing a paralysing sense of failure.

'Mum,' said Hannah, emboldened by the darkness and the weird hour of the night, 'is this what it felt like when Dad left?'

Fran half turned, and in the darkness Hannah couldn't read her expression. She held her breath, waiting for a thread of contact, another loop in the reknitting of their relationship.

Fran sighed and stuck her hands into her hair. The moonlight caught the wryness in her face. 'I'm not being disingenuous, Hannah,' she said, 'but I can't really remember.'

Chapter Ten

If she was being absolutely truthful, Hannah didn't have vivid memories of her father, other than his insistence on ordering the *Guardian* from the newsagent (clear evidence of his latent Communism), and a few choice catchphrases. 'Just what I'd expect!' was one. 'That's typical Linton thinking!' was another, an implicit insult that enraged both Dora and Hannah. Aside from his compost heap in an unused corner of the garden, when Keith moved out he left no trace on the house, which had been Dora's anyway; also, as Dominic was a male version of Fran, and Hannah was the dark-eyed image of her grandmother, he left little trace on his own children. The night before he left, Hannah found her mother furiously snipping away at a pile of school nametapes, turning Dominic and Hannah Marshall-Kirk back into Dominic and Hannah Marshall. It seemed to Hannah that her mother had snipped him out of her life just as easily.

The nametapes were all Hannah really remembered about Keith's departure from the family home; it seemed as though he had been there one day and gone the next. Since the arguments that had ricocheted through closed doors stopped at the same time, and Fran's weight went back up to nine stones, Hannah didn't press her for details. Fran once tried to take her and Dominic to a family counsellor, her conscience pricked by a new government report about the high incidence of shop-lifting in divorced children, but was defeated by the idea of someone in the town knowing her business. In that respect, she and Dora were in unusual harmony.

Much later, it struck Hannah as unfair that her father never phoned or wrote to them. At the time, it seemed easier just to get on with things. Divorce in Linton was uncommon, but she did know one or two kids whose fathers only saw them at weekends; sometimes she spotted them in the booths at the Coffee Pot Café, eating knickerbocker glories with grim determination. If Fran was with her, Hannah used to turn quickly at the door, and ask to be taken to Linton's version of a Wimpy bar ('Would you like a knife and fork with that, pigeon?') instead.

Keith and Fran's separation came as little surprise to the neighbours. Fran might have believed she was keeping herself to herself, but little got past Mrs Tyson, who could read minute signs of domestic unrest – spare beds used, meals left on plates in the fridge – like a Roman pontifex interpreting chicken entrails. The plain fact of Fran's insisting on Marshall-Kirk as her married name had been indication enough for Mrs Tyson's darker predictions. Keith Kirk was sorely lacking in what was known locally as 'gumption' (or, for variation, 'nous') and Hannah overheard more than one conversation in the Coffee Pot where his and Fran's university degrees were blamed specifically for the marital breakdown.

'He may have letters after his name but that don't mean he knows owt about women,' Mrs Tyson had informed Hannah at the time, by way of dour comfort. She was meant to be spring-cleaning

Rose View. A poisoned-chalice Christmas gift from Hillcrest. 'As I say, men are like that, pet. Think on. Clever girls are easiest fooled.'

Looking back as an adult, Hannah acknowledged that Keith's defeat had been only a matter of time in coming. Men didn't count for much in their family, unless they were worth hanging on to for some specific reason, and since Fran was cleverer and better-paid than Keith, his days had always been numbered. Hannah surmised that he must have seemed a better catch in Manchester: ten years her senior, university research fellow, her supervisor.

As soon as they were married, though, Fran became the supervisor, especially after their return to Linton (why, Hannah didn't know). From then on, she had shouldered the burden of defending Linton's legal aid clients, and Keith had devoted more time to lecturing in the home than in higher education. But Fran had inherited her attitude to husbands from Dora. After enduring a combined thirty years of wedlock, both Arthur and Keith were referred to only in passing and then usually in connection with a set of shelves that had not been put up properly, or a disastrous driving holiday. Most of the photographs in the family albums had been taken by Arthur or Keith, so all pictorial records focused on Dora, Fran, Hannah and Dominic – and, frequently in the background, Faith, Constance and Louise, smart as paint in their tweed suits and pearls, never looking a day older or younger than sixty-seven, no matter when the picture had been taken.

Keith, at least, had made some small effort at parenting, even if it was limited to bedtime lectures about Linton's role in the slave trade and the importance of recycling plastics. Hannah had no first-hand memories of her grandfather, who had died before she was born. Dora didn't exactly keep a shrine to her late husband, habitually referred to as Poor Arthur or sometimes, in Fran's case,

Poor Dad. That was about as far as they went in terms of sympathy.

Like Keith, Arthur had failed to make much impact on Rose View: apart from two photographs (featuring him with the Duke of Gloucester, and with some new-fangled pit machinery) and a presentation barometer, there was little to show for his fifteen years of marriage to Dora. Fran excepted. All three photographs were kept in Rose View, not in Dora's cottage, and only Fran remained as living proof that he'd ever been there.

Consequently, as a child Hannah relied on her books for male role models. At least she could choose them: the Hardy Boys, Sherlock Holmes, Just William, even Snoopy, with his typewriter and his dark, cold, windy nights. She grew up in a town run by matriarchs, surrounded by old women, harangued on feminist principles by her mother, and taught by a series of annoyed female schoolteachers, until the idea of meeting a man in Linton (who was 'any good for owt') seemed about as realistic as it was for Sleeping Beauty. There were many times, doodling idly at the back of a French class, when Hannah wished she could just fall asleep, wake up and find a handsome prince there, to save the interminable boredom of waiting for one of the Linton frogs to turn into something more promising.

Hannah knocked on the back door of Hillcrest and shivered as the wind whipped in off the sea and went straight down the back of her neck. It was no good, she thought. If she was going to stay into autumn, a trip to Hawkshead for insulated thermals was unavoidable.

She gazed out towards the Isle of Man while somewhere deep inside the house Mrs Graham-Potter made her stately way to the door. The sky and sea had turned the same washed-out grey colour, which meant a bigger storm was brewing. The wind was blowing so hard that the waves were going sideways, edged with lacy white spray. Hannah thought of the coal seams stretching out like knobbly fingers under the seabed and shivered again, but from the inside out.

When the door finally opened it wasn't Mrs Graham-Potter, but Mrs Tyson.

'Hello, Mrs Tyson,' said Hannah.

Like her own mother before her, Mrs Tyson, had 'done' for Hillcrest for nearly twenty years, but only the rooms that Mrs Graham-Potter allowed her into. This was a regime begun by Faith, who had been even more draconian about maintaining the thick curtain of privacy that surrounded various parts of the house. From what little Hannah had seen of the place, she'd always thought that cleaning it must be a pretty thankless task – all that wood and brass and carpet – but Mrs Tyson liked to give the impression that it was an easier job than tackling Rose View because at least Mrs Graham-Potter didn't insist on biodegradable cleaning materials and trips to the recycling bins.

'Hello, Hannah,' she said.

'How are you?' Hannah began dutifully, although she wasn't sure she wanted to know. Mrs Tyson's daughter, Leanne, had been in her class at school, and had produced an unexpected baby at the same time as Hannah was turning huge profits on leather A-Ha bracelets for the school's Young Enterprise efforts. There was an understanding locally that if you asked about other people's news, it was a precursor to showing off about something of your own. On the other hand, not asking would be rude.

'I'm well, thank you,' said Mrs Tyson, making no move to let her in.

'And Leanne?' Hannah shifted from one foot to the other in the biting wind. Mrs Tyson, she noticed, stayed within the minuscule warm zone of the kitchen, arms folded across her ample chest.

'Leanne's well, too. Getting married Friday.'

Hannah raised her eyebrows in polite surprise. Then lowered them in case it looked like she was surprised in a bad way. 'Um, I've come to see Mrs Graham-Potter,' she said. 'I'm . . .' She was about to say, 'going through her paintings,' but some native instinct for secrecy broke through and closed her mouth.

Mrs Tyson's own eyebrows, plucked by an over-eager Linton beauty therapist in 1976 and heavily pencilled in compensation since, lifted.

Fortunately, before either of them could press for more information in a wordless eyebrow interrogation, the tiny figure of Louise Graham-Potter appeared. She was dressed in a neat wool twinset, the colour of cherry lips, over a mulberry tweed skirt, and her hair was freshly set. Rissini's sent one of the older stylists to the house to set it on Fridays, as they had since 1959. Only the old-lady clumpiness of her shoes betrayed her age. 'Hannah, dear, you don't have to use the back door like a tradesman,' she said.

Mrs Tyson sniffed loudly.

Hannah managed a nervous smile and shouldered her bag for confidence. It was a nice leather Bill Amberg satchel that she'd bought to boost her self-esteem when she'd started working with smart blonde girls who acted as if they had better paintings at home. The conker-brown satchel had been a starting point for her own new London personality, but she felt she really needed it now, even if it only contained her file pads and felt-tip pen set.

'Mrs Tyson, if you've finished with the vacuum cleaner, would you make us a pot of coffee?' announced Mrs Graham-Potter regally. 'Hannah must be frozen, walking through that wind. We'll be in the drawing room.'

Mrs Tyson bit her lips until she was almost gurning, and swung round, muttering something about manners and real ladies. Hannah caught something about jumped-up folk who knew no better as she stamped off into the kitchen and started crashing kettles about.

Mrs Graham-Potter sucked her teeth briefly with annoyance, muttered a few choice words of her own about staff, then turned briskly and vanished into the house.

Hannah hesitated, not sure where her loyalties were meant to lie, then heard Mrs Tyson turn up the radio. The local station's *Midday Mart* filled the kitchen.

Hannah opened her mouth to say something apologetic, but then couldn't think what would be appropriate. Oh *God*, she thought, Dora would know how to defuse this tension. Any adult would. I'm nearly thirty and nothing is any clearer. It was clear though that her presence wasn't required or desired there so she followed Mrs Graham-Potter's soundless steps through into the dark passage that led to the secret, untouched-by-Linton-cleaner part of Hillcrest.

Since Mrs Graham-Potter hadn't emerged from her room before Hannah had let herself out earlier in the week, head spinning with faces and questions, she thought it best to start with some evidence of her work so far.

She popped open the clasps of her satchel and took out the list of notes she'd made on Fran's computer. 'I've been on the Internet, and found recent auction prices for some of the artists represented in the collection – not that it's a guarantee,' she added, 'but it gives you a rough idea of what's here. I've listed most of the paintings from the drawing room and what I think would be a guide price at auction. Of course, this doesn't include the personal pictures of the family, but I think you should consider talking to the Records Office about having them scanned, with the Musgraves being such an important part of the town's history.'

'Goodness, you have been busy.' Mrs Graham-Potter held out a hand.

Hannah gave her the list. 'I, er, didn't know quite how you wanted to do this. Would you like me to present you with all the details at the end, or would you like it room by room? Most of the information I can get from the Internet, but I did wonder if there was a household record of acquisition, some guide to who bought what. That would speed everything up considerably.'

Mrs Graham-Potter was scanning the pages, as if she was looking for something. Hannah felt a strange certainty that Mrs Graham-Potter didn't know what it was.

'Good,' she said eventually, handing back the list with a wintry smile. 'You're very thorough. Like your mother in that respect, aren't you? But not like dear Dora. She's always been a featherbrain.'

Hannah smiled uncertainly. Was that rude? Or just posh-family joshing?

'I'm so sorry that I wasn't able to finish explaining the family photographs,' Mrs Graham-Potter went on. 'It's such a bore being old, and prone to these sudden attacks. However, I do think that if you're to draw some kind of conclusion about the artistic judgement of the family, I should explain a little about the Musgraves. How they came to be here, and so forth.'

She gave Hannah a close look. 'Unless I'd be covering familiar ground?'

'I can honestly say that I know practically nothing about the Musgrave family, beyond Constance's *découpage* skills in my nursery and Faith starting the children's Sunday School,' said Hannah, with what she hoped was friendly lightness.

Mrs Graham-Potter held her gaze for a micro-second longer than was comfortable.

'Well, we should start with their own portraits.' She inclined her head. 'I'm no artist, but I imagine you'd pick up more than I would from their . . . What's that dreadful phrase television people use now? From their *vibe*?'

Hannah shared Mrs Graham-Potter's amused shudder at the dreadful phrase and the television people, and suppressed her own at the thought of going back into that creepy room, full of staring, scowling Musgraves.

'That would be very interesting,' she said politely. At least she wouldn't be on her own. 'I thought at the time the portraits were very ... arresting. Either the artists were exceptionally good, or there was a strong family personality for them to capture.'

Mrs Graham-Potter raised her eyebrows. 'Indeed.'

Hannah let Mrs Graham-Potter lead her to the study. For such an old lady, she was remarkably agile.

The study was dark and cold, with no motes of dust spinning in the shaft of weak light coming through the net curtains. From the moment she stepped into the room, she felt the eyes following her, assessing her, watching her, making her skin prickle. Mrs Graham-Potter's presence didn't change that.

Get out a notepad, be business-like, she told herself, but her fingers fumbled on the clasps of her satchel.

'Shall we start with this portrait?' Mrs Graham-Potter indicated the large photographic study above the desk.

Hannah noted that she skipped the older portraits of Musgraves in Regency wigs and limpid empire-line frocks, going straight for the modern-day industrialists. 'Who's this?' she asked, clicking her pen. 'It must be one of the first photographs taken round here, is it?' She'd guessed it to be around 1850, 1860.

'I should think it was. The family were ahead of their time, keen to be the first in the county with new developments. Sir Joseph and Isabella, Lady Musgrave.' Mrs Graham-Potter pointed to each. 'He was made a baronet for his services to industry. They were Faith and Constance's grandparents. The family nose, you see. Very straight. You'll notice that Constance got her lovely hair from Isabella's side of the family.'

Hannah murmured politely at Isabella's mad blonde coils, wrapped like snakes round her head, but she could see the family resemblance more in the fierce expression of Joseph Musgrave's eyes. Faith's eyes. They glared out of the portrait just like Faith's burned out of the school photographs.

'Joseph was responsible for keeping the coal side of the family business profitable and investing in machinery to keep the mines up to date,' explained Mrs Graham-Potter, in her precise tone. 'He invested in the railways and, of course, contributed to the harbour development. That's where a lot of the family wealth came from originally, you know – shipping and coal. Isabella was wealthy in her own right. Her people owned cotton mills in Manchester. She and Sir Joseph met in Grange-over-Sands, I believe, at a spa.'

'Was it a long marriage?' asked Hannah. The stiff body language, combined with the *faux*-naturalistic setting, suggested that they had met only minutes previously at the woodland tree stump against which Joseph was propped on his mighty elbow.

'*Everyone* had long marriages then,' replied Mrs Graham-Potter icily. 'There *were* no divorces round here. Goodness, no. Respectable families would go to any lengths rather than have their dirty linen aired in public. We didn't dwell on problems, the way young people do now. People only remarried if their spouses died, and there were children to consider.'

Hannah took this as a slight, on behalf of her mother.

'And did they have many children?' Apparently not if Isabella had had enough time to arrange her hair into such architectural splendour.

'Nine. Eight sons and one daughter.'

'Bloody hell!' said Hannah, without thinking, and put her hand over her mouth immediately. 'Um, sorry.' Isabella's faraway expression now became clear. She really didn't want this man any nearer to her than he had to be.

'Joseph, Samuel, John, Derwent, Carlisle, Thomas, Benjamin,

Isaac and Catherine. There were three others, more sons, but they died in infancy.' Mrs Graham-Potter lifted a hand towards a series of smaller silhouettes hanging in a long vertical line next to the marble fireplace. 'You may want to make a note of those, by the way. They're exceptionally good quality. I believe Isabella commissioned a French silhouettist, from Paris.'

'Someone from Paris came up here?'

'No, of *course* not.' Mrs Graham-Potter sounded mildly exasperated. 'The family had a large residence in London. They didn't *live* up here. Good heavens, no.'

Ah, thought Hannah, the famous London house. Quite why living in London was now considered so *outré* when the Musgraves had had a house there all along, she didn't understand.

She didn't mention that she'd already seen the painting of the house upstairs, suspecting that she'd learn more by playing dumb: Mrs Graham-Potter struck her as the sort of person who liked to be in charge of dishing out information, and would dish out more according to how much you made her feel in charge.

'They didn't live here, even though they owned the mines?' she asked innocently.

'Why on earth would they? None of the better families round here did. Of course they had houses here, but the time they spent in them was . . . well, limited. They hired agents to take care of their business affairs. My great-grandfather was an agent, you know, for Joseph Musgrave's father.'

'Really?' asked Hannah, interested, but the old lady was sweeping on.

'The Musgraves had a lovely townhouse in Wilton Place, in Knightsbridge, where the children grew up. There's a painting of it somewhere in the house.' She made a vague movement of her hand towards the upper storeys. 'It used to hang in here, but

Constance didn't care for it, so Faith moved it after their father died. The family owned quite a lot of property in London. Lady Musgrave inherited some warehouses, I believe, and Sir Joseph invested in quite a large area of . . .' Her voice trailed off. 'Well, I don't remember where it was.'

'Who owns it now?' asked Hannah, making a discreet note. 'Is it still somewhere in the family? It must be worth an absolute fortune.'

Mrs Graham-Potter looked evasive and picked a few dead leaves off the aspidistra in the mahogany planter. 'Most of the London property was sold when the family lost money in the depression,' she said. 'I don't recall whether it was still in the family by the time Faith and Constance were born.'

'But *any* property in London now is like a gold mine,' said Hannah. 'Even in the really rough areas, you know, like the East End – even the sweatshops no one wanted to go near ten years ago. Honestly, you wouldn't believe how hard it is to get started on the property ladder there. All those warehouses are selling for millions as loft apartments.'

'I wouldn't know about that,' said Mrs Graham-Potter, and Hannah felt the mood between them chill.

She looked down at her pad and wished her notes looked more professional. Either that, or that the whole situation could be less formal. It really was hard to know how she was meant to respond to a woman whom she'd known slightly for thirty years, who must know everything about her own family, including all the little details that Dora wouldn't discuss. It didn't matter how smart her satchel was, everything Mrs Graham-Potter did or said made her feel as if she was the one being assessed, not the paintings.

Hannah cleared her throat and reminded herself that, although she might feel like a miserable failure, everyone else in this town thought she was hopelessly over-qualified for normal life. 'Um, OK, then. Those miniatures look rather interesting . . .'

But Mrs Graham-Potter hadn't finished with the family lecture. Soundlessly, she had moved to the other side of the study, looking at the large portraits that hung above the mahogany roll-top desk, her head on one side like a bird.

She glanced at Hannah, her expression guarded. She nodded at the portrait, and obediently Hannah took up her pen again. 'Then there's Sir Samuel Musgrave, Faith and Constance's father. I don't think he was expected to inherit, being the youngest of the brothers, but there really was a dreadful lot of bad luck in the family. In the end, he was the last male Musgrave in the line, when all's said and done. Not that he'd have thought so when that was painted, I dare say.'

Hannah picked her way carefully across the room, avoiding the numerous small tables, primed with stacks of books just asking to be knocked over. She sensed that they hadn't always been there, that this study had once been tidier than it was now. There was an odd crossness about the atmosphere, as if the oak-panelled room itself were trying to expel the clutter.

She stood in front of the portrait, near enough to Mrs Graham-Potter to smell the faint odour of mothballs underneath the Shalimar. Together, they gazed critically at the portrait.

Samuel had eschewed the modern photographic medium for something more stately and less available to the masses: he'd chosen to be depicted in oils, against a background of teeming mines and rolling hills. One hand was laid gently on the head of a Dalmatian, presumably to represent his paternal qualities. The other was shoved in his pocket, presumably keeping tight hold of his cash.

Faith and Constance's father, thought Hannah, and shivered as a draught caught her skin.

Ever since her own father left, Hannah had developed a secret habit of casting replacements. John Major had been a favourite for a long time: kindly smile, and good at cricket. Sean Connery had been another – although it was impossible to imagine Fran putting up with James Bond's unreconstructed sexist ways. Spotting nice men had become a habit, on the bus, drinking coffee, to the point where she could tell in an instant whether she'd want them for a father or not. But Samuel Musgrave chilled her blood. He didn't look like the kind of man she'd want for a father, or even consider worth painting – except that he had a sizeable fortune.

She wasn't even sure she'd want him near children. 'What happened to all his brothers?' she asked.

'They died,' said Mrs Graham-Potter.

There was a short pause.

'How?' Hannah prompted.

'Oh . . .' She flapped her hands dismissively. 'I think a couple went into the army and were killed in the Crimea. Isaac left home at sixteen, went off to America and wasn't heard of again. Carlisle was the London property agent for a long time, but he died at his club. There was a bit of gossip about that at the time, by all accounts, but it turned out to be malicious rumour. An unhappy woman, I believe, or her husband. I don't recall what happened to the rest. Poor Derwent was a mining engineer, and was caught up in a pit collapse in one of the Etterthwaite pits, I do know that. That finished Isabella off. She always liked Derwent best.'

'It seems very unlucky,' said Hannah, scribbling down these details.

'Well, life was very hard. If people caught diseases, they usually died. If they were injured, well . . .'

Hannah looked into Samuel Musgrave's face. It wasn't a huge leap of the imagination to imagine him picking off his brothers, working his way up the line of succession, making sure of his inheritance . . . 'I suppose that's why they had such large families?' she asked. 'To be on the safe side?'

Mrs Graham-Potter raised her eyebrows at the implications. 'If you want to put it like that.'

Not so different from the miners in the cramped pit cottages then, thought Hannah. Safety and income in numbers.

'What did you mean when you said about him being the end of the line but "not that he'd have thought so"?' she asked, unable to tear her gaze from the painting. Surely Faith and Constance had had brothers? 'Didn't he have any sons of his own?'

She might not like the look of him, but there was something in the coal-black eyes that held her attention. The haughtiness unbalanced an otherwise weak face. Musgrave's hair, like his mother's, was blond, but looked insipid, incongruous with such dark eyes. He wasn't handsome, but there was something compellingly masculine about him. It was all contradictory.

'Well, no. He had eight healthy sons – and two daughters, obviously.'

'Eight?' How had such a massive family dwindled into three old ladies rattling round this barn of a house? Hannah thought of the photograph hidden away upstairs, of the tense picnic at Thirlmere with the two lone boys hovering behind their unhappy-looking mother and nervous sisters.

'I wish you wouldn't repeat everything I say, dear,' said Mrs Graham-Potter tetchily. 'It's making me feel like a school-teacher. Yes, he had eight sons. Joseph, Young Sam, Derwent, William, Merlin, Hartley, Alfred and Henry. All dead by 1919, unhappily enough.'

Hannah's pen flew across the page, marking spidery new strands of family tree. She stopped suddenly. 'Wasn't it very confusing, having two lots of Josephs, Derwents and Samuels?'

'Not really. Their uncles . . . didn't survive long enough for it to be awkward. It wasn't unusual to have the same names repeated in each generation, you know. There was a very high mortality rate. And not many suitable male names.'

'But for them *all* to die! Again!' Even by Linton standards of low male life expectancy this was unlucky, especially with their money and influence to protect them. 'How did that happen?'

'The war,' said Mrs Graham-Potter, simply, and sat down in the wing-chair by the fireplace. For the first time, Hannah thought she could see traces of sadness soften the sharp features, revealing a shadowy hint of the youthful beauty she must once have taken for granted. Of course, she would have known all the lads: she would have danced with each one, knitted socks for them to take away to France. These were boys she'd have expected to grow old with, perhaps even marry, whereas Isabella's eight lost sons were only names.

'I'm sorry,' said Hannah, impulsively.

Mrs Graham-Potter turned her head from side to side, as if she could see them all in front of her again. She put up a hand to her face, then let it fall back into her lap. 'They went together, as so many boys did round here. They wanted to set an example to the rest of the men. Samuel wanted them to stay, to make sure the mines were running properly – no one would have complained at that – but Ellen, their mother, said they should go.'

She gestured towards a smaller portrait above a bookshelf. Ellen Musgrave was small and soft-featured, more like Constance than Faith. Her little round face almost disappeared into the high neck of her purple dress, and she seemed too shy to meet the artist's gaze. Hannah guessed that she, too, had had a father who was big in cotton.

'Jos, Sam and Derwent were killed in the same week in France, November 1914. Will died at Ypres in 1917, just before his twenty-first birthday. Merlin was wounded in a skirmish in Belgium, on Valentine's Day in 1918, and we never heard what happened to Hartley.' The words flowing from Mrs Graham-Potter's mouth stopped in a dry hiccup of sadness, and she had to pause to collect herself.

Hannah knew better than to interrupt.

'Hartley simply vanished. The letter we had from the commanding officer, informally, you understand, was that he was there when they were marching out of the trenches, but the next minute he was gone, and there wasn't time to look for him. Faith tried to find out afterwards, dragging Constance out there with some people from the War Graves Commission, but there was nothing to go on. He died too late, you see, for anyone to have any time to bury him. If there was anything of him left to bury.' She paused again.

After another moment's silence, she added, 'Alfred and Henry, the twins, were too young to join up, thank Heaven, but they got flu when it went round the country in 1919.'

'Oh, no,' breathed Hannah.

The old lady sighed bitterly. 'They used to say that if you didn't lose someone in the war, you lost two when influenza went round. The town lost a lot of miners who'd been retained to keep the pits running. It went through those colliery streets like wildfire. That's what poor Merlin died from too, in the end, influenza. He was the only one who came back. He survived a big shelling offensive, with just a bullet in his shoulder. We thought it was a miracle. But it wouldn't heal properly, so they sent him home, and we were going to nurse him here.'

Her hands fidgeted in her lap, and the diamonds sparkled unexpectedly in the shadowy room.

Hannah could feel heavy sorrow filling her chest, as if all the tears wept over letters, opened and read here in the study, were trapped in the fabric of the curtains and between the pages of the books, and were now seeping through the darkness and into her skin.

She didn't trust herself to speak. Mrs Graham-Potter seemed lost in the wastelands of her own memory, hardly noticing if she was there or not.

'Flu was *rife* in the town, and Faith and Constance were helping out in the soup kitchens, mixing with all the roughest sort of people day and night. We even had a few wounded soldiers staying here, when the hospital had more flu cases than it could take.' Mrs Graham-Potter pursed her lips. 'Merlin was on his way back, with special dispensation to be nursed at home, but Ellen wouldn't let him come here until the house was quarantined properly. She was worried about the girls, you see. Didn't want them to give it to him when he was so weak. He caught it from a nurse in the convalescent hospital in Kent. Died on his way back, from complications.'

Hannah caught her breath. 'Poor Faith! And Constance!'

Mrs Graham-Potter bit her lip. 'They *adored* their brothers. Good heavens, all the girls did! They were handsome, good, strong boys. Not like the surly louts you see hanging around Linton these days. They played cricket for the town team, you know, when they were back from school, and rugby too. Rugby union, of course,' she added quickly, 'not league. They were beautiful men. Merlin was especially good-looking. He had the face of an angel.'

Hannah suppressed a smile. It had occurred to her that maybe Merlin Musgrave, rather than a shared enjoyment of lacrosse, had sparked the friendship between Constance and Louise.

'Are there no photographs of them here?' Hannah looked around the shelves but could only see Faith and Constance's dark eyes staring out at her.

'No. Lady Musgrave wouldn't have them downstairs. She put them all in her room, around her dressing-table. When she died, Faith wanted to bring them down again, but Constance wouldn't have it.'

'Really?'

Mrs Graham-Potter sighed. 'Sometimes you don't want to be reminded. When you get older, you'll realize that some memories are better in your head. They're more private that way.'

Hannah let that go, not knowing how to respond. 'Were you all still at school during the war? You didn't have to volunteer to do war effort things?' She tried to work out how old they would have been then. Thirteen? Fourteen?

'Goodness, no! Certainly not. It was a horrible time. Lady Musgrave . . .'

A sarcastic cough announced the arrival of Mrs Tyson with the coffee-tray. She had made the etiquette decision that Hannah's junior, yet guest, status warranted smart mugs, but not cups, and had slammed a couple of slices of fruit cake on to a plate (no cake knives). This display of reluctant waitressing, almost worthy of the Coffee Pot, was hampered by the fact that there was no available space to bang down the tray, so she compromised by pushing it into Hannah's hands, forcing her to stuff her notepad under one arm and lose the last traces of dignity she felt she had. 'I'll finish the windows at the back and then I'll be off,' she grunted, permitting herself a good look round a room she wasn't normally allowed into.

'You do that,' said Mrs Graham-Potter tightly.

She waited until Mrs Tyson's firm tread had retreated a safe distance down the hall.

'Just put it down somewhere,' she said to Hannah. 'Anywhere.'

Hannah moved some books off the desk and set it down carefully. She didn't want to stop Mrs Graham-Potter's flow of memory for the sake of a cup of coffee. This was more information than she'd ever had about the villa's history, and her imagination was hungry for scraps of detail to flesh out the empty house, the people who had sat in the chairs or made notes at the desk. At any moment, Mrs Graham-Potter might move on to Dora, and her childhood, spent playing in the garden, running around the long corridors, growing up in this mausoleum. Had she been a comfort to Ellen after her sons had died? Had Samuel Musgrave liked her? Where had she fitted in?

'So there was no existing heir to take over the family business after the war?' she asked carefully. 'Did all the sons die before—'

Mrs Graham-Potter interrupted her: 'Sir Samuel died shortly after the Armistice. I don't think he ever got over the injustice of all the miners being kept safely here, working to keep the coal supply going, when his boys had to go and die. Of course, he didn't survive to see the influenza epidemic.' Mrs Graham-Potter's mouth twitched. 'That would no doubt have made him feel a little better. Evened things up a bit.'

Hannah wasn't sure what to make of that. 'And Lady Musgrave? Ellen?'

Again, the long sigh. 'Oh, she died in 1921. She practically lost her mind, poor soul. It was a very difficult time, what with one thing and another. We were all . . . rather disarranged by the time it came to a close. Ellen was always highly strung. I suppose now you'd say she needed psychiatric care, but then she just had to get over it as best she could. She spent a lot of time travelling. Spas were fashionable. She went to most of them.'

'Did Faith and Constance go too?'

'No. Faith thought they were so much hogwash. Still, there was some light at the end of it all,' said Mrs Graham-Potter, lifting her mug off the tray despite a slight tremor in her hand. She paused significantly, as if the information wasn't to be offered lightly.

'And that was?' asked Hannah.

'Well, when all the dust had settled, Faith, Constance and I went to Cambridge University. Faith had always been keen, but her parents wouldn't hear of it. Now there was no one left to stop us, you see, and the boys' arrangements had already been made,' said Mrs Graham-Potter, and hid her face behind her mug so that Hannah couldn't read it.

After a few minutes of less taxing conversation about the weather, Hannah felt dismissed, but on the way downstairs it occurred to her that, in this swift recent history, Mrs Graham-Potter hadn't mentioned Dora.

'Face of an angel, my aunt Fanny,' Mrs Tyson was muttering, as Hannah came back into the kitchen with the coffee tray. 'As evil a bastard as any of the—'

Hannah would have liked to hang about and hear more but as ever, her heavy tread gave her away and Mrs Tyson swung round as if on castors. 'How long have you been earwigging?' she demanded, going bright red in the areas of her face that weren't already bright red.

'How long were *you* earwigging?' replied Hannah, emboldened by a rare sighting of the moral high ground.

Mrs Tyson made a huffing noise and folded her arms across her bosom. 'It's not my place to make comments,' she said.

Hannah gave her a look.

'Well, it's not,' she repeated. 'But it's not right that she should put such downright lies in your head when you've no other way of knowing what they were like. And I don't think I'm speaking out of turn when I say that.'

Hannah deduced, correctly, that this was payback for being forced to serve elevenses like a parlourmaid.

'So why don't you tell me what they were like?' she said encouragingly. 'Would you like me to make a pot of tea?'

Mrs Tyson grunted.

Hannah took her time finding the teabags and the milk, and when she'd brought the big teapot to the table, Mrs Tyson was sitting down, and her mouth was twisting in a manner that suggested inner turmoil.

'Now, don't get me wrong, I'm not saying they were all horrible,' Mrs Tyson began, with absolute fairness that Hannah knew, from eavesdropping at the Coffee Pot Café, inevitably preceded a ruthless character assassination. 'Constance was a lovely lady. Kind as anything, and no side to her at all. And that Ellen, her mother, God rest her, had a good heart too, my mam always said. Even Faith . . .' She sniffed. 'Well, Faith had her faults, but she did a lot for them as had nothing round here, with her sick visiting and her art classes. Damn sight more than her father ever did.'

'Really?' said Hannah. 'I thought he owned the mines? Or at least some of them.'

'Aye, but what did he do? Where's the hospital? Or the welfare hall? Or the workers' library?' Mrs Tyson looked fierce. 'You're meant to look after the folk whose hard graft's buying your fancy houses in London, not leave them in filthy hovels wi' no running water.'

'Oh,' said Hannah. So they were evil Catherine Cookson-type land-owners. She added a pinch of salt, but said nothing.

'There's a reason they had money to burn,' Mrs Tyson went on. 'He was *mean*. They were all mean, the Musgrave men. Except when they were buying their title down in London.' She snorted. 'That's why Linton's got no facilities worth speaking of – they never put up the money for owt they couldn't get the benefit from. I don't know why her ladyship's defending them – Faith never did and they were her own flesh and blood. Bloody snob. "I can't recall", my foot!'

Mrs Tyson was getting redder in the face.

Hannah sipped her tea and made a diplomatic face.

Mrs Tyson struggled with her discretion for about ten seconds, then jabbed her finger on the worn pine tabletop. 'It's a long while back, but everyone else in this town knows where Sam Musgrave's brothers died. Benjamin got the clap from one of them fancy whorehouses in London, and Lady Musgrave wouldn't have him back in the house. Jack got into a big fight down on the docks – and you might well ask what he was doing there in the first place – and had his head cracked open. Derwent were that useless as a mining engineer that he couldn't even spot fire damp when it blew up in his face, and took twelve good lads with him and all. Down the Samson Pit. Always been unlucky, that one.'

Hannah wasn't sure what response was expected from her, if, indeed, she was meant to make one, so she just nodded.

Mrs Tyson, though, was happy to let her tea cool while she carried on, uninterrupted. She counted off each of Samuel's brothers on her thick fingers, snapping them into her palm as they were dismissed.

'Aye, they were the talk of the town, them Musgrave lads. Legendary. Tom and Jack were packed off to the army because they were too useless to have around, Carlisle got mixed up in a divorce scandal with some MP's wife, and shot hisself.' Mrs Tyson lifted her eyebrows meaningfully. '*Or so they said at the time.*'

Hannah widened her eyes.

Mrs Tyson nodded, as if to confirm all the worst things Hannah might be thinking. 'Only that Samuel was smart enough to keep himself out of trouble long enough to inherit.'

'He looks smart,' said Hannah.

'Smart, aye,' agreed Mrs Tyson, 'but a nasty piece of work.'

Hannah could see a pattern emerging. 'In what way?'

Mrs Tyson sucked her teeth and looked towards the door that led into the rest of the house. The kitchen was huge, designed to service a household that entertained in splendour, and they were sitting at the old table by the window, which was some way from the door. Even so, she dropped her voice to a low mutter. Hannah knew without being told that Mrs Graham-Potter, with her ethereally light step, could materialize silently anywhere.

'As I say, my mother was their housekeeper for years here, and her aunt Lizzy had worked here as a parlourmaid before that. Lizzy came home one night, white as a sheet, wouldn't go back. Wouldn't say why neither.'

Hannah took this with another pinch of salt. 'Wouldn't say why' didn't necessarily mean that at all. The only person she knew who would genuinely refuse to reveal unspeakable horrors, under pressure, was her grandmother. Most other people just used sworn secrecy as a sort of advertising trailer. 'What did she see?'

'Something in his rooms. The old man's. He was very odd, you know.' Mrs Tyson's lips clamped shut. 'You don't spend all that time in London without getting into bad ways. No offence, like.'

'None taken,' murmured Hannah. She was willing to put aside small personal insults for this unauthorized view – it would certainly explain why so many doors were locked.

'You see things, when you're tidying folk's houses,' said Mrs Tyson darkly. 'And in those days, they'd carry on as if the servants weren't there. Didn't care what they saw, because we didn't matter. How they carried on with their friends, now that was a different story. Poor Lizzy saw things that I'd bet my life Isabella didn't see.'

'Did she see something in his rooms?' asked Hannah. She tried to make her voice casual.

There was silence. The kitchen clock ticked loudly.

'Whips,' said Mrs Tyson eventually. 'Curled up like adders in a box, she said. She wouldn't talk about the rest.'

The hairs on the back of Hannah's arms prickled.

'Made a lot of money from slaves, did the Musgraves,' said Mrs Tyson, 'and not just them poor darkie souls they had in their ships all them years back either. The things I've heard about their dealings in London, some of the things that went on in their posh house—' She clamped her lips shut again.

'What happened to Lizzy?' asked Hannah. 'Surely she couldn't just walk out? What did she do for money?'

Mrs Tyson regarded her levelly, considering how much to tell. 'Lizzy couldn't *walk out*, God bless her soul,' she said. 'Couldn't walk at all, hardly. Old Joe Musgrave found her in his room. She was only dusting. But by the time he'd finished with her, they had to get one of the stable lads to carry the poor lass back down t' hill. That far from dead, she was.' She held up a finger and thumb to demonstrate the girl's hair's-breadth grip on life.

Hannah gaped in horror. 'But her father . . . Surely . . .'

'Dead at thirty. Her brothers were of a mind to go up there and sort him out, but they worked in the pit, didn't they? Any sign of trouble and Musgrave used to close the mines. All of them. That's why there's never *been* much trouble. Mind, I don't know if that's gospel about the whipping,' Mrs Tyson added. 'Lizzy always was sickly.'

They drank their tea in a silence thick with lurid thoughts, broken only by the rattle of the cat-flap when the blackest of Mrs Graham-Potter's cats slunk into the kitchen and disappeared like a shadow.

Hannah thought of the old tea caddies and the inlaid humidors in the hall, and the men's hands that had opened and closed them, and the women's hands that had cleaned them. Hands that had run up the banisters. Hands that had opened the brass doorknobs. Hands that had touched Ellen and Isabella and the servants. Hands that stretched out from the past to meet hers as she listed their possessions and put a market value on their worth, just as they'd assessed and acquired the contents of their home.

'What was so bad about Samuel Musgrave? The son?' she asked, to stop the shiver running through her.

'Oh, he was a bad 'un, too,' said Mrs Tyson, as if Samuel Musgrave was a *real* villain, unlike his mildly wayward father. 'Through and through. He had some nasty habits, some like his dad's and some of his own.' She narrowed her eyes confidentially. 'The problem with all them Musgrave men was they thought that because they had money they could disregard people, like they didn't matter. And Samuel, he liked to think he was a real lord of the manor. You've seen that portrait of him – lord of all he surveyed.' Mrs Tyson snorted in disgust.

'It is, er, rather pompous,' said Hannah.

'Thought that his rights extended to the miners' wives as well as the men, if you know what I'm saying.'

Hannah flushed, despite herself.

'Ironic, isn't it?' said Mrs Tyson, helping herself to another mug of stewed tea. 'No sooner had Faith and Constance been round with charity baskets than their father'd be in, having his way with the women while their men were down his pits. Soon as the cage went down, so did his breeches.'

'That's terrible,' said Hannah. She knew better, though, than to ask why no one had done anything.

'I've nowt against them lasses,' added Mrs Tyson. 'As I say, the women of the family were always well meaning,' her brow darkened, 'if a bit fey. But what can you do with men like that? No wonder they never married. Reckon Faith and Constance were much better off on their own. Even with that one around.'

She jerked her head towards the door, having first checked that Mrs Graham-Potter hadn't materialized.

'Do you mean Mrs Graham-Potter?' asked Hannah. 'But I thought . . .' She wasn't sure what she thought, so she let the sentence trail off.

'Well, she's no class.' Mrs Tyson managed to stir her tea in a dismissive way. 'But she knows how to jump on other folk's backs. Moved herself in by degrees when they were all at school. Never left. Orphaned, they reckon. I'd give my eye-teeth for a quick sken at the will.'

The clock struck three o'clock, loud chimes that reverberated round the room. They made the old service bells, still lined up above the clock, hum in a ghostly echo: Drawing Room; Blue Bedroom; Study; Library.

The Sewing Room bell jangled.

Hannah jerked with shock.

'Aye, it does that,' said Mrs Tyson. 'There's a fault in the wiring. Whole house needs seeing to. It's a death-trap.'

Hannah couldn't take her eyes off the bell as it subsided into silence.

Mrs Tyson gave her a hard stare, and seemed to remember, all of a sudden, who she was talking to. 'Anyway,' she said, stiffly, 'I'd best be getting on. I've a fair amount of washing to do.' She rose to her feet with a double creak of the knees.

Hannah leaped up and gathered the mugs. 'You get away, I'll wash the tea-things.'

Mrs Tyson folded her arms. 'I'm not ashamed of what I've just said, but it might be better if you don't, er, repeat it to your grandmother. I daresay she'll have a rather different view.'

Again, there had been no mention of Dora. No unauthorized version of where she'd come from, no conjecture about who she really was. But, then, would Mrs Tyson tell her anyway?

Hannah stopped with the tea-things in her hand, and thought about where Dora fitted into this confusion of gossip and doctored family history. She had never mentioned Samuel Musgrave, or indeed any male Musgrave, to her. Dora's omissions, though, were usually more telling than her verbal assaults.

'I won't say anything,' said Hannah, and started to run the hot water into the big stone sink.

Chapter Eleven

As a little girl, when Hannah read a fairy story involving a house in the woods, she invariably thought of Dora's cottage, even though it wasn't in the woods, really, and stood no chance of being visited by anyone more scary than her mother bearing the Sunday papers. It wasn't made of gingerbread either, but there was something mysteriously neat about it, with its large sash windows edged in blue paint that never flaked, unlike the permanently scabbing sills at Rose View, and its garden of rose bushes that proliferated with musky flowers and rambled up one side of the cottage; the buds tapped at the windows when the wind blew, and their fragrance curled into the rooms. It might have been built for a princess to fall asleep in or a beautiful maiden to live there in secret until her prince came and swept her away.

As she got older, Hannah didn't think of it in such fairy-tale terms, but a faint cloud of magic clung to it. Dora's cottage always smelt like fresh washing and flowers; whereas Rose View reeked of Keith's post-school chain-smoking and Fran's lentil experiments. It was a happy place. Dora was certainly happier there than she had been in Rose View. Hannah was happier there than in Rose View which, although it was a big house, was not big enough to contain Keith and Fran and the dust-storms of frustration that whirled around them until Keith had left. Afterwards Fran, seemingly now addicted to stress and arguments, accepted a series of complicated long-running compensation battles on behalf of families affected when a disused ventilation shaft collapsed, taking with it four streets of hastily erected Victorian miners' cottages on the outskirts of the town. From the subsequent breakdown in communication between Rose View and the gardener's cottage, Hannah deduced that the Musgraves were in some way involved.

Having signed up for five A levels (English, French, German, History of Art and General Studies), Hannah's time was rigorously divided between school (9 a.m. – 3.30 p.m.), the Coffee Pot Café (12.30 p.m. – 2 p.m., and 3.30 p.m. – 5.45 p.m.), Dora's cottage (alternate evenings) and Rose View (8 p.m. – 8.17 a.m.). If she could have got away with spending only sleeping time at home, she would have done it, but Fran was draconian about keeping regular (silent) family meals, and splitting household tasks between her and Dominic, even though Mrs Tyson was coming in twice a week. There was a lot of brass to polish.

Dominic, who had abandoned his media-studies course for a year off, had observed that what they were really polishing was Fran's social conscience. It had earned him a long, agonizing lecture; a clip round the ear would have been preferable.

If she could have spent all her waking hours in the Coffee Pot Café, revising with Fiammetta, Hannah thought she would have been perfectly happy. They spent hours together, giggling at anything, anyone. It was easy to be happy with Fiammetta. The painful certainty that this was the best time in her life sat in her chest like a hot, knotted ball all the time, and that feeling intensified when they were in their regular window booth, empty cappuccino cups stacked on their set-text books, mocking the boy racers driving past the window on the Linton lap, going round and round the town's one-way system in their low-slung Golf GTis.

Hannah knew she wasn't going to fail her exams, and she knew she was on the verge of leaving the narrowness of Linton, spreading her wings and flying somewhere where no one would mock her for the way she spoke or the things she said. But that wasn't what made her feel so intensely jittery.

Behind the revision lists and crib sheets jostling for space in her head there was a faint but disorientating hum, like a cattle stampede on the distant horizon; a murmur that things weren't right. Hannah tried to push it aside, but it wouldn't go away so she piled work and deadlines on top of it until all she could think about was what was in front of her.

Everything was about as perfect as it could be. By now she was even one of the cool older girls at school, more by dint of staying on to the sixth form than by *being* cool. Her workload was massive, but she found the actual learning of it easy; she had the best friend anyone could want, and she alone of all her class didn't have to spend every evening working in the supermarket for extra allowance. (Fran was keen, but Dora expressly forbade it.)

Yet behind all the things that should have made her happy the tiny niggle knotted her stomach in premature nostalgia for this summer, like a fiery dash of Tabasco in an innocuous sauce.

Even upstairs in her room Hannah could hear Fran arguing over the phone with Keith. Fran had refused to discuss it, but from what she could piece together from Mrs Tyson, Dominic and some judicious eavesdropping, after turning invisible for several years he'd met someone else and now wanted a proper divorce so he could have another family. Presumably one that wouldn't give him as much trouble as theirs had.

She sighed and reached for her Walkman. At least she only had to listen to one side of the argument now. Both her parents were trained to make themselves heard at the back of rooms and consequently could project throughout the house without trying. And without, Hannah thought, being aware that they were doing it.

She stared at the text in front of her. The most important thing was to focus on matters that could be resolved by learning all the questions first. *Twelfth Night.* It wasn't improved by the Smiths running over the top of it to blank out her mother yelling. When the song finished, she heard Fran bellow, 'I am not going to sign these papers just to make you happy, you bastard!' and wondered if there was a way of taping songs with no pauses between.

Hannah's heart wasn't in the revision, and she knew it. She had the kind of brain that only needed to look at something once for it to be imprinted, and she was going through the motions of revision only because she was scared not to. Everyone else at school was winding themselves and each other up into simmering hysteria; it seemed like tempting Fate not to do the same.

Hannah looked at her revision timetable: this was her last evening with *Twelfth Night,* and she didn't have the exam for another six weeks. Her eyes unfocused with second-hand panic.

She didn't want this term to end.

Outside, the tide was coming in noisily and the raucous shrieks of seagulls suggested that the fishing-boats were arriving back in the harbour. A note fell out of her textbook, and she unfolded it carefully to read it once more before it went with the rest into an old cigar box. Hannah hated throwing away Fiammetta's notes.

Fiammetta had beautiful handwriting and she always used a fountain pen, which gave even her most scrawled jottings a certain cachet. Precocious Hannah had learned to write joined-up before she left primary school, and her writing bore the neat functionality of Mrs Pritt's cursive classes.

The note was one that they'd passed back and forth during double English that afternoon, negotiating when would be a good time for Fiammetta to cut Hannah's hair – on the quiet, naturally.

'If you want me to do your hair,' Fiammetta had written, 'it'll have to be round at your house, or in the Coffee Pot. I don't want Mum finding out I know how to do it. She'll have me enrolled at the college before you can say Vidal Sassoon. Tomorrow evening OK?'

Hannah's neat answer confirmed that, yes, it was. She was looking forward to it. Fiammetta was good with her scissors, despite her refusal to join the family business. The sniping with her mother had now turned into a full-scale battle of wills, and Hannah had made the ultimate sacrifice, a few months ago, of allowing Fiammetta to perform a disastrous tint on her, just to prove how much of a liability she would be in the salon. It had taken the combined skills of the entire salon to put it right, and Allegra Rissini was still apologizing to Dora every time she went in for her weekly set, which was now 'on the house' for life.

Fiammetta and Hannah agreed it had been worth it. This time, Fiammetta had agreed to try some highlights in Hannah's mousy fringe. The sun didn't spend long enough in Linton to achieve the effect naturally.

The click and silence at the end of the tape revealed that, downstairs, Fran and Keith were still hard at it, pursuing new and ever more acidic ways of ending their marriage.

'I have better things to do than argue with you about maintenance for two children you've never given a damn about!' yelled Fran's voice. 'I'm fighting to rehome families with no roofs over their heads!'

Hannah winced and looked at her watch. Half ten. Dora would still be up, and would probably make her some decent coffee.

She took off her headphones, closed *Twelfth Night*, climbed out of the bedroom window, then down the sturdy apple tree so she wouldn't have to walk past the kitchen and force her mother to pretend she'd been watching television with the volume turned up.

At the end of the garden, lights were shining through the cottage's curtains, and Hannah thought she could hear the faint sound of music. Dora kept late hours.

Between the back of Rose View and Dora's door lay a dark and shifting garden, where all the leaves bore slicks of soaking Linton rain. It was exactly on nights like this, Dominic had said, that the White Lady could be seen. Bright nights where you could see the moon twice: above and reflected in the sea.

A gust of wind whipped out of nowhere, rustling the trees and shifting all the shadows round again.

Hannah focused on the yellow rectangles of light as she marched down the path and through the orchard; she wouldn't let herself run, because that would be giving in to the whispers at the back of her mind that things were watching her from the bushes.

In the back of her mind, she could hear Dominic's soft voice still. The corniness made her smile in daylight, yet whenever she had to walk through the garden at night . . . 'The White Lady, running through the garden to her lover, already dead in the cottage, with her murderous and angry father by his side . . .'

'No!' Hannah said, and quickened her step on the wet grass.

She had never seen the White Lady, but it was easy to imagine her. It was a clear night and the moon seemed unusually large in the navy blue sky, looming over the harbour like one of Fran's cheap paper-globe lampshades. The kind of moon you watched from an upstairs window, imagining someone else looking at it too, when they couldn't be with you . . .

Don't be ridiculous, Hannah told herself. There's no evidence at all for ghosts. And if you can't prove something, it can't exist.

Sticking religiously to the facts had done Hannah a lot of good in the past few years. From being 'over-imaginative' as a child, she had become a stickler for proof and evidence as a teenager, and her mind refused to range beyond that. Even her artwork had metamorphosed from curlicued illustrations of fairy-tales to a near-obsession with black-and-white photography, usually of household objects taken from challenging angles. She had even suggested to her mother that she might think about training to be a solicitor. Hannah could tell Fran hadn't known whether to be pleased or not. When Dora heard, she had been insistent that Hannah shouldn't waste her life 'tidying up after other people'. Dora, it seemed, was keen for her to pursue a more artistic career, claiming it ran in the family. Where she'd got that from, Hannah didn't know, unless Dora was referring to her own cheesy memorial verses.

While sea damp crept through her battered trainers and into her socks, and the breeze made the bushes shift in an unsettling way, she kept her mind trained on real, reassuring facts, like the cast of *Twelfth Night*:

Orsino, Curio, Valentine, Viola.

But even with these characters forming a wall against her imagination, scary little thoughts snuck in like draughts under a door: what was that moving in the Hillcrest bushes? A Musgrave cat skittering up towards the villa? Would a White Lady float through the air towards her, or would it carry on walking on the path it was accustomed to?

Hannah gulped.

The Captain, Sir Toby Belch, Maria.

Recently, facts hadn't been quite enough, and that was worrying with her exams days away. Several times Hannah had caught herself pondering thoughts that didn't seem to fit inside her head. Sensuous, dark thoughts, that made her squirm and blush with unexpected arousal. She felt as though she was experiencing someone else's daydreams. They were even more unsettling at night, when her fettered imagination roamed free across her mind. Often she dreamed she was naked in the garden, and Fiammetta was there too, with faces and voices she knew she'd never heard before rushing up at her, changing as she looked at them. Sometimes she was jerked awake by the embarrassing weirdness of it all.

Her breath was coming quickly as she almost trotted towards the cottage. When she reached the gravel that marked the official garden path, she could hear Dora singing along to *La Traviata*, each beat punctuated with an almighty bang.

Hannah knocked on the front door. The wind rustled through the garden and she steeled herself against a strong impulse to turn and look behind her. She had to wait a few bars before Dora stopped slamming away at whatever she was beating long enough to hear her knock. Then the door opened.

'Hello, darling,' said Dora. Her eyes were glittering, and she was wielding a steak tenderizer.

'Hello,' said Hannah, and took care to wipe her feet on the mat as she went in.

Dora's cottage was surrounded by foliage on the outside and filled with plants inside. Her conservatory, with its long french windows and skylight, was covered on one wall with certificates from the Linton and District Agricultural Show, which she dominated with gracious autocracy. Roses, sweet-peas, dahlias, and her speciality, huge hanging baskets, foaming with red and pink busy-lizzies.

Tonight she was arranging a bunch of white and pink roses, which lay all over the kitchen table, their stems broken.

'Would you like a cup of tea?' asked Dora.

'Yes, please.'

'How's the revision going?'

'Oh, you know.' Hannah pulled a face.

'Well, it's good for you to have a change of scene now and again, isn't it?'

Hannah mumbled a response and pushed her nose deep into the velvet centre of a pink rose until the fragrance filled her head.

'What is it tonight?' Dora poured Hannah a cup of tea from her large teapot. '*Twelfth Night?*'

'Yeah.'

'You're so good at English, though, darling. Nothing for you to worry about there.'

Hannah put down the rose and stirred her tea with a surly expression. She heard that phrase a lot. Rather than reassuring her, it tightened the screw. If anything happened and she dropped down to Bs, Fran and Dora would have her checked over by a specialist to explain why.

'I thought you had orchestra tonight?'

'Cancelled because of the exams,' lied Hannah. She eased off her wet trainers under the table.

'Oh.' Dora opened a packet of French Fancies and arranged them on a plate. 'I thought I saw you in the Coffee Pot Café with Fiammetta.'

Hannah flushed. 'You might have done. We had a coffee after school. We revise in there,' she added defensively.

'You're spending a lot of time with her,' said Dora, with studied disinterest.

'She's my best friend,' Hannah replied. She began biting the icing off a pink cake. Dora knew they were her favourites and that Fran had banned them from the house after the latest tartrazine scare to have swept through the *Guardian* health section. Hannah appreciated little thoughtfulnesses like that; right now, a salmon pink French Fancy was a lot more consoling than one of Fran's bracing pep talks about her STEP papers.

'It's not . . . good to rely on just one friend, though, you know,' said Dora. 'Especially female friends.'

Hannah gave her a piercing look. 'I don't think there's much danger of me spending time with any other kind, Granny.'

Dora had the grace to blush.

'None of the boys in my class even talk to me,' Hannah went on. 'They don't like girls who are taller, cleverer and, oh, yes, *heavier* than they are.' She finished off the French Fancy in one bite.

'There's no need to be so hard on yourself,' said Dora automatically. 'You're a bonny girl. When you get to Oxford, you'll be making them wait in lines, see if you don't.'

Hannah didn't dignify the comment with a response.

'But I do think it might be a good idea to have some other friends too.' Dora edged the words into the conversation, in the same way she arranged her flowers for the best effect. 'Women can share the most wonderful . . . closeness, but don't always make the most straightforward friends. They remember everything, for a start. And . . .'

Hannah saw from the faint flush on Dora's cheeks that she was trying to hint something embarrassing, but didn't feel inclined to help her out.

'And people can be very cruel,' she said eventually. 'I speak from experience.'

'Really? What experience is that?'

'Well, Constance, you know, was terribly close to Louise Graham-Potter, and people used to . . .' Dora raised her eyebrows to illustrate a point she didn't wish to make verbally.

'There's nothing wrong with Fiammetta,' said Hannah, stoutly. She had a suspicion of where this might be going, and didn't want to hear it. Dora could be a terrible snob. 'She understands me. We have fun together.'

'As long as—' Dora stopped herself.

'As long as what?' asked Hannah, curiously.

Dora bashed some more stems and said nothing.

Whenever Hannah thought of Fiammetta from that moment on, as she did often, her mind went straight back to Dora's cottage, the smell of wet roses and the background murmurings of Italian opera. It was from that moment that a vague sense of intrigue about her friendship with Fiammetta began to take a more solid form.

Although Hannah was spending most of her days up at the villa, walking through the rooms with her notebook and having the occasional cup of coffee with Mrs Graham-Potter, Fran's brooding was becoming impossible to ignore. She refused to admit to Hannah that anything was wrong, and Hannah was still too wrapped up in her own misery to want to delve into her mother's.

She'd deduced that the problem was of a medical nature when she picked up an answering-machine message one night, confirming Fran's appointment at the hospital for tests, but even when she passed on the message, Fran wouldn't expand, and they ate their beans on toast in haughty, if secretly relieved, silence.

In the morning, Hannah decided to give her mother a bit of space and have breakfast at the cottage with Dora, even if it meant forgoing her usual lie-in.

There was a chill in the air that cut through her fleece as she strode briskly through the orchard, and the tang of ozone was strong. Mrs Graham-Potter's cats were stalking some poor creature through the rosebushes; they stopped for a moment to glare defiantly at her as she went past. Hannah gave the bush a shake: the leaves rustled and a thrush flew away over the wall towards the sea.

Despite the early hour, Dora was up and about: she went to bed late and got up ridiculously early. A hangover, she always said, from living near the pits. Once up, Dora didn't see the point in tiptoeing around for others: Hannah could hear music coming from the cottage when she was only half-way down the path. It was Maria Callas, Dora's favourite.

Hannah gave their three-knock code – how did Dora get those roses to climb round the door when Fran could barely get hydrangeas to survive the sea blast? she wondered – and let herself in without waiting for a reply.

'Good morning,' she shouted over the music. 'Do you mind if I turn Maria down? It's a bit early for me.'

'Oh, hello, darling!' said Dora, waving in greeting. She was wearing a pair of pistachio green rubber gloves festooned with extravagant cuffs of plastic lace. 'Yes, do, by all means.'

Dora celebrated the onset of winter by planting bulbs on the kitchen table, a ritual she performed with great glamour and mystery. A fleet of troughs stood waiting to be filled with hyacinths, which she had lined up next to bright illustrations of their mature glory, and a series of clinical-looking gardening implements, with green plastic handles. She had chosen the dramatic, not entirely spring-like colour scheme of blood-red and deep purple flowers in bone-white troughs. A copy of *Birdsong* lay on the draining-board, the marker no further than the first three pages.

'I like them to have a little Callas before they go to sleep for the winter,' she said, stuffing a bulb into the compost. 'It makes them come up very bright.' Her one concession to neatness was an old copy of *The Times* spread over the table, but it was liberally sprinkled with John Innes compost and the translucent skins that some bulbs had shed.

'There!' She tamped down the compost with a firm hand and put the finished trough to one side. 'Nice and warm. Do you remember how you'd come down here when you were little and help me?'

Hannah nodded. 'I do. I remember that hand cream you used to make me put on afterwards. It gave me a rash.'

'Would you care to make some tea, darling? Thank you. We had some happy times together, didn't we?' said Dora.

'We did.' Hannah went to fill the kettle. Fran occasionally said the same thing – 'We had some happy times, didn't we?' – but it always sounded to Hannah's ears as if she needed reassurance. Dora said it with a conspiratorial wink: most of their happy times had involved trips or indulgences that Fran would not have countenanced.

'So, what brings you down here, when you could be having muesli and a breakfast debate with your mother?' asked Dora, pulling another trough towards her. Her hands hovered over the purple, then the red bulbs, like a child in a sweet shop, wavering between sherbet dabs or cola bottles.

'I thought I'd like to see you for a change.'

'That's very kind of you.' Dora pursed her lips in a complicit smile. Her lipstick was poppy red, the colour of femmes fatales, and adulteresses. She was wearing more makeup than Hannah would put on for a night out and it was only eight in the morning. 'But I don't believe it for a minute.'

'No, it's true,' said Hannah, busying herself with the tea-caddy so Dora wouldn't catch any trace of a white lie.

'Well, it's lovely to see you all the same,' said Dora. 'Have you to myself for a little while.'

She carried on planting and humming along to Maria Callas while Hannah made the tea and assembled the cups on a tray. Dora was a tea connoisseur: breakfast tea at breakfast, Earl Grey in the afternoon, Assam after dinner, all loose leaf and stored in old tea-jars bought from Addison's the grocer's when it closed down.

'Take it through to the sunroom, darling.' Dora took off her gloves and threw them on to the table. 'I can't be bothered tidying up midway through. And it's nice to drink your morning tea listening to the sea, isn't it? I bet you missed that in London.'

Hannah realized that she hadn't had her usual 'I'd be on the Tube by now' thought and, for a second, couldn't recall what time she used to set off for work.

Dora smiled enigmatically, as if she could read her mind.

The long windows in the sunroom looked out towards the harbour, where the street-lights were still shining out of the morning gloom. Signs of life were few and far between on the quayside, apart from a few dedicated joggers and dog-walkers.

'Granny, I need to ask you something rather delicate,' Hannah began, when they were settled in the big armchairs, staring out towards the dock, rather than at each other.

'Go on,' said Dora. 'Have a Puritan biscuit.'

Hannah took a Rich Tea from the proffered tin and nibbled it while she tried to think of the best way to get a straightforward answer.

'Is Mum ill?' she asked at last.

Dora dunked her biscuit. 'I don't know the answer to that.'

'Well, is she or isn't she? I can always ask Mrs Woodward at the book group. I'm sure she'll know.'

Dora sighed. 'Your mother is a . . . very private person. She likes to keep personal matters to herself.'

Hannah knew where Fran had got that particular trait. 'But is she ill? Surely she'd tell you.'

'Why don't you ask her?'

'I've tried,' said Hannah. Then, conscious that she hadn't tried very hard, she added, 'But you know what she's like.'

'I know she's been up to the hospital for some checks.' Dora pressed her lips together. 'But you mustn't worry, women her age go through all sorts of disturbing phases. There *is* no trouble-free age to be a woman, let me tell you. And it would be just like Frances to feel she should be entitled to beat the menopause.'

Hannah sank back in her seat, and considered this. It made sense. 'Well, that would explain the bad moods and weird behaviour.' It didn't explain Mrs Armstrong's concern, though.

'Darling, how would we tell the difference?' said Dora. 'Why she can't just give in gracefully, I don't know. She's been grilling me about what it was like when I went through it – did I have hot flushes, did I have dizziness.'

Hannah pulled a sympathetic face.

'I think she's bought a book about it.' Dora rolled her eyes. 'Fancy someone writing a *book* about the menopause. Surely a pamphlet would suffice. In my day, we didn't talk about bodily functions *at all* unless we were securely inside the four walls of a doctor's surgery. And even then we'd try to exercise some discretion.'

'Which is why so many women died of perfectly curable diseases,' Hannah chided her. 'Don't pretend to be all prim. I know you're not, really, you're just enjoying the sensation of thinking like Mrs Jordan.'

Dora tried to frown, but couldn't. 'Oh, don't. Janet Jordan? Really! I mean it, though. Your mother has become obsessed with medical details. It's just like her vegetarian craze all over again. Do you remember? We were all going to die of hardened arteries unless we ate her soya cake.' She huffed out a sigh. 'I don't mind telling you that we had to have words about it the other day.'

'Really?'

Dora nodded. 'She came down here and positively *interrogated* me about family ailments. Implied I could be harbouring all manner of genetic idiocies.'

'And what did you tell her?' Hannah tried to keep all emotion out of her voice. This wouldn't be about whether Poor Arthur had been susceptible to varicose veins. Dora and Fran had wrangled over Dora's uninterest in her parentage for years: Dora absolutely refused to discuss her family background, about which she claimed to know very little beyond what was already in the public domain, and Fran resented her mother's lack of curiosity about something she felt she had a right to know.

'I told her that if she wanted to go off and have lots of blood tests done that was her business. At my time of life, it makes little difference to me what's going on inside.' Dora looked affronted.

Hannah sipped her tea and tried to be tactful. 'Far be it from me to be on Mum's side for once, but maybe, you know, if she thinks she's got some rare syndrome . . . She's probably decided she's the only woman in Britain with elephantiatis or something.'

'I can assure you she's not.'

'How do you know?'

'Because if your mother does have some rare disease, she'll want to be the first to beat it with soya milk alone.'

For a few minutes they drank their tea in silence, and Hannah contemplated all the medical implications of not knowing who your parents were. She was surprised that it had never occurred to her before now, but it might have repercussions for her as well – not so much now that Toby had put any baby plans off the agenda.

Toby, thought Hannah. She tried to dredge up a feeling of resentment that he was probably revising his no-kids stance with Jennifer but, to her surprise, she couldn't. She actually didn't care. Hannah put aside that revelation for closer examination later. What were the diseases that went down the female line – haemophilia? That one the royal family had? Fran would rather go mad than have some tyrannical blood disease in common with Queen Victoria. Then again . . . 'Maybe you should—'

Dora cut her off. 'There's nothing I want to know.'

'Granny, I understand that, but there's a difference between – between not wanting to know for emotional reasons and finding out if there are any major illnesses in the family.' Hannah thought hard. 'They might've asked her to find out if there's something serious they can rule out or not. Is that it?'

'I haven't asked.'

'Why not?'

'Because that's her business, and this is mine.'

Hannah stared at Dora, unsure what to say. Was her grandmother scared of finding out more than she wanted to know?

Or was she just digging in her heels on a point of mother/daughter principle?

'Hannah. I'm a stubborn old woman, but it's just the way we were all brought up.' Dora poured herself some more tea through her pewter strainer. It was a dark orange-brown colour, like liquid amber. 'There are things it's better not to know about, and that's an end to it.'

'How can you say that? If you ignore things, they only cause more problems later on. Nasty psychological problems. She could be giving herself terrible psychosomatic symptoms just worrying about it.'

'Nonsense.' Dora stirred milk fiercely into her tea. 'When I was growing up, horrible, unspeakable things happened, every single day. Things you'd shrink from now. Men were suffocated by gas in the pits. Young lads had their arms torn off by machinery in the steel works. Women much younger than you were worn out trying to feed eight kids, screaming day in day out, and then they threw themselves into the dock. There were no social services then to sort out lives for people. None of this *claim* mentality. When something terrible happened to you, you just put it to the back of your mind and got on with your life.'

Dora sounded as if she were speaking from bitter experience, but Hannah had no idea what she meant. Arthur hadn't mistreated her, and she certainly hadn't wanted for anything. She could hardly claim the Musgraves' series of losses as her own.

Dora was still smarting. 'And that's why, at this time in my life, I don't take kindly to your mother, *my own daughter*, telling me that I've got it all wrong and should be asking questions and digging up the past.'

Dora's cheeks were flushed and, in the meagre morning light, her age showed through the artful makeup.

'Did something terrible happen to your parents?' asked Hannah, boldly. It wasn't easy to ask personal questions of either her mother or grandmother, but somehow Dora seemed less vulnerable, less likely to change before her eyes. And she had gone so far now, it would be pointless to leave without asking. 'Is that what you're getting at?'

'I don't *know* who my parents were,' she said. She spoke lightly but the pain was evident on her face. 'Faith and Constance brought me up, and that was good enough for me. I don't see the point in finding out now.'

'Even now that Faith and Constance aren't here to be upset?' asked Hannah gently. She didn't see why they would be upset, anyway — wasn't it natural for an adoptive child to want to know about their beginnings, however disadvantaged?

'No,' snapped Dora.

There was silence between them.

Hannah felt ashamed of her curiosity. It seemed base next to her grandmother's dignity. She put her hand on Dora's. 'Granny, I didn't mean to upset you. And I really don't mean to pry, if that's what you're thinking. I just don't *know* anything.'

'And how much do you know about your other grandmother?'

'Not very much,' Hannah admitted. Keith hadn't been much of a one for family, and still wasn't if his lack of communication was anything to go by. 'That she died of lung cancer before Dom was born, and she lived in Wolverhampton.'

'And has that lack of knowledge blighted your life?'

It was Hannah's turn to redden. 'Well, given that I don't know a great deal more about my dad, no, not really. But I do feel that I'm . . . missing something other people have, you know, to look back on. To compare themselves with.'

'Who needs to compare themselves with anyone?'

'Not everyone has your cast-iron confidence,' Hannah retorted.

They glared across the coffee table, each thinking privately how like Fran the other was.

Dora squeezed Hannah's hand and sighed. 'Oh, I don't mean to bark at you, darling. I'm not trying to *hide* anything, don't think that. Quite the opposite.'

She looked out at the harbour and then looked back at Hannah. 'I'm *happy* to tell you all I know myself, what little there is. I mean, I'm sure you know it already. When Faith and Constance, and Louise, of course, came back from Cambridge – they went to Newnham after the war – they had a baby with them. That was me. They brought me up in the villa, and never once mentioned where I'd come from, and I never asked them. And, barring a few little squabbles of the kind that any family has to endure from time to time, we were perfectly happy.'

Hannah wasn't sure that that was the whole story, but she believed her grandmother about the mutual lack of enquiry. She could imagine the polite wall of silence, built up on each side. 'I just don't understand why you were never curious.'

'*You've* never asked me before, have you?' Dora raised her eyebrow.

Hannah ignored her. 'But you *never* wondered who your parents might be?'

'Not once. It's only now that people are so obsessed with *finding out*,' said Dora, bitterly. 'That was your mother's generation, always *finding out* and demanding this and demanding that. As if everyone has a *right* to know everything about everyone else, even private matters. They weren't so good at dealing with what they found out, though, were they?'

'What do you mean?'

Dora shook her head. She lifted her hand as if she was going to say something else, then smiled brightly in a let's-change-the-subject-now-and-talk-about-gardening fashion.

The smile faded a little when Hannah put her finger on her chin and launched into more questions. 'But weren't the people in the village curious?' she asked. 'About where you'd come from?'

'Oh, they were curious, all right.' Dora sniffed. 'They were *burning* with curiosity, but how could they ask? One *didn't* ask questions like that. And you know exactly what they're like round here. Sometimes one has to wonder whether they want to know the truth of the matter when making it up is so much more interesting.'

Hannah was too polite to ask directly what people had said, but Dora read it in her expression.

'Oh, well, Faith and Constance did a lot of charity work in the town after their father died, and I imagine the more generous gossips had it that I was a foundling from one of the poorer mining families, brought in out of Christian charity.'

Hannah didn't say anything. It sounded unlikely, given Dora's natural haughtiness – but stranger things had happened.

'The *less* generous put it around that I was Faith's . . . mistake.' Dora tensed. 'She was the suffragette, after all. The local campaigner for women's rights. And she had a mind of her own, which is, as you know, considered a dangerous thing round here for a woman. There were *limitless* variations on who the father might be. Daughter of a lecherous Cambridge don, or a philandering minor royal – at least they had the grace to let Faith aim high in their little fantasies.'

'How do you know they said all this if no one told you?'

Dora held her head up proudly. 'Oh, one always knows about whispers. Children often repeat things their mothers say without knowing how hurtful they're being.'

'They said that to your face?' Hannah couldn't imagine anyone daring to.

'Not to my face, no.' She sighed. 'But I spent a lot of time in the garden when I was a little girl, like you did, and we had a very deaf old cook – Mrs Farthingale. The servants had to yell pretty hard to gossip to her, and she yelled back. With the range full on for baking or washing, the kitchen was like a furnace most days, so they kept the back door open. I heard a great deal. More than they'd ever have dared to say if they'd known I could hear them.'

'Poor little girl,' said Hannah.

'Do you know, I haven't even told your mother some of that?' said Dora, sounding surprised at herself.

'Have you ever thought that she might, you know, understand you better, if she did know things like that?'

Hannah saw from the defensiveness that rose in Dora's face that this was rather too close to counsellor-speak for comfort.

'Frances is the reason I never believed Faith could be my mother,' said Dora, heavily. 'Faith and I understood each other perfectly, shared the same interests, never had a cross word. On the other hand, I've never, ever understood Frances, and I doubt now that I ever will. I imagine you and your mother are no different.'

'Oh dear,' said Hannah. She looked at her watch. 'I should get a move on. Mrs Graham-Potter's expecting me at half ten.'

'Where have you got to in the great collection?'

'Artistic representations of the Lakes past and present, mostly bought by Joseph Musgrave, possibly by the yard, to go with the watercolours of the Lakes and the occasional stuffed animal of the Lakes. It's got to the point where I'm praying there'll be some disgusting Victorian pornography to break the monotony.' Hannah rolled her eyes. 'I'll just go to the loo before I head over there.'

Dora started to gather together the tea-things, humming to herself. As Hannah went down the narrow hall to the bathroom, she heard Maria Callas being turned up again in the kitchen.

It had been Dora who taught her to flush the loo while she peed, to avoid any embarrassment to those listening.

The bathroom in the cottage was cramped compared with Rose View's, but it had been one of the few of its time in Linton to have been built with an indoor lavatory as well as a bath; both were decorated with blue flowers painted on the enamel. Dora had covered virtually every inch of the walls with framed postcards and little paintings, some of them rather *risqué*.

While Hannah was washing her hands, her eye was caught by a bold outline sketch she hadn't seen before, of a naked woman stepping out of the bath, holding up a towel to dry her arms.

She stepped nearer to see it better, and a pulse started throbbing in her throat – the pulse that started up whenever she was allowed to handle something of real value at work. The lines were bold, and it was clearly just a dashed-off little sketch, but the style was familiar, and startlingly intimate: obvious affection turned the ungainly pose into an elegant uncurling of curves and shadows. The woman's face was hidden by a fall of hair, which covered more than the towel did, but her unselfconscious air made it private and sensuous.

It looked very much like a Matthew Fisher.

Hannah shook the water off her hands and hurried back to the kitchen, fizzing with excitement. It was so typical. Days and days of notating endless nonsense up at Hillcrest and the first item of real interest turned up in Dora's bathroom.

'Granny?' said Hannah. 'That picture in the bathroom, of the lady getting out of the bath. Where did it come from?'

Dora had started on her bulbs again and was making holes in the earth with her trowel. Callas was on loud. 'The bathing beauty? It was in the house when I came. I found it in a cupboard.'

'It's very good,' said Hannah. Of course it would be in the house, if Matthew Fisher had lived there. She considered telling Dora who the artist might be, but decided to save that until she was surer. If she was right, it might be a nice little nest egg. And while she was on the Internet surfing for Sheila Fell prices for Mrs Graham-Potter, she might be able to find out who the woman in the picture was.

'It's rather lovely, isn't it?' said Dora. 'But . . . private. That's why I keep it in the loo.'

'It's beautiful,' said Hannah.

'I like it,' said Dora.

If it was undiscovered work, or had a history to it, it might be worth even more. Maybe Mrs Graham-Potter could shed some light on the woman's identity. Cheered by this thought, Hannah picked up her satchel. 'Thanks for breakfast,' she said, and dropped a kiss on her grandmother's head as she went.

'My pleasure,' said Dora sadly, but then her expression returned to its usual inscrutability.

Chapter Twelve

Hannah was listening to the early-evening news on the radio and peeling potatoes for a stew when the phone rang.

She guessed it was for her mother, who was locked into her study wrestling with a child-custody case involving two childhood sweethearts from Hannah's year at school, and let it ring, assuming she'd pick up her own extension.

Hannah didn't feel like talking to anyone anyway – it had been a long day – especially London friends – until she had some kind of glamorous story to explain her extended absence – or Toby. But, then, who would be phoning her apart from him? Most of her friends had sheered away when his affair with Jennifer had come to light; she'd left others behind with her gym kit and spare biros when she'd walked out of her job.

The phone carried on ringing.

Not that they'd been real friends, she thought. Not like Fiammetta.

'For Christ's sake, pick it up!' yelled Fran.

Reluctantly Hannah did so. 'Hello?' she said, trying to sound as much like Fran as possible so she could pretend Hannah was in Barbados, if necessary.

The salon noises in the background – chit-chat bellowing over the sound of hair-dryers – gave Fiammetta away before she spoke. 'Han?'

Hannah nearly dropped the phone. 'Oh, God, it's you – I didn't think you'd – hang on a second.' She kicked the kitchen door shut.

'How's your hair?' There was a familiar laugh in the voice.

Hannah looked at it in the window reflection. It had gone flat, despite her efforts with Fran's heated brush, but the style was still there. The low fringe still looked moody, rather than scruffy. 'Well, I don't look like I just stepped out of the salon, put it like that.'

Fiammetta laughed. 'That's what everyone says. It's a trick we use to make you come back. Special hairspray.'

Hannah caught sight of her hands – red and rough. She thought of Fiammetta's soft white fingers. 'I thought you were just being polite when you said you'd call,' she said jokily, then realized she'd sounded rude.

There was a pause at the other end of the line, in which Frank Sinatra and Nelson Riddle's swinging orchestration could be heard above the dryers.

'Well, I wasn't going to. Then I thought how nice it was to see you after all this time and . . .' Fiammetta trailed off. The salon doorbell jangled in the background. 'I thought you were very brave to come home, and face the past, and if you could do that, I could too. It's healthy to put things behind us, and start again.'

Hannah was momentarily confused. She'd told Fiammetta she'd come back for a break, hadn't mentioned Toby, or her job let alone any darker thoughts.

But Fiammetta had been right: if there was one thing Hannah was determined to do it was to start afresh, doing what she wanted, and not hanging on to old ideas.

'No,' she said slowly. 'You're right.'

'Good.' There was audible relief. 'So, do you still want to go out for a drink?'

'Yes,' said Hannah, 'but you'll have to choose where we go. Everywhere's changed so much.'

'OK. Why don't you meet me at the salon after work tomorrow and I'll make a snap decision?'

'Fine.' Hannah's pulse skipped. That was easy.

'Great! Look forward to it. See ya,' sing-songed Fiammetta, the way all the girls in Tesco did.

'See ya,' replied Hannah, and put down the phone.

See ya? How long was it since she'd said 'see ya'?

She remembered that she'd said it to the girl in the Coffee Pot when she picked up the cakes for tea.

It was all coming back.

'Who was that on the phone?' Dora breezed into the kitchen with a bunch of magenta-pink roses wrapped in newspaper. Hannah guessed she'd be staying for supper, and that was her contribution.

'Fiammetta.'

Dora had taken off her Dannimac and was reaching for a vase in one of the tall cupboards. She hesitated. 'You're seeing her again?'

'Yes. For a drink.' Hannah didn't add 'tomorrow', and felt guilty for holding back information.

'Oh.' Dora's fingertips touched the lip of the nearest crystal vase ('from the London house') and she pulled it towards her. 'Do you think that's a good idea, darling?'

'Why wouldn't it be?'

'Well, after everything that happened . . .'

Hannah examined her grandmother's face. It seemed guileless enough, but there was something else too. Something Hannah couldn't read.

'I don't see why not,' she said. 'It was a long time ago and we've all changed since then. It feels like a different life.'

'Quite,' said Dora. 'All the more reason to move on from it. There's no point letting the past rule your future.'

'Look, I know you didn't like her, but she was my best friend,' protested Hannah.

'Was she, darling?' enquired Dora, coolly. 'But, really, what kind of friend allows their best friend to stuff herself with sleeping pills and leaves the country before she comes round? Not one I'd want.'

Hannah's cheeks reddened as if she'd been slapped.

'That's just what *you* say, though!' she retorted, without thinking. 'That's just your version of events!' Her face flushed as her brain caught up with what Dora had said.

'And did she call? Did she bother to get in touch with you afterwards? I don't call that the kind of friendship worth getting upset over.'

Hannah stared at her grandmother in disbelief. Just as casually as she'd ask what was for supper, Dora – *Dora*, who refused point-blank to talk about her own murky origins – had reached into the locked cupboards of Hannah's past and pulled out a hidden subject that hadn't been touched for over ten years. Hannah blinked at the shock of feeling a cluster of forgotten thoughts rush in on her brain. Instinctively she looked at the door, which was still ajar.

From the study Fran's muttering and paper-rustling were audible.

Dora pushed the door shut. 'Don't worry. She doesn't know the whole story.'

'I thought we agreed that we'd never talk about that again,' said Hannah, painfully. 'You know I don't remember much about it.'

'We did. I've never breathed a word to anyone. But if you must come back to Linton – and I don't see why you shouldn't when your home's here – then I can't stand by and let you expose yourself to even more hurt. Not when you came here to get over one heartbreak. I'm sorry to be so cruel, darling, but there it is.'

'If you have such a problem with Fiammetta – *still* – then why did you make me an appointment for her to cut my hair?' demanded Hannah.

For a moment, Dora looked shifty, but it quickly mutated into serenity. 'Oh . . . I wanted her to know how well you were doing. Your wonderful job in London.' She smiled her forgive-me smile, the one everyone found so hard to resist, even in the face of appalling liberty-taking. 'It was catty of me, I know, but I wanted her to see that you'd moved on and were only here for a break. She's in Linton for life.'

Hannah looked out of the window to where Mrs Jordan was labouring up the hill with a reluctant Daisy.

What Dora meant was the absolute opposite: that she had wanted Hannah to see how dead-end Fiammetta's life was. Spiteful. 'That's very thoughtful of you,' she said, 'but I have to make my own decisions about who I see. It's part of the growing-up process.'

Dora opened her mouth, and looked as if she was about to carry on. She stopped herself, and closed her lips, very deliberately, then turned away and filled the vase with water at the sink.

The silence glittered with disapproval, and Hannah was hurt. 'Don't be cross with me,' she said, fighting to keep the pleading from her voice. 'But I'm not a little girl any more.'

Dora didn't turn round. 'You weren't a little girl then.'

Hannah didn't trust herself to say anything in reply to that, so she left the room.

At the sink, Dora made a small but eloquent noise of frustration.

Hannah arrived at the salon three minutes late. She'd planned to leave Hillcrest by four, to give herself time to decide whether to be late or not, but Mrs Graham-Potter had kept her back, wanting to know her opinion about some worthless pencil sketches of herself 'by a well-known Parisian artist'. Since Hannah had finished cataloguing the drawing room, the living room, the study and most of the hall, Mrs Graham-Potter had expanded her original brief quite radically. Three or four times a day now, she would materialize at Hannah's side, bearing a piece of Linton china or an old photograph for inspection, usually with an illustrative anecdote regarding the wealth or taste of the Musgrave family. At this rate, Hannah had concluded, she was going to be cataloguing the whole house and drawing up a Musgrave family tree to boot.

There hadn't been time to go home and get changed, so she was still dressed in the jeans and shirt she'd been working in all day. Maybe that was a good thing, she thought, running her hands through her hair to dishevel it. Nice and casual. The jeans had been ridiculously expensive. Although they were now dusty, they had been designed to look fairly ruined – a concept she hadn't even tried to explain to Fran.

Hannah took a deep breath, and pushed open Rissini's door.

The bell clanged overhead, making escape impossible.

'Are you here for the model night?' asked Marina, the receptionist.

Hannah looked into the salon, where several nervous teenagers were clustered around the basins, making tentative snipping motions with their new scissors. In the chairs, Mrs Woodward, Mrs Hind and two other elderly ladies were engrossed either in gossip or back issues of *Take A Break*. Mrs Woodward's hair, Hannah noticed, was several disconcerting shades of grey, ranging from ash blonde to slate to gunmetal. They weren't yet swathed in the green plastic capes, and there wasn't any soothing music playing.

'No, I'm not,' said Hannah thankfully.

At that moment, Fiammetta swept out of the back room, her eyes sizing up the salon like a general reviewing troop deployment. She was wearing a black T-shirt and black jeans, but with bright green stiletto heels. Her dark hair swung from a high ponytail, tied with a pink silk cyclamen and black liner was flicked in a chic tick at the edge of her brown eyes. Hannah sighed at the ordinariness of her own scuffed cowboy boots.

'All right, ladies, let's get moving, shall we?' said Fiammetta. 'Hello, Mrs Woodward! Very brave of you to come back for a second go! Thank you so much for putting faith in Stacy. I know she'll do me proud.'

The girls jerked to attention and put away their scissors.

'Be with you in a moment,' Fiammetta mouthed to Hannah.

Mrs Woodward gave Mrs Hind a very obvious nudge and nodded towards Hannah, then Fiammetta, in order to draw her attention from *Take A Break*'s 'My Child Is A Sunny Delight Monster' to the real-life problem children in front of them. If Fiammetta saw this, she ignored it.

'Now, tonight we're just doing simple trims and washes, which, for a change, Columba is going to supervise.' Fiammetta turned round. 'Columba!' Her elder sister slunk out of the back, waving away the clouds of smoke from around her head.

'I thought you were taking us tonight,' complained the tallest trainee. 'You said we were going to do disconnected cutting.'

'Well, there's been a change of plan,' said Fiammetta, brightly. 'Now, I'll be inspecting these when you're done, and I don't want any repeats of last time, Stacy. Columba will be keeping a close eye on you, and you know Mrs Woodward is a very special client.'

Mrs Woodward directed a fierce stare at the teenager, who rolled her eyes and had the grace to look embarrassed.

'Good. Now, have fun!' Fiammetta leaned behind the counter, switched off Radio One and put on a Dean Martin CD.

'Lovely!' said Mrs Hind.

'See ya!' carolled Fiammetta.

'See ya!' chorused the trainees.

'Are you really going back to check on them?' asked Hannah, once they were safely inside the Bond, the new brass and glass wine bar near the harbour. It had been built inside one of the old bonded rum warehouses, hence the name; so it wasn't inappropriate that it was full of wines and spirits once again.

According to Fiammetta, who seemed to be a regular from the way the barman greeted her, their early arrival meant that they'd grabbed the best table: a plush-lined booth with a sculptural steel candelabrum hanging precariously overhead and a wide view of the rest of the room. She drained her large white wine. 'No way. Columba can sort them out. She pretends she hates doing training but she loves it really. Gives her a chance to yell and not get yelled back at.'

'Are you running the salon now?' Hannah was curious. If Fiammetta was in charge, maybe it wasn't such a U-turn on her original plans for world domination.

She smiled wryly, showing small white teeth. 'I suppose I am. Mamma's practically retired now, apart from her regulars, and Dad's always just done the barbering side. Idle bastard. You want another?' She nodded towards Hannah's glass, which was still half-full.

'No, I'm OK.' Hannah knew from bitter experience that it only took two glasses to get her to the falling-over-on-the-way-to-the-loos stage. Embarrassing, really, given the amount of drinking practice she'd had recently, although it was largely home-based and therefore without stools and people to negotiate. 'The glasses are big here, aren't they?'

'Gets us drunk faster.'

'Faster than drinking it straight out of the bottle?' Hannah grinned. 'Last time I was out drinking in Linton, glasses were shunned as a soft southern affectation.'

Fi's smile faltered, then turned rather metallic. 'Linton's coming up in the world, Hannah. We've got Sky telly and QVC these days, you know. It's not the backwater you remember.'

Hannah flushed. 'I never said it was.' She raised her palms in appeal. 'Oh, God. I never could say the right thing. Don't you start. I can't believe how touchy everyone is.'

Fiammetta picked up her empty glass and began to lever herself out of the booth. 'Should I get a bottle? It's cheaper.'

Their eyes met. Hannah knew that whatever came out of her mouth next would decide the way the whole evening went. She was already surprised at how easy it was, picking up like this, but then, she supposed, the ice had been broken by the haircut. And they had always got on so well, before all that weirdness. Maybe meeting old friends like this *was* easier when you were a bit older, a bit more practised at social drinking and chit-chat.

'Yeah, why not?' she said. 'Get a bottle.' She grinned. 'I'll get the next.'

While Fiammetta was leaning on the counter ordering the wine, Hannah cast a discreet eye around her. It was just starting to fill up with Linton's aspirational crowd: the solicitors with fat-knotted ties, the managers from the town-planning department, the odd journalist from the local paper, all drinking shorts at the bar so they could see who was coming in and out.

None of them looked at her, she noticed.

Time was an odd thing, thought Hannah, after another glass of wine. It really did feel as though she and Fiammetta had only seen each other days before. It was so easy to talk to her. And once she'd put the confused circumstances surrounding the end of their friendship to the back of her mind, as Fiammetta seemed to have done, it was almost possible to imagine that they'd parted as friends.

A warm, optimistic feeling spread through her, along with the wine. There was so much to catch up on, she thought happily, then bit her lip. If she could stay sober enough to edit her own recent history into a more flattering shape.

'More?' Fiammetta was gesturing with the bottle.

'Oh, er, yes, please. So what happened to bring you back to hairdressing?' asked Hannah.

Fiammetta filled their glasses. 'Oh, God. I don't know. I worked in Manchester for a while after my degree, didn't really settle, mainly thanks to Mamma and her constant reminders about my true vocation. That, and the subscription to the *Linton Gazette*. Then the company I was working for got bought out by some American firm, possibly at the instigation of my mother, and about a week later Maria announced she was pregnant and couldn't cut hair any more.'

She rolled her eyes. 'They offered me another position, but it would have meant moving to America. In the end, it was a straight choice between Seattle on my ownsome, but with the entire family still on my back, or coming back to Linton and giving myself a break.'

'Families, eh?'

'It's not for ever,' said Fiammetta quickly. 'I like Linton and everything, there's nothing wrong with it, but I'm only doing this for another year or two. I've got plans for my own IT consultancy.'

'Really?' said Hannah.

'Yeah, really.' Fiammetta looked cross, but then smiled. 'Anyway, you're not one to talk, are you? So, come on, why have *you* come back? And you can tell me the honest version, if you want. I'm highly unlikely to go running to your mother.'

'Well . . .' Hannah considered how much Fiammetta needed to know. The reasons ranged themselves in front of her like unwished-for tarot cards: Toby, her job, London, loneliness, that hollow sensation of not being exactly who she thought she was. A tremor ran across her skin at the clarity of her thoughts. Maybe it was the wine – or that she wasn't having to filter everything through her mother and grandmother's expectations.

'Oh, Han. How bad can it be? Did someone discover that you failed your driving test first time round and you've come here to escape the shame? Or have you slept with some sleazy MP by accident and need Dora between you and the gutter press?'

Hannah smiled through a warm haze of wine and nostalgia. She'd never felt under any pressure with Fiammetta to be anything other than herself. They had been such good friends: so close that she could extrapolate whole sentences from just one word and the shades of Fiammetta's expression. Close enough to share secrets and worries and observations that neither would have breathed to anyone else. Whole chunks of her adolescence only existed in her and Fiammetta's minds. Then, in a snap of the fingers, it had all gone and she wasn't sure she remembered exactly how any more.

'No,' she said. 'None of the above.' Hannah took a deep breath and dived in with the truth. 'I came back because my boyfriend had been seeing someone else behind my back, and about a fortnight after we split up, I found out that they'd got married. It was someone I'd worked with, so that spoiled my whole job for me and it seemed obvious, at the time, that I should pack it all in and come home for a bit.'

'Shit,' said Fiammetta. She refilled their glasses. 'Had you been going out for a long time?'

'Quite a while, but it was always very on and off,' Hannah admitted. 'I was never sure about him. I mean, he had a great job and he was very good-looking but . . .'

'He was the kind of man your granny would have picked out for you? Rich and good-looking and entirely suitable for such a clever girl?'

Hannah was startled by the accuracy of this observation. It had never occurred to her, but it was true. Despite her derision, had Dora actually met Toby, she would have sung his praises constantly. Not that she wanted to admit that.

'Well, no. Not really. He wasn't exactly . . .'

'Yes, he was. And what about the job?'

Hannah noticed that at least Fiammetta had asked those questions in the right order of importance. 'It was a good job,' she said ruefully. 'Working at Christie's, liaising with clients, preparing big international picture sales mainly. I started off earning nothing, being a dogsbody, but I was starting to feel as if I was getting somewhere.' She took a gulp of wine. 'But it was making me feel, I don't know, kind of stupid.' She knew she'd never admit that to her mother. 'Something wasn't right. And, hey, there are other good jobs.'

'Not here.'

'I didn't come back to look for a job here. I came back for a rest.'

Fiammetta snorted. 'You came back to get your next set of instructions, you mean.'

'What?'

'Oh . . . Sorry if that sounded rude.' Fiammetta didn't sound apologetic. 'But it seems to me that you ran out of items on Fran's to-do list. Get a good job. Find a nice man. Get a nice southern accent.'

'I do not have a southern accent!' protested Hannah.

Fiammetta made a little scoffing noise. 'Only teasing. So, what are you going to do now, then? I don't suppose your mother wants you to stay here too long, does she? Doesn't want you catching apathy from the rest of us.'

'She's happy to have me at home for a while,' lied Hannah.

'And Dominic?' Fiammetta looked at her fingers.

Hannah wondered why she suddenly seemed nervous. Had she had a crush on Dom? Something twisted inside her and she couldn't put her finger on it. 'Well, he's in America.' She didn't say how much she missed him. 'He sends cards on birthdays and Christmas, you know. Very happy, big flat. Writing for various magazines.' Hannah looked closely at Fiammetta. 'Why do you ask?'

Fiammetta blinked and smiled. 'Oh, just interested in your fascinating family. Still on the same familiar terms with Mr Jack Daniels and Charlie, is he?'

'I don't know what you mean,' said Hannah. She felt a sharp, unexpected jealousy: that Fiammetta might have known a side of her brother that she hadn't. Or was it the other way round? 'Did you . . .' The idea was weird, and refused to go away. 'I didn't know you and Dominic—'

'Oh, no,' said Fiammetta too quickly. 'God, no. He's really not my type at all.'

But the image of Dominic and Fiammetta, her brother and her best friend, had lodged in Hannah's mind like a speck of dust in her eye. She didn't like finding out things like that. It changed her memory, made it shifty and unreliable. She pushed it away and tried to be light again. 'Dominic doesn't like to be typecast,' Hannah replied. 'His repertoire's clearly huge.'

Fiammetta tipped back her head and laughed. The light caught the pale skin above her T-shirt. A little diamond crucifix sparkled in the hollow of her throat. 'I bet your mother doesn't know that.'

'She doesn't *want* to know. Anyway,' said Hannah, 'I hardly think I'm the only one under the thumb when it comes to family instructions, Hairdresser Girl. Or is it Perm Princess?'

Fiammetta pulled a rueful face and tipped her glass towards Hannah, then took another gulp. '*Touché*. But great idea for salon T-shirts. Perm Princess. I'll talk to Columba about it.'

'She can be Foil Freak,' suggested Hannah.

'Crimp Queen's more her style.'

'It's so nice to see you again,' said Hannah impulsively. 'Really.'

'Well, I have to say I didn't think I'd ever see *you* again,' said Fiammetta.

Hannah made an ambiguous noise. There wasn't much point demurring; after she'd moved to London *she* hadn't expected to see anyone from Linton again until well into the next life. It wasn't as though she'd had many friends to bump into. 'But I hoped I'd see you,' she heard herself say. 'At some point.' Oh dear, thought Hannah. Have I reached that stage of drunkenness already? Where thoughts slip out before you have time to review them?

Fiammetta was apparently wrestling with the right thing to say but managing to keep the rough workings in her head instead of blurting them out.

'What?' asked Hannah. The final T trailed off in a semi-sibilant hiss, self-consciously northern.

'You.' Fiammetta made a sweeping gesture of dismissal that nearly cleared the table of glasses. 'It *always* amazed me, your imagination.'

'But I don't have much of an imagination.'

'That's exactly what I mean! Your negative imagination. It's amazing, the way you can just push things out of your mind like they never happened.'

Hannah didn't need her to spell out this oblique reference: she knew exactly what she was talking about. The accidental overdose after her A levels. And it was true. She *had* managed to edit those few nights from her life – quite literally, since she had no memory at all, apart from the details Dora had supplied, and Hannah had always harboured doubts about those.

'But you know I don't – *can't* remember what happened,' she protested.

'I'm not talking about the overdose on its own, Hannah! I mean the emotions and the – the – everything that led up to it! I don't understand how you've managed to gloss over something that should have changed your life! It's like you've just put it all in a box and closed the lid, and now you're pretending it's not there!'

'I don't know what you mean.' Hannah couldn't help hearing Dora's voice again: *What kind of a friend allows their best friend to stuff themselves with sleeping pills and merely stands by?*

'Hannah!' Fiammetta closed her eyes tightly. She had very long black lashes. She rubbed her temples with her delicate hands.

Hannah was struck dumb by how beautiful Fiammetta was. Too exotic and gorgeous for Linton's rain-stained greyness. Even with her eyes closed, her face seemed animated, with its slanted dark eyebrows. But when Fiammetta opened her eyes again the ferocity in her expression was disconcerting.

'Hannah,' she said, 'if you've come back to start again, as I think you have, then you really need to *face* what happened. You can't just skim over it. Tell me, honestly, has your granny ever told you what she said to me when she found you after your overdose?'

Hannah shook her head. 'No, listen, it wasn't a proper overdose, it—'

Fiammetta didn't wait for her to carry on. 'I can assure you it was. Your grandmother practically accused me of murdering you. How can I forget something like that? She didn't believe me when I told her how miserable you were – she wouldn't even *listen* to me. She blamed me for the whole thing, said it was my fault for leading you into bad ways. She wouldn't even let me give you proper resuscitation. She *even* accused me of—' Fiammetta put her hand over her mouth with a mad laugh. 'Oh, what's the point?'

'You were there? She accused you of what?' stuttered Hannah. The seat seemed to be plummeting beneath her like a fairground ride. 'You never told me this.'

'When was I meant to? I was specifically instructed never to come near the house again.'

'Oh, God, Fi. She didn't mean it. She was so upset, you know, about everything. I know she doesn't show it, but that's just the way she was brought up.' It was odd how distance gave you such detachment, thought Hannah. She could see it exactly, as if it were a picture she was examining: Dora raging away, struggling between shame and distress, trying to find someone to blame for the inexplicable collapse of her golden girl. 'But surely Mum . . . ?' Her voice trailed away. Fran, the voice of reason, hadn't known, hadn't been there.

Fiammetta's expression changed and her eyes flicked evasively towards the empty wine barrels hoisted in the eaves. 'Your mother didn't come into it. Dora didn't think she needed to know. We agreed it would be best if she thought you'd just got the bottles mixed up in the bathroom. I can't believe all this . . . *subterfuge* is still in place! How on earth can you carry on with secrets like that coming between you?'

Hannah breathed deeply, trying to process this startling new information. Something deep inside her subconscious recognized all this as probable, much as her mind was denying it.

'Do you remember *anything* about that night?' Fiammetta demanded. 'Tell me what you remember.'

Hannah put down her drink. The music in the bar suddenly seemed very loud. 'I only know what . . . Granny told me. And what you told me.'

That last bit was a courtesy. Hannah had barely seen Fiammetta afterwards, and it hadn't been the same. She wanted to say, 'So why did you take off to Italy with your family, if you really cared about me?' but she didn't want to spoil the easiness with which they'd slipped back into each other's company.

Fiammetta was waiting for her to go on.

'Well, you know things hadn't been too great at home,' said Hannah slowly. She didn't want to let too much slip out, just because she was drunk. 'I was under a lot of pressure with all those A-levels. Mum was working on some big compensation suit. And I remember . . . I remember that week I'd had a row with Granny.'

'About?'

'I don't remember.'

But Hannah did remember. It had been a snappish row, about the amount of time she and Fiammetta spent together. Hannah rarely argued with her grandmother, and had assumed Dora was jealous or lonely or something. Fran was going through an abrasive phase, resentful of the new woman Keith wanted to be free to marry, and wound up about the cases she was co-ordinating; she'd abruptly suspended all family dinners because she was 'too busy'. A minor ventilation shaft had fallen in at the end of the garden, ruining Dora's favourite rosebed. Their little chats had grown more distant as Hannah's workload increased, and then this row had blown up out of nowhere.

As if I wasn't confused enough already, thought Hannah, bitterly. *As if I didn't have enough to worry about.*

She was aware of Fiammetta's gaze on her and pulled her attention back to the pine table in front of them. The fittings were all brand new, but the surface was already scarred with initials and burn marks. 'Um, well, then fast forward to me waking up in Dora's bed with everyone around me, looking terrified. I thought I'd died. Then the phone rang and I knew I couldn't be dead.' She grinned wryly. 'No phones in heaven, see?'

'You don't remember me pulling you out of the bath? Or Dora coming and finding you lying there with no clothes on?' Fiammetta's voice rose. 'You don't remember driving to the hospital in Dora's car because she wouldn't call for an ambulance, even when you weren't responding?'

Hannah shook her head. Fiammetta had *been* there?

'I sincerely hope you don't remember the stomach pump,' said Fiammetta, incredulously.

Hannah shook her head again, and her fringe fell into her eyes. 'It's so weird hearing you say all this, Fi, because it doesn't even sound like me. It sounds like it all happened to someone else.'

'Hannah.' Fiammetta leaned across the table and dropped her voice to a low, urgent murmur. She tapped a finger just in front of Hannah's glass. Her short red nail clicked on the pine surface. 'Believe me. You swallowed an entire bottle of sleeping tablets, took off all your clothes, ran a warm bath – with bath oil – and passed out. That was definitely you. And you definitely wanted to do it at the time.'

Did I? wondered Hannah. She threw the idea into the deepest corners of her mind, but couldn't find any echo of recognition. Nothing at all. It might have been someone else Fiammetta was talking about, not her – it just didn't fit.

But, then, the human brain was capable of blotting out all sorts of things, she reasoned. Maybe that's what had happened. Maybe it was a momentary earthquake in my brain; no one had ever mentioned it at home, and gradually all the pain and shock had slipped beneath the surface of everyone's minds, and vanished.

'Oh, my God. You're a great family for ignoring things,' said Fiammetta, heavily. 'Do you use decimal currency, or are you all pretending we're still on the Imperial system?'

Hannah felt a tremor of emotion rising in the back of her mind and seized on it, only to realize it was mild embarrassment. 'You took me to the hospital with no clothes on? Which doctor was it? Was it someone I knew?'

'Christ,' said Fiammetta, and downed the remnants of her wine. She lifted the bottle to see how much was left, and sloshed the last inch or so into their glasses. 'Hannah, you can't just ignore a huge crisis in your life because it doesn't fit in with the way you want to see yourself. Do you have any idea how fucked up it can make you in the long run?'

She followed that up with a sarcastic expression, as if it were already obvious.

'This isn't *Trisha*,' said Hannah primly, and cringed to hear herself sound so much like Fran.

'No wonder you came back here when your relationship broke up. Would you like Dora to invent a better explanation for that too?'

'Don't talk about her like that,' Hannah snapped. 'It's not fair. I've never heard her side of this, not properly. I'm sure there were perfectly good reasons for what happened.'

'Yeah, right.' Fiammetta pushed her hair behind her ears as if she couldn't quite believe what she was hearing. 'But I think you should talk to her. Honestly. Find out why she only wanted you to know half a tale.'

'Mmm.' Hannah couldn't imagine that conversation. It didn't matter how close she and Dora were – sometimes closeness didn't come into it. Or, rather, closeness led to a sense of mutual protection that stopped them revealing darker things. It had always been easier to talk to Fran about bodily topics, partly because Fran, the modern parent, was so determined to tackle embarrassment head-on and brush it aside with frankness and information. Hannah felt a reticence with Dora that had nothing to do with squeamishness: she wanted to keep their relationship pristine, and not sully their mutual adoration with any acknowledgement of failure or frailty. And that included crushes, feelings of terrible despair and low grades.

In fact, now she thought about it, neither Dora nor Fran wanted to discuss those particular topics. So they'd never existed.

'I take it you're not going to go back and check on Columba's progress?' she asked brightly.

Fiammetta looked at her watch and gaped. 'No! Do you have any idea what time it is?'

'Half nine?'

'No, it's a quarter to eleven.'

The last-orders bell rang at the bar as if in illustration and a wave of suits swept forward to get a last round in.

Hannah shrugged. 'Time flies.'

'It does indeed.'

There was a moment or two of awkward silence. Hannah's stomach still churned with contradictory emotions, all curdling together.

'So, if you're back I suppose I'll be seeing you around?' said Fiammetta, reaching for her jacket.

Hannah touched her newly cut hair. 'Six to eight weeks, isn't it? For a trim?'

Fiammetta smiled. 'Hopefully before that.'

'Yeah,' said Hannah. 'Hopefully.'

Chapter Thirteen

When Hannah had told Fiammetta that her first memory of the 'incident' was waking up in the big bed in Rose View, surrounded by the concerned faces of her immediate family, she wasn't exactly telling the truth.

Her first memory was, in fact, of being woken up by the sound of distant shrieking, not in Rose View but in the private patients' ward at Linton Infirmary.

To begin with, she wasn't sure where she was. It was the light that first dragged her into consciousness, before the shrieking registered. Hannah's whole body felt surrounded by an intrusive white light, burning through her eyelids and buzzing at a high pitch in her head. At first she thought she had died, and this was the blinding white light everyone talked about on television specials about the afterlife. If she could only hold on through it, Poor Arthur would no doubt appear, holding out his hand to welcome her through to the Things You Wanted to Know about Grace Kelly's Car Crash and Other Unanswered Questions reception area.

Not that the thought appeared in Hannah's head in such specific detail. Her brain seemed to be working at a tenth of its normal speed. It took her several minutes to formulate this idea and another five to concentrate on something other than the buzzing in her ears.

When Hannah could gather her thoughts again, though, she realized that the white light was, in part, a headache so intense that it was registering in her brain only as light. The other light source, established by forcing one eye open, was coming from the sunlight streaming in through the window and bouncing relentlessly off the white walls, the starched white sheets and the white curtains around her bed.

She wasn't in heaven. She was alive, in hospital.

And the person holding on to her hand wasn't Poor Arthur, it was his extremely earthbound widow.

'Hello, darling,' said Dora. She looked as if she hadn't slept for days. Her lipstick was bleeding round the edges and her clothes were crumpled. Other than that, she gave off the air of being perfectly normal. She even had a paperback book on her knee. *The Turn of the Screw*, by Henry James.

'Granny?' croaked Hannah. She tried to turn her head to look at Dora, and a red hot pain shot down her throat.

Somewhere down the corridor, the shrieking continued.

Dora grimaced in irritation at the noise and poured Hannah a cup of water from the jug by her bed. 'The maternity ward is next door, I'm afraid. They've moved them in here, near the private patients' wing. I hope they haven't been disturbing you. Here, try to swallow a little of this.'

She put her arm round Hannah's shoulders and lifted her up so she could drink.

Another wave of pain went through Hannah's body, but this was a duller ache across her shoulders, more purple than the pain in her throat. The water stung her parched lips and made her throat burn.

'Your throat will be a bit raw where they had to put the tube down to pump out your stomach, you know,' said Dora, matter-of-factly. 'Very messy, but it'll heal soon. Amazing how the mouth can heal so much quicker than the rest of the body.'

Hannah looked down and noticed that her arm was bandaged too. What the hell had happened?

Dora put the glass back on the table and leaned towards her, taking Hannah's hands in her soft ones. 'Now, listen, darling,' she said. 'Your mother went home a little while ago to have a rest and I think we need to have a little talk.'

'What happened?' whispered Hannah, with a huge effort. It hurt to speak, but she needed to know what she was doing in here before Fran got back.

Dora inspected her face with the same eagle-eyed look she had used when, as a little girl, Hannah denied knowledge of missing biscuits despite being covered in crumbs.

Hannah stared back at her.

'I found you in bed at home,' said Dora eventually, once she was satisfied that Hannah really didn't know. 'I assumed you'd had one of your migraines because you'd taken one too many of your mother's painkilling tablets. Thank God you had the foresight to leave the bottle by the side of the bed so when we brought you into hospital the doctors knew what they were dealing with.'

Hannah shut her eyes and the humming pain intensified. That didn't sound right.

'But you're fine now. No harm done.'

Hannah felt her hand being patted. No harm done? she thought. *No harm done*, and I'm in hospital feeling like this? And would they have pumped my stomach for one extra painkiller?

That didn't sound right at all. She searched for some memory of coming home from school, taking the tablets, even having a migraine.

But there was nothing. It was as if someone had Tippexed out her memory, leaving blank whiteness. She tried to dredge up an image from beneath it, but it was like being asked what her earliest childhood memory was. She knew the kind of images she'd *like* to see flashing up before her eyes, but nothing came.

She could vaguely remember walking back up the hill with her books, thinking about her English exam, but as that was all she ever thought about it didn't pin down a time. Did she see Mrs Jordan with her dog? But that could have been any day for the past ten years.

All Hannah could find in her mind was a fire blanket of unspecific sadness, covering any flicker of memory.

Dora stroked her hands. 'Don't think about it, darling. The mind sometimes works in funny ways, but it's always for the best.'

A thought burrowed its way out through the whiteness in Hannah's head. 'F'mmetta?' she croaked.

Dora's expression tightened. She kept her voice as kind and calm as before, but her comforting smile no longer reached her eyes.

'Gone on holiday to Italy, darling. With her mother and sisters. I dare say she'll be back for speech day.'

Hannah slumped into her pillows as if she'd been punched. Suddenly everything ached twice as much. Fiammetta? Gone?

What had happened while she'd been unconscious?

'Oh, look! Here's your mother!' said Dora brightly.

Christ, thought Hannah, and felt thankful that she couldn't really talk. Hopefully, the proximity of the maternity ward meant that a high-decibel showdown would be postponed until she was sent home.

Fran's lace-up shoes could be heard down the hall, clipping along at a brisk pace.

'Be brave,' muttered Dora. 'Remember, you just took one pill too many. Let me deal with this. And don't say anything.'

Fran's cheery smile wavered when she walked into the room. She hurried in, clutching a bunch of flowers, wrapped in smart paper from Julie's Florists, and went over to the bed to hug her daughter. She paused when she saw the bandages and bruises, and leaned over carefully to deposit a kiss on Hannah's head.

Hannah smiled weakly, which resulted in tears forming at the edge of Fran's eyes. But Fran was made of stern stuff, and sniffed them away. 'Hello, love,' she said, distracting herself by stuffing the flowers into the vase by the bed. 'You've given us all a big fright, but you're going to be fine.'

'Thanks to my private medical insurance. Oh, Fran, dear,' said Dora, 'while you're still on your feet, do you think you could get me a cup of coffee? I'm parched.'

'Oh, er, yes, all right,' she said. 'Hannah, can I get you anything?' Hannah shook her head.

Fran nodded towards the flowers. 'I went to Julie's,' she said. 'You pay a bit more but they last longer. White roses are your favourites, aren't they?'

Hannah croaked, 'Thank you.'

Fran's eyes filled again, and she turned and left the room.

'Blames herself,' said Dora. 'And I haven't the faintest idea what she was thinking of, going to that ridiculous florist. The roses in my garden are at their peak. She could have had her pick.'

Hannah glared and gestured towards the notebook on the bedside table.

'What?' said Dora.

'The notebook,' croaked Hannah, and Dora passed it to her wordlessly.

She picked up the pen stuck through the spiral spine; it would be awkward writing with her left hand, but panic at Fran's imminent return urged her on. She had more questions than she could comfortably voice.

'What really happened?' Hannah wrote in messy print, underlined twice, and shoved the pad towards Dora.

Dora looked stricken, but Hannah glared until Dora picked up the pen and started writing. When she passed the pad back, Hannah read, 'I found you in the bathroom. You had taken all your mother's sleeping tablets. I brought you straight here, in my car, and they pumped your stomach just in time. You are very lucky to be alive.'

Hannah read the words in shock. They didn't mean anything to her, and she had an overwhelming yearning to go back to sleep. Images kept floating in and out of focus at the back of her mind – the dark trees in the garden coming to life, dead children, feeling too hot – but she didn't know where they were coming from. All her A-level set texts jumbled up with some dreadful lurid paperback horrors. As soon as she thought she was closing in on something that might give her a clue, it slipped away from her. Her body and brain were numb with drugs and exhaustion.

'It's best if you put all this behind you,' said Dora, as if she could read her mind. 'Your mother's going through a difficult time with this compensation nonsense she's working on, and she'll blame herself for being too busy to notice. I know it's nothing to do with that, but that's how she'll see it.'

'Why?' scrawled Hannah, thinking she could hear Fran's footsteps coming back down the corridor. She pushed the notepad on to Dora's lap.

Dora pursed her lips. 'I haven't the faintest idea. I imagine you made a mistake with the label.'

To the extent of taking all the tablets?

Hannah wished Fiammetta were here to talk to. As her friend's face appeared in her mind's eye, she felt a terrible pang of longing and misery that burned across her body then disappeared again into numbness.

'The sooner you forget about it, the sooner you can carry on with your life,' said Dora, ominously. Then she smiled. 'Just think, you've the whole summer to relax before you go off to Oxford.'

Hannah opened her eyes long enough to give her a withering look.

'Don't be like that,' said Dora, cheerfully. 'I don't doubt for one second that you're going to get your grades. Your mother's certain too.'

Hannah grabbed the pen and wrote 'Fiammetta' on the pad. She couldn't have gone to Italy, not without saying goodbye. Hannah added, 'Does she know?' and thrust the pad back at Dora.

Dora's sunny expression vanished behind a cloud. 'She does know, and she's gone off to Italy with her family, as I said before. Some friend she is.'

Fran's footsteps prevented Dora saying more, but her expression was pretty eloquent.

'I couldn't get proper tea, just tea from a machine,' said Fran. She was carrying two cups and a bag of Minstrels under her arm.

'Did you speak to one of the private nurses?' asked Dora. 'I'm sure they'd have made you a proper cup.'

'Mother, I wouldn't ask a nurse to make me a cup of tea!' said Fran. 'They've got far more important things to do.'

'It's their job to take care of people,' said Dora loftily. She took a sip of the proffered cup and pulled a face. 'Euch.'

'What?' demanded Fran.

'I wouldn't give it to Mousy.' Mousy was Dora's superior cat, offspring of an equally superior villa tabby called Mitford. 'Wait here. I'll just have to go out for supplies myself.'

Before Fran could stop her, Dora had swept out of the room and her heels clicked down the corridor like spent bullet cases, fading away as she marched out of earshot.

'How are you, love?' asked Fran, stroking the hair off Hannah's forehead the way she used to when Hannah was little. She seemed less tense without Dora on the other side of the starched bed, but looked exhausted. There were hollows under her cheekbones that clouds of inexpertly applied pink blusher failed to hide, and shadows under her eyes.

''M OK,' said Hannah.

'We had such a shock, but you're going to be fine now.' Fran squeezed her hand.

Hannah nodded.

'You'd tell me, wouldn't you, if there was something ... something bothering you?'

She looked so mortified that Hannah nodded harder.

'You have to be careful with my prescription drugs,' Fran went on. She flushed guiltily. 'I'm not saying you should use any at all. I know sometimes Dominic . . .' She looked cross with herself and started again, her voice a shade higher this time. 'Some of them are stronger than others and, well, the dispensary sometimes reuses my bottles, so you mightn't have taken what you thought you'd taken.'

Hannah didn't believe this for a minute. Mrs Woodward was a Tartar for sterilization and hygiene. Did they think she'd had her brain pumped as well as her stomach?

She examined her mother's face. What exactly had she been hiding in the bottles? And what was Dom doing, sneaking pills? There was so much she didn't know about him now.

'You know I've been under a lot of stress recently, what with one thing and another, and Dr Andrew prescribed me some, um, new tablets, to help me, well, sleep, and—'

Please don't tell me any more, Mum, thought Hannah, desperately.

'I don't think I want to take them for much longer, because counselling is the real answer to most problems.' Fran's voice rose like a child's and she looked at Hannah beseechingly.

Hannah met her eyes with a steady expression: Fran knew she had to talk about something emotional and messy and was hoping that she could somehow circumvent it telepathically. She was fine on the technical value of discussion, if conducted under the supervision of a trained professional, but didn't like to practise it so close to home.

'I know something's wrong, love,' Fran went on. 'You've been very quiet recently. I know you've had your exams. Maybe we've been pushing you too hard but . . .' she looked sick, but forced herself on '. . . if there was a problem, and you didn't feel you could talk about it with me, would you think about talking to someone else? Someone professional?'

Hannah tried to look innocently shocked.

Fran seemed to gather herself. 'Listen, love. I just want to say this while she's not in the room, but your grandmother's very upset. I know she looks as if she's fine but she's concerned about you, about all the pressure you're under. She thinks it would be a good idea if we went on holiday as soon as you're better. Together, you know, as a family. Dora says she'll treat us.'

Hannah looked at her. It was late in the day to start having jolly family holidays, but if it would make everyone happy, who was she to stop them?

She nodded. There was nothing she wanted to do here, if Fiammetta had gone off to Italy.

Her heart ached at the still-sharp discovery that she'd been abandoned by the one person she needed to talk to now. The one person she *could* talk to, now that Dominic had left.

Maybe Dora was right, she thought, watching relief spread across Fran's face. Maybe the sooner she forgot all about it, the easier it would be for everyone.

Chapter Fourteen

As the days turned into weeks, characters came and went on *The Archers*, which she'd started listening to with Dora over a cup of tea and Puritan biscuits, and Hannah fell back into a routine: the lulling, low-key rhythm of Linton life.

There was a lot to be said, she thought comfortably, for coming home. It was nice to go for a drink with Fiammetta in the Bond, and wind up the local wannabes with their shiny BMW Compacts parked outside where the coal ships used to dock. It was nice to help her mum out with the shopping at Tesco, arguing about GM foods and how you could now get fresh coriander in Linton. It was even nice, in a way, to feel that she was bringing something back to life at Hillcrest, handling little paintings and pieces of china that had lain ignored for years, waiting for someone else to see them and admire their neat framing or unusual markings.

Although she was now familiar, if not exactly relaxed, with the sudden draughts of cold air that rushed past her ankles, and the strong scent of roses or tobacco that sometimes flooded a room, Hannah still felt as if she was being watched. Not by Mrs

Graham-Potter, who spent hours in her chair in the airy drawing room, reading or just staring out into the garden, or by Mrs Tyson, whose approach was easy to detect from the vibrations in the floorboards. At first, she thought it was just the inherent spookiness of the big, quiet rooms; often, she'd spin round, convinced she was about to catch someone sitting in the chair behind her. The rooms were crammed with so much stuff that, as in Rose View, the mirrors sometimes appeared to reflect movement in the corner of her eye – and were empty when she turned to look. Once or twice Hannah thought she heard breathing, and her heart speeded up with panic, until she realized it was her own, unusually loud in the echoing room.

It was the study that gave her an unsettling answer. The eerie sensation of being watched was particularly intense in there, where little natural light permeated the net curtains, and the dusty aspidistras in the mahogany planters seemed to suck all the oxygen out of the air. The portraits were commanding, running back to 1704, she knew now, but once she'd noted them with Mrs Graham-Potter, and fastened their details on the family tree she was annotating, they had lost their initial power to unnerve her.

It was something else, something smaller but more creepy. Hannah felt as if the room was waiting for her, holding something secret inside it that she had to uncover and explain. She wasn't afraid of atmospheres, having spent her childhood in echoing, creaking rooms, yet she put off her examination of the various family portraits for as long as she could, finding more and more to do in the hall, in the drawing room and the library upstairs. But she knew she couldn't avoid the study for much longer, if she ever wanted to think about leaving.

One morning, when the sun was making a rare appearance over Linton, bathing the dark wood surfaces with unusual lightness, Hannah steeled herself and stepped into the study to assess how long it would take. At once, she saw what had unsettled her: the bookshelves were full of photographs, set back a little so as not to be immediately obvious. Frozen faces gazed out with dark eyes from every shelf and surface.

Like her own family album, the groups were dominated by women: Faith, Constance, Louise, Ellen, people she didn't know in scenes of Linton that were still vaguely familiar. It was almost as if every photograph in the house had been collected into that one room. They were smaller, less formal versions of the photographs hanging on the walls upstairs, but all bore the clear message: we are a smart family. Parties, presentations, boating trips, groups posed around cars and hounds. They covered a wide span of years, as the young women turned into the stout, tweed-clad ladies Hannah remembered, but in nearly every one, Faith was either laughing, or glaring, and Constance's limpid eyes were fixed to the floor, or gazing at her sister or Louise Graham-Potter with unconcealed devotion. Mrs Graham-Potter always looked the same: picture pert, with an identical smile. Like Wallis Simpson, she seemed to have researched her best side, and presented it at every opportunity.

And behind each of these pictures was a ghostly secondary presence: the photographer, who stood now somewhere just behind Hannah. Had Samuel Musgrave taken these pictures? Or one of the handsome dead brothers, unaware that he'd never see them framed? A male friend? Just by standing and looking at these spotlit moments of the Musgraves' lives, Hannah felt as if she were stepping into them, colluding with the images they were choosing to present to the world.

She shivered. She would have liked to turn them to the wall while she worked, but she couldn't. She didn't want to stay in the room any longer than she had to.

With shaking hands, she gathered the miniatures of Isabella Musgrave's unlucky sons and took them into the sunnier drawing room. The light was better, she explained to Mrs Graham-Potter, as she studied the dead blue eyes of the identikit blond angels.

The mornings and nights crept in as autumn approached, darkening the gloomy oak-panelled corridors still further and sending a damp wind whispering through the orchard that hurried along the falling leaves, making a sound like constant rainfall. This pleased Mrs Tyson and Fran almost as much as it depressed Hannah, who sometimes woke with a start, feeling her life in London slipping away with each darker morning. Then she would snuggle further into her flannel sheets, push away the thought, and wait for Fran's mug of tea to arrive outside her door.

'I don't mind the warm,' said Mrs Tyson, spooning sugar into her first cup of tea, 'I'm not saying that, but you know where you are with winter. How's that grandmother of yours?' She took a thoughtful slurp and observed Hannah beadily over the top of her mug. It said 'World's Best Nan' in cartoon script.

'She's fine, thanks,' said Hannah. Since the day when she had thought it prudent to bring a packet of biscuits with her to 'share' with Mrs Tyson a cup of tea had been waiting for her in the kitchen when she arrived at half past nine. Hannah wasn't entirely taken in by this show of solidarity: Mrs Tyson was a satellite in Mrs Woodward's gossip network because she had access to significant houses in the town and her husband was a caretaker at the school.

She sipped her tea and wondered what Mrs Tyson was fishing for now. 'She's just finishing off her reading for the book group tomorrow.'

'The book group, aye.' Mrs Tyson produced a meaningful sniff. She wasn't a member. 'Be nice if we all had time to sit around talking about books. Some of us have livings to earn.'

Hannah pulled her conciliatory face. Fran insisted that Mrs Tyson was exploited labour; Dora considered her staff. Hannah wasn't sure where she should pitch her opinion and had played safe by not having one.

'Better get upstairs,' she said. 'Told Mrs Graham-Potter I'd have this done in a few weeks and it's taking me ages.'

'There's a lot to get through, all right.' Mrs Tyson squinted at her. 'There's cupboards I'd say's not been opened since their Constance died.'

She had dropped her voice, even though the door was shut – evidently Hannah wasn't the only one to have been conditioned into thinking the house could hear. 'And not many know this, but there were cupboards only she had the keys to. I don't reckon her ladyship even knows about them. And I wouldn't like to guess what might be in there.' She sat back on her stool, to see what Hannah's reaction would be. Clearly a lot of guessing *had* been going on.

'Really? How, er,' Hannah chose her words carefully, 'do you know that?'

'Faith Musgrave,' Mrs Tyson nodded, 'she didn't trust Mrs Graham-Potter, I reckon. Well, I mean, she wasn't family, was she? I reckon Faith knew that one'd outlive poor Constance, and didn't trust her sister not to clat about any secret documents or what-have-you. Lovely woman, Constance, but soft as a drayhorse.'

'How do you mean, she didn't trust her?' asked Hannah, curious. 'Why wouldn't she?'

'Well,' Mrs Tyson pulled a face, 'them being sisters. Never come between sisters, that's what I've always said. Constance was close to Mrs Graham-Potter, but Faith wasn't so keen. She was a shrewd judge of character, that one.'

'So I hear,' said Hannah.

'She knew a thing or two, did Faith. And they never lost money in the depression like everyone else did, no matter what she says upstairs.' Mrs Tyson nodded. 'Mark my words, it's just well hid, I reckon. Sitting on God knows what, that one is. She wants to find out as well.'

Hannah couldn't tell whether Mrs Tyson had meant that in the usual sense, that Mrs Graham-Potter *wanted* to know, or in the northern sense, that she bloody well ought to find out. As she was struggling with the linguistics, it dawned on her that she was the conduit Mrs Tyson had been looking for. She would not dare to poke around herself, but Hannah had a licence to do so. The expectant expression Hannah noted above the rim of the mug confirmed this.

'I can't imagine Mrs Graham-Potter not knowing exactly what's in the house,' Hannah said. 'She's lived here nearly all her life, after all.'

Mrs Tyson sniffed expressively. 'They didn't always get on, her and Faith Musgrave. Not by a long chalk. I'd imagine there are a fair few things that one doesn't know about.'

'Well, there's a lot we all don't know about,' said Hannah. 'Doesn't mean we'll find out, does it?'

She swilled out her mug in the stone sink.

'That depends,' said Mrs Tyson darkly.

Hannah took a deep breath, swung open the study door and stepped inside with what she hoped was a purposeful air.

Immediately she could feel the eerie sensation of all the hidden eyes in the room training on her.

If I'm going to do anything useful in here, I've got to challenge this head-on, she thought. And what are they, after all? Only photographs. She went over to the bookshelves, collected them, took them to the desk and laid them in a pile. They were much less threatening like that, and the frames weren't as imposing. Some of the heavy silver ones were moulded, hollow at the back, with primitive fastenings holding the photographs inside. Others seemed more solid, with proper hallmarks – the kind that should have been displayed in a lavish cluster on top of a grand piano. Maybe Mrs Graham-Potter would like a list of these for valuation, she thought.

She picked up the one on top of the pile: Constance, aged about seventeen, sitting on the steps of a red-brick building, cuddling a spaniel on her knee. She and the dog shared the same trusting expression of doe-eyed eagerness. Hannah wondered whether the building was the school that had been knocked down to make way for the supermarket. It would be interesting to know, and might help confirm the date of another photograph in the kitchen, a rather good shot of the high street that Mrs Graham-Potter wanted to give to the town archive. It looked about the right date – if Constance was in her late teens, then it should be some time after the First World War, and she'd guessed, by the buildings, that the photograph of the high street must be from about the same time.

She turned the frame to see if it would be easy to open. Faith had annotated most of the pictures in the house: no doubt date, place and time would have been neatly printed somewhere.

The picture was held in by a simple flap. Hannah pulled it gently and the back came apart, revealing several layers of cardboard as well as the photograph behind a heavy rectangle of dusty glass. As she separated out the layers, she noticed that a yellowing page of newspaper was flattened against the card. It had been folded several times and Hannah opened it carefully. It felt as if it might crumble into dust in her hands. It was a page from the *Linton Chronicle*, 18 August 1919, filled with closely typed columns in no apparent order, details of the week's events, advertisements, births, deaths, arrests and sport crammed into as small a space as possible – presumably, Hannah thought, to save precious paper so soon after wartime.

Each segment of news was given equal billing in typeface and size, and Hannah had to run her eye down all the columns to work out why the page had been saved.

5 swarms of bees for sale. Prize-winning honey.
Linton Hall.

Etterthwaite family honours 4 sons lost in French
infantry charge

Subscription monument to local regiment unveiled.

Miss Constance Musgrave commended by the Mayor of
Linton, Mr Michael Strong, for her bravery.

Bravery? thought Hannah. Constance? A little shiver ran through her, and she squinted to make out the tiny print.

Miss Constance Musgrave, younger daughter of Sir Samuel Musgrave of Hillcrest Villa, Linton, and 9 Wilton Place, London SW1, was commended yesterday by the mayor for her considerable presence of mind and bravery in saving the life of her spaniel, Jem. When the small dog fell into the harbour while walking along the Sugar Tongue at high tide, Miss Musgrave, with no thought for her own safety, dived in at once and pulled him out. She was herself rescued by a friend. Both dog and mistress are now perfectly safe and well with no ill-effects from their ducking.

In honour of the event, Miss Musgrave's father, Sir Samuel, has presented the town with a commemorative lifebelt to be kept on the harbourside in case of such emergencies.

Miss Musgrave is well known in the Linton area for her charitable works, with her sister, Faith. The Musgrave sisters are responsible for the establishment of many improving schemes for the workers in their father's mines and are the founders of Linton's Woollens for War knitting effort.

Hannah's brow creased. This wasn't the Constance she had known. Constance the demure milkmaid leaping into the harbour to save her little dog? Who'd have thought it? She didn't look the type for mad acts of bravery. Although she did look the type who'd care more about animals than people.

Fran would doubtless make a lot of that, given the number of pit disasters in the tough years after the war.

She picked up the photograph and looked at it more closely, searching Constance's placid face for clues. It wasn't easy to equate this beautiful young girl, with round eyes and apple cheeks, with the slow old lady she'd become. Maybe the eyes were the same. Hannah tried to make the two match. Constance had the kind of eyes that would always look sad, no matter how happy she was, she decided. She looked melancholy here, and she was only seventeen or so, and as beautiful, in a limpid way, as she'd ever be.

'Why so sad?' Hannah asked the picture.

'The war, of course. And Linton has never had a particularly *carnivale* atmosphere.'

Hannah gasped and almost dropped the photograph. She spun round on the oak office chair, and saw Mrs Graham-Potter standing in the doorway.

Her heart jumped in her chest. 'How long have you been there?' Hannah demanded, forgetting to be polite.

'Oh, just a few seconds. I don't like to stand for too long and you seemed so intent. I didn't creep in, you know.'

'I didn't hear you,' said Hannah, lamely. She could hardly accuse the woman of sneaking about in her own house. Sweat prickled in her armpits.

Mrs Graham-Potter gave her a chilly smile. 'Are you looking at that picture of Constance? It's one of my favourites.' She closed the door behind her and walked towards the desk. Her feet, in pink shoes, made only the ghost of a sound on the parquet. 'May I see?'

Hannah handed it to her.

'I remember the day when this was taken,' she said, holding the photograph by the edges and staring into it.

'Is it outside the school? That was why I was looking on the back,' Hannah added quickly.

'It was.'

'Was it . . .' she gestured towards the newspaper '. . . was it taken before or after this incident in the harbour?'

Mrs Graham-Potter's face darkened. 'I beg your pardon? Which incident in the harbour?'

'Constance leaping into the dock to save her little dog. It's in the paper, I thought it was terribly brave . . .' Hannah ran out of words as Mrs Graham-Potter's eyes grew steely.

'Where did you read that?'

'There was some newspaper tucked into the back of the frame. There's an account of the incident and it mentions the mayor commending her. Mr Michael Strong.'

'Oh.' Mrs Graham-Potter made a gesture of dismissal. 'Michael Strong was a terrible old fool. Thought he was dreadfully grand because his father had made a fortune importing fancy soap from America. Ha! He only made his money from other people's filth, and drove around as if he owned the place.'

Hannah had found that Mrs Graham-Potter's reluctance to talk about the past could be circumvented by dropping an easy target in her path. In that respect, she was really not dissimilar from Mrs Tyson – or Dora, for that matter.

'There was a little ceremony, wasn't there?' she went on spikily. 'Does it mention the presentation water bowl Samuel Musgrave had installed on the harbour walk for thirsty dogs?'

Hannah peered at the paper. 'No, just the lifebelt.'

'That would be in next week's, I imagine. They've always liked to spread their news thin.' Mrs Graham-Potter tutted and tapped her foot, but she didn't put down the photograph.

'Was he a dog-lover, then, their father?'

She snorted. 'Him? No, he could be a dreadful hypocrite. Constance's father hated Jem. Used to aim little kicks at him, if he caught him in the house. Said it was a woman's dog and not fit to be fed.'

Hannah goggled. 'But didn't he have a dog of his own, in the portrait?'

There was a brief pause, during which Mrs Graham-Potter recovered her normal composure. 'Oh, that was *Czar*. Czar was a pedigree Dalmatian, quite different. Besides, Sir Samuel was a very busy man, under a great deal of pressure for most of his life.' She changed the subject abruptly. 'I see you're getting along quite well. If you would excuse me, I'm going to lie down.'

'Of course,' murmured Hannah, even though her mind was teeming with questions.

When Mrs Graham-Potter left, as soundlessly as she'd come in, Hannah put on her Walkman to lighten the atmosphere in the room. It helped for a while: the familiar cheeriness of Radio One reduced the forbidding desk to a mere piece of furniture, and hearing her own voice singing along gave Hannah more of a tochold in her own world, and stopped the dark eyes in the pictures dragging her into theirs.

But after twenty minutes or so, as the sun went in, and the shadows returned slowly to the mirrors Hannah's nervousness also returned, along with a vivid image of Constance flailing around in the muddy depths of the harbour, her skirts filling with seawater and oil leaked from the ships.

There was just something *wrong* about that, she thought.

Faith would have dived in, to save a dog, and even Mrs Graham-Potter, if there was something in it for her.

But Constance?

She went back to the desk and looked at the photograph again. Constance's arms were tight around the spaniel's neck, clutching it to her like a baby. Well, perhaps she didn't get much affection at home, thought Hannah. If the mother was frail, the father a pig, and all her brothers had died, was it so odd that she had been very attached to her dog?

No, she thought. If Hannah had had a dog, she'd probably have been the same.

Even so, the image niggled for the rest of the morning, and Hannah went through the room more systematically than normal, noting artists, dates, subjects, making *aides memoire* for the Internet searching she would do later.

As she picked up and examined old directories and leatherbound surveys from the shelves, her mind didn't stray into the fascinating shadows of who might have bought the book, or how it might have ended up there, as it often did now the house was starting to come alive to her, offering tantalizing clues to its past, and the scenery of her grandmother's youth. All she could think of was the strange expression on Mrs Graham-Potter's face when she saw the newspaper cutting again, over the chasm of eighty-odd years.

Was it fear? Or suppressed sadness? Or just shame that her own memory was failing, and she'd forgotten?

The sound of the vacuum stopped at twelve o'clock, indicating that Mrs Tyson was due for a break. Even so, Hannah forced herself to wait until half past before she went to the kitchen for some coffee and a chance to get the full story. She didn't want to look overly keen, but the possibility that Mrs Tyson might fill in the gaps of Mrs Graham-Potter's discretion made her trot along the worn hall carpet.

Too late. The back door was shut and locked, and Mrs Tyson's pinny was hanging on its hook.

Hannah was embarrassed by her disappointment that she couldn't pump Mrs Tyson for biased information about her own family. What was she turning into, Mrs Woodward? Would Fran know anything more about Constance's life-saving? Probably not. Dora might – but getting her to talk about her childhood was like pulling teeth, and the pained expression she adopted gave Hannah the unpleasant feeling that she was somehow upsetting her. You're making a mountain out of a molehill, she told herself. That's what Toby would say.

But I don't care what Toby would say any more, she reminded herself.

Hannah made a cup of coffee. She wondered if her gossip hunger was a sign that she was turning native.

Chapter Fifteen

Despite Dora's elephantine hints, neither Fran nor Hannah had been to recent meetings of the book group, so they had missed Mrs Cowper's observations on *Five Quarters of the Orange* and *Birdsong*. Fran claimed she had better things to do than sit around discussing soft furnishings with a lot of old women. Hannah said she'd love to go but didn't think she could contribute enough to the gossip, and would have to fall back on discussing the book, which was clearly not the done thing.

The day after she had found the picture of Constance in the study, Hannah woke up feeling drained. She couldn't face another silent day in the villa, sitting in the past. Not being a skiver by nature, however, she felt obliged to provide a solid community reason for not being there and, much to Dora's delight and surprise, she walked down to the cottage after breakfast and volunteered to take her to the book group, which was being hosted by Mrs Kelly, of the green cords and primary-school manner.

'So have you read this book, then?' asked Dora, as she got into the passenger seat of her MG. She slammed the door because it was her car and she could.

'Which book is it we're subjecting to literary scrutiny today?' asked Hannah, adjusting the mirrors carefully. Driving Dora's car was an honour, accorded only after several assessment trips into town in Fran's infinitely more expendable Saab.

'This week it's *Bridget Jones's Diary.*'

'Who chose that?' Hannah backed the car out of the drive and narrowly avoided Betty Fisher, who was hauling her Alsatian up the hill. Hannah had never seen an Alsatian look cowed before.

'Does Betty Fisher ever go to the book group?' she asked. 'They always seem to be expecting her, but I wouldn't have thought it was her thing at all.'

'Oh, I don't know. She likes to come now and again, throw some barbs about. Poor woman really is mentally unbalanced. They'd like to exclude her, but they don't know how. Or they're too scared to.'

Dora was reapplying her lipstick in the vanity mirror. 'She might have enjoyed *Bridget Jones,*' she went on. 'Plenty to carp at there. I think it might have been Judy Hind who picked it – you know, trying to be with it. Or maybe Edith Cowper. She can be a real twine. Sometimes she just suggests books so she can have a really good snipe at them. If she were a man I'd swear she was a misogynist.'

'Being a woman is no barrier to that,' muttered Hannah.

Mrs Pauline Kelly, Other Half of Ray, Mam of Craig, Carla and Cherry, Nan of Cairo-Rose, Scott and Baby Ray, and Surrogate Mum of the Reception Class, lived in the 'new' development: it had been converted in the early seventies from Banner's flourmills, which had run all hours in the days when Linton ground its own flour and sent it off round the county to be baked with the spices and rum that had 'fallen over the side' of the trade ships. Most local specialities had a significant rum ingredient: the thinking behind this was that the evidence could be eaten before the Customs and Excise men came round.

It was amazing, Hannah thought, as she searched for a parking space, that Linton's tall ships could roam all over the world, getting the dust of the Indies blown into their holds and their sails bleached by the sun, then come back to a port where even then people thought the wearing of red shoes was a sign of dangerous attention-seeking.

Antigua Close was a classic example of this great Linton paradox. It had been named after one exotic destination of those ships, yet consisted of houses that could have belonged anywhere, built in an era when the town was ashamed of its shabby Georgian centre and longed to look like somewhere a bit go-ahead, like Milton Keynes.

Mrs Kelly's house was instantly identifiable: four blue book-group hatchbacks were parked outside and there was an ostentatious climbing frame in the front garden, not dissimilar to the one Hannah remembered from primary school.

'Of course, your mother protested about the flourmills being demolished,' said Dora, as Hannah tried to find reverse. 'It was 1974. She was protesting about everything that year. Then you were born and she really had something to protest about. She chained herself to a door, until it collapsed, and she had to be taken to hospital to be cut out of it. She made the front page of the *Linton Gazette*.'

Hannah had a vision of Fran's face, covered in brick dust, thwarted but still raging, aghast that she was to be in the paper for a comedy moment instead of a legitimate protest.

'Of course, she was right, really, the council shouldn't have knocked them down,' Dora went on.

'I should think so too!' said Hannah, parking next to Mrs

Woodward's Vauxhall Corsa, leaving a conservative amount of space to avoid potential damage to Dora's precious car. Mrs Woodward lived on a farm and had learned to drive on a tractor. 'It's part of the town's heritage. They should be proud of things like the flourmills. You can't just go—'

'Well, I suppose that's true, yes,' agreed Dora, mischievously, 'but if they'd left them where they were, they could have converted them, like they did with the bonded warehouses at the harbour side, and got hundreds of thousands for them. London prices! Such views. Not like these hamster wheels,' she added, with a contemptuous sneer. 'They could have paid off some of those debts they've run up with the sports centre.'

Hannah stared wordlessly at her grandmother. It was bad enough yuppies buying the miners' cottages, but exploiting town heritage then forcing up the prices so locals couldn't afford housing was unforgivable.

Dora's blue eyes were wide with sincerity. Then she cracked. 'I'm joking, you pudding.'

'Are you?'

Dora flipped down her sun visor for a final check on her makeup. 'Hannah, I'm relying on you to have a sense of humour.'

'Ah, well. I've been practising switching it off specially for this afternoon,' said Hannah, and got out of the car.

They waited at the frosted-glass door until Mrs Kelly's trim figure materialized behind it. 'We thought you weren't coming!' she carolled. She had long ago mastered the teacherly skill of disguising criticism behind wide smiles and all-encompassing plural pronouns.

'Would we miss this?' Dora asked.

Hannah said nothing: it was the Prime Minister of Barbed Compliments versus the Duchess of Irony.

'Well, we did think you might find us a little lowbrow after your friend Laurence Sterne,' Mrs Kelly replied, with just a hint of tartness, and swung the door open to reveal an array of family groups photographed in Linton's Studio of Memories that rivalled the Musgrave collection.

Dora graciously crossed the threshold.

Mrs Kelly's house smelt of cleaning products and homemade soup. Mr Sheen had certainly popped in for a visit before the book-club ladies.

'Now, come through to the lounge and we'll make a start,' said Mrs Kelly.

The rest of the book group – Mrs Cowper from the library, her dwarf-like 'odd' sister, Hettie, Mrs Hind from the WI, Mrs Woodward from the surgery, Mrs Jordan from the post office – were already there. They were seated around a glass-topped coffee-table, staring morosely at two plates of biscuits. There was no sign of Betty Fisher, who was presumably still being hauled up Linton Hill by her dog. No one made any reference to her absence.

Mrs Kelly's child-control had an equally subduing effect on old women: no one had started on the biscuits or poured the tea. They weren't even gossiping. Copies of *Bridget Jones's Diary* sat on their laps like exam papers.

Hannah felt prematurely embarrassed for everyone: the ladies, Bridget, Helen Fielding and, most of all, herself.

'Hello, Dora, love!' said Mrs Hind, in her jovial boom. Twenty years of projecting across the Linton Amateur Dramatic Players theatre had left her without an informal indoor tone, and she had developed a habit of conducting all conversations in Musical Comedy Tone No. 1 – a mildly feminized 'hail fellow, well met'.

Dora winced at the endearment but smiled, then let her eyes wander obviously around the room in search of a comfortable seat.

Immediately Mrs Jordan leaped up from the armchair of Mrs Kelly's three-piece suite. 'Here you are, Dora, have this one!' She twitched down the skirt of the little suit she was wearing: early mornings in the post office and varicose veins meant she generally stuck to slacks.

'You're so kind.' Dora beamed, and lowered herself elegantly on to the seat, putting her slim knees together so that her legs slanted and her ankles touched.

Now that her grandmother was seated, Hannah could feel all eyes upon her and awkwardly edged round the table and chairs to perch on the arm of Dora's leatherette throne.

'Now!' Mrs Kelly entered with one hand spread wide in welcome and a hot water jug in the other. 'Let's fortify ourselves with some tea and a digestive biscuit, then get going, shall we?'

There was a more enthusiastic rustling of books than there had been for *Tristram Shandy*. Mrs Cowper, in particular, looked fit to burst. She reached into her handbag and took out a notebook, which she folded back to the appropriate page with a sigh of malign anticipation.

'Who'd like to start? I can see Mrs Cowper's keen,' said Mrs Kelly, pouring tea into cheerful Denbyware mugs. She looked up and around the group and unerringly went for the one person who didn't want to say anything. 'So what about . . . Mrs Jordan? What did you think?'

'Oh, er, I can't say I was that struck,' stammered Mrs Jordan, flipping through the pages for inspiration.

Mrs Kelly compounded her discomfort by giving her a cup of tea to hold at the same time. 'Oh, er, thank you,' said Mrs Jordan. 'What lovely china.'

'So, you weren't that struck,' Mrs Kelly repeated. 'Well, it's a start.' She looked round the group brightly, to show she was making a little joke. 'But can you be a *little* more specific, Janet?'

Hannah realized why she loved books but avoided book groups. It was like being back at school, but voluntarily and with points to score off each other, rather than the Northern Examining Board.

'Well . . .' Mrs Jordan flushed '. . . I know it's very *with it*, but really, I . . . For one thing, I can't say I myself was that impressed by illustrating the cover with a young lady smoking. It doesn't set a very good example to young folk today. It's irresponsible.'

'Very much so,' said Mrs Cowper eagerly. 'Even the brightest young women still seem unable to appreciate the health warnings about cigarettes.'

Everyone's gaze swung to Hannah, who stared them all out as best she could.

Bloody Mrs Armstrong, she thought.

'And she *counts* the cigarettes in the book too!' went on Mrs Cowper, with only the briefest glance at her notes. 'And she overeats, and drinks to excess virtually every night, and is so rude about her mother!'

'I found the spelling *very* annoying,' chimed in Mrs Kelly, nibbling a biscuit. 'It's so hard to teach children how to spell correctly when they're all texting each other with abbreviations and so on.'

'And her friends were such sluts!' Mrs Cowper steamed on. 'And I, for one, hardly think it's healthy for a single woman to be spending so much time with homosexual men. It sends out quite the wrong message. No wonder she can't get a man. They probably all think she's a Sapphic.'

Hannah spluttered. Half the old ladies in the town lived together, and if spending time with other women made you a lesbian, then some kind of geriatric orgy was permanently under way at the Coffee Pot Café.

'Please try not to get crumbs in the chair, Hannah!' Mrs Kelly reminded her gaily. 'That goes for all of you! Otherwise you can go round with the Dustbuster before you leave.'

Dora looked at Hannah with merriment in her eyes, but Hannah refused to rise to the bait. They'd only just started and there'd be at least another hour to be got through.

'As I say, I pity young women today if this is the attitude they have towards their lives,' said Mrs Cowper. It sounded a lot like a prepared conclusion to Hannah. 'The trouble is that they all think being happy is a right, and it isn't. When we were young, there was far more to worry about than how much you weighed, or whether you had a boyfriend. We worried about being warm, or having enough food. If you were happy it was a *bonus*.'

Hannah doubted this but didn't say anything. It sounded like one of Fran's favourite rants. There was a general tendency, she'd noticed, among the book-group women, to fantasize collectively that they'd grown up in the 1840s rather than the 1940s.

'You don't think, then, that maybe it's meant to be ironic?' suggested Dora.

Mrs Cowper harrumphed. 'I don't think so.'

'It doesn't really matter, because it's *made up*,' said Hannah, before she could stop herself. 'And she isn't meant to be some kind of role model – she's *meant* to be a complete loser.'

'There's no need to be smart, Hannah,' said Mrs Kelly, primly, grabbing the opportunity to regain control of the discussion. 'It's a perfectly reasonable observation. It is, after all, meant to be a book about the tedious minutiae of a modern woman's life.'

'Yes, but within the structural bounds of fiction,' said Hannah. She cursed the instinct that had made her mouth open – she didn't want to get embroiled in explaining fuckwittage to the Linton book group. 'It's meant to be within the diary tradition of . . . I don't know, *Pamela* by Samuel Richardson, or, well, *Tristram Shandy*, I suppose.'

A stunned, defensive silence fell over the lounge. No one wanted to revisit *Tristram Shandy*.

'It's a comedy about how little people really know themselves, even if they spend all day reading *The Road Less Travelled*,' she stumbled on.

Blank and suspicious silence.

'Oh, *can* we do that one week, Pauline?' said Mrs Cowper. 'It really is a very spiritual book.'

'That's not what the vicar says,' hooted Mrs Hind. 'He told me it's a load of—'

'If we try to finish with this book first?' Mrs Kelly smiled icily.

'—jolly old cobblers and he prefers *The Little Book of Calm* in his little boys' room any day!'

'Hannah!' said Mrs Kelly. Her voice evidently came out louder than she'd intended, since she then modulated it into a sweeter tone. 'Do you want to go on?'

Hannah had the distinct feeling she was merely being invited to display the full length of her rope before they hanged her with it, but played her final card anyway: 'It's really based on *Pride and Prejudice*. You know. Mark . . . Darcy?'

Honks of derision.

'You can't tell *me* that there is any relation at all between the great Jane Austen and this . . . badly written nonsense!' hooted Mrs Cowper.

'Adaptation and pastiche is nothing new, Kathleen. What about *West Side Story*?' suggested Dora.

'You can't say that this is anywhere *near* as good as *West Side Story*!'

'Oh, I agree,' chimed in Mrs Jordan. 'Those lovely songs. And the dancing! You just don't get anything like that nowadays.'

Four or five separate conversations immediately arose to dispute the varying qualities of Irish dancing versus ballet, Gene Kelly versus Fred Astaire, whether the Irish immigrants on the far side of town had or had not danced down Jericho Street in a huge *Riverdance* formation one St Patrick's Day before the war, and whether it was possible to put on a decent production of *West Side Story* utilizing the somewhat limited talents of the Linton Tap and Ballet School.

'Do they *ever* talk about the book?' Hannah asked Dora, during the ensuing cacophony.

'No. This is something of a record,' said Dora. She broke a digestive biscuit in half, shook off the crumbs over the side of the chair, then dunked a piece in her tea while Mrs Kelly was telling Mrs Jordan about the very expensive hotel their Craig had put her up in, and Mrs Jordan was not mentioning the fact, well known to everyone else, that he'd only done it so she wouldn't have to stay with him and the common-law partner she didn't know about.

'In what way?'

'Well, they've clearly read the book, since they hated it so specifically.'

Mrs Cowper shushed for silence, taking great delight in catching Mrs Kelly as the last one still talking.

'. . . and we were very lucky because his friend Pietr was in town and he's an expert on Broadway musicals, but – I'll tell you later. After we've finished discussing the book,' said Mrs Kelly, quickly.

'Maybe you can tell us, Hannah,' said Mrs Cowper, 'is this really how young women are, these days? I mean, it could only be set in London. I dare say young women round here are too busy earning a living and bringing up children to be writing down their fat grams.'

Hannah reddened under the attention and considered for a moment. The eyes turned towards her clearly expected her to say no, it wasn't, not in her world. She twisted the gold ring on her finger. It would be easy to say yes and be done with it, then all their assumptions about London could be confirmed in one fell swoop. But where would that leave her? An idiot, like Bridget?

Then she thought of Toby, and of how she had failed to notice that she'd been living in a dream world of her own making, right up to the point where he'd told her he and Jennifer were going to get married. A dream world bolstered by her prosaic imagination, which could only work on what was there and not on what might be. More than that, she remembered how bitterly lonely she'd felt, having to pretend to all and sundry that everything was fine and that her life was just as golden and successful as ever.

At least Bridget had ended up with Mark Darcy, no matter how much of a fool she made of herself.

But did she really believe that catching a Darcy was going to make her happy? Really happy? Something stirred inside her.

'Well?' said Mrs Kelly, impatient to get back to tales of Scott.

'It's not that simple . . .' began Hannah, squirming. 'Young women today are expected to have wonderful careers that, er, *previous generations* of women couldn't have, but at the same time they're meant to maintain the happy family lives that you . . . er, previous generations of women devoted all their time to keeping up. And we're also meant to have as much fun as men, and drink as much and, um, have lots of, um, boyfriends . . . Only we've got to do everything all at once, and when it doesn't work out, we blame ourselves for wanting it in the first place and feel bad for being greedy. It sometimes feels like the goalposts keep moving. And not many women I know are eight stone nine,' she finished lamely.

'Evidently,' said Mrs Woodward, giving her a long look as she reached for the digestive biscuits.

'What rubbish!' exclaimed Mrs Kelly. 'I mean, you've managed it, haven't you, Hannah? You've got a wonderful job and a nice flat, and I daresay she's got a decent young chap, hasn't she, Dora?'

Hannah flinched.

Dora didn't look at Hannah, but her dry hand touched her fingers. 'I wouldn't know,' she said coolly. 'I don't like to pry in my family's private lives.'

'Evidently,' said Mrs Woodward again, but much quieter.

The meeting ground to an abrupt halt when Mrs Kelly's phone rang and it was Carla. Their Scott needed taking to judo because Carla was late home from work and her Glenn was, as Mrs Kelly explained, 'temporarily without a car'.

'Temporarily without a driving licence more like,' muttered Mrs Woodward, as she levered herself off the sofa. 'Claiming it was diabetes, my backside.'

'Don't forget – next week it's *White Teeth* by Zadie Smith,' said Mrs Cowper, brightly, as everyone shuffled to the door.

'I think we're going away next week,' said Dora to Hannah, in a conversational tone that fooled no one.

Chapter Sixteen

Fran was less than impressed with Hannah's news from the book group. 'They're a bunch of dried-up old prunes,' she said. 'I hope you told them exactly where to go, with their ill-informed personal comments.'

'No, I didn't,' said Hannah. 'And you wouldn't have either.'

'I would,' said Fran.

Hannah pulled a disbelieving face behind her back.

They were walking along the Ramble Way, above the harbour. It was narrow, which meant that Hannah often trailed along behind Fran's long strides, but she didn't mind: she didn't want Fran to see she was getting out of breath keeping up with her.

'You wouldn't,' argued Hannah. 'We all know what we'd say to these old bags in theory, but no one ever does. That's why they're still ruling the roost in the library and getting away with murder.'

Fran, who was fair, made a noise of reluctant agreement.

They were almost at the crest of the hill now, and the sea glittered in front of them. The sun had inched out from behind the clouds; it sparkled on the windows of the harbourside houses, and in shards of light on the waves. Hannah's heart filled with an unspecific feeling of elation and belonging.

'Did your grandmother not offer her thoughts on women's independence?' asked Fran.

'No,' said Hannah, still gazing out at the sea.

'You surprise me.'

'I think she was hoping I'd give them the full benefit of my university education. I could see they were waiting for me to make a mistake and show off,' she said. 'I never know what the right thing to say is. If I get it right, I'm showing off, if I get it wrong, universities don't teach you anything.'

'Ignore them,' said Fran. 'I do.'

'She had a very nice house, though,' said Hannah. 'Mrs Kelly, I mean. Like a little palace.'

Fran made a snorting noise and skipped a stone down the hill.

'Have you been down on the harbourside recently?' Hannah asked. 'The new warehouse developments look really smart.' Despite herself, Hannah could imagine living in one of those nice flats – on the top floor with a panoramic view of the harbour. You could eat your breakfast watching the boats going in and out with seagulls trailing after them. You'd feel as if you owned the harbour, as though all the boats were coming in for you. 'They'll be selling like hot cakes, won't they?'

Fran had gone very quiet.

'Mum?' Hannah prompted her. 'You know the ones I'm talking about, don't you? The ones down by the harbourside?'

'I know them,' said Fran, grimly.

'It's amazing when you think of all the industries Linton used to have, even before coal took off,' Hannah went on, oblivious to the expression on her mother's face. 'I've been flicking through some of the old town directories up at the villa. Flourmills, tanneries, potteries . . .'

'You know what they really had in those flourmills?' said Fran.

'Flour?' replied Hannah. 'Grindstones? Stock piles of the "nowt that they don't tek out"?'

'*Before* they were flourmills.'

Fran's flinty tone made Hannah turn and look at her in surprise. Her eyes were burning with anger.

Hannah wondered what it was like to face her mother in full flight in court, and abandoned every slick joke that had just occurred to her. 'No, you've got me there,' she said. 'Tell me.'

'There were slaves,' said Fran, and bent to look for another stone to skim down the hill.

Hannah stared at her mother's narrow back, weighing this comment against what Mrs Tyson had hinted about the Musgraves' involvement in slavery, and against her mother's known enthusiasm for taking offence on other people's behalf, often without a shred of evidence. 'Are you sure?' she asked, and immediately wished she hadn't.

'Am I sure?' snorted Fran. 'Excuse *me*. You don't have the monopoly on knowledge round here.'

Hannah felt wounded. Fran was the one who had always told her not to listen when everyone else made her miserable for being a swot.

'It just seems . . . unlikely, that's all,' she said. 'I can't imagine . . . slaves in Linton.'

'Why not? There's been trade here since the seventeenth century.'

Hannah opened her mouth and closed it again. She couldn't think of an answer that wouldn't sound either glib or racist. 'Are you sure they weren't just *part* of a trade triangle and didn't actually arrive in—'

'Hannah, slaves didn't just come here,' said Fran. 'They left from here too.'

'Oh, Mum, are you sure that's true? I mean—'

'How much do you really know about this town?' demanded Fran. 'Beyond the nice parts – the station, the gardens, that little coffee shop you like to go to. Rissini's, which does London cuts for Linton prices. There's more to this place than just its architecture, Hannah. Does it never occur to you to wonder where the money for all the nice white houses *came* from?'

'From the mines,' said Hannah, feeling oddly defensive. 'And the shipping trade.'

Fran made a dismissive noise. 'And the rest. It never strikes you as grotesque that the nice houses are built directly over a catacomb of mines where men worked all the hours God sent for a pittance?'

A picture of the cross-sectioned honeycomb of tunnels beneath the town flashed into Hannah's mind – from a school textbook? – and the stony footpath seemed to shift beneath her feet. She closed her eyes and saw the cross-sectioned town falling in on itself like a scarf pulled down into a magician's fist.

'It's dirty money,' Fran was saying. 'All filthy with coal dust, blood and slavery. Doesn't matter how white they paint the houses, they're dirty underneath. And nobody's hands are as dirty as those of the Musgraves, in their lovely big house, all paid for with other people's sweat!'

'Mum—'

'You remember that big compensation case I was handling when you had your A levels?'

Hannah nodded.

'Well, that was all down to the Musgraves not putting in enough proper underpinning when the seam was sunk, then jerry-building the houses on top. And then there's all that business about whether they were responsible' – her fingers made quotation marks in the air – '"indirectly" for the Samson Pit disaster. Money can get you out of anything, but people don't forget. Who in their right mind would want to be related to *them*?'

She sank on to a bench with a bump.

'Mum, are you OK?' asked Hannah. 'Please tell me the truth.'

There was a long pause.

'No.' Fran put her hands to her head. 'I'm ... No, not really. Sorry. I've had a long week, love. We're under a lot of pressure at work and it's been very—' She jerked her chin up. 'Listen, I should really tell you. So you know. I've been to the hospital for some more tests, love.'

'Oh,' said Hannah. She tried to look surprised. 'What kind of tests?'

'Did you know already?' Fran's eyes narrowed. 'Has your grandmother been talking to you about it?'

'No,' said Hannah. Then she saw it was pointless to try to cover up, and added, 'Not really. She wasn't sure,' Hannah balked at referring to Dora's menopause theories, 'what was wrong.'

Fran sighed. 'She's being unbelievably selfish, Hannah. She's adamant that she doesn't know anything about her medical history and has no intention of finding out. I mean, I know she's an old lady, but sometimes I wonder if there's a bit of senile dementia creeping in.'

'I honestly don't think so, Mum. Really.'

'Well, it's world-class obtuseness, then.'

'Maybe there are things she doesn't want to remember,' said Hannah, thinking of how Louise Graham-Potter's practised serenity had crumpled when she recalled all the dead Musgrave boys, a generation of romantic possibilities wiped out. 'Or maybe she really doesn't know.'

'Oh, *someone* knows where Dora came from. You don't think that Faith Musgrave would take a baby from anywhere, and bring it up as her own?'

'Well, there must have been a birth certificate.'

'Yes, there was. Don't you remember the fire?'

'No,' lied Hannah, wanting Fran to tell her the story from an adult point of view, in case there were things she'd missed.

Fran gave her a hard look. 'Well, I suppose you were too little to know what was going on. Can you remember the night Faith Musgrave had her stroke?'

Hannah looked doubtful.

'The night you nearly fell out of the bedroom window?'

Hannah nodded.

'Well, that was it. Still don't know what prompted it. I think Faith must have had bad news from the doctor – she'd been ill for a long time before that – and there was all sorts of to-ing and fro-ing between her and Constance, but the upshot was that Faith gave Dora an envelope with her birth certificate and a letter and photographs and everything, explaining where she'd come from and how she'd ended up being brought up by them.'

'And?'

'And,' said Fran, through gritted teeth, 'Dora made a bonfire in the garden and burned it without opening it. She can be very selfish, and was brought up to do exactly as she likes. I can understand why she might want to blank out where she came from, rather than deal with it, but I don't think she has the right to erase our past too.'

'Can't you get another copy of the birth certificate?'

'She won't tell me what name she's registered under.'

'What?'

'Hannah, that's the kind of secretive old *biddy* she can be.' Fran sighed. 'And you could get away with anything, in those days, if you had their money and position. The Musgraves paid for a new roof for the church the year Dora got married – and the vicar never asked any questions about her birth certificate. Just waved her straight in. She thought it was hysterical.'

'Poor Arthur,' said Hannah.

'Poor us,' said Fran. 'Don't ever let me get like that.'

'I won't,' said Hannah. 'So, this problem . . .'

Fran put her chin in her hands. 'It's not just the medical thing either, to be honest. Though that's getting . . . a bit more urgent. I just . . .' She sighed crossly, as if she couldn't believe what she was saying. 'I know I've always said it didn't matter, but sometimes I really wonder where I'm *from.*'

Hannah's skin crawled at the unfamiliar note of sorrow in her mother's voice. Fran's attitude to life had always been terrier-like: quick, cross and nippy. It didn't leave room for self-pity. Hannah suddenly realized how lonely her mother must have been all the years she'd been away in London – living on her own, divorced and defensive, with no real girlfriends, and only her own secretive, private mother for company. Even she spent most of her social time up at the villa.

'But you're from here,' she said. 'From Linton.'

'Am I? How do I know that?'

A huge seagull flew past their heads, its wings an easy metre across. Up close, its white feathers looked like polished marble.

'We must be,' said Hannah. 'I can't imagine being from anywhere else. Don't you feel a . . . um, bond with this place? You know, with the harbour and the sea, and the houses and the sound of people's voices?'

Hannah stopped, aware that she was starting to sound bathetic. Georgian houses, however pretty, and the dourly stoic people of Linton weren't exactly Ben Nevis and the view over Waterloo Bridge at midnight.

'To be honest, Hannah,' said Fran, 'I don't really know what I feel. There's a lot of myself that I don't like, that doesn't feel like me, and I've no one to blame it on but Dora and me.'

'And Arthur.'

'Poor Arthur,' said Fran automatically. 'God. He had no idea what he was letting himself in for. It must have looked like such a good deal on the surface – own house, rich family, pretty wife.' She skipped another stone down the bank.

'Were you close to him?'

'Not really. I used to think that the mines ate men, you know, like the Incas made human sacrifices. I thought that's where the men had gone when there was a pit disaster. I used to add Dad in at the end of all my prayers, pray that he wouldn't be taken away. I didn't know he worked at the mine offices. He never talked about what he did, he just left the house at half eight and came back at half six.'

Hannah tried to imagine her mother as a child, and couldn't.

Fran let out a sigh. 'I don't know how you can feel so reassured coming back here. I'd want to run away as far as I could, if I were you. I suppose it's nurture over nature.'

'Sorry?' said Hannah.

'I mean, you grew up here, so you think you have roots.' Fran swung an expansive hand over the harbour. 'Maybe two generations back is enough to make you feel you belong. But I don't know where my roots *are*. I don't even know if they're not just a sentimental invention to justify keeping in touch with families.'

Hannah didn't know what to say.

They looked out to sea, where a yacht was approaching the harbour, tacking quickly across the denim-blue waves.

'Do you think Granny doesn't want to know who her parents were in case they were miners, or something?' she asked, thinking about the long mine seams stretching out beneath the water. At the back of her mind, she could hear Mrs Tyson's dark hints about Samuel Musgrave and his predatory visits to the pit cottages while the miners were sweating underground. Surely Faith and Constance wouldn't have taken in one of their father's bastards?

'It wouldn't bother me,' said Fran, grimly. 'Rather that than one of the Musgraves.'

'Mmm,' said Hannah.

'I doubt that she's ever really thought about it. You know what she's like. She was Faith and Constance's little princess, had everything she wanted, probably pretended in her own mind that she was a lost child of the Russian Revolution . . . Don't take this the wrong way, but your grandmother's one of those people who's perfectly content to exist in her own world as long as she's at the centre of it.'

'I'm a bit like that,' said Hannah.

'No, you're not.'

Hannah thought about what Fiammetta had said, about her ability to forget chunks of her life. 'I think I am.'

Fran put her arm round Hannah's shoulders. 'No, you're just going through a tough time. Come on, before you know it you'll be back on your feet, down in London, getting another job. You're a winner, love.' She squeezed her encouragingly. 'There's a life for you outside this place.'

Like there once was for you? And for Dad? But Hannah held her thoughts inside her head. She didn't want them flying out to ruin this rare moment of intimacy with her mother.

Instead she smiled weakly and laid her forehead on her mother's wiry shoulder. She smelt of fresh washing powder and stale coffee.

'Come on,' said Fran again, getting up from the bench. 'I'll buy you a cappuccino at the Coffee Pot. And one of those disgusting fondant fancies you like.'

Fran left Hannah to finish her coffee after despatching a decaff *latte* and a rock bun at lightning speed. As she swirled the last mouthful of coffee in the cup, she opened her bag, took out a little pill-box and swallowed three vitamins, two Nurofen and a precautionary

Rennie, then left, promising she'd be back in time to make 'something nice for supper'.

Hannah sincerely hoped she wouldn't.

The café was emptying and she would have liked to linger and watch the first lunchtime customers come in, but she knew she was expected up at the villa and didn't dare disappoint Mrs Graham-Potter. Not to mention Mrs Tyson.

The latter was polishing silver in the kitchen when Hannah let herself in, and muttering crossly to herself about the devil and idle hands. 'This'll be worth a pretty penny,' she said, as Hannah filled the kettle to make some tea. 'I'd say it'll have come from the London house. You'd know more than me, though.'

'Looks like it,' said Hannah. She picked up a monogrammed silver hot-water jug and scrutinized the hallmark. The quality was obvious, and it wasn't a showpiece — it had been used regularly — for tea parties on the lawn in summer maybe. It was so much easier to imagine the Musgraves' elegant life when the props were still here, waiting to be brought to life. If only the people who had used them were less shadowy.

'Makes you wonder what happened to the rest of it,' said Mrs Tyson. 'I can't see them selling owt.'

'Why not?'

Mrs Tyson sniffed. 'Didn't like anything to get out of their hands, did they? Look at your grandmother. They didn't even want her living where they couldn't see her.'

'Well, that's one way of looking at it, I suppose,' said Hannah.

Mrs Tyson rubbed away at her coffee-pot irritably. 'Even when they got young lasses pregnant, they couldn't let well alone.'

Hannah put down the hot-water jug and looked in her satchel for her notebook. 'How do you mean?'

'Well, let's just say it wasn't only the silver that got moved back and forth between the houses.' Mrs Tyson smiled at her own discretion, then spoiled it by explaining, 'The maids – when Dirty Joe had had his way. Faith's grandfather,' she added, seeing Hannah's brow crease. 'With the whips. He sent the poor lasses to the London house to work until they had the baby, then get rid of it, pretending he was doing them a favour.' Her lips pursed. 'Some didn't come back, said they'd got a job in a factory. That'd be the shame, though. Folk remember things like that.'

Hannah scribbled this down, but turned the jug over so it looked as if she was noting the mark. 'And Samuel Musgrave? Did he send maids down there?'

'I'd say so.'

'How interesting,' said Hannah. It was odd that they were sent down to London to escape gossip when that was where the social grapevine was; maybe he even got a charitable spin from it, 'saving' fallen maids from local gossip about their miner sweethearts. She grimaced. Maybe *that* was why the painting of the London house wasn't displayed so prominently – if Faith and Constance had known about these secrets being swept under the carpet, and were ashamed. Maybe their brothers were guilty of it too. But, then, they were both spinsters and, if her own clam-like family was anything to go by, they might have been unaware of the whole thing.

She clicked her pen shut and lifted the jug. 'Nice bit of silver, this,' she said.

Mrs Tyson grunted and set to on the teapot.

Mrs Graham-Potter was nowhere to be found, so Hannah made her way upstairs. She hadn't had any specific instructions about what she should look at up there, beyond the family photographs in the corridors, but she was curious about the bedrooms. They were the private part of the house, where no visitors had to be impressed, where the clothes would be, the beds and the little accoutrements of feminine life.

Part of her – the part still hooked on ghost stories – hoped that the rooms would have been left as they were when the old ladies died, with traces of their breath still on the air and pale hairs still caught in the silver-backed brushes. But as she made her way up the stairs and the usual gust of cold draught caught her ankles, she told herself not to be ridiculous. Faith had died over twenty years ago, and Constance ten years later. There wouldn't be any trace of them left in their rooms, just as her own room had been tidied by Fran minutes after Hannah had left home. At the time she'd been offended that her mother couldn't wait to eradicate her; now she wondered if she had been claiming it back for herself.

Hannah turned left down the corridor after the landing, away from the family photographs and the locked doors, and cautiously turned the first brass doorknob she came to.

It opened with a gentle squeak and she stepped inside, holding her breath.

Without knowing why, she sensed that this had been Constance's room. It was spacious, as all the rooms in the house were, but it didn't have a commanding sea-view or even a sweeping vista of the garden. Instead, it looked out down the hill into the town, with the fells in the distance and the tall steeple of St Peter's visible over the tiled roofs of the terraced streets. A bedroom, thought Hannah, for a fifth or sixth child, who wouldn't make a fuss.

It was calm, though, and the faint traffic noise made it seem more alive than other parts of the house. There wasn't a great deal of furniture besides a double bed with carved rosebuds on the oak headboard, a solid-looking wardrobe and an elegant dressing-table, on which Hannah was delighted to see a set of silver-backed brushes and some intriguing little boxes.

She took out her notebook. There were several brisk hunting scenes in oils hanging on the rose-sprigged wallpaper, and a set of pretty samplers. One had been sewn by Catherine Margaret Musgrave in 1869, another by Lettice Arabella Musgrave in 1807 and a brighter, newer one, by Constance Ellen Musgrave in 1911, on which the words to the Lord's Prayer were generously surrounded with nautical knots and the Linton bear emblem.

Hannah sat on the dressing-table stool and noted it all down, querying whether these were by the same artist as the hunting oils she'd noticed by the cloakroom. When she looked up again, her attention was drawn to a large family Bible that sat on a side-table by the bed. It was huge, about two feet by eighteen inches, and a good five inches deep, bound in tobacco-brown leather with a tarnished silver clasp. Hannah ran her fingers over it, and realized it was locked.

Of course it would be locked, she thought. The master of the house would have had the key and unlocked it for readings on Sunday, and for ceremonial inscriptions of births and deaths. But where would that key be now?

She looked impatiently around the room. The boxes on the dressing-table. Of course.

There were only cotton reels and abalone buttons in the first, and an assortment of silver buckles in the second, but in the third, underneath several rolls of ribbons, there was a tiny embroidered bag. Hannah undid it with trembling fingers and tipped out a pair of screw-backed marcasite earrings and a small key.

It fitted the Bible's little lock and turned with a satisfying click. The front page released the smell of old paper and sea damp.

As she'd guessed, the frontispiece was elaborately engraved with the Musgrave coat-of-arms and the family tree as it had stood in 1805, when the Bible had been acquired from a bookseller on King Street. Even here the curious Linton blight on men was in evidence: there was a dull repetition of the same boys' names – Samuel, Derwent, Carlisle, Joseph – as they were born, then died before the line could extend through them.

Hannah turned the page where Victorian births had been recorded. Here they all were as babies, those faces that now glared out of the portraits in the study: Sir Joseph, the first baronet with the hard stare and the aggressively smart clothes, born in 1829, the third of five boys, married in 1857 to poor blonde Isabella, who had started producing infants at the tender age of eighteen and hadn't been allowed to stop until she was thirty. Joseph Alexander, 1858; Samuel Jacob, 1860; John Michael, 1862; Derwent Patrick, 1864; Carlisle James, 1865 . . .

Hannah winced. Until Catherine Margaret, the last in 1869, there must have been barely three months when Isabella wasn't pregnant.

And then the same thing again with Ellen, Constance's mother. Married to be a brood mare – to no avail. Hannah's heart ached for her. All that discomfort and distress to produce eight sons, only to watch helplessly as they died.

She shivered.

Constance had pressed flowers between the pages of the Bible, faded pansies and Michaelmas daisies from the garden, now nearly embossed on the closely printed lines. The book was almost thick enough to take a rose without it showing when it was locked.

As she turned the pages, holding the flowers in, the book fell open in the middle of the Song of Solomon; a page marked with a photograph. Hannah held it up to the light.

It was Constance, aged about seventeen, holding a small dog on her lap and looking unusually bright, sitting on a bench that Hannah recognized as being outside the Miners' Welfare Hall, which was now a council crèche. Standing awkwardly by her side was a tall youth on the verge of turning into a man; his face was handsome in a craggy way, with intelligent-looking eyes and a firm mouth. There was something familiar about him, although he clearly wasn't a Musgrave brother – the clothes were too shabby for that and his thick hair was dark.

Hannah scrutinized the faces – he must have been about twenty. She turned it over and read the pencilled words, in Constance's small handwriting: *Constance, with Matthew Fisher, Miners' Welfare Hall, 1918.*

How curious, thought Hannah. How would Constance have known Matthew Fisher in 1918? The first paintings she had found on the Internet were dated from about 1927 onwards – and it would hardly have been appropriate for Constance Musgrave to be socializing with a miner before he had the credibility of his art to compensate for his working-class roots. And hadn't that been more to do with Faith than Constance?

She looked at the stone-built hall in the background, pretty much unchanged, and remembered something Dora had said about Faith and Constance running art or reading classes for the miners. Presumably they'd have been held in the welfare hall. Had Matthew Fisher been one of their star pupils?

Curious, she thought again, and curious that Constance had kept that photograph locked in her Bible.

It seemed sacrilegious to take it out so she put it back carefully where she'd found it, and carried on turning to see if Constance had hidden any other little fragments of her private life.

Hannah's ears twitched for the sound of Mrs Graham-Potter's cat-like approach. This felt too much like snooping, and she wondered if she'd fallen into her grandmother's habit of over-dramatizing everything, but at the back, she found a handwritten letter folded flat to blend with the pages of the book.

She took it out and scanned the elaborate office-script writing. It was from the Musgraves' solicitors in London – she made a mental note to take the details for further reference – and was addressed to Faith.

Dear Miss Musgrave,

Further to the instructions from your mother of the 17th
inst, in my most regrettable capacity as executor of your
late father's estate, I have made arrangements for monies
to be made available to you while in Cambridge, in addition
to accounts at the appropriate London establishments,
with which I am sure you are already familiar.

Hannah looked at the date: September 1919. Some months after
Samuel Musgrave had died. That must have been a terrible year for
Ellen: losing her husband, her last two sons, then her daughters
leaving for university. No wonder she'd gone off her head.

She scanned the rest of the letter, which was a gloopy mixture
of obsequiousness, condolence and legalese, until her eye stopped
at a sentence which struck her as odd.

Please find enclosed herewith details of your travel
arrangements to Cambridge later this month, and two
railway tickets.

Only two?

Surely there would have been three? If the three friends went
together, then would not their arrangements have been made at the
same time? Presumably the orphaned Louise would have had her
financial affairs – or what money she had – arranged by Samuel
Musgrave's lawyer? Or was this some form of snobbery, whereby
Faith and Constance had first-class seats and Louise had to make
her own way?

Hannah tried to pinpoint what was making her feel as if she was
missing something. Amid the long words and complicated
sentiments, something wasn't being mentioned.

She put the letter back in the Bible, and locked it carefully, then replaced the whole thing on the table. It weighed a ton.

She put her hands on her hips and stretched her aching back, letting her gaze roam around the unassuming room – not what one might have expected of a lady with Constance's income, but perhaps in keeping with her quiet, demure character.

There was a door on the far wall that Hannah thought must lead to a bathroom or dressing room. She walked over to it and tried the handle. It opened, and led into a blue-tiled bathroom, dominated by a large claw-foot bath and several brass towel rails. A small circular window, like a porthole, let in light from high up in the wall, and a large mirror, decorated with leaping dolphins and yellow sea-shells, reflected her face.

Hannah was filled with an unexpected sense of joy at the pretty little room. Then she noticed another door on the other side of the room.

She hesitated, then went across to it and tried the handle. She expected it would lead into an airing cupboard full of monogrammed linen sheets, but instead, she saw a bed. And on the bed, above the silky ivory coverlet, lay Mrs Graham-Potter with a compress over her eyes, her chest rising and falling.

Hannah blushed and put a hand to her mouth to stop herself gasping aloud. Even asleep, Mrs Graham-Potter popped up where she least expected her.

Then the old lady raised a spindly hand from the coverlet to the compress and turned her head in the direction of the bathroom.

Hannah pulled the door shut, as softly as she could, and slipped across the bathroom tiles, holding her breath in case her feet made a sound. In Constance's room, she picked up her notebook, went out and closed the door quietly. Then she tiptoed down the main staircase and returned to her legitimate study of the family through their collection of silver tea services.

But at the back of her mind there was a chilling conviction that Mrs Graham-Potter had known she was there, just as she seemed to know where she was throughout the house. That she would know, yet let it hang unspoken between them, made Hannah feel uneasy, as if she were being drawn into all sorts of secrets she didn't understand but would be expected to keep.

Chapter Seventeen

Hannah wondered if it was worth trying to probe Fran about the implications of the solicitors' letter but it was difficult to get any straight answer out of her regarding the Musgraves. She would have asked Dora, but she was presiding over a meeting of the Linton and District Agricultural Show committee, which had recently elected her chairman in a late but cunning attempt to put an end to her winning streak in the horticulture sections.

Hannah had a pot of tea ready when Fran returned and a plate of toasted sandwiches, but her mother was even less chatty than usual, and failed to rise to Hannah's conversational bait. Hannah wondered if the mysterious test results had come from the hospital, but Fran's expression didn't invite enquiry. When Hannah made a few half-hearted attempts, she bit them off.

Consequently, it seemed easier to ask about the Musgraves.

'When did Louise Graham-Potter move in with Faith and Constance?' she asked.

If she was surprised by the question, Fran didn't show it. Her eyes barely moved from the local newspaper, open beside her plate. 'She's always lived there, I think.'

'But since when?' Hannah persisted. 'What about her parents? Or her husband? Mrs Tyson said something about her being orphaned.'

Fran put down her knife and fork. In the Marshall household this was a sign of deep thought. 'I think she *was* orphaned young, now you mention it,' she said. 'There might have been a car or train accident. Her family had worked for the Musgraves, I think, in the past and she was always friends with Constance. There would certainly be enough room for her in that house. And, God knows, they could afford a little generosity. You should ask your grandmother, but I can't guarantee she'll know either. Louise is terribly private about those kind of things.'

'So would all Mrs Graham-Potter's affairs be managed by the Musgrave's solicitor?' Hannah asked. 'I mean, would they have made all their arrangements for university together?' she added as artlessly as possible.

Fran was chewing, and making fierce tutting noises at the editorial column, which meant that her brain was now engaged with the council's fight against mandatory parking charges. 'Yes, I suppose so.'

And aside from another reprise of 'Don't Let Life Pass You By In Linton' that was the end of the conversation.

The next day, Hannah sat on the dressing-table stool and noted down details of the hunting scenes in Constance's bedroom, having first established that Mrs Graham-Potter was taking tea in the drawing room with Dora and wouldn't disturb her. Her mind wandered to the conversation she'd had on the Ramble Way with her mother. Conversations with Fran were like treacherous coastlines: the stiller the water seemed on the surface, the more rocks and becalming reefs were hidden underneath. Hannah tried to see into her mother's mind but, to her mild shame, all she kept coming to were the little criticisms of herself, which lingered in her mind, like burrs. It might not have registered with Fran, but her casual dismissal of Hannah's precious sense of place hadn't had the bracing mental effect she'd intended: rather, it had plunged her into another maze of self-examination, with frustrating secrets and silences at every turn.

Did she have a real spiritual bond with the place, Hannah wondered, or was she just borrowing the faded glory of the town's history to supplement the warm sense of belonging that anyone else would find in their own family tree?

Hannah didn't like the implication of that. It wasn't her fault the family tree had odd, sawn-off branches.

She sat on the lumpy bed with her notebook, and stared out of the window. After Samuel's death, Constance could have picked any room, and yet she'd kept this one, with its good view of St Peter's steeple. She'd certainly chosen a bed that was only one step above sleeping on sack-cloth and ashes. One night in this, thought Hannah, shifting uncomfortably, and you'd definitely be on your knees, most likely at the chiropractor's.

She couldn't imagine her grandmother or the Musgrave sisters worrying about what they should do with their lives – as if having a degree and not using it was a criminal offence. What *had* they done? Come back from Cambridge, part of a tiny, revolutionary elite of women graduates and got on with raising Dora.

If, of course, they *had* all gone to Cambridge.

Hannah sighed and stared out of the window to the church. It must have been easier, in some respects, when there were clear rules for good and bad behaviour, and indiscretions could be wiped away with regular church attendance.

Constance had been good, everyone agreed on that. Faith had

been less good, stroppy even, but her relentless improving seemed to have balanced that out.

Hannah's eye fell on Constance's Bible, where she had left it on its table. A money spider was crawling over the metal binding.

St Peter's, Linton's Anglican church, stood back from the smart Georgian high street, near Rissini's and opposite the town bookshop. It was solid and squat, made with stone from the nearby quarry, decorated with maritime motifs in recognition of the industry that had paid for it. Thanks to the determined efforts of the church maintenance committee, pink and orange flowers blazed from sculpted beds year-round, even in the face of Linton's hostile weather – helped by the criminal element of the population: most magistrates were also associated with the town council so the majority of community-service orders sentenced local ne'er-do-wells to several hours of intense gardening.

Hannah could hear a confirmation class winding up as she approached and redirected her steps to the back of the church so that she could wander through the graveyard before she went in. There was something satisfyingly morbid about the heavy collection of mossy tombs and Victorian angels. The sense of forgotten misery appealed to her current frame of mind.

St Peter's limited graveyard space was filled with the imposing tombs of Linton's merchant families, who had been savvy enough to pay up-front for eternal grave space in the eighteenth century. Everyone else was buried in the overflow graveyard on the other side of town.

The Musgraves, naturally, had a memorial tomb, which Hannah now inspected. Few of the senior Musgraves actually lay in it – they had been buried in London – but their presence was felt on huge marble slabs. John and Sarah Musgrave were the first incumbents, dying in 1738 and 1757 respectively, and were followed by a series of offspring bearing confusingly similar names. A whole side appeared to have been devoted to Musgraves killed in battle, of which there were many.

Constance's was the last name to have been carved into the stone, beneath Faith's; in an eerie display of foresight, John and Sarah Musgrave seemed to have judged precisely the space needed to contain their dynasty.

Hannah lingered among the child graves, all mossy angels and grieving stone terriers, then, hearing the class filtering out into the street, she turned back and pushed open the side door into the church.

Inside it smelt of polish, in the same way that Catholic churches smelt of incense: the heavy oak pews, shining brass and parquet foyer gave the parish ladies something to do when they weren't scouring their own homes with religious fervour.

Hannah walked down the side aisle, trying not to let her boots make loud clicking noises on the metal memorial tablets that paved the floor. Already, she could feel calm seeping into her brain as the bustle of the high street receded.

St Peter's was bigger and more ornate than she remembered. She admired the quiet dignity of the solid pillars holding up the fanned ceiling, and felt a little guilty that she'd never visited it much after her own confirmation classes. The windows were particularly beautiful; high, pointed Gothic arches filled with jewel-bright glass pictures. Like the station, the civic hall and the library, the church windows had been ostentatiously sponsored – not, however, by local tradesmen eager for new business but by the smarter families, canny enough to buy recognition in this world and the next at the same time, and thereby getting excellent value for money.

Hannah's eye went automatically to the biggest and most elaborate window. As she had guessed, it had been placed there by the Joseph Musgrave, Faith and Constance's grandfather, in memory of his own father, whose excellence was described in a Latin inscription on a wall plaque nearby.

The stained glass had been cleverly designed to make the most of weak light, with expense no object: rich crimson and indigo panels made the window glow with imperial importance. When she got up close, Hannah saw that part of it depicted St Patrick leading the snakes into the water – a tribute, she guessed, to the thousands of tons of Linton coal exported to Ireland, which had made the Musgraves' fortune. Her gaze on the coiling black snakes, slithering into the aquamarine water, she thought of what Mrs Tyson's Lizzy had seen in Joseph Musgrave's room, and shuddered.

What good were the most devout windows in the church if no one had a kind word to say for you after you'd gone? she wondered. But then again, once the gossips had gone, and their stories with them, there was only your version left, if you took care to make it permanent.

Hannah slipped into a pew half-way down the nave and positioned herself carefully on an embroidered kneeler, provided by the local Women's Guild. It was designed for devotion rather than comfort, and could only have been less comfortable if it had had spikes. She stared up at the large rose window above the altar and tried to empty her mind to make room for divine guidance.

She concentrated on the colours in the glass.

So.

The distant sound of traffic crept into her consciousness as her ears adjusted to the silence.

She waited patiently for a message to filter through the ether to her.

Nothing.

She tried reciting the Lord's Prayer in her head, coming unstuck half-way through as usual, and panicked that maybe if you didn't say it right, it didn't count. She followed that up with a quick extempore prayer about how sorry she was to have let everyone down, and how much she would appreciate some suggestions as to what she should do next.

After about ten minutes in which the numbness of her knees made it difficult for her to keep her mind clear, Hannah thought she could detect a mild sense of divine disapproval, but it turned out to be one of the church ladies coming in with new flowers for the altarpiece.

She gave it another five minutes, then decided to go to the Coffee Pot for a cappuccino. On her way out, she dropped some change into the roof-fund box, and guiltily lit a candle for her mother's malady.

'Where did you get to today, then?' Fran stepped back from the stove to pour the soup into two bowls. She did it with grim fairness, dividing up the chunks of vegetable equally. She had correctly identified it as 'fancy' soup. Hannah had bought it and left it in the fridge: Fran wasn't letting her contribute to the housekeeping in case it set up any expectations about her staying, but Hannah was starting to miss proper food.

'I spent the morning up at the villa, finishing off Constance's room. I hadn't realized there were so many little prints and things in the corridors. There's so much stuff you don't even notice. It's going to take ages.'

Her mother put the soup in front of her. 'The amount of clutter in that house,' she said, helping herself to bread. 'It was OK when there was an army of servants to clear up after those three, but now! Poor Irma Tyson. I'm sure Louise doesn't pay her enough.'

Hannah stirred her soup and wondered how Fran would take a suggestion about *crème fraîche*. With extreme resentment, no doubt. 'I went to the church as well, this morning,' she said.

Fran paused with her spoon half-way to her mouth. 'Why?'

'I wanted a bit of spiritual guidance,' said Hannah.

Fran rolled her eyes. 'I thought we agreed that the institution of religion is just a way of keeping the lower classes subjugated and breeding regularly. Didn't we teach you that at home?'

'No,' said Hannah. '*You* said that. Dad wasn't so sure.'

'Yes, but your father wasn't so sure about anything, as it turns out, was he?'

Hannah clenched her jaw. She didn't want to have a big theological discussion, and if her mother thought part of the coming-home deal was to provide her with an ethical-argument partner it would be kinder to set her straight right now. 'Mum, I just wanted somewhere quiet to think.'

'You went there hoping for some kind of answer, didn't you?' asked Fran, with a shrewd look.

Hannah blushed.

'Don't feel bad about it.' Fran blew on her soup. 'That's why ninety-nine per cent of believers go. It's like the National Lottery – they go in the hope that this week will be the one in which the Virgin Mary appears and tells them the password to eternal life.'

'You're very cynical.'

'Not as cynical as some. And I need to be, in my line of work.'

They ate their soup in reasonably companionable silence while Fran listened to the local news, and Hannah flicked through the evening paper.

'Anyway,' said Hannah, once the travel reports started, '*you* were the one who went to the spiritualist church. That's *much* worse than going to St Peter's for a bit of light meditation.'

'Is it?' Fran's expression was, if not shifty, then at least ambiguous.

'Well, yes. It's all jiggery-pokery.' Hannah widened her eyes with shock at hearing herself use such a classic Linton expression. God, it was a slippery slope. Another week and she'd be tearing into Nick Hornby with the book-group ladies.

'That depends on how you look at it,' said Fran calmly. 'It's not completely different – both believe in the afterlife but with the spiritualists you get some kind of evidence. Feedback.'

'When was the last time you went?' asked Hannah.

Fran spread some low-fat Flora on her bread. 'I can't remember. Years ago.'

For some reason, Hannah didn't believe her. 'Will you take me? As part of my search for inner peace?'

Fran thought about it. 'OK,' she said, finally. 'If it'll get you sorted out and back to London and a proper life.'

A few days passed in which Fran might have changed her mind, but she didn't. She would still have gone even if she had changed her mind: she wasn't the sort of person to go back on an agreement once it was made, even if it revealed itself subsequently to have been a bad idea.

The Linton Spiritualist Church held services twice a week, scheduled to fit in between *Countdown* and *Coronation Street* and allow time to get the tea on. Unlike St Peter's stolid high street presence, it was almost hidden, at the far end of the market-place between an old temperance hall, now derelict, and a fishmonger.

'Is this it?' asked Hannah. She peered at the dusty glass-fronted noticeboard, which was advertising a bring and buy three weeks previously and the funeral arrangements for two regular attendees. Both events seemed to be taking place at St Bride's Catholic Church.

Hannah wasn't sure what she'd expected from a spiritualist church, but she'd hoped for something a bit more dramatic than a Scout hut.

'Well, you don't want to make too much of a show, do you?' said Fran, defensively.

'I didn't think that was a problem for the kind of folk who go to spiritualists,' said Hannah. 'I thought that was the whole point. At least in *church* the vicar keeps quiet about what your dead rellies think you should be doing with your life.'

'Don't be smart,' snapped Fran, and pushed open the door.

If Hannah had been hoping the drab exterior might hide a magical cornucopia of mysticism on the inside, she was disappointed. A half-hearted attempt had been made to jolly up the drab interior with mother-in-law's tongue plants on the window-sills, but any cheery effect was counteracted by the curling first-aid posters instructing bystanders on what to do in the event of heart-attacks, choking or animal bites.

'The spiritualists share it with the St John's Ambulance Brigade,' explained Fran, 'alternate Mondays and Fridays.'

'Maybe we've been misunderstanding all these years, and the real congregation is from the Other Side and they're here already, packed in to the rafters just waiting to get in touch with us.'

Fran gave her a look. 'All right, so maybe some of it's a load of tosh, but don't forget this is very important to a lot of other people.'

Their voices were loud in the empty hall.

'All right, all right,' said Hannah. 'Just trying to lighten the tone.'

'Just like your grandmother. No idea when to be serious,' Fran muttered.

Hannah thought Fran was rather tense for someone who thought maybe it was all a load of tosh. 'Shall we sit down,' she asked, 'or are there are specially designated chairs? Maybe we'd be sitting in the medium's chair without realizing and start transmitting, like a radio that— OK, sorry, I didn't mean . . .'

The door creaked and rattled, and Mrs Jordan from the post office peered in. She was wearing a turban.

'Hello, Mrs Jordan,' said Fran, briskly.

Mrs Jordan looked surprised to see them standing there. 'Oh, hello, Fran. Hello, Hannah. I didn't know . . . I thought that . . .'

Fran smiled encouragingly but didn't say anything to help her out. Mrs Jordan inched her way into the hall rather self-consciously.

'How are you getting on, Hannah? I heard you were doing a little job for Mrs Graham-Potter,' Mrs Jordan began, with a certain delicacy. 'Was it Faith's artworks you were looking at? It's always been said that there are some very valuable paintings up there . . .'

'That's right,' said Hannah, as Fran aimed a none-too-subtle nudge at her arm.

'I'm sure it's nothing that Mrs Graham-Potter wants discussed,' said Fran. 'For insurance reasons, if nothing else.'

Mrs Jordan looked shocked at the very idea. 'Oh, of course not!'

Hannah swung round to see where this sudden vehemence had come from – when Fran had stormed in from court that afternoon, the Hillcrest art collection had been 'nothing more than a pile of old junk'. Hannah had noticed she had a habit of taking swipes at the Musgraves in the privacy of her own home (built by them for Fran's mother), but defending them as primly as Dora in public.

The door opened again, and a few more village ladies came in. Hannah didn't recognize them, but Fran smiled politely.

At that point, a door at the back of the hall opened and three women emerged in a silent line.

Mrs Jordan quivered with anticipation.

'Mrs Hartley,' muttered Fran, 'from the Grange. She taught domestic science at the old girls' school. And Miss Rouse. Her companion.'

'Mm,' said Hannah, none the wiser. Her attention had been taken by the woman with them. Her skirt was a dramatic purple tweed, which indicated she probably wasn't from Linton. At last, she thought, someone who looked like she might be in touch with the other side.

'We'll sit down,' said Fran, and steered Hannah firmly towards the end of a row of chairs.

'Now, listen,' she hissed, as more old women started to slide into the hall, 'don't say anything, don't make fun, and don't ask stupid questions. Don't do *anything* to attract attention to yourself.'

'Why?' asked Hannah. 'Are you worried about hearing unsavoury details about Granny from Poor Arthur? Do you think the worm might turn now he's safely on the other side?'

Fran's face twisted as if she'd swallowed something unpleasant. 'No, I'm just . . . Oh, forget it,' she said, and sank back in her chair. 'Just don't show me up. And switch off your mobile phone.'

On the small platform, Mrs Hartley and Miss Rouse were bustling about, arranging some kind of altarpiece. Hannah stopping inspecting her mother's stony face for clues and looked instead at the gorgeously enamelled triptych the ladies were unfolding on the table. It was highly incongruous in the drab setting: peacock blue, gold, and mother-of-pearl haloes. Clearly someone with a bit of money had believed in adding some mystery to the Scout hut.

'Mum, is that . . . ?' Hannah began, but Fran nudged her to shut up.

Mrs Woodward from the dispensary, warmly wrapped in a hand-knitted scarf and beret combination, slipped into the seat behind them.

'Hello, Fran. Hello, Hannah,' she mouthed, and settled herself back, ready to absorb information like a journalist at a press conference.

Behind them, the door closed and Hannah thought she heard the faint clink of a lock. Or it might have been the latch.

Mrs Hartley coughed modestly and spread out her hands in welcome to the hall. Hannah wished Fran hadn't told her she was a domestic-science teacher. 'Welcome, one and all, to Linton

Spiritualist Church. Tonight we're very lucky to have an old friend with us . . .'

'I thought that was the whole point,' muttered Hannah, and got another sharp nudge.

Mrs Hartley waved her hand expansively towards the woman on her left. 'Mavis Todhunter, who's come all the way from Spennymoor.'

A murmur of approval went round the group, as Mavis Todhunter raised a beringed hand. Hannah recognized the murmur as an indication that some real mediumship would be in evidence: anyone born within a five-mile radius of the town would know the ins and outs of the families already, without the need for any spirit assistance.

'First, though, let us sing hymn number nine, "God Who Sees and Does Not Speak".'

'That could have been your grandfather's theme tune,' muttered Fran, as everyone shuffled to their feet.

Miss Rouse, seated at Mrs Hartley's right with her knees close together, reached down and pressed play on her tape-recorder. After a momentary skirl of tape noise (possibly the end of the previous hymn) a Bontempi organ blared out with a series of notes that sounded as though they were being played at random.

Hannah did not know the tune or the words, but her mother was singing with gusto.

'"God who sees and does not speak, Smite the vain and cheer the weak,"' bellowed Fran. '"Halt us in our selfish ways, Shake us on our idle days."'

Hannah realized that it was years since she'd heard her mother sing. She had a pleasant voice, strong and confident. As she attempted to follow the vagaries of the tune, her gaze moved discreetly around the room. There must have been thirty-five women in there – where had they come from? – all dressed in the aubergine and moss green uniform of the local over-fifties. Most of them were wearing hats. Two had brought their knitting, one had a huge cassette recorder on her knee, and all wore a hungry, hopeful look that perhaps secrets might now be revealed.

Suddenly Miss Rouse bent down and stopped the tape-recorder. 'Actually, I think that was "Be My Torchlight in the Dark",' she said, to no one in particular.

'Without further ado, I'd like to get on to the main event of the evening,' said Mrs Hartley. 'Mavis will lead us in a short prayer, and give us a brief talk on some of the illuminating messages from the beyond to those who have not yet passed over. Then there will be a display of mediumship and she will answer any questions you may have.'

Purple tweed skirt aside, Mavis Todhunter wasn't how Hannah had imagined a medium. There were no flowing robes, no turbans (unlike much of her audience), not even a jazzy sweatshirt to demonstrate her otherness. On closer inspection, Mavis looked like a smartly dressed farmer's wife, albeit one with more makeup than normal.

The congregation lurched painfully to its knees for the prayer and sat impatiently through the talk. Then it assumed a grave air of religious solemnity to disguise its palpable lust for gossip.

'We ask spirit to come among us tonight and share our thoughts and hopes . . . fears and expectations . . .' Mavis lifted her arms so that the loose sleeves of her blouse fell back, revealing a man's watch on her chunky wrist.

A frisson of anticipation ran through the congregation.

'Ooh, no . . . Not you . . . What?' muttered Mavis, apparently to someone standing just behind her left shoulder. 'I'm getting someone,' she announced. 'It's a man . . . called Jack.'

At least five women let out sighs of anguished delight.

'*Jack*. Get away,' said Fran, under her breath, but Hannah could see her eyes were gleaming with fascination.

'It's for you, dear,' said Mavis, bearing down on Mrs Jordan.

'But I don't know anyone called Jack,' she protested guiltily.

'Are you sure now?' Mavis circled her left index finger round her left palm as if she were trying to remove a stubborn stain.

'Yes!'

'Well, he knows you.'

A prurient murmur ran round the hall.

'I can't think why!' stammered Mrs Jordan.

'He says he was a mate of your dad's. Down the Samson Pit.'

Mrs Jordan's face creased as she tried to remember someone called Jack who might or might not have known her father in the two years he worked in the mine before a startled pit pony broke both his legs and effectively retired him to the post office and permanent marital warfare.

'Jack . . . Bragg?' she hazarded, as if politely trying to guess the name of an unexpected party guest.

Mavis closed her eyes and rotated her head. 'Is it? Is it? Yes, it is. He's saying something about a dog, and that they're very happy now.'

Mrs Jordan's worried face brightened under her turban. 'Are they?' she asked hesitantly. 'Are they really?'

'Aye,' nodded Mavis. Then conceded, 'Well, as much as can be expected, like.'

Mrs Jordan clasped her hands over her handbag and sat back dazed in her chair. 'No one's ever come through for me before,' she said, forgetting to be solemn and religious. A sudden thought struck her. 'Does this Jack Bragg lad know what happened to that tea-caddy Mother said she left the keys to her jewellery box in?'

Mavis clapped her palms to her face, and mumbled over her left shoulder again. 'No,' she said eventually. 'Sorry, love. He's gone, like.'

'Fancy,' observed Mrs Woodward acidly.

'There's someone else here, though.' Mavis squeezed her eyes shut. 'It's another man . . . called Bill.'

Another round of gasps.

'Oh, for God's sake,' muttered Hannah. 'Bill! Half the men round here were called Bill. She's not making it hard for herself, is she?'

'*Well*,' hissed Fran, 'who were you expecting? Winston Churchill coming through to say what a nice job they're making of the harbour redevelopment?'

Bill, it turned out, was there for one of the middle-aged ladies sitting at the back with her sister. He'd been a foreman on the docks but rather than being killed by falling off the ladder while dead drunk, as had always been thought, the ladder had collapsed while he was climbing it dead drunk. 'You might want to look into that,' advised Mavis, her watery blue eyes taking on a more practical focus. 'There might be something in it, he says. Negligence.'

'Good to know the Linton compensation culture continues from beyond the grave,' muttered Fran.

Several more manifestations followed, mainly men to reassure widows that they were happy and not going hungry, some with opaque messages about 'getting to the truth' that had Mrs Woodward's knee twitching with curiosity.

Then, as Hannah had resigned herself to spiritualism being a mildly spooky version of the book group, the atmosphere abruptly changed. The air felt heavy around her, and she felt unaccountably nervous. She looked round, wondering if anyone else had felt it.

Mavis's eyes snapped open and she stopped swaying, casting worried glances instead to every corner of the room.

Hot water trickling through the ancient central heating was audible in the silence. Every eye was fixed directly ahead, at the three figures on the platform. Behind them the bright enamel on the triptych glowed intensely in the gloom.

'Come forward,' said Mavis bravely. 'Who have you come to speak to?'

There was a terrible pause in which Hannah half expected to hear a voice booming out from behind them, or a series of scurrying whispers. Unconsciously she clutched Fran's arm.

Mavis appeared to be listening, and didn't relay what she was hearing, as she had with the parade of Bills and Johns and Jacks. She looked as if she were being told off by a teacher. Once or twice she flinched and put a hand to her throat as if she were choking. Then she pressed her lips together and shut her eyes, then opened them slowly. Hannah felt Fran's arm shake and realized that Mavis's gaze was coming to rest on them. Her heart pounded in her chest.

'I don't know your name, love . . .' said Mavis, haltingly, then winced as if someone was shouting in her ear. 'Hannah. Is it Hannah?'

Hannah was scared now, barely able to breathe.

'I'm getting someone for you, dear. I'm getting the name – Bert? Does that mean anything to you?'

'No,' croaked Hannah. Her mouth was dry and her pulse was beating high up in her throat. Suddenly she felt scared, ashamed of doubting.

'He's talking about his daughter. He's unhappy about something that happened to his daughter while he was down in that pit.' Mavis shook her head. 'Now, is that your grandmother, maybe? I'm getting the name . . . Mary? No, Molly. He's very angry about something that happened to her, something that he couldn't stop. He's angry with himself and he's angry with . . . Samuel? Does that mean anything?'

Fran's hand gripped hers so tightly that Hannah could feel her rings digging into her fingers. 'No,' she whispered.

'Ooh,' said Mrs Todhunter, almost to herself. 'I feel like I'm in the dark, I can hear water all round me. Now, something about his daughter. I'm getting a big house, a big dark house, not round here, though, in London. And I'm getting the name Eagle – an Eagle Street? Does that mean anything to you?'

No, thought Hannah, gritting her teeth to stop them chattering. Sorry, she wanted to say, sorry, sorry, sorry. She didn't know why.

'He says you've to ask yourself questions.' Mavis's face creased with effort. 'He says something about faith. You've to have faith? Is that it?' She went quiet. She was swaying now. 'I can't . . . I'm getting the image of a fire? Very hot. Very . . .' Her swaying intensified and she sat down with a bump on the chair nearest Mrs Woodward.

Gradually, Hannah felt the air clear around her. She breathed in and out deliberately to calm herself.

'That's it.' Mavis put her hands to her head and let out a long sigh. There was a sheen of sweat on her forehead and upper lip, and damp patches on her blouse. She was exhausted. 'What was it like? Did it ring any bells?'

'Well,' murmured Mrs Woodward automatically, but without her usual brio.

No one else dared speak. The atmosphere was thick with nerves.

On the platform, Miss Rouse and Mrs Hartley sat still and waxy white with shock. They looked exactly like the tweed-clad dummies in Jean's Fashions on the high street.

Hannah's legs twitched with the need to get up and run around, yet her whole body was paralysed. This must be how the women had felt when they heard about the collapse in the mine, she thought, and immediately wondered where it had come from.

Hannah was aware of movement next to her. To her surprise, Fran rose and marched to the front, the heels of her court shoes clicking briskly on the sprung floor of the hall. She watched in dumb amazement, much like the rest of the women, as her mother seized the flailing attention of the group and pulled it smartly back into the realms of sensible committee procedure.

'Thank you, Mrs Todhunter, for an interesting display of mediumship.' Fran took the woman's clammy hand and half turned to the congregation. 'I'm sure everyone here will join me in a round of applause, and we do hope that your journey back to Spennymoor will be a safe one. Hannah, put the urn on.'

There was a smattering of applause.

All eyes in the hall swivelled from Fran to Hannah, but for once Hannah didn't notice. She stood up, knees almost buckling, and made her way to the trestle with the cups on it. She switched on the urn and ate three custard creams in one go, crumbs spilling down her jumper.

Murmurs of muted library conversation sprang up like little waves.

Hannah heard the court shoes approach the tea table, and smelt her mother's light cologne. 'Why did you do that?' she asked, under her breath.

'Do what?' Fran was glaring at the urn.

'Stand up like that. In front of everyone. Poor Miss Rouse looked like she was going to burst into tears.'

'Someone has to, Hannah. We can't all wait for someone else to take charge. There, it's boiling.'

Hannah flipped the tap on the urn and made tea with shaking hands. This triggered a Pavlovian reaction in the women and an orderly queue formed at the other end of the trestle. Not, Hannah noticed, too close to her and Fran.

'Can you explain any of what she said?' she asked, in a low voice, before Mrs Woodward could get close enough to earwig.

'Some of it,' said Fran. Her lips were a tight red line. 'Not all. Cuthbert Fisher was Matthew Fisher's father. He was killed in that pit collapse. I assume all that was about Molly Fisher getting pregnant while she was working up at the villa. Probably thought Faith should have done something about it. But you can't believe everything you hear at these things. I've no idea about that house, for instance. They just guess half the time.'

Hannah stared at her mother in amazement.

'Don't mention this to your grandmother,' said Fran quickly, before Hannah could say anything. 'She doesn't need to know. There's nothing she can tell you, and even if she could, she'd just say some things are best left in the past where they belong. God knows, she's refused to give me more salient information than that over the years.'

Mrs Todhunter was still sitting on the platform when Hannah took her tea over. 'Thanks, love,' she said absently, without removing her hand from her forehead. 'You know I don't like to – to say negative things, or pass on frightening news, but sometimes . . .' She rubbed her eyes. 'That came through very strong.'

Hannah wasn't sure what to say. Her curiosity was securely matched by outright fear.

Mavis drank some tea, and grabbed Hannah's upper arm. 'Listen, love,' she said, urgently, 'you be careful.'

'About what?' asked Hannah.

Mavis gazed at her for a few charged moments. For the first time since she had come to Linton, Hannah felt conscious of problems beyond her abilities, and felt cold inside.

'It's all very well digging in your family tree,' said Mavis, 'but people bury the past for a reason. I've seen it before. Remember that.'

'Aye,' said Hannah, then corrected herself. 'Er, yes. Yes, I will.'

'I didn't want to say, in front of your mother,' added Mrs Todhunter, 'but you're not happy, am I right?'

'Um, I don't know what you mean.'

Mrs Todhunter gave her a friendly look. 'Be true to yourself, pet. You'll never be happy unless you're true to yourself.'

'Is someone telling you that?' demanded Hannah. 'Or is that just you?'

Mrs Todhunter blinked. 'That's just me. Now, is there another cup of tea? I feel quite refreshed.'

Without a word, Hannah went back to the urn, her head full of questions she didn't want to think for fear of having them answered.

Chapter Eighteen

'Who on earth chose *Lady Chatterley's Lover*?' asked Hannah, as she negotiated her way over the Linton roundabout *en route* to Mrs Hind's house. During rush-hour, the streams of early-morning traffic, meshing into each other on autopilot, made the roundabout run like a watermill; outside rush-hour when Linton's army of elderly women emerged to go about their leisurely business in brand-new hatchbacks, it wasn't easy to get across: politeness seemed to take precedence over the Highway Code.

'No, it's *you* first. You've got *priority*,' mouthed Hannah, flashing her lights at the two old ladies in the blue Polo, who were letting her out.

They flashed back and smiled.

'Oh, I don't remember who chose it. Didn't we escape before they went through the rota? Mrs Cowper, I'd say. It's her brand of salaciousness disguised as classic fiction.' Dora was gazing out of the window and running a finger over her lipstick.

'I'd have thought *Lady Chatterley* was rather racy for the book group.' Hannah accelerated to get on to the roundabout and narrowly missed a tractor taking the inside line past the polite old ladies.

'Darling, it's the only book they haven't all had to go out and buy, believe me. It's on their bookshelves, even if it's turned the wrong way round. Take the back road up to Judy Hind's. You don't want to get stuck behind all these doddering old women.'

Hannah indicated left and accelerated up the coast road, which had originally been built to link the farms on the outskirts of Linton with the harbour and market. It had been barely used since the new bypass swept traffic straight into the centre. Despite Linton's Georgian urbanity, the harshness of the northern countryside began almost immediately outside the town, with sturdy Herdwick sheep dotting the hillside. Hannah hadn't been along here since Dora had taken her pony-riding on the fells, and now she had odd little flutters of *déjà vu*, passing smart out-of-town Victorian doctors' houses and crooked trees she'd last seen as a child. Little had changed.

Judy Hind lived in the hamlet of Nether Linton in an old stone farmhouse down a narrow lane between fields full of cows on one side and sheep on the other. The road was liberally scattered with cowpats and sheep droppings.

'Can we leave before it gets dark, please?' asked Hannah, as the MG bumped and rattled its way over the uneven track. 'I don't fancy reversing down here and meeting a tractor coming the other way.'

'Oh, you should do what I do and just shout out of your window that your reverse gear is broken,' said Dora. 'Most farmers round here don't mind reversing for a lady, I find. Now, can you get me as near as possible to the door? I don't want to ruin my shoes.'

Hannah dropped Dora off at the stone front steps, then drove round to the back of the house, where a previous Hind had thoughtfully tarmacked over a large section of garden to provide better access for farm vehicles. She parked next to a Land Rover – leaving a cautious space between.

Dora was waiting for her at the front door with her handbag under her arm. She was smacking her lips in a manner that suggested she'd just reapplied her lipstick. 'Are you fit?' she asked, grinning fiendishly so that Hannah could confirm she didn't have lipstick on her teeth.

Hannah nodded, trying to remember the last time she'd worn lipstick. It seemed like a long time ago. 'Um, the book-group ladies – they do understand that I'm not back for good, don't they? I mean, you have made it clear that I'll be going back to civilization at some point?'

Dora gave her a funny look. 'But you keep telling your mother that you're quite happy to stay here for ever.'

'Well, that's what I tell *her*,' Hannah said. 'I don't necessarily want this lot to think that.'

'You're a funny one,' said Dora.

'You know where I get it from,' said Hannah, and gave the prehistoric doorbell a decisive prod. Somewhere deep in the house a buzzer sounded.

The door opened wide. Mrs Hind's square figure almost filled the space, like an animated wardrobe draped in heather tweed.

'Dora! Hannah!' she exclaimed. 'Jolly nice to see you both! Thought I was going to be stuck with Kathleen Cowper and her Hettie!' This last comment was delivered in an aside – but one designed to be heard at the back of Linton Memorial Theatre.

'Hello, Judy,' said Dora.

'Hello, Mrs Hind,' said Hannah.

'Well, come on in.' Mrs Hind swung the door open and they squeezed past her into the hall, where various flats from the theatre were propped up against the wall, leaving the standard farmhouse arrangement of Lakeland prints and walking sticks on the left side, and the red-light district of Venice on the right.

'We're just having a cup of tea while everyone arrives.' Mrs Hind extended a dramatic arm. 'Do go on into the sitting room and join the fray.'

'Too kind,' murmured Dora.

The Cowper sisters were sitting on the sofa in front of a roaring fire. Kathleen had a pile of notes and the *Linton Chronicle* on her knee; Hettie appeared to have shrunk further into herself, and was wearing several layers of clothes, topped off with a purple knitted hat that bulged in odd places, as though she was hiding things under it.

'Hello, ladies,' said Dora, in her most charming voice. 'How are you keeping in this cold weather?'

'I'm fair frizz,' said Hettie. 'It's starving out.'

Hannah wasn't sure there was a conversational response to that.

'Now, then,' said Mrs Hind, steaming in with pots of tea and coffee. 'Who's for tea or coffee, and who's for something stronger? Dora?'

'I'll have a black coffee, thank you, Judy.' Dora had settled herself into the nicest chair by the hearth, with her old copy of *Lady Chatterley* on her knee. Hannah knew it was a first edition, because Dora had shown it to her when she was little. Faith, apparently, had been friendly with its publisher, who'd sent her a copy.

'Hannah?'

'Tea, please.' She held up a china mug. 'It doesn't taste the same in London,' she added, diplomatically. 'The water's been through the system too many times!'

Mrs Cowper shuddered daintily, but Hettie let out a throaty chuckle.

'Is there any milk, please?' asked Hannah.

'Oh, damnation! Isn't there always something you forget?' said Mrs Hind, jovially, as if she were about to break into song.

'Hannah'll go and get it, won't you, darling?' said Dora.

'The milk's in the larder, dear,' bellowed Mrs Hind. 'The larder? It's the door in the kitchen that doesn't appear to lead anywhere. Chop-chop! Everyone will be arriving soon! Don't want to keep Janet Jordan from her cup of tea.'

Reluctantly, Hannah left the warm circle of the fire and went back into the hall, down the narrow passage that led to the kitchen. There wasn't much sign of Mr Hind in the house: he reared sheep and goats for cheese and milk, and kept himself to himself. Only the odd pair of enormous Y-fronts drying on the radiators gave away his presence.

She went down a little flight of steps into the kitchen: a stone-flagged, worn pine affair, which most of Wandsworth was trying to create, albeit without the strong smell of sheepdog and the piles of *Linton Gazette*s to keep out the draughts. Mrs Hind's kitchen was the warmest place in the house: a big green Aga pulsated with heat in the corner, with an earthenware bowl of bread dough on one hot-plate cover and a huge ginger cat curled up on a tea-towel on the other. Both were rising gently.

Hannah lifted the black iron latch and went into the larder. It was colder than most domestic fridges and about twenty feet long. Mrs Hind was a keen baker when she wasn't murdering Gilbert and Sullivan operettas, and the high shelves were lined with rows of jam-jars and old Coronation biscuit tins going rusty round the bottom. Some still bore entry stickers from the local agricultural show, or were marked 'Honey Fruit' or 'Cherry Plain' in confident capitals.

Hannah's mouth watered. Throughout her childhood, she'd wished that Fran was more of a home cook. Constant exposure to boarding-school stories had made her something of an expert on tuck-boxes, and she dreamed of midnight feasts – opening studded trunks and handing out jam tarts, jars of honey, and tins of homemade ginger snaps that would win her instant friendship and devotion. Organic flapjacks didn't win any friends, not the way Fran made them. They were always the last things to go at the harvest-festival sale.

Hannah wondered if Mrs Hind had anything in the tins at the moment. She had overslept and hadn't had time for any breakfast, then missed lunch, as Dora swept in, hat on and car keys jingling, at half past one. A rumbling stomach, she reasoned, would only give the book group something to make nasty remarks about and, frankly, she wanted to put off discussing D.H. Lawrence's earthy approach to *al fresco* sex with them for as long as possible.

Carefully, so as not to make a noise, she eased the lid off a Lady Diana Spencer tin and the sweet smell of fresh pastry rushed out. There was just enough light coming through the ventilation holes in the door for Hannah to see that she was holding a tin of home-baked custard creams. Her favourites. She took two and put them on the side, then hastily took another. She put the lid back on and replaced the tin on the shelf. Better eat them here, she thought, and leaned against the wall.

Mrs Hind's custard creams deserved any prizes they won at Linton Show. They melted in the mouth. If they had a failing, Hannah conceded, it would be that you couldn't dunk them in your tea without leaving a visible slick of fat. And you couldn't easily eat more than two or three – so they were almost dieting biscuits.

As she was scraping off the filling on the second biscuit with her front teeth, Hannah heard the sound of sensible lace-up shoes approaching from the hall. She froze.

It was too late to sneak out, and from the muttering going on, a conversation was in progress.

'I think it's very odd.' That sounded like Mrs Jordan's timid voice, but unusually emphatic.

'What do you mean, Janet?'

Was that Mrs Kelly? Hannah leaned closer to the door.

'Well, I say Lola's got a nerve,' said Mrs Jordan.

'How do you mean?'

'Insisting on doing *Lady Chatterley*. With Dora here, and Hannah.'

Hannah thought it was considerate to think of her own innocence but a bit late to be worrying about Dora's.

'Oh, I don't know.' An audible sniff. 'There's far too much pussy-footing around that one as it is, if you ask me.'

Do they mean me? Hannah wondered, then realized that as far as this lot were concerned, there was only one She and that was Dora.

A pause. 'That's not like you, Pauline.'

'What do you mean by that?'

'Oh . . .' Hannah could almost hear Mrs Jordan blushing '. . . being catty. I'm sure no one wants to bring all that old gossip up again. I daresay poor Dora will be very embarrassed, and Hannah probably doesn't even know. I'm sure it never even occurred to Lola.'

There was a significant clatter, as though cups were being banged on to a tea tray with unnecessary vigour.

'And I've always doubted it myself.' Mrs Jordan's voice wavered. 'Faith Musgrave was such an upright woman . . .'

'Oh, Janet!' said Mrs Kelly.

Hannah could see the bright smile that always came on to disguise a vinegary dose of cattiness.

'Janet, handing out sweets to Sunday schools doesn't mean you're Mother Teresa! My nan had to go without her lunch for weeks so Mam had a new pair of shoes for Faith Musgrave's Christmas-homily tea party. Smart, they had to be, just to go to some sermon! Then at the end of telling them all only good girls got into heaven, that Faith Musgrave gave out Christmas treats like she was the queen. My mam never forgot it.' Audible sniff. 'Made her feel like a charity case. She promised my mother her children would never go.'

'But everyone went,' Mrs Jordan protested. 'My mother went too, and her sister used to be in service up at the house and—'

'My da always said that if it wasn't for him and his mates risking their lives down that pit for pennies, them Musgraves wouldn't have had a brass farthing to offer us at Christmas.'

'Oh, Pauline, now . . .'

'And all the time she was acting like she was setting us an example, there she was, carrying on like a common tart! No better than she should be!' Mrs Kelly had dropped her usual anodyne love-of-all-people tone. It was the first time Hannah had heard her have a specific opinion on anything outside the primary-school curriculum. 'So don't tell me what can and can't be discussed in front of Madam Dora!'

'Pauline!'

'She might act like she's the Queen Mother, but I wouldn't have had her upbringing for all the tea in China. All those men up and down at the house the whole time! You know what everyone used to say, don't you, about those parties they had? No wives invited. And the amount of—'

'Pauline! I don't think we should continue this conversation!'

There was some bad-tempered clattering.

Hannah fervently wished they *would* continue it. What on earth was it about?

'Now,' said Mrs Jordan, 'we'd better hurry up. I know Judy's keen to get finished before Bob comes in from the milking.'

In the pantry, Hannah listened as the footsteps faded away. Her eyes were now properly accustomed to the dark and she could see the rows of jugs hanging from hooks off the jam shelves. She took down a blue and white striped one and filled it with milk. To her surprise, her hands were trembling. What had they meant? What didn't they want to talk about in front of Dora – and her? Wasn't all that vitriol towards Faith bad enough?

Hannah wiped her mouth on the back of her hand to erase any tell-tale crumbs, but as she was pushing open the door of the larder, her eye fell on the custard-creams tin again. One more wouldn't hurt, she thought. To calm my nerves.

Just then, more footsteps approached down the kitchen steps and she was trapped again.

'. . . very good of you to think of making nibbles, but I knocked up a few biscuits last night, listening to *The Archers*.'

Oh, shit, thought Hannah. It was Mrs Hind come in search of the milk herself.

'It's no bother, Judy. I don't like to come empty-handed, as you know.'

Who was that? Hannah froze with half a biscuit in her mouth. It sounded like Mrs Woodward from the dispensary. What had she brought? A handful of anti-histamines? A Tupperware box of inhalers?

'I did want to have a quick word with you, in private, actually.' It *was* Mrs Woodward. She had a way of dropping her voice that made her sound discreet yet allowed her words to carry perfectly across the room.

'Good heavens! How mysterious! About what exactly?' boomed Mrs Hind.

'Well, I did wonder about today's novel for discussion.'

There was a long pause, in which Hannah assumed Mrs Woodward would be supplementing her remark with eye-rolling and nodding. She would have looked through one of the ventilation holes in the door, but didn't want to draw attention to her presence, covered, as she was, in biscuit crumbs. Anyway an eye at the hole would be hopelessly *Scooby-Doo*.

'Let the dog see the rabbit, Lola!' urged Mrs Hind.

'Excuse me?'

'Explain yourself, dear.'

'Well, as I say,' Mrs Woodward continued, with delicate reluctance, 'I chose *Lady Chatterley's Lover* when it looked as though Dora would be on holiday for this session.'

Long, meaningful pause.

'You've lost me.' Hannah was grateful for Mrs Hind's obtuseness, feigned or otherwise.

'You *know* what I mean . . .'

''Fraid I don't, dear.'

'The *Matt Fisher* business, Judy!' exploded Mrs Woodward. Her voice echoed round the kitchen. 'All that talk about Faith Musgrave keeping Matthew Fisher on as a gardener when really she was carrying on with him in that cottage.'

'Oh, that . . .'

What? thought Hannah, startled.

'With his wife barely cold in the ground! And him one of her father's miners too! Hardly what you'd call appropriate.'

There was another pause. It was clearly an issue that rankled with ladies of a certain age. So much for the sisterhood. Hannah sucked her biscuit, rather than crunching it.

'Oh, I see what you mean,' mused Mrs Hind. 'I suppose it is a bit D.H. Lawrence. Now you mention it, he did have an earthy quality. Very good-looking, all things considered. Always hoped he'd join the Amateurs. But that's all in the past, isn't it? I'm sure Dora wouldn't know anything about—'

'Well, that's just it.' Mrs Woodward was practically hissing with excitement. 'There's always been all that speculation about whether he and Faith . . . you know . . . and then Dora came along . . .'

Hannah nearly choked on her biscuit.

'Dearie me!' hooted Mrs Hind. 'You do read a lot of those dreadful paperback romances, Lola. I've never heard such nonsense in my life!'

'*Lots* of people think that.'

'Well, I'm not lots of people, and you shouldn't be either. I don't think Dora will give it another thought. Unless you carry on acting in this ridiculous cloak-and-dagger manner.'

Mrs Woodward sniffed. 'I'd have thought that you, of all people, would have had a little more imagination, Judy. These things often happen.'

'Not in Linton, dear.'

Hannah now felt sick, and indignant on Faith's behalf. Then she remembered the little sketch in Dora's loo, the naked woman getting out of the bath with delicious abandon – and none of the grandeur she associated with Faith Musgrave. That was surely one of Matthew Fisher's pictures, and it looked very much as if it had been painted from life.

A tingle ran over her.

'Did you see Hannah on your way in?' Mrs Hind was asking. 'I sent her to fetch the milk. The child must have got herself lost.'

Hannah panicked and nudged a couple of tins off a shelf.

'What was that?'

'Oh, rats, I dare say. We've been plagued with them since Ginger Tom had his balls off. I think he's turned effeminate.'

'No, there's something in your larder, Judy.'

'Do you think so, dear?' Mrs Hind's feet clumped towards the larder and, in desperation, Hannah shut her eyes and slid down the wall as if in a dead faint.

The door opened and strong light flooded in. She tried not to let her eyelids twitch too obviously.

'It's Hannah!' exclaimed Mrs Woodward.

A dark shadow fell over Hannah's face and she assumed that someone was leaning over her. It occurred to her that Mrs Hind might employ some forthright farming methods of first aid – a firm slap or, at best, the contents of the milk jug over her head – so to be on the safe side she creased her brow and murmured vaguely.

'Hannah? Hannah, dear!' A large hand applied itself to her brow. 'Are you all right?'

'Hannah! You should let me through, Judy, I'm a trained St John's Ambulance first-aider!' said Mrs Woodward.

Sod that, thought Hannah, and opened one eye. 'Oh . . . Mrs Hind? I . . . I don't know what happened . . . I felt very dizzy and . . .'

Hannah saw them exchange a meaningful glance: it was quick and furtive – Mrs Woodward coloured faintly – and contained a hidden implication that neither wanted to voice but couldn't resist acknowledging.

Maybe it was just the embarrassment of being overheard bitching about her grandmother, she reasoned, and concentrated on looking brave.

'Do you feel all right now, dear?' asked Mrs Hind.

'I think so,' said Hannah, but in a tone that suggested otherwise.

'Perhaps you're anaemic?' said Mrs Woodward, regarding her healthy pink cheeks doubtfully. 'You had that funny turn when you were at school, didn't you? After your A levels.'

'Lola! That's enough. Here, let's get you up.' Mrs Hind offered a hand, which Hannah grasped. It was warm, reassuring, and surprisingly soft.

'What's that on your jumper, dear?' asked Mrs Woodward, as Hannah rose unsteadily to her feet in the manner of Bambi taking his first steps.

'Um . . .'

'Oh, dear, dear.' Mrs Hind brushed her down as if she was a pony. 'You're covered in dust! Was it just a sudden wobble? Can I get you a glass of brandy? Or a cup of tea?'

'I think a cup of tea would be fine,' murmured Hannah. 'And a sit-down.'

'You have been under quite a bit of stress recently, Hannah,' said Mrs Woodward. Her eagerness to prove the first-aid training temporarily made her forget what little tact she possessed. 'It could be that the trauma of losing your job and coming home is catching up with you.'

This shameless attempt to provoke a reaction didn't escape Hannah; only Dora and Fran knew the truth, but that wouldn't stop Mrs Woodward's gossip mill turning overtime.

'Now then . . .' said Mrs Hind, with a warning glance. 'I'm sure that's none of our business.'

Mrs Woodward looked down at her feet, and when she met Hannah's gaze again it was with all the briskness and artificial concern that Hannah recognized from the dispensary. 'When did this happen, Hannah?' she asked. 'Have you been in there long, do you think?'

'Now . . .' said Mrs Hind.

'It matters, Judy, if she's been passed out – a long time or not,' said Mrs Woodward, defensively. 'Her blood sugar might have diminished to dangerous levels.'

Hannah knew this was her chance. She looked between the two women and wondered if they saw her as an adult at all. It didn't feel to her as if they did. *She* didn't feel like one. Everything seemed to have been going on over her head from the moment she'd stepped on to Linton station platform.

'Hannah?' prompted Mrs Hind.

Hannah looked at one, then the other.

Why don't I know the answer to this? she wondered, then

immediately thought, How do I ask my grandmother if she was an illegitimate child?

Suddenly Hannah understood the frustration her mother must have felt for so long.

'Hannah?' Mrs Woodward held up three fingers. 'Are. You. All Right?'

Hannah shook her head, then nodded, and let Mrs Hind lead her through to the sitting room. Mrs Woodward followed with the milk jug.

By now the rest of the group had arrived, and a little forced conversation was taking place. It was silenced by Hannah's appearance at the door.

'So!' said Mrs Hind, in a hearty voice that fooled no one. 'We're all here? And we've all got some tea? Shall we get started? Who'd like to lead us off?'

'Let me,' said Dora smoothly. 'It's one of my favourite novels.'

Mrs Kelly coughed, but no one looked at her.

Hannah looked at Dora sitting opposite her, holding court over the proceedings, directing the discussion with the casual art of a conductor. They might resent her for that easy social dominance, these old women with roots going back further than hers in Linton's dark soil, but they couldn't help bowing down before it.

'Hannah's funny turn' gave Dora an excellent excuse to leave Mrs Hind's well before it got dark, but Hannah had the distinct impression that any debate about Lawrence's portrayal of passion crossing the class divide had only really got going once they were well down the lane.

'Thank God for that,' said Dora, through a fixed grin of cordial thanks. She stopped waving at Mrs Hind on the steps and relaxed into her seat. 'I thought we'd be there for ever. There's a limit to how much grinding and clanking of two-stroke brains one can take.' She tucked her book into her handbag, patted it, and offered Hannah a mint. 'So, how are things up at the villa?'

'Oh, fine,' said Hannah.

'Has Louise shown you any of the studies Matt Fisher did of the harbour? I think Faith used to have them in the library.'

'I've only seen the one in the study.' Hannah turned her head. It had struck her as odd that there weren't more Fishers around. If Faith had been his patron, surely there would be more paintings elsewhere in the house. 'Mrs Graham-Potter didn't mention any more. They're not there now.'

'Oh. How odd. They're rather beautiful, I think,' said Dora, 'as far as I remember them. I suppose they were all put away when Faith died. Too many memories for Constance, and rather too stark for Louise. Too real. She prefers her Lakes in nice colours, and Matt wanted to paint what he saw on the docks – the sweat and misery of eking out a living. Clogs were never Louise's cup of tea.'

'I *know*,' said Hannah. 'I've seen a *lot* of sunsets over Crummock and not a single one through a light blanket of rain and cloud. I mean, artistic licence is one thing, but re-creating an entire weather system is another.'

'Pretty, though,' said Dora.

'Yeah, but not real,' Hannah retorted.

Dora leaned one elbow on the window and touched the pearls at her neck thoughtfully. 'Well, maybe not. But it was hard, you know. I suppose it's not so odd to want to be surrounded by trickling streams instead of reminders of how difficult things were.'

Hannah flicked a look at her. Dora's moods were unbelievably changeable. And she didn't recall hearing that anything had been hard for Mrs Graham-Potter. 'Where do you think they are? Should I ask to see them?'

'I'm sure she'll show you them in her own good time.' Dora gazed out at the rusty bracken on the hillside, then said, in a more playful tone, 'Ask her about the satin party shoes she had dyed in London and sent back first class on the train.'

'Sorry?'

'Ask her about the parties they used to have in the summer, with their friends from university.' Dora relaxed into her seat. 'They used to come up from London, with all the new books and records you couldn't get here, and baskets of fruit from Covent Garden market, and stay for days. Wonderful parties. Constance liked to cover the tables with flowers and hang little paper lanterns in the apple trees by the french windows – so pretty. I used to look out of my bedroom window and imagine the fairies had put them there. Then I'd see people wandering around, drinking and chatting all night. I used to watch out of the window for hours until I fell asleep.'

Hannah tried to picture such hilarity in the solemn rooms of the villa, and failed. 'Didn't you get in the way?'

'No,' said Dora. She sounded surprised by the question. 'Children didn't then. When I was old enough to hold a proper conversation, I was allowed to join in.'

'Mum used to make me recite things at parties,' said Hannah, glumly. 'I used to think she was showing off, but now I know it was to avoid talking to people herself.'

'Anyway,' said Dora, sweeping on with her recollections, 'when everyone arrived, I'd have to go upstairs and Mrs Tyson – not our Mrs Tyson, her mother-in-law, Enid – would bring me some supper on a tray, but she'd bring it on the special dinner service they were using downstairs, you see, so I'd have a treat too. It was duck-egg blue, with a tiny gold shell pattern round the edge. Very old. Part of the enormous service they had in the London house. I've often wondered where that is now . . .'

'Granny,' said Hannah, 'when did Mrs Graham-Potter move into the villa?'

'She's been there as long as I can remember, darling. Her mother died in an accident when she was sixteen, seventeen, and there was some business with her father that was never talked about it. I suppose he shot himself. But he was an old family retainer, so Louise was scooped up and taken in. They were like that.' Dora paused. 'Well, Faith and Constance were like that.'

Hannah processed this information. There was still something missing. Something that didn't add up. Was that how Dora had come to be there too? Scooped up? She wanted to know, but couldn't find the right words to ask without causing pain.

'Why do you ask?' added Dora.

'Um . . . I found an old letter up at the villa, hidden in a Bible,' she said. 'From their solicitors, about arranging money and so on while they were up at Cambridge. I just got the impression that, well, there was something odd about it.'

'Like what?' Dora sounded cagy, but Hannah had no alternative now but to press on.

'Well, odd that someone had kept the letter, for one thing, and locked it away. And also why would he only arrange for two train tickets? If Louise was living with them, and left from here with them, then surely there should have been three tickets? I just . . .' Hannah stopped herself saying, 'Did Louise Graham-Potter actually go to Cambridge?' although it was what she was thinking. Instead she said, 'I haven't come across any degree certificates.'

'But women weren't awarded formal degrees for quite a while after they were there,' Dora pointed out.

'No, I suppose not.' Hannah didn't reveal her other confusing discovery: when she'd been looking through Faith's wardrobe she had found two undergraduate gowns hanging like sleeping bats between the tweed suits and neat satin blouses. Just two.

Didn't it fit with everything else she'd pieced together about Mrs Graham-Potter? The scrambling need to keep up with these two confident rich girls, never quite managing it, but always appearing immaculate throughout? Maybe she'd gone away at the same time, let everyone think she was with them, then come back also at the same time. In fact, thought Hannah, pleased with her own cunning, maybe she'd gone to the London house, and brushed up her social skills, perhaps even looked for a husband. After all, who would know in Linton, especially if there were no degree certificates to be framed and hung up?

'I don't even know what her maiden name was,' she said aloud.

'Heslop. Louise Heslop. Not quite so grand, is it?'

'What was *Mr* Graham-Potter like?'

Dora's lips curved in an enigmatic smile. 'Somewhat forgettable.'

'Well, presumably not to *Mrs* Graham-Potter,' said Hannah, impatiently. If Dora had a fault it was this irritating habit of talking in cocktail-party epigrams about serious matters.

'No,' said Dora thoughtfully. 'I'd say she found him somewhat forgettable too.'

'In what way?' said Hannah.

'I don't recall meeting him,' said Dora. 'She went away for a little while, not long after Cambridge, and came back with a wedding ring and a double-barrelled name but, sadly, no husband in tow. Or, indeed, any pictures of him.' She twinkled. 'I shall say no more than that.'

'Why not?' demanded Hannah.

'Because – as the lady herself has always made perfectly plain – it's none of our business.'

Hannah recognized one of Dora's brick walls – in this case, possibly one that disguised her own lack of information. But in the back of her mind, another piece of the villa's complex jigsaw of social order and politely ignored secrets slotted into place.

They crested the top of the hill into town and the panorama of the harbour spread out in front of them: the rows of terraced pit cottages lined like tight frills down the valley, giving way to the bright colours of the old town below. The sun had come out, and the harbour looked like one of Mrs Hind's over-vivid backdrops for the Linton Amateurs.

Hannah indicated to turn down their road.

Dora sighed unexpectedly. 'Would you mind if we drove round once more, darling?'

'Are you all right?' Hannah looked at her with some concern.

Dora patted Hannah's knee. 'I'm fine, thank you, darling,' she said. 'Just enjoying the drive.'

Chapter Nineteen

Hannah had only just settled down to her morning cup of tea with Mrs Tyson, and was wondering how she could work the conversation round to Matthew Fisher without being too obvious, when Mrs Graham-Potter emerged from the shadows of the hall at the kitchen door. She was immaculate in heather tweed, her hair a fluffy tribute to a recent Rissini home visit. Hannah had the impression she'd been waiting for her.

'If you'd like to make a start on Faith's room today, Hannah, I should be grateful,' she said. 'There's a good deal of interesting work in there. I should imagine it will take you a few days.'

Hannah smiled tightly. She didn't want to let on that she'd slipped into Constance's room already, uninvited.

Mrs Graham-Potter turned to leave, then paused. 'You really don't have to drink your tea down here,' she added lightly. 'You're very welcome to have it with me in the drawing room. I'm sure Mrs Tyson wouldn't mind bringing you a tray.'

'That's very kind,' said Hannah, in what she hoped was a unilateral way.

Mrs Tyson muttered darkly to herself.

* * *

Faith's room was at the top of the stairs, the largest of the bedrooms with a huge bay window that gave a sweeping view over the gardens running down to the sea. Evidently, unlike Constance, she'd had no qualms about moving into a better room. It had a peaceful, airy atmosphere and smelt of the sea without being damp like some of the others. There was a chair in the window, with a small table bearing a broad copper dish of old cotton reels and embroidery paraphernalia, and a well-stocked bookcase next to it. Unlike the leatherbound wall-to-wall books in the library, all the titles on this shelf looked well thumbed, including, Hannah was pleased to note, a dictionary and a copy of *Gone With the Wind*.

The room was dominated by a magnificent oak four-poster bed, carved with berries and leaves in the Arts and Crafts style, and hung with crimson brocade curtains. Although it was old, it was clearly much newer than the rest of the heavy Victorian furniture in the house; Hannah guessed that Faith had bought it for herself when the villa became hers.

That was reasonable, she thought. Much as she loved Fran, she blanched at the idea of inheriting her parents' bed, with all the huffy nights and badly feigned sleep that must have permeated its fibres.

Faith's four-poster was more of a bower than a bed: Hannah could imagine her taking a leisurely breakfast on a tray, reading a paper and dealing with correspondence, drawing the curtains to keep the world at bay. The pillars reached nearly to the ceiling, and the sides were hidden by a mossy-green coverlet that reached the floor, trailing little fronds of candlewick on to the threadbare Axminster.

Hannah thought about having a quick bounce, but some respectful impulse stopped her. Instead she walked over to the window and abandoned herself to the view. She could see Dora in her garden, happily decapitating her roses in a new all-weather cape, while her washing fluttered discreetly behind the cottage, red knickers and vests just visible. Beyond that, someone in a green anorak was walking a dog along the harbourside (Mrs Jordan? Betty Fisher?), and a police car slowly drove to the lifeboat station at the far end of the quay where a couple of youths were doing something highly suspicious with a wheelie-bin.

Really, thought Hannah, you could watch this for hours. If you were Mrs Tyson, of course, she added guiltily.

She balled up her scarf, her phone and her knitted hat and put them in the dish so she wouldn't forget them when she went home for lunch. Then she opened a new page in her notebook, now nearly half full of scribbled prices and notes of websites, and walked slowly round the room, mindful of the creaking floorboards, and examined the small framed pictures hanging in little groups on the dark walls.

She knew at once, from the clean style and strong black lines, that it was Matthew Fisher's work, and wondered why Mrs Graham-Potter hadn't led her to them sooner. These small studies were in an entirely different league from the tranquil lake scenes in the drawing room.

There was beauty here too, but it was dark and bleak, capturing the power and effort of men at work on the dock, loading the coal ships and winching grey cargo off the steamers, while the spoked wheels of the pit workings rose in the background and white seagulls floated overhead.

It wasn't Hannah's area of expertise, but Fisher's figures reminded her of Lowry's: unromanticized stick people, cogs in the bigger machinery of the dock, but each one different in a tiny detail of dress or stance, each individual strain noted. It wasn't a pretty vision of the docks, no sugar-coloured houses or bunting here, but there was a grim dignity in the way all the colours in the overall greyness were hard-earned – the dull red of the crates or the occasional splash of gold in the ships' livery.

Fisher's paintings articulated something Hannah felt about her home town, but couldn't wrestle into words.

These, presumably, were the paintings Dora had mentioned in the car, the ones that had been a little too real for Constance's conscience and Louise's aspirations.

Hannah revised her opinion of Faith, as her eyes moved slowly around the images, letting the shapes and colours burn into her mind and connect with her own feelings: Faith Musgrave hadn't been just a do-gooding social interferer, with an amateur taste in art. If she'd done one useful deed with the Musgrave fortune, it had been in allowing Matthew Fisher space and time to develop his talent into something so powerful.

The starkness and honesty of what he had chosen to record touched Hannah's own confused reaction to the place: pride that hard work had created something of grace, yet guilt in seeing beauty in other people's struggle. She wondered how Fisher had felt when he saw the pictures hanging on Faith's wall, considering his own complicated position between the mining community and the mine-owners.

Something was buzzing, like a fly banging against a window-pane.

Hannah's head swivelled. The room was empty.

The buzzing noise continued, louder and more urgent.

She swallowed and tried to control her racing pulse. There would be some logical explanation for this. Some tiny localized tremor, maybe, or a heavy load on a train.

There was another sound now, tuning in with the buzzing – was a bell ringing in the kitchen?

She held her breath. Downstairs in the kitchen, one of the bells was definitely jangling, as if someone was yanking on the bell pull in an imperious frenzy.

Her eyes shot to the old rope pull, which hung next to the four-poster, well within reach for Faith to summon a maid on a whim.

Downstairs the bell clanged relentlessly.

Her heart hammered in her chest and she rose unsteadily to her feet. The temperature in the room had dropped, and the buzzing was even louder.

Hannah took a step towards the window, trying not to look in the mirror, scared of what she might see in it – in the other mirror world of the villa. As she stepped away from the window, Hannah realized that the source of the buzzing was the brass dish on the dressing-table, the one that was full of buckles and cotton spools. It was vibrating, almost visibly.

Abruptly, the ringing stopped downstairs, leaving a dull hum on the broken air.

Be careful, she thought.

Hannah put both her hands on the sides of the bowl and held it, feeling the metal vibrating on her fingers. Then she forced herself to look down into it. She saw that it was vibrating because her mobile phone was in it, with the ringer switched off. She picked it out with trembling fingers.

'Hello?' she said.

'Hannah?' said a familiar voice.

'Hello, Fi,' she said. Warm relief trickled through her body. 'God, you gave me a shock.'

'Why?' Perry Como was singing in the background.

'Oh, just this old house.' Hannah felt nervous even saying it, and couldn't make it come out as a joke. 'It's trying to expel me, I think. It's turning me a bit mad.'

'Listen,' said Fiammetta, 'I was wondering if you'd like to come down to the salon and be a model for our students. We're doing intensive treatments so they can't wreck your hair or anything.'

'Oh,' said Hannah. 'What's the worst that can happen?' She couldn't help thinking about the unnamed disaster that had befallen Mrs Woodward, and required remedial treatment.

Fiammetta made an impatient tsking sound. 'Worst-case scenario: your hair gets an overdose of vitamins and strength-building minerals. And it's not like you don't need that anyway. Your hair's in a shocking state.'

Hannah thought about it briefly – some of those trainees had looked dangerously casual – and then, for the sake of seeing Fiammetta, said, 'Yeah, OK. When?'

'Tomorrow night. About six-ish?'

'Fine. Should I bring anything?'

'Just yourself.'

'OK,' said Hannah. Her gaze returned automatically to the dockers on the wall, hauling coal on the same granite harbourside she could see from Faith's bedroom window. 'See ya.'

'See ya.'

Hannah took a step back to the pictures and slipped the phone into her back pocket. She imagined Matthew Fisher sitting with his sketchbook on the docks, where the fishermen and the tourists sat now, choosing what to keep in and what to leave out.

She wondered again why Mrs Graham-Potter had waited so long before sending her to this room. Didn't she know how valuable the pictures were? Maybe it had been a test: she had wanted to see whether Hannah was clever enough on the run-of-the-mill stuff before she let her see the true gems of the collection.

Or was there a darker reason? Had she wanted her to make the connection between Faith and Matthew Fisher – and the privacy of Faith's bedroom?

It would be like her, thought Hannah. It was a delicate little hint, but a hint all the same. Everything Mrs Graham-Potter did was careful, and neat.

'Model night?' asked Marina, her pen poised over a short list.

'Er, yeah,' said Hannah.

'Rather you than me.'

Fiammetta was at the other end of the salon, dividing oil into small bowls, flicking the bottle each time, with a swift, decisive movement. She waved at Hannah, held up a finger, mouthed, 'One minute!' and indicated that she should join the other ladies at the cutting stations.

Hannah slid into the last seat, nearest the window.

Inevitably, Mrs Woodward was seated next to her.

'Hello, Hannah,' said Mrs Woodward. She dropped her tone confidentially. 'How are you feeling after your funny turn at Judy Hind's?'

'Oh, I'm fine now,' said Hannah. 'I think it must have been something I ate.'

Next to her, Mrs Bradley, one of the church wardens, was pretending to be scandalized by a copy of *Cosmopolitan*, but her ears were virtually flexing in her efforts to eavesdrop.

'Well, Janet Jordan was rather worried that you might be anorexic, with all the stress you've been under, but I said you wouldn't be one of those.' Mrs Woodward gave Hannah's sturdy legs a hard stare. 'Much too . . . sensible.'

'Mmm,' said Hannah.

'How's your grandmother?' asked Mrs Woodward. Her tone was so neutral that Hannah knew she was fishing.

'Oh, she's fine, thanks,' she said artlessly, then added, 'Well, she is now.'

Mrs Woodward's eyebrows arched.

'She was a bit upset after the book group,' Hannah went on innocently. 'I think it was something to do with . . . Oh, look, Fiammetta's ready now!'

Mrs Woodward turned to Fiammetta as frustration froze her face like a Botox overdose.

Fiammetta clapped her hands and smiled at the assembled victims. 'OK,' she said. 'We're going to cover treatments tonight and pressure points on the scalp.'

'Is that some kind of skin disease?' enquired Mrs Bradley.

'Massages,' tutted the girl stationed behind her.

'Oooh, I say!' Mrs Bradley rolled her eyes in a game fashion and nudged Mrs Woodward.

'We're lucky this evening to have Hannah Marshall with us,' said Fiammetta. 'Hannah has had her hair done in many fancy establishments in London, and I hope all you trainees will do your best to meet her high standards.'

'Meet her fancy prices, more like,' said Mrs Woodward. She raised her voice. 'You want to charge her London prices, love.'

Hannah thought that if one more person cracked a joke about London prices, she'd start up with London sign language.

'Oh, I will,' said Fiammetta. 'And, since she's the expert, why don't I use her as a guinea pig? Come on, gorgeous, let's have you.'

She pointed at the nearest basin, and Hannah walked over to it self-consciously. Fiammetta flipped a towel round her neck, and lifted her hair, which fell into the basin in a dirty-blonde pool.

Hannah hoped Fiammetta could tell she'd washed it that morning. She wasn't sure where to look: at Fiammetta, which would give the class an unprecedented view up her nose, or out towards everyone else, which would give her an unattractive double chin.

'First of all, we're going to wash the hair with a detoxing shampoo.'

Hannah could feel the water rushing past her ears as Fiammetta ran it over her fingers, waiting for it to warm up.

'Hannah's hair is fine and prone to stress breakage, as you can see . . .'

'Thank *you*,' muttered Hannah.

'. . . so we'll start off gently because, God knows, she can't afford to lose more than she already has.'

Hannah heard a ripple of titters, and fixed her eyes on the ceiling fan.

Fiammetta's fingertips worked quickly round her head, distributing the minty shampoo, then lathering it up: little circles at her temples, longer scratching rakes around the back, and firm whirls to spread the lather. Hannah's shoulders relaxed and dropped in a warm wave of pleasure.

The water rushed round her ears again, as Fiammetta rinsed.

'Now, can you all see how much hair's coming away as I do this?'

Hannah couldn't, but she could guess from the murmurs of surprise and mild revulsion.

'What causes hair loss?' Fiammetta demanded. 'Stacy?'

'Stress, poor diet, smoking, pregnancy . . .' Stacy trailed off.

Fiammetta's hands patted Hannah's scalp. 'Does any of that sound like you?'

'No,' said Hannah firmly.

Mrs Woodward coughed in an I-beg-to-disagree fashion.

'Anyone else? More reasons for hair loss?'

There was silence.

'Poor thyroid action,' murmured Hannah, since no one else was going to. 'Lack of vitamin B complexes.'

'Very *good*,' said Fiammetta. 'Is there anything you don't know?'

Hannah only just stopped herself informing Fiammetta that since her hair had started coming out in small but disturbing clumps, about six months previously, she'd become something of an expert on hairloss.

'So when you've towelled off the excess moisture from the hair . . .'

A soft towel was wrapped round Hannah's face and agitated. Hannah breathed in spring-fresh Lenor.

'. . . then we apply a conditioner and use the time it takes to work on the hair to massage the client's scalp. Because . . . ?'

'Scalp massage brings the blood back to the follicles, which can stimulate hair growth,' chorused the trainees.

'Good.' The towel was removed from Hannah's face. 'And why do we towel the hair first?'

'So excess moisture doesn't dilute the effect of the conditioner.'

'Very good! Stacy, put that spray down when I'm talking to you.'

The herbal sweetness of rosemary and lime filled Hannah's nose as Fiammetta poured out the treatment oil. She could hear the slippery snaps as she worked it between her palms, warming it up.

'Now, watch what I'm doing. You need to have your client nice and relaxed.'

Fiammetta's fingers pressed and kneaded around Hannah's hairline, sending little tingles of pleasure down her neck. The fingertips found distinct points and pressed, then moved a fraction of an inch and pressed again, hard into Hannah's scalp, hitting the exact spot between optimum pleasure and acute pain. An image of the phrenology head that sat on the piano in Rose View (Fran's head, Dora's piano) swam into Hannah's mind, and she imagined the precise squares that Fiammetta's fingertips seemed to be finding on her scalp. She wondered if she was deliberately choosing between 'calm' and 'alert', 'hair growth' and 'self-abandonment'.

Hannah closed her eyes and submitted to the sensation of satisfaction and peace that was spreading through her.

She wondered if Fiammetta did this in bed to her boyfriends, finding the pressure points for 'arousal' and 'submission'. The thought made her flush.

The fingertips hesitated and Hannah heard a familiar tsk of annoyance.

'Stacy, you can't see what I'm doing if you're sitting there chatting to Kelly! Now, do you want to gather round so you can see what I'm doing to Hannah's scalp? You stay where you are, ladies.'

Even with her eyes shut, Hannah could feel the press of bodies round the chair and smell the faint aroma of cigarettes and CK One, and she felt somewhat embarrassed that she could be experiencing such a range of intimate emotions so close to Linton's entire hairdressing college course.

'There.' Fiammetta's fingers divided her hair, stroking it into a tight parting. 'Can you see how her scalp's turning red, with all the blood returning to it?'

That would be my whole head blushing then, thought Hannah.

'Now we rinse it off, and you can get on with putting the colour conditioner on, as we did at the start of the month.'

Warm water rushed round Hannah's forehead and she felt Fi's strong fingers massaging the oil out of her hair. Her scalp was tingling, but so was the rest of her body.

How long is it since anyone touched me? Hannah wondered.

Months.

She was almost pleased to have the towel wrapped round her head again.

Fiammetta reappeared in front of her. 'Hannah, you don't mind if I hand you over to Linzi at this point, do you?'

Linzi, the eldest trainee, stood a little behind her, biting her nails. She had enviably long legs, displayed in the black Lycra bootlegs that formed the Linton uniform, and no visible buttocks. Her hair was jet black, and cut in a low fringe over her eyes, which made her look like a skinnier, younger Chrissie Hynde. Hannah thought of pointing this out by way of an ice-breaking compliment, but immediately realized, with a lurch of depression, that Linzi was too young to know who Chrissie Hynde was. 'Of course I don't mind,' she said.

Fiammetta leaned between the two of them and whispered, 'Since we go back a bit, I've given you the one with the best track record. Linzi's the only one who's passed all her modules with no need for outside medical involvement.'

Hannah's eyes, round with horror, met Fiammetta's in the mirror.

'Only joking!' Fiammetta let out a wicked laugh.

Linzi pulled a face, which might have been a silent laugh or an unamused pout. The inherent sarcasm of the Linton teenager made it impossible to differentiate. Fiammetta pointed a comb at Linzi. 'I'll be back to check on you, lady, so no funny business.' She stalked to the other end of the salon, making minor adjustments to the trainees' shampooing technique as she went. 'Now, who's in charge of making coffee tonight?'

Linzi began to comb the colour treatment through Hannah's hair.

'I don't know what she said to you but I'm perfectly capable,' she said defensively. 'I won't be as good as them London stylists, but there's nowt wrong with my cutting.'

'I'm sure you're extremely capable,' said Hannah, soothingly. 'Fiammetta was telling me how good you were, and you know she has very high standards.'

Linzi worked and combed. 'I like your boots,' she said eventually.

'From Top Shop,' lied Hannah. They were actually from J.P. Tod's, but that wouldn't cut any ice here. In fact, it would probably cause a flash-freeze. 'They do great designer knock-offs, don't they?'

Linzi met Hannah's eyes in the mirror and smiled. 'Have you known Fiammetta long, then?'

Hannah could tell from her tone that she'd obviously decided she was no threat. There was, after all, a large Top Shop in Linton high street. 'We were at school together.'

'Was she always as bossy as she is now?'

'Er . . . she used to be a lot worse, actually,' said Hannah.

'Really?'

'Really.' Hannah thought of Fiammetta's exasperated reorganization of the Coffee Pot ordering system when she'd worked there.

'God.' Linzi searched through her trolley for the clingfilm to wrap round Hannah's head. 'She'd do my head in. Once a week in here's about as much as I can take. She's a good hairdresser, though, like,' she added hastily. 'She's got customers coming from miles round. And she could charge loads more than she does, I reckon.'

'Fancy,' said Hannah.

'I'm going to wrap your head up now to intensify the treatments,' said Linzi, remembering her training, 'and put you under a turbo-dryer. Can I fetch you a tea or a coffee?'

'Coffee, please,' said Hannah. 'Milk, no sugar.'

Linzi pulled a turbo-dryer to the chair, fitted it over Hannah's head, set the timer to ten minutes, and dumped a pile of *Vogue* and *Elle* in her lap. A moment or two later, she returned with a white china mug of scalding hot, but very good filter coffee. 'I'm going in the back now to text my boyfriend,' she said reassuringly, 'but if you want anything, just give us a shout, eh?'

Next to Hannah, Mrs Woodward was having a blonde conditioning treatment, and simultaneously pumping Mrs Bradley for information about her recent knee replacement.

Seeing Hannah was now free, Mrs Woodward abruptly abandoned Mrs Bradley and yelled, above the roar of the dryer, 'Was it something we said that upset your grandmother? The other day?'

Hannah pointed at the turbo-dryer engulfing her head like an alien brain-scanner, and rolled her eyes apologetically.

Mrs Woodward slumped back in her seat, defeated, then turned back to Mrs Bradley. 'So how long did you say you were you on the slab for then, Janice?'

After ten minutes the timer shrieked, and after twelve, Linzi came back and turned it off with a practised stab. She flipped away the dryer and prodded uncertainly at Hannah's scalp.

'Do you have training every week?' asked Hannah.

'Yeah, but it fits in really well with Kieran, because he's got rugby down the road and he comes and picks me up. Mind, it's not good for your social life, this job, because the nights folk want their hair done are nights you want to go out yourself. Stacy and myself, we were here until eight last Friday, doing straightening.'

'Does Fiammetta always stay to supervise?' asked Hannah, thinking of her casual abandonment of the group to Columba's tender mercies.

'Yeah, most times,' agreed Linzi.

'Doesn't that affect her social life?' asked Hannah disingenuously. She hadn't spent weeks around the likes of Dora without picking up a few tactics. 'Doesn't, er, doesn't her boyfriend mind?'

'She doesn't have one,' replied Linzi. She pulled an 'aww' face. 'Bless. Keeps herself very private, like, but I'm fairly sure there hasn't been anyone special. No one ever calls on her, not that I've seen.'

'That's a shame,' said Hannah.

'I know,' agreed Linzi, nodding emphatically. 'And she's getting on, now. I mean, she looks wonderful for her age and everything, but she's nearly thirty.'

'I know,' said Hannah.

'Oh, sorry, no offence,' Linzi added hurriedly, 'but round here all the decent lads get snapped up early. I should know. Mind, you get the odd ones coming available if things don't work out first time round.'

'That's encouraging to know.'

Linzi flicked at Hannah's hair with a tail-comb. 'Mind, Fiammetta's dead fussy. She could have gone out with loads of dead nice-looking lads, but I don't think they were good enough for her. She's like that. Very high standards. She had a bad do with some virus a while back, and I think that might have left her a bit, you know, not interested, so to speak, and then there was some business with her sister. They fell out quite badly after she got pregnant and Fi had to come back from Manchester. There was maybe someone there, but we've never met him. Her mam's always going on about leaving it too late, but I don't think she wants to go out with anyone from round here.'

'Quite right too,' said Fiammetta's voice.

Linzi jumped and dropped the comb. It stuck in the back of Hannah's head, where gravity yanked it downwards, taking several of Hannah's precious hairs with it.

'Ow!' Hannah grabbed at the back of her head.

Fiammetta gave Linzi a dark stare, and disentangled the comb. 'Have you checked the drier for hot towels?'

'No,' yelped Linzi.

'Well, go and do it. And you can clear the hair out of the plugholes. And make sure Kerry hasn't done her usual on Mrs Wakeham.'

Hannah tried to catch Linzi's eye, so she could pull a face of apology but she had slunk off, muttering. 'Aww,' she said. 'I was just getting to the juicy stuff.'

'Bloody little gossips.' Fiammetta picked up strands of Hannah's hair and tested them in her fingers. 'Old biddies don't just become biddyish at sixty, do they? Some start training at sixteen.'

'She was just telling me that you've auditioned and rejected all that Linton manhood has to offer.'

'Which took all of ten minutes.' Fiammetta tutted, took out her comb and started redistributing Linzi's colour conditioner. 'She's got this all over your ears. You look like one of the seven dwarfs.'

'So there's no one on the scene now?' Hannah tried to make the question sound casual, but she couldn't ignore the way the pulse in her neck had started to throb.

'No.'

'Never?'

Fiammetta searched busily in the trolley for something she couldn't seem to find. 'There was someone, a while back, but it didn't work out and I don't agree with casual sex. It's never that casual.'

'So how come this lot don't know?' asked Hannah, emboldened by not having to look at her. 'They seem to know everything else.'

'Listen, did Linzi ask you whether you were allergic to anything? After Mrs Woodward, they should be more careful.'

'Hey!' said Hannah. 'Don't change the subject. You've had the full story of *my* sorry existence since I left here.'

'You know what?' said Fiammetta.

Mrs Bradley and her trainee returned from the basins. They didn't disguise their interest in the conversation going on at the next chair.

Fiammetta smiled sweetly at Mrs Bradley, glared at the trainee, then turned back to Hannah and dropped her voice. 'You know what? The thing I am most proud of is that I've managed, against all the odds, to throw a shroud of discretion over my life. It's been hard at times, but I've managed it. Yes, it's true that I'm not seeing anyone at the moment and, no, I don't really want to talk about it. Especially in the middle of training night at the salon, oddly enough.'

'And how is that different from me refusing to face up to my past?' demanded Hannah.

'It's *totally* different.'

'*How?*'

'In that I don't have anything to hide.' Fiammetta walked over to another trolley and took her time coming back.

When she did, their reflections glared at each other. Hannah felt she was at an unfair disadvantage: her head was wrapped in clingfilm, and her mascara had smudged where Linzi hadn't been too careful with the dribbling conditioner.

'Have you spoken to your grandmother yet?' asked Fiammetta, in a very low voice. 'About . . . your little factual discrepancy?'

'No.'

'I think you should.'

'I need to find the right time.'

'Do you want *me* to speak to her?'

'No!' said Hannah, so loudly that Mrs Bradley looked up from her *Now* magazine. 'No,' she repeated, more discreetly. 'There are other things I need to sort out first before I get into that kettle of fish. And she has a lot on her mind right now. My mother, for a start.'

'But surely it must affect the way you think about her, knowing that she lied to you? Doesn't it make you wonder what else you don't know the truth about? Like—' Fiammetta stopped, but Hannah knew what she had been going to say. Ever since Fiammetta had flung open that window of doubt, flotillas of nagging questions about every aspect of her life now drifted in her mind as she was about to fall asleep.

Had Dad left for the reasons Fran gave at the time or was there something else?

Was there some *other* reason that Dominic hadn't come back after college, and had gone to work in America?

Why had Dora wanted her to think she'd only taken one extra tablet, and why hadn't she mentioned that Fiammetta had been there?

And, most importantly, what had Fiammetta been doing there in the first place?

Hannah wished that the spiritualist had been able to come up with some practical information the other night. Stuff that she actually needed to know but couldn't ask without upsetting the delicately balanced understandings that kept her life at this level of comfort and familiarity.

Fiammetta stopped combing. 'I *will* speak to her, if you don't,' she said, in a low tone. 'There's no point you coming back here otherwise. It's just a holiday. You're not achieving anything.'

'That's not true.'

'For fuck's sake,' hissed Fiammetta, 'you've got to sort this out, or I'll just have to do it for you. I care about you, Hannah, believe it or not. You can't base the rest of your life on a lie.'

Hannah looked at Fiammetta in the mirror. She had the kind of assured, sculpted looks that had made her seem twenty-five at eighteen, and now she'd always look twenty-five. In that respect she hadn't changed much at all. But she was somehow different in the salon: more professional, more sure of her own knowledge and her own limits. Rather than making her seem stuck, as Dora had hoped, seeing her in the salon felt natural. Her outlines were sharper: she was an adult, rather than the teenager Hannah had pictured in her mind when they spoke on the phone. But actually, thought Hannah, when you look in the mirror, we're *both* adults. Maybe it was being surrounded by old women that gave you a distorted sense of your own youth.

Fiammetta threw the clingfilm into the bin and wiped her hands on her black overall. 'Have you spoken to Toby since you've been in Linton?'

Hannah was wrong-footed by the sudden change of tack. 'Er, no. Well, there didn't seem much point.' She wasn't going to tell Fiammetta that Toby had evaporated from her life without leaving a trace.

'Oh?' said Fiammetta. She raised her dark eyebrows in an unspoken question.

'Oh what?'

'Oh, nothing.' Fiammetta slipping her fingers into Hannah's hair and began to dig them into her scalp, raking them down to the nape of her neck and back up again, creating furrows of colour conditioner and pink skin. She pressed her thumbs into the hollow of Hannah's temples, lacing her fingertips along the middle of her skull.

Hannah shut her eyes against the white shiver of pleasure that bloomed like a rainbow behind her eyelids, then spread down into her neck and tingled along her spine.

Toby, she thought, and had to make an effort to picture his face. It was weird how his voice had faded in her mind since the night of the mysterious telephone call. If, of course, it had been him. She didn't really believe it had, but that was the anaesthetizing effect of Linton blocking out the painful memories of what she'd left behind in London. Blocking out all memories of everything, with its demanding litany of gossip and complicated petty histories, and social debts owed and paid, and its proud disconnection from life anywhere else.

And that was a good thing, surely.

The massage stopped. Hannah opened her eyes, and saw Fiammetta watching her in the mirror. Her head was tilted in a private question, but her fingers remained on Hannah's head, as if she were trying to discern her thoughts through the hair.

'Don't try to read my bumps,' said Hannah, self-consciously.

Fiammetta pulled an inscrutable face. 'Too late, honey.' She removed her fingers, and made Mickey Mouse ears behind Hannah's head. In the mirror, her dark eyes held Hannah's less confrontational gaze. But Hannah refused to be stared out, and Fiammetta was the first to look away.

'So, unlike me, you don't take orders from your parents, you don't have a problem with your stalled love-life and you're utterly at one with yourself,' said Hannah. 'Know what? I really don't understand what's keeping you here.'

Now Fiammetta held Hannah's eyes for fractionally longer than was comfortable. 'I'd say it's probably the same thing that brought you back,' she said. 'Come on, Linzi will rinse you off.'

Chapter Twenty

The card arrived in the first post, just before Fran left for work. Hannah was still eating toast in her pyjamas, which made her feel at an immediate disadvantage. It was the kind of postcard she would have preferred to read fully dressed. She crunched her toast slowly as she studied the message. 'Oh,' she said aloud, without thinking. 'Oh . . .' She didn't know whether she meant, 'Oh, good' or 'Oh, shit'.

'Don't just stand there,' said Fran, going through her own post. 'I don't have time for drama. Read it aloud.'

'"Having a lovely time on St Lucia, wish you were here, love Dominic."'

'I know it's not from Dominic,' said Fran. 'Don't bother lying to me. I can smell lies – lies, false alibis, and recreational drug use. It's my job.'

Hannah sighed and flipped the card towards her. 'It's from Mandy, my flatmate. Our lease runs out in a month's time, and she and her boyfriend want to take it up. On their own.'

'And?'

'And . . . maybe it's a good idea.'

'What?' Fran put down her bills. 'But you won't have anywhere to go back to.'

'Well, it's an expensive area, Mum. Very convenient for the City, apparently. And I can't afford to stay there without a job, can I? Besides,' Hannah raised and dropped her hands, 'I don't know. Bad memories. Maybe it's better to make a fresh start somewhere else.'

'I hope you're not planning to make it here.' Fran narrowed her eyes. 'Because that would be an old start, wouldn't it? Not a fresh one.'

'Thank you,' snapped Hannah. 'I'm not entirely stupid.'

'As I've said before, I just don't want you getting cut off.' Fran picked up her jacket. 'I've been in your situation and it's my duty as a mother to stop you making my mistakes. It's your duty not to irritate me by making me watch them all over again.'

'Mum, there are slackers in London too,' protested Hannah. 'You want to see the number of my friends who haven't the faintest idea what they're doing with their lives.'

'I don't mean that. I mean, it's all about attitude, isn't it? Motivation. There's none of that here, people can just *drift* for years. I don't want the forest growing up around you like Sleeping Beauty while you day-dream up at the villa until you can't get out.'

'No chance of that,' said Hannah, ignoring the little voice at the back of her mind that was reminding her it was now over six weeks since she'd spoken to anyone in London. On the other hand, her hair loss had now slowed to a pace that Fiammetta insisted was normal. She didn't think the two facts were unconnected.

'Especially when there's no chance of Prince Charming coming along to save you any time soon,' added Fran. 'Sorry, but.'

Hannah winced. 'Thank you very much, Mother.'

Evidently Fran saw her mistake. 'Look, I'll see you tonight, love,' she said. 'I might be late back. I've, er, got another appointment with a consultant. But we can talk about this later.'

'I'd rather not,' said Hannah. 'Mum?'

'What?'

Hannah held up her briefcase and papers, which Fran had left on the table. 'And you're still wearing your slippers.'

Fran looked down at her feet. 'So I am,' she said.

Hannah thought about Mandy's postcard while she drank her mid-morning tea, sitting in the window of Faith's room, looking out at the thrushes flocking around Dora's bird table. At least she'd had the grace to send her a nice postcard from the National Gallery: Ophelia, drowning in the river.

It was a bit off, thought Hannah, that Mandy hadn't phoned to discuss her plans – she had her mobile number, after all, and it was a big assumption to make that she wouldn't be coming back.

Well. To be fair, she conceded, maybe she had left London in a bit of a state. Three days in her room without coming out, refusing to eat or take phone calls, walking around as if she was blindfolded. She hadn't dealt with any of it very well. She'd behaved like a zombie toddler, in fact.

Maybe Mandy didn't want to talk to her.

Hannah cringed a little, thinking about the night she'd fallen asleep in the bath after drinking a bottle of wine.

Hannah didn't want to talk to Mandy either, now she thought about it.

She sipped her tea and tried to remember what she had left in her room in London. Nothing she needed, obviously. It felt like a different life, one she could turn her back on easily while she was here.

In the garden, the blackest cat sprang out of a rosebush in pursuit of a lone thrush, which took to the air in panic.

In a matter of weeks, Linton now seemed more like a refuge than a no-alternative escape. Hannah wondered if this was part of growing up. All right, so the shops weren't up to much, her mother was acting strangely, and she'd failed in her jogging attempts, but her social life had picked up nicely, her hair looked better than it had for years, and she felt she was finally getting somewhere in chipping away at the walls surrounding her grandmother's origins.

When they were revealed, Hannah was sure everything else would fall into place and the remaining emptiness that hung about her would disappear. And then something would show her what she should do – as she'd hoped would happen at the spiritualist meeting.

For the moment, as she looked out at the dim shape of the Isle of Man on the horizon, she didn't want to look that far ahead.

Fran came back earlier than Hannah had expected, and caught her going through the store cupboard, throwing away out-of-date tins, including a surprising number of spice jars with price tags that included halfpennies.

'Shall I sling these, or give them to the Linton museum?' asked Hannah. Then, on getting no response, she looked more closely at Fran. 'Mum? Are you all right?'

'No.' Fran's face was pale and drawn.

'Mum! What's the matter?'

Fran sank on to the chair and dropped her briefcase. 'You remember I said I'd gone for some tests the other day? Well, the good news is that I'm not late-onset diabetic, anaemic or senile.' She rubbed her eyes, smearing her scant eye-shadow. 'The bad news is they don't know what *is* wrong. And I have to make an appointment with the psychiatric consultant.'

'What kind of symptoms have you been having?'

'Oh . . . I've been forgetting things, having terrible black moods. Not feeling myself. None of the tests have come up with anything, but that doesn't make me feel any better.'

'You're run down,' soothed Hannah. Now that she finally knew something was medically wrong, she wanted to push it back into its box. 'You work so hard. And me being back home is a terrible stress on you. You're worrying about my life, as well as everything else.'

'My God, you're just like Dora,' snapped Fran. 'Quick flash of concern, then bring the conversation straight back to yourself.'

'How?' Hannah frowned. Wasn't that a proper adult response, taking some of the blame for Fran's stress? Then she understood. 'Oh, I didn't mean . . . I mean, it's all tied up together, isn't it? God, I'm sorry.'

'No, forget it.' Fran smiled bleakly. 'Actually, I don't really want to talk about it – so maybe we're both turning into Dora.'

Hannah bit her lip. 'Wouldn't it *help* to talk about it?' she asked. 'I mean, *everyone* forgets things now and again. And we're a terrible family for – for bad moods, all of us. Wouldn't it make everything seem less serious?'

'No,' said Fran. 'It would make it seem more real. I don't want to be going mad, thank you. I just want to feel normal.'

Hannah put her arms round her mother and hugged her as tightly as she could. 'Mum, you'll be fine, you're just tired.'

Fran said nothing and stared at the calendar on the back of the kitchen door. The illustration for October was a photograph of St Peter's Church, with the Musgraves' window glowing in a rare shaft of sunlight.

Dora didn't come up to Rose View for supper, although Hannah could see her in the cottage, moving back and forth in the kitchen carrying terracotta plant pots.

Hannah had sensed a mild *froideur* emanating from her grandmother since she'd resumed her friendship with Fiammetta. She'd had to turn down an offer of supper and opera appreciation a few nights back because she and Fiammetta were going to see a film at the new multiplex; Dora had been arch and distant ever since, to the point of not even asking her for a lift to the next book-group meeting (*Hidden Lives* by Margaret Forster) because she didn't think it was 'Hannah's kind of thing'. None of this made Hannah any more keen to reopen old wounds but, in a grim way, it tended to make her believe Fiammetta was right.

Fran didn't want any supper, and went up to her study after *The Archers* with two sheaves of other people's problems. Hannah made herself a banana sandwich and ate it reading the local paper. There were still no jobs she could do, but now she found that annoying rather than a relief.

Mrs Kelly, she noted, had started writing a summary of the book-group meeting for the arts page. It fitted in nicely between the reviews of local band nights at the Fox and Hound ('Bloodaxe played with their usual ferocity to a crowd of over twenty "headbangers" . . .') and advertisements for brass-band concerts in the civic hall. Significant portions of Mrs Kelly's copy, Hannah suspected, had been lifted from the book's cover and welded on to more personal observations, judging by such jarring sentences as 'The essence of humanity in all its fragility is juxtaposed with sweeping panoramas of shattered geography. Mrs Kelly suggested that it would make a nice film, if rather gruesome!' The phrase 'Mrs Kelly suggested' appeared roughly every three sentences. Mrs Hind and Dora seemed to have been excised altogether.

Oh, God, thought Hannah, with a pang of nameless dread. *I now know people in the local paper well enough to see when they're making stuff up.*

At half past ten she made a cup of coffee for herself and took one up to Fran.

As she walked into the study, Fran closed the web page she was looking at. Unfortunately, her lack of skill with the computer meant she closed her e-mail application by mistake, leaving Net Doctor Mental Health Issues on the screen.

Hannah's heart sank and she made an internal note to do a cache check when she went on the Internet to go through her day's notes from the villa. 'Brought you a coffee,' she said.

'Oh, er, thank you.' Fran moved her papers, trying to make a space for the mug on her cluttered desk. 'I was looking on the Net for some background information on a case,' she added hurriedly.

'Really?' Hannah turned away so that Fran could close the window properly. Out of habit, adopted during the hours of assessing pictures at the villa, her eye fell on the framed collage that hung next to the door. She'd never spent long enough in Fran's study to look closely at her mother's collection of bits and pieces. Fran eschewed pretty pictures in favour of facts: she had three framed front pages (Margaret Thatcher's resignation, Princess Diana's funeral and the collapse of the Berlin Wall), her university degree certificate and a couple of Christmas cards Hannah and Dominic had made at school.

The collage by the door consisted of pale fawn and brown penny stamps with Linton postmarks, neatly cut from envelopes and arranged in circles, mosaiced at intervals with darker blue and green receipt stamps; curly Victorian office writing rippled over the queen's head, and round the edge there were circular postmarks from Liverpool, Manchester, Bradford and Carlisle, dating from 1840 onwards.

'What's this?' asked Hannah.

Fran swivelled on her chair. 'What? Oh, it's something one of the managers got the miners to make during the depression when there wasn't much work up at the pit. Louise Graham-Potter was throwing it out after Constance died. Chucking it out! God, that made me so angry.'

'The miners made it?'

'Yes.' Fran scooted her chair back to look at it. 'They weren't running full shifts when business was bad. The men had to turn up at the pit head for work at five in the morning – walking *miles* some of them, from Etterthwaite and further than that – and the foreman picked out the ones he needed and the rest had to go home. And they all had wives and kids to feed. It's made from letters that came into the mine offices – shows you the sort of world Linton had in those days. I'd like to think Arthur commissioned some others like it, but I've never found any in the house.' She shrugged. 'Are you going to tell me what it's worth?'

'I can't,' said Hannah, 'only in money terms, and I wouldn't even know that. It isn't about money, though, is it?'

There was a little silence between them.

'Are you off to bed?' asked Fran brightly. 'Early night?'

Hannah looked at her watch; it was ten to eleven, not late by her standards in London, where she'd read or talk until one, but she felt sleepy so much earlier here. The sea air, Dora always said.

'I might have a bath first.' She squinted at Fran. 'Don't be too long yourself. You don't get enough sleep. I've heard you wandering around in the night.'

'Yeah, yeah,' said Fran. She turned back to the collage. Her eyes were hooded and thoughtful.

Hannah went to leave, then, remembering something, added, 'Have you seen my mobile around? I need to recharge it.'

'No,' said Fran, snapping to attention. 'Where did you have it last?'

'Well, if I knew that I wouldn't be looking for it, would I?' Hannah mentally awarded Fran ten points for being totally predictable.

'Is it in your coat pocket? Or your bag?'

Hannah thought hard, trying to pin down the flutter at the back of her mind, and finally succeeded. 'Oh, damn,' she said, seeing the phone quite clearly in her mind's eye. 'I think I've left it up at the villa.'

Fran looked at her watch unnecessarily. 'It's a bit late now for waking up Mrs Graham-Potter, don't you think? Can't it wait until morning?'

'No,' said Hannah, at once. What if Fiammetta rang or texted her? 'No, I need it. I've got a key. She'll never know I've been in. Mrs Tyson says she takes enough sleeping pills with her cocoa to doze through the arrival of the Four Horsemen of the Apocalypse.' Hannah checked her pocket for her keys.

Fran peered at her over the top of her glasses. 'Are you expecting a call? I thought you'd run away from all communication.'

'No,' said Hannah. 'And no.'

'We haven't talked about your flat, have we?' said Fran. 'What you're going to do about giving up your lease.'

'I'll be back in ten minutes,' Hannah said firmly, and slipped out of the room.

Hannah marched through the garden with more bravado than she felt. It had stopped raining but the grass was wet and water dripped from the dark branches on to her hair. Clouds scudded rapidly across the sky, sometimes obscuring the moon. As breezes shivered through the trees, the rustlings from the orchard sounded as if someone might be hiding but not bothering to be secretive about it.

'Oh, get a grip,' Hannah said aloud, and regretted the nervous way her ears pricked for any response from among the trees.

She ploughed on through the overgrown grasses of her mother's garden. The paths were so familiar to her that she didn't need to

look where she was going, and instead kept her eyes fixed on the
long windows of Hillcrest, half dreading, half hoping to see some
figure standing there, looking out towards the flat horizon of the
Irish Sea, as Dominic had promised.

There was nothing in the windows tonight except the occasional
reflection of the moon.

As she got nearer, Hannah's fingers closed round the keys in her
pocket. She knew exactly where her phone was: on the table in
Faith's room, by the window. She could remember leaving it there,
because reception in the house was so erratic, and that was one of
the only places where she could get a signal. Hopefully Fiammetta
hadn't rung and drawn attention to it. Hannah bit her lip. Her
voicemail message was very London – fake posh and offhand –
and she wasn't sure she wanted Fiammetta to hear that old version
of herself.

Hillcrest's white exterior caught what little moonlight there was,
and slicks of rain made the black paint of the back door gleam
darkly. Hannah hesitated. Now she thought about it, this was a
weird thing to be doing, letting herself into Hillcrest Villa, through
the back door, like a burglar or a servant. Despite the adult privilege
of holding her own key, she felt seven years old again.

But then, she thought, shaking off a shudder, it wasn't as weird
as going round to the front, knocking on the door at this time of
night and explaining what she wanted. If Mrs Graham-Potter
actually *came* to the door.

No, Hannah told herself, I can get in and out without waking
her. It'll be kinder to do it this way, rather than frighten her with
knocking and peering through the windows.

There were faint signs of light deeper in the house as she
unlocked the door and pushed it open.

'Mrs Graham-Potter?' she murmured experimentally. There
wasn't any point in waking her up, but if she heard movement

downstairs . . . Hannah wouldn't have been surprised if she kept Samuel Musgrave's Purdey under her bed.

There was no reply, but somehow the silence in the house wasn't absolute, rather as if it was breathing, making faint noises in its sleep, as the water-pipes and wooden window-frames contracted in the cold night air.

Sleeping, maybe, but Hannah felt the house was aware of her presence. And if it could dream, about the people and the parties that had filled the staircases, about the arguments contained behind doors quickly pushed shut, and the moments of private joy ingrained in the thick fabrics, then what revealing flickers of the past would it choose to show her about Dora?

Hannah's breathing quickened with fear. I need to get my phone, she thought sternly, dragging her mind back to practicalities. *I need to go in and get my phone.* It's only a dark house, for God's sake.

Silence. One of the cats came slinking from the shadows of the kitchen and, with a sudden rush of speed, slipped between her legs and out into the garden, where it vanished into the bushes with a soft rustle. Hannah jumped, and cursed it under her breath, more to relieve the pounding in her chest than anything else.

Gently, she pushed the door shut. Dead leaves had stuck to her jeans, and she pushed off her trainers so that she did not trail mud over the polished floor. She wrinkled her nose. The kitchen smelt of fish – boiled for the cats – and china dishes had been left stacked on the side for Mrs Tyson to do in the morning. Mrs Graham-Potter, it seemed, did not have supper beyond a cafetière of coffee.

'OK,' Hannah whispered. A light shimmer of fear had settled on her skin. There was something over-familiar about the movements she was making, the night-time smell of the house – she couldn't put her finger on what it was, but it was unsettling. Dominic's voice was loud in her head, talking about the haunted corridors and all the rooms they'd never been in. Although the logical part of Hannah's brain knew that the easy way to stop it would be to throw on the lights and call Mrs Graham-Potter's name as she did so, something wouldn't let her. Her mother or grandmother might do that, but she didn't have such confident control of the situation.

Hannah padded down the hall, averting her gaze from the mirrors, repeating, 'It's just a house, it's just a house.' She looked at her feet as she walked past the hunched shapes of the coats hanging on the hooks in the hall. The sound of her footsteps changed as she went from the parquet to the threadbare hall carpet, then over the newer rugs near the study.

She peered into the drawing room, in case Mrs Graham-Potter was still up, dozing in her chair. Moonlight, mixed with a distant street-light up the road, cast a pale orangy glow through the net curtains. The three armchairs were grouped companionably around the unlit fire, like the three old women who used to sit in them. Their high wings meant that Hannah couldn't see whether Mrs Graham-Potter had nodded off there. She took a hesitant step into the room to see better and, for a chilling second, felt positive that all three were occupied. Her breath stopped and she could hear the blood beating in her ears.

Her eyes skittered across the room in search of movement. Was that . . . ? The cushions on the chair nearest the fire seemed to be moving, as if someone were shifting in the seat, trying to get comfortable. Or stand up.

Before she could breathe, or summon the courage to scream, a car drove down the hill, flooding the room with white light. The glass eyes of the stuffed owl glittered. As the shadows moved round the room, she could see that the chairs were empty. Not even a cat to disturb the cushions.

She clung to the door-frame.

Don't be so ridiculous, she told herself. Frightening yourself like this. You're far too old to be behaving like a child.

But this time she didn't say it aloud.

She went to the stairs, found the first step and reached for the mahogany banister. It was smooth under her fingers, leading upstairs like a ribbon.

She shut her eyes as she climbed up, knowing, as she went, which photographs she was level with. The lacrosse team, the whole-school photo, the debating team: all those fierce eyes staring out at her from the long-exposure pictures. One of those little girls asleep somewhere in the house; the other two still there in shell form, their clothes hanging in the wardrobes, their combs arranged on their dressing-tables, their spirits wandering around the rooms where they'd laughed and entertained and swallowed their secrets.

Stop it! Hannah reprimanded herself. This is just what Dominic used to do, and he was only winding you up.

At the top of the stairs the stained-glass window let in the street- and moonlight in monochrome pools that fell on the polished wood of the blanket box.

Concentrate on that, she thought, the number of times you've seen that in the daytime, looking perfectly normal. She forced herself to think about Mrs Tyson, carting the Hoover from room to room, complaining under her breath about her veins. About Dora, having coffee and polite conversation in the drawing room. Real people, living people.

Yet Constance and Faith, in their youth, were becoming as real to her as her grandmother, and here in their shadowy house, with the constant whisper and murmur of ancient pipes and sea breezes finding their way through old windows, they didn't seem gone. More eerily, what if she saw a fragment of her own grandmother's childhood caught in the fabric of the sleeping house – Dora as a little girl, running down the corridors from her nursery, watching the party below through the banisters on the landing?

Hannah shivered. Her hand was on the doorknob of Faith's room. With an effort she turned it and went in.

The room seemed different in the dark, and the huge bed dominated it with a nearly human presence. She could see her phone on the table by the bay window, and was grateful for the sight of something that connected her with her own real world.

She kept her eyes fixed on the window now and didn't look at the bed again. She couldn't remember if its curtains had been drawn when she was in earlier that day, but they were now. The room smelt of the heavy old fabric, and of the beeswax on the dresser and wardrobe. Like the flowers in Dora's garden, the house seemed to let out its smells at night. Hannah tried not to think of the hands that had rubbed in the wax, or the sleepy breaths that had floated up into the hanging fabric – she concentrated only on the fixtures and fittings she'd been listing.

That's all there is in this room, she reminded herself – fixtures and fittings.

It was too dark to see the paintings on the walls, but traces of light gleamed off the frames, reminding her that they were there. She thought of Matthew Fisher, and wondered if he would stay in the house as a spirit too, or if he would go back to the pit cottages where he had grown up. *Could* he stay here, alongside the ghostly traces of Samuel Musgrave, breaking things in his blind rage, or Joseph, prowling the servants' quarters in the attics for unsuspecting housemaids? Hannah shuddered.

As she walked towards the window she saw her own ghostly reflection approaching, faintly lit by the moonlight, which caught on her watch and on the buttons of her jeans and jacket. She focused on it to stop her eyes flicking to catch any movement behind her.

Within a few steps she was at the window, standing so close that she couldn't see a reflection. The view swept over the orchard, taking in Dora's little cottage and the inky sea, where the lights of a few fishing-boats twinkled beyond the harbour.

Hannah breathed slowly, staring out at the horizon, letting her hands rest on the window-frame. The twitchy fear melted out of her chest and was replaced by a comforting sense of place that swelled through her body, and weighted her down.

I really belong here, she thought. There isn't any point in trying to go elsewhere. *This is my home, this is where I'm safe.*

A strong feeling of security welled inside her. *This is my home, this is my place.*

She had no idea where it was coming from, but the words were loud and clear in her head, spoken with the same calm conviction that she'd heard as a child, hiding in the cupboard in Rose View.

This is where I'm safe, this is where I'm from. This is mine.

It was almost as if the house were speaking to her.

Hannah jerked abruptly out of her trance, and became aware once more of her wet jeans. She caught her breath: something was moving in the garden. 'Oh, God,' she breathed. Was this going to be the ghost, reappearing for her like some old Pathé newsreel, triggered by her presence in Faith's room, disturbing the layers of time and dust that had settled over past disruptions?

She gripped her phone.

It was hard to see where the movement was coming from among the shifting trees and bushes, but she knew something was down there, and not just one of the cats.

It was a person.

Hannah squinted into the darkness. A figure was moving through the orchard, gliding along without a torch, partially hidden by the branches and small trees. It was tall, and pale, and moved as if on tracks, quick and sure. As if it wasn't touching the ground.

It was heading for Dora's cottage.

'Granny!' Hannah couldn't shift her gaze from the garden, even though she now felt utterly vulnerable, standing with her back to the rest of the room, away from the bedroom door and what might lie beyond. Somehow it seemed more dangerous to take her eyes off the garden.

The figure passed behind some trees, then emerged again and reached the little rosebeds outside the front door where it seemed to hesitate. Hannah squinted again. It seemed smaller now, and lighter; a woman's shape.

It knocked on the door. There was an agonizing pause that lasted for ever before the door opened and Dora appeared in her long dressing-gown.

Then Hannah realized, as Dora ushered the figure inside, that the shape was Louise Graham-Potter.

Chapter Twenty-one

The next morning Hannah walked into Faith's bedroom as quietly as she could, treading carefully on the patches of carpet she knew would creak under her trainers, clutching a bunch of flowers from Dora's garden. Now it wasn't a collection of sleeping memories she was afraid of disturbing, but a real woman, albeit one clinging with frail hands to the living side of the house.

Louise Graham-Potter was asleep, a doll tucked up in Faith's big double bed. The mossy coverlet seemed too heavy to lie over her, and her face was grey and pinched. Hannah hoped she was asleep — there were no signs of life.

Mrs Jackson, one of the carers from the old people's home a few doors down, was only a slightly more positive bedside companion than the Angel of Death. She was sitting awkwardly on a wicker-backed chair, as if she expected it to collapse any minute or, alternatively, for Louise to spring to life and take her to task for slouching in the company of a lady. She was reading a third-hand copy of *Woman's Own*, open at the astrology page and, with every other glance, sneaking a look at Mrs Graham-Potter.

Her eyes lit up with relief when she saw Hannah's solid presence by the door.

'She made a real fuss coming in here,' she whispered, 'but the doctor insisted. He said it would be warmer, what with the fire.'

They both looked towards the black grate. Hannah felt a twinge of fear at the sight of the hot flames in the dry room. There was so much dryness in this house – wood, paper, furniture – that it was easy to imagine it burning like an amaretto paper, flying up into the air then disappearing.

'I don't know what's brought this on,' Mrs Jackson went on. 'It seems to have been very sudden. Dr Gale said she was talking about being out too late in the garden. But we know she can't have been out, don't we? She doesn't go out.' She dropped her voice. 'I've seen this so many times before. I do hope she's not . . . you know . . . becoming Unreliable.'

Without realizing it, Hannah pulled Fran's mild-disapproval face. It was strange to hear someone talk about Mrs Graham-Potter as though she was just another old dear in the village, to be looked after and patronized into manageability.

'I'm sure there was a good reason for whatever she said she did,' said Hannah. 'What did Dr Gale suggest?'

'That she's got a chill.' Mrs Jackson sniffed. 'As I say, it could be anything. Sitting in a draught. Or forgetting to close a window. And her age, of course.'

She didn't apportion blame, but Hannah knew what she'd be thinking. *Someone should be living in with her.* Not Dora, because she was far too old; not Fran, because she had a full-time job fighting crime. *Me*, she thought, with a pang of guilt.

'And did Dr Gale leave any instructions?' she asked.

'Just to keep her warm and keep an eye on her.'

'No medicine or anything?'

'No. But he did say to . . .' Mrs Jackson dropped her voice '. . . to let him know if she starts rambling. It can be a short step for these old dears, you know, from a little chill to . . . more serious ailments. Terrible how quickly they can go downhill. We see it a lot, you know.'

'Yes, well . . .'

'She's had an amazing run, hasn't she?' Mrs Jackson shot a calculating look over Mrs Graham-Potter's fragile form. 'How old is she? Nearly a hundred? Still, I suppose she didn't have what you'd call a hard life.'

Hannah goggled, amazed as ever by the easy way rudeness could be sugar-coated with concern in Linton. 'And what do you mean by that?' she asked.

Mrs Jackson was already getting her bag together, folding *Woman's Own* neatly to fit. She looked up in surprise. 'Oh, nothing, dear,' she said. 'Just that she's led the life of Riley, really.' She gave Hannah a book-group smile and rolled her bag of mint imperials tightly shut. She didn't offer Hannah one.

The room smelt different this morning, perhaps because of the fire crackling in the grate. Hannah presumed Mrs Tyson had laid it, although there'd been no sign of her downstairs. A spark leaped out onto the green tiles, fizzled and died.

Mrs Jackson tutted. 'You want to get a fireguard up here.'

'Aren't you going to stay?' asked Hannah. Her stage-whisper echoed round the high ceiling.

Mrs Jackson sniffed again — part of the language of disapproval round here, thought Hannah. If you didn't know, you'd be forgiven for thinking there was a permanent outbreak of flu.

'I've things to attend to at the hospice.'

'Of course.' Hannah smiled politely. Gossip to pass on to Mrs Woodward up at the surgery, more like.

'I'll see myself out,' Mrs Jackson said. 'Better if you stay with her.'

Hannah started to rise but Mrs Jackson beat her to it.

'Just give me a ring if . . . if, you know . . .' She pulled a 'sad' face and disappeared, leaving a faint aroma of old ladies and mints behind her.

As soon as the door shut downstairs, Mrs Graham-Potter's china blue eyes snapped open, like a doll's.

Hannah was preoccupied with stuffing Dora's flowers into a jug without breaking the stems or spilling water everywhere, and missed this. When she turned to the bed, she was a little startled to meet the direct gaze, but recovered well.

'Hello,' she said. She put the vase down on the bedside table, remembering at the last moment to slip a crocheted mat underneath it. 'You gave us all a bit of a shock but you're in good hands now.'

She stood back from the bed, pleased that for once she'd come out with the right grown-up comment. Somehow it was easier to slip into the old-lady routine with Mrs Graham-Potter in bed and out of her smart suits.

In fact, it was startling how much she *did* look like an old lady now. Age had crept into her skin and round her eyes. Maybe Mrs Jackson was right: maybe this was the beginning of a very quick descent, like Dorian Gray when he'd slashed the painting.

'Oh, please. *Hannah.*' Mrs Graham-Potter rolled her eyes witheringly. 'Why do you think I've been pretending to be asleep all morning? The drivel I had to put up with! That stupid woman.'

Every other word was breathy, but Mrs Graham-Potter's voice was still full of her usual disdain. 'Why *will* people of that type insist on treating you like an imbecile just because you're in bed? Exactly the same when Faith had her stroke. As if her brain . . . had gone overnight.'

Hannah was frantically trying to recall what Mrs Graham-Potter might have overheard while it had been assumed that she was out for the count.

'And that doctor!' Mrs Graham-Potter went on. 'I felt like saying to him, "Where did *you* get *your* degree from, then?" Off-comers, these new ones. Forget that I'm not one of these bovine old women.'

Hannah looked away, not wanting the old lady to see the doubt that had crept into her face at the mention of the degree. Maybe if you told yourself something over and over again, it became part of your life. Did it really matter to anyone else if it wasn't true?

'Why didn't you say you weren't asleep?' Hannah stammered.

'Because I've got a mild *chill*, not senile dementia. I'll be perfectly all right in a few days and then—' She broke off to cough, which soon turned into painful retching.

Without thinking, Hannah slipped on to the bed and put one arm round her shoulders, holding a towel to the old lady's mouth to spare her the indignity of the bucket that Mrs Jackson had left by the bed. 'Careful, now,' she said. 'Careful.'

The hacking stopped, and Hannah touched away the strings of saliva hanging from her mouth. The lips looked odd without their sheen of lipstick, more like an old turtle's.

Mrs Graham-Potter put her hands to her face. Hannah was terrified she was crying, because she had no idea how to react. But when she brought the hands down to the quilt, her scornful expression had softened a little, more when she met Hannah's fearful eyes. 'Hannah, there's something I need to discuss with you . . . on your own,' she said. 'Your mother isn't likely to come over this morning?'

Fran had left the house early, a long time before Hannah had risen, even before the milk float had rattled up to their door. The three bottles had been waiting on the step when Hannah made herself breakfast: a pint of skimmed for Fran, the pint of semi-skimmed that Fran had ordered every other day for Hannah, and the pint of full-fat that the milkman left at their door for Dora to collect, since the cottage had no access road.

Fran never usually left so early. If it wasn't court, it would be a hospital appointment. Hannah pushed that thought away.

'Well, I think she's busy in court,' said Hannah, 'but I'm sure she'll be along later to see if there's anything you need.'

'No, I'm glad it's you. Wanted to talk to you.'

Mrs Graham-Potter appeared to be working a thought back and forth in her mind. Unlike Mrs Tyson, she didn't move her mouth like a cow chewing the cud while she did so.

Hannah didn't rush her, and instead let her gaze roam around the room, in search of things she'd missed off her list. Faith's room, unlike Constance's sparsely furnished cell, was full of stuff that no one had dared move after her death. There was a jointed artist's model on the mantelpiece, made from dark, polished wood; it had been left posed in a defensive crouch. Faith's, she supposed, from her art class. It looked valuable. Hannah made a mental note to add it to her list.

Mrs Graham-Potter coughed and lifted her head with some effort. Hannah waited, and watched as her gaze flicked repeatedly to the Matthew Fisher dock paintings and away again.

'I haven't been entirely honest with you, Hannah,' she said finally, 'and there are things we need to discuss. While I still can.'

Hannah wondered if this was going to be the moment.

'There are some paintings that I'm afraid I've kept back from you.' Mrs Graham-Potter paused. 'Now, you'll think I'm a dreadful old prude, I expect, but it's always been . . . a most sensitive matter in the family, and I needed to be certain that you would handle it properly.'

'Oh,' said Hannah.

Mrs Graham-Potter raised a hand, then placed it unexpectedly on Hannah's. It lingered there for only a few seconds but Hannah felt her dry touch burn on her skin. Mrs Graham-Potter had never touched her before. She was not a touching person.

'I'm not as stupid as Mrs Jackson imagines. I know I don't have much time left.'

'No, no,' soothed Hannah automatically, but stopped when Mrs Graham-Potter glared at her.

'I haven't. Last night probably didn't help, but who knows if it would have made any difference? I'm ridiculously old. Too old.' She paused for breath.

The fire crackled, and Hannah thought how companionable this would be in any other circumstances. Instead, despite the bright sunlight and the warmth, she was aware of a chill in the room.

'I need you to help me through to the sewing room.'

The sewing room? thought Hannah, with a shudder. Whose bell rang and rang in the kitchen? 'Where's that?' she asked. 'Mrs Tyson mentioned there was a problem with the wiring for the servants' bell in there. Is it locked up?'

Mrs Graham-Potter's face betrayed nothing. 'I wasn't aware of any problem with the bell. It hasn't been opened for some years, no. I'll show you. Help me, will you?'

Mrs Graham-Potter eased her legs out from under the heavy covers and, with a huge effort, put her small feet into the slippers by the bed. She was wearing a chic pair of old silk pyjamas, cut like a Chinese mandarin suit, with black frogging at the front. Hannah bet that Mrs Jackson didn't see a lot of old women dressed like that. She took the dressing-gown from the back of the door and helped Mrs Graham-Potter into it. She wondered if she should bring forward the wheelchair that Mrs Jackson had carted up from the old folks' home.

'I suppose she thinks I need that now, does she?' rasped Mrs Graham-Potter, with her old acidity. 'They're all like that in the home. Want to reduce you to a level they can deal with. I need my keys.'

She clung to the carved oak bedpost with determined grace.

'Where are they?' asked Hannah.

'In my room. On the dressing-table.'

That was a real concession to her weakness, thought Hannah, as she slipped into Mrs Graham-Potter's room, opposite Constance's. Allowing someone else to root around in her things. And it was a sign that she must have been rambling if she had allowed Dr Gale to put her to bed in Faith's room, she mused, as she looked for the keys amid the pots and perfume bottles on the cluttered dressing-table. Downstairs, no one was even allowed to sit in Faith's *chair*.

When she did lay her hands on the keys, they weren't the bunch Mrs Tyson had, but a larger collection on an old-fashioned chatelaine ring.

As Hannah weighed them in her hands, she thought of all the doors and boxes and cabinets and cupboards in the house that were locked with these keys. There were more than fifty, of all shapes and sizes, none labelled. When Mrs Graham-Potter dies, no one will have a clue what these are meant to unlock, thought Hannah. Or what was worth locking up in the first place.

In her absence, Mrs Graham-Potter had wrapped herself in the dressing-gown and was looking determined. They made their way slowly down the long landing. Hannah wasn't sure how best to help elderly ladies along when they were weak on their legs: she ached to pick Mrs Graham-Potter up and carry her like a rugby ball. Her own pulse was racing at the thought of what might be inside the room and it was all she could do not to run.

At the end of the landing, Mrs Graham-Potter turned right, and went down a little corridor that Hannah hadn't noticed. It had no windows and only one door at the end. 'Now, then.' She fumbled with the keys, trying to remember which fitted the lock. Her hands were shaking with the effort, but Hannah waited until the old lady offered them to her with a weak smile before she gently took them and tried first one, then another.

The seventh fitted and turned with a satisfying clunk.

Hannah waited for Mrs Graham-Potter to lead her in.

'Go on,' she said. 'Open the door.'

'Are you sure?' said Hannah. If she had kept this room a secret for all these years, she had to be sure it was the right time to let it go.

'Open the door, Hannah,' she said impatiently. 'I know what's in there.'

Hannah grasped the doorknob, feeling its brass coolness against her palm, and turned it. The door opened without a creak, releasing stagnant air that smelt of old newspaper and unbeaten rugs.

Hannah stepped inside.

It was another large room, with tall sash windows that looked out up the hill. Filigree net curtains obscured the view, although the shafts of sunlight were strong enough to show the motes of dust sent spinning by her entry. Three leather armchairs were grouped around the marble fireplace, in an empty echo of the drawing room, and white sheets hung over some sizeable pieces of hidden furniture. What immediately caught Hannah's attention were the dusty stacks of paintings propped up against the salmon-pink walls.

Cautiously she walked across to the nearest and pulled the first picture towards her. It was big and square, framed in simple black satinwood. Elegant but stark, with neat tape fixings on the back.

Hannah's heart hammered with the instinct that the painting she was holding would reveal something that couldn't be ignored and put back once she saw it; that somehow it would spill out a secret about her own history that her grandmother couldn't or wouldn't tell. Before she turned it round, Hannah carried it to the armchair, where it would be in the best of the winter sunlight, and set it down.

Then she turned it round and stepped back.

The painting was by Matthew Fisher, Hannah knew straight away. It had his distinctive bold outlines, and strong blocks of colour that glowed off the canvas. But instead of the fishing-boats and spindly pit workings she'd seen in Faith's room, these images were of a woman, stretching herself over an unmade bed, unashamedly naked. She wasn't a skinny virgin, or an art-school model, but a woman of about thirty; her thighs were strong and her long stomach had a ripeness that reminded Hannah of papayas. Dark blonde hair spilled around her face in dishevelled coils and she smiled with a confident directness that burned off the canvas. Even if her cheeks weren't flushed with tell-tale rosiness, it was clear from her eyes, if not her nakedness, that her lover had just left the luxuriously rumpled sheets.

Hannah's own cheeks flushed: she felt she was looking over the artist's shoulder at a creature half real and half his own adoration of the subject.

'It's Faith,' said Mrs Graham-Potter, flatly.

'Faith?' But Hannah could see it now: Fisher's honesty was just as exacting as it had been in capturing the individual stoicism of the rough dockhands. He might have loved her, but he hadn't flattered her into unrecognizability: her legs were sturdy, rather than slender, and her strong nose hadn't been shaded away. More than that, the expression in the dark eyes was a classic Musgrave challenge, even if the pose was something Hannah would never have associated with Faith in a million years.

She wondered how long Faith had lain on the cooling bed like that, exposed and open, letting her lover find every curve and line of her body, confident that he was capturing more than just the physical record of her form. Or maybe it wasn't a pose. Maybe it was a fleeting image he'd carried in his head for days and days, the slightest detail seared on to his mind's eye.

Hannah swallowed. It was an astonishing picture: astonishingly erotic, astonishingly well executed, astonishingly personal.

'Matthew Fisher painted this, didn't he?' she said, and Mrs Graham-Potter nodded.

'It's the most beautiful thing I've ever seen.' Hannah's voice echoed in the room.

'Do you think so?' Mrs Graham-Potter exhaled heavily. 'I'm afraid I can't see it like that.'

'Well, I know it's quite . . . explicit but—'

Mrs Graham-Potter interrupted her with a wave of her hand. 'I don't mean . . . Seen all that before.' She hobbled to the nearest armchair, clutching the shrouded furniture for support, and sank into its depths. She and the chair let out a sigh.

'Are they all of Faith?' asked Hannah, eagerly.

'Have a look.'

She went back to the first pile, picked up the next picture, and set it against the wall. It was Faith again, pinning up her hair at her dressing-table, the one that was still in her room: her supple back had the elegant curve of a cello, rising from a silky pool of discarded paisley dressing-gown. In the next, she was sleeping, curled up on a sofa; in another, she sat at the table by the window in her room and stared out to sea, while a vase of fading white tulips threw pale light on to her high cheekbones, matching the ageless beauty of her proud forehead with their own brief moment of perfection. It was a classic pose, but she wasn't the demure little woman waiting for her husband to return from a voyage: she was the owner of the ships, or Helen of Troy, or Elizabeth I, and there was an imperiousness in the expression that was curiously ambiguous.

Hannah turned over painting after painting until she was surrounded by a Faith Musgrave she had had no idea existed. The Faith Musgrave Hannah had thought she knew was stern, moral, faintly patronizing with her soup kitchens and Sunday School outings for the deserving. She had reams of serious books that she'd read and discussed. She was always fully dressed, usually in riding gear.

Yet Matthew Fisher had captured something utterly feminine, even more so than her beautiful sister's pink and white loveliness. And Faith seemed to exude a confident allure that was as challenging as the glare of any male Musgrave in the portraits in the study.

'Do you not like them because they're not of the Faith you knew?' asked Hannah. She was itching to see the rest, but if they were embarrassing to Mrs Graham-Potter she'd have to wait.

'They're evidence of a terrible mistake,' said Mrs Graham-Potter, stiffly.

'They're very valuable,' said Hannah. 'I mean, there's so little of his work in the marketplace, and he's really starting to pick up interest overseas. I found one of his seascapes for sale on the Internet in America for well over five thousand pounds and it was just a small sketch. These are worth . . . I don't even know . . .'

Mrs Graham-Potter managed a smile. 'Yes, the irony hadn't escaped me. I hate the awful things, yet they're worth a fortune.'

But you didn't hate them enough to destroy them. Hannah began to do the maths in her head.

There were fifty, maybe sixty large paintings here, not to mention the ones in Faith's room. And with the provenance . . . 'So why didn't you sell them?' she asked. The answer occurred to her immediately, but she wanted to hear it from the old lady.

'Why didn't I sell them?' Mrs Graham-Potter's breathy voice lifted with incredulity. 'Sell them? And let everyone know that Faith Musgrave had had a love affair with a married miner, and lay around the house like a whore in a seraglio?'

'But he wasn't a miner,' said Hannah. 'I mean, he *was* a miner but he was an artist too. That's nothing to be ashamed of.'

'If you'd had to live with the scandal hanging over you, you wouldn't be so glib.' Mrs Graham-Potter wheezed, but waved away Hannah's anxious hand. 'And she wasn't so open about it herself. Kept him a secret, down there in the garden, pretending he was just the groundsman.'

Hannah wondered for whose benefit that was, considering the whole town had apparently known what was going on, and still talked about it. 'But after she died? Surely it wouldn't have mattered then?'

'It did to us. We were the ones who had to face out the gossip, you know. Constance put them in here and locked the door. That one,' she indicated the nude on the chair opposite hers, 'used to be in Faith's bedroom. Constance hated it. Said there was something about the expression that reminded her of their father.' Her face darkened. 'I can see it too, you know. A certain . . . cupidity.'

'I know what you mean,' said Hannah, slowly. 'Has anyone else seen these? I mean, does Dora know they're here?'

'No, she does not,' snapped Mrs Graham-Potter. 'No one's seen them. They're not fit for public viewing.'

There was a silence as they both gazed at Faith sprawled on a scarlet bedspread. Outside, the lunchtime traffic was crawling up the hill.

Mrs Graham-Potter looked away first. 'Can you take this down, please? It's . . .' Her voice trailed off.

Hannah moved the picture and propped it against the wall, so only the neat framing work on the back was visible. Fisher seemed to have done it himself, from the initials and the date. It was the art equivalent of processing your own private snaps instead of taking the films to Boots.

'What would you like me to do with them?' she asked. In an illuminating instant, it dawned on her that this was what the whole 'valuation' scheme had been leading up to. Forget the stacks of anodyne Lakeland scenes and the trinkety milkmaids. It was all about the discreet solving of a knotty family problem that would leave Mrs Graham-Potter quids in and sweep yet another secret under the carpet.

'I'd like you to find out how much they're worth, and dispose of them for me,' said Mrs Graham-Potter, without a trace of shame in her voice. 'Preferably overseas, if that could be arranged.'

Hannah marvelled at the very Linton assumption that anyone outside a five-mile radius of the town would know who Faith Musgrave was, let alone care what she looked like naked. The fact that 'this miner' was already more famous than Faith Musgrave would ever be had apparently escaped both Constance and Louise.

'I don't know how long that would take,' Hannah began. 'There are . . .' Another thought had presented itself, curling around and spreading insidious roots in her mind. 'Surely Dora should see them before they're sold?'

'Why?'

'Well,' said Hannah, slowly, 'aren't they part of her, um, heritage?'

'I hardly think this is how she would like to remember Faith.'

'Well, no, but this is art,' replied Hannah, as fast as she could, without seeming rude. 'This is a significant body of work by an important local artist. I realize that it might not be the way Dora remembers Faith, but surely . . .' She trailed off. More to the point, she reasoned, if Dora was the named ward of the Musgrave sisters, were these pictures in fact Mrs Graham-Potter's to sell?

'When were these painted?' she asked.

Mrs Graham-Potter coughed fractiously and wrapped her dressing-gown tighter round herself. 'I don't remember. Before the war?'

'When he was living down at the cottage?'

'I imagine so.'

Hannah left the stack of paintings and went to sit in the armchair opposite Mrs Graham-Potter. Seeing how chilled the old lady was, she got up again, took one of the blankets off a chest of drawers, and tucked it round her shoulders.

'Thank you,' said Mrs Graham-Potter.

She seemed to be shrinking by the minute, but her eyes were still as sharp and quick as they were in the old photographs, where she stood between Faith's confident presence and Constance's protective arm. Fran would go mad if she knew I'd let her out of bed, she thought. 'Why don't you tell me how Matthew Fisher came to be living down there?' she asked.

Mrs Graham-Potter waved a dismissive hand. 'Oh, it was a very long time ago.'

'But I'm interested,' said Hannah. 'And there's only you left who really knows what happened. And if you don't tell me, then it'll just disappear and the paintings won't mean the same.'

A wry smile appeared on Mrs Graham-Potter's turtle lips. 'That was what we hoped.'

'Please,' said Hannah. 'What's the harm now? I feel as if I've come so close to her, touching all her things and walking round her house. It feels odd not knowing about this central part of her life.'

There was a long pause, as though the truth that had been buried for years in the old woman's mind was rising back to the surface like a barnacle-encrusted whale coming up for air.

But it was coming, Hannah could tell. It had something to do with Mrs Graham-Potter's visit to Dora the previous night, with the closed curtains and locked door at the cottage when she'd called round that morning. She held her breath and didn't dare say anything in case the wrong word changed the old lady's mind.

When Mrs Graham-Potter did speak, her voice was so faint that Hannah had to lean forward to catch the words.

'Faith met Matthew Fisher at her art class. She began one in 1917, when she was still only seventeen or so.' She folded her hands in her lap. 'She joined a group of local ladies who used to run various night classes for the miners at the welfare hall, reading and so on, so they could improve themselves. Don't know how she thought art would benefit them in the pit, but that was Faith. I suppose Matthew was handsome, in a rough sort of way. Not like the Musgrave boys – they were what I'd call handsome, golden hair, clean-looking. Matthew was . . . surly.'

She fell silent and fidgeted with her diamond rings. Hannah sensed the delicate social gulf between Louise and the two sisters: their brothers, after all, were what she would have aimed at, not a miner who was only a few social steps below where she'd risen from.

She also thought of the photograph of Matthew and Constance, sitting on the bench outside, and the ambiguous expression on Constance's face. The beginnings of their friendship – a friendship of which Louise hadn't approved, perhaps.

'Matthew's sister, Molly, was a parlourmaid here, until she fell pregnant. They lived up on New Row, where that supermarket is now. Eight of them in a little house. Molly's baby was absorbed into the family, I understand, another younger brother. It happened a lot, in those days,' she added, seeing Hannah's sympathetic expression. 'Those sort of people were used to it. Faith used to visit them when the shifts were cut back at the pit, with food and so on for the babies. Constance didn't like to go up that end of town. It was very rough, you know, but Faith wouldn't listen to her.' She sniffed, not so very differently from Mrs Tyson. 'We knew why later, of course. It wasn't enough for her to see him once a week at the art class.'

'But wasn't he married?'

'Not when she first met him,' said Mrs Graham-Potter. 'But we went away, you know, to university, and when we came back, he'd got himself tied up to one of the kitchenmaids here. Shelagh Connelly, her name was. Pretty Irish girl.' Her accent was slipping, letting in a shade of harsh Linton vowels.

'And?' said Hannah. Her mind was racing with dates, trying to fit this flurry of events into some kind of order, alongside the possessions she'd already documented in the house: the girls going to university, Faith's art classes, Constance's mysterious leap into the harbour, the last twin boys dying of flu, Samuel Musgrave's death, Ellen's retreat to health spas . . .

'And Faith didn't give art classes any more, not after university. I did tell her at the time that it wasn't what men needed. After that it was all reading and writing. Matt had a living to earn, a family to support. I dare say university knocked some of the more Lady Bountiful ideas out of Faith, but I did say . . .' The lips set in a grim line and Mrs Graham-Potter's eyes were unfocused. She was probably hearing the arguments all over again in her mind.

'I, well, I meant Shelagh, actually,' said Hannah, after a moment's pause.

'Oh! She caught diphtheria, along with half the town in 1923. It went through the pit streets like *wildfire*. Awful sanitation in those slums. Dirty. All three of Matthew's children caught it, then Shelagh, and when Faith found out, she moved them all into the gardener's cottage so she could keep an eye on them.'

'She didn't worry about catching it?'

Mrs Graham-Potter laughed, a dry sound like rustling paper. It wasn't a kind laugh. 'Faith never worried about catching anything. Influenza, diphtheria, lice. She didn't even worry about going round those houses, offering help to widows whose husbands had been killed in her father's pits. I'd say that required far more bravery than cleaning up after the sick.'

'Did you go too?'

Mrs Graham-Potter gave her a look. 'I wasn't so daft.'

Hannah was taken aback by the fury in the rheumy eyes. 'I take it they died, then? Shelagh and the children?'

'They did. Matthew wasn't allowed to go back down the pit in case he spread germs to the rest of the lads. That was when he started painting those pictures of the docks. There wasn't much work going anyway.'

Hannah thought of the heartbreaking collage on the wall of her mother's study, the big fingers arranging the stamps with laborious care. At least Fisher had had an alternative. She wondered if there had ever been any bitter aftertaste of charity in Faith's support of him; or if the feelings he and Faith had had for each other had spoiled his success.

'And they fell in love?' asked Hannah.

'I suppose so,' said Mrs Graham-Potter, grudgingly. Her lips shut tight.

'And he stayed there for the rest of his life?'

The old lady nodded.

Frustration gripped Hannah, but she tried not to let it show on her face. What was the point of being delicate now, so many years later, with everyone concerned dead and beyond embarrassment? She wanted to know *how* this passion had bounded over the high walls of expectation; whether his maleness or her social status had taken the initiative; with what tiny gestures this sensitive man had demonstrated his feelings; and how it had felt for Faith to see how she was driving his creative vision. She longed to know what Matthew Fisher had done to turn efficient, independent Faith into the sprawling concubine on the unmade bed; and what Faith had seen in him to encourage the first sparks of talent into such accomplishment.

But thanks to Louise and Constance having locked all this away, no one would never know, and the only indication that they'd ever met was a collection of pictures that Louise Graham-Potter wanted to sell out of the country so that she could draw a veil over the affair.

'He clearly adored her.' Hannah nodded at the paintings.

Mrs Graham-Potter shuddered.

Hannah wished she didn't have to drag the information out of this crabbit old woman, but there was no one else to ask. And the questions she really wanted to ask were too big, too impertinent – too destructive.

'Mrs Graham-Potter, why were you in the garden last night?' she asked, quietly.

'I beg your pardon?'

'I saw you, down at Dora's cottage.' Hannah didn't want to add where *she* had been to see this.

The old lady dropped her gaze to her liver-spotted hands, folded neatly in her lap, as they had been in her schoolgirl debating photographs. Then she raised her head, so that her sharp chin pulled taut the loose skin on her neck, and said, 'I went to talk to Dora. I know she keeps very late hours.'

'You went to tell her about these paintings?'

'It's very hard, Hannah, when you're obliged to keep secrets that aren't yours to keep,' she went on, a touch of petulance creeping into her voice. 'It isn't up to me to decide when to tell Constance's secrets or Faith's. The fact that they're not here doesn't make it any easier. And we were brought up to believe that some things are best left in the past.'

'But it makes such a difference with these,' said Hannah. 'Their provenance is what makes them so *special* as a private collection. Matthew Fisher could become a very significant artist. He's already sought-after. I realize it's all very personal to you but, as a curator,

I've got a different kind of responsibility. And I'd be failing in that if I didn't ask you about how they came to be the way they are.'

'Is it really so important?'

'Well, yes.'

Mrs Graham-Potter sank back into the depths of the leather chair and closed her eyes, gathering herself.

Hannah knew she was watching the last turns of an old lady's mind, and that it was cruel to press her when she was so weak. The fight had gone out of her. But this devotion to discretion only had true value in the quick moment when it came to a choice between telling or concealing. The years when the truth could come out another day had trickled away. Now it had come down to a blunt decision between loyalty to dead friends and honesty to those who were left, and Mrs Graham-Potter didn't look strong enough to make it.

'Paintings aren't the only things that need provenance,' said Hannah.

Mrs Graham-Potter opened her eyes. 'Dora was told about her parents,' she said. 'Faith put it all down for her in a letter, with the pictures from her childhood, and she chose not to know. That was her decision, and she made it.'

'What about us, though?' Hannah demanded. She felt as if she were standing on the edge of the cliffs outside. 'What about Mum?'

'That's not in my hands,' said Mrs Graham-Potter, and relief was audible in her voice.

Chapter Twenty-two

Having supported Mrs Graham-Potter safely to her room, and instructed Mrs Tyson to check on her every half-hour or so, Hannah returned to the sewing room and, with trembling hands, began to turn each picture to face out until she was surrounded by images of Faith Musgrave.

There was one pastel study of her lying on a bed with a child curled up asleep next to her, like a little dog. Hannah recognized the bedroom at once: Dora now slept in it in the gardener's cottage. The windows were the same, even down to the tendrils of blown roses in the background and the familiar solid oak of the bedstead.

The little girl, she guessed, was Dora.

She studied the picture hungrily; there were so few images of Dora as a child, but Matthew Fisher had caught enough of her likeness for it to be unmistakably her – the wide-spaced eyes, closed here with long dark lashes, the pouting red lips half open, as if she were mumbling in her sleep. What moved Hannah most was the casually tender way that Faith's hand lay on her arm.

How could anyone deny Dora this? thought Hannah, with a

rush of hot indignation. There was such obvious devotion here, not just between Dora and Faith but from the shadowy third participant as well – Matthew, sitting a few feet away, probably on the bed with them, probably barefoot, like Faith, painting not just what he could see but also what he felt for the woman and child in front of him. It was impossible to remove him from the picture, just as it was impossible to remove him from their lives.

Hannah could see a difference between the paintings created in the cottage and those done in the house. In her own four-poster bower Faith was imperious; in the cottage she was softer, more beautiful, and the lines flowed with a different confidence. This was where Faith was free to be herself, to unbend with the man she had chosen. In Hillcrest, she had to live according to what was expected of her – as far as she could bear to. Her father's shadow hung over each part of her life, with those of all the other Musgraves: acquiring, commanding, opening fêtes and deciding livelihoods. In the cottage, surrounded by trees and roses, in earshot of the sea, she was Matthew's lover, and that was all. No wonder she looked as though life was bursting out of her.

There were so many paintings, sketches and studies stacked around the walls. Faith had allowed him to draw her in any way he chose, throughout her life, and he must have painted on most days. The whole of their long affair had been gathered up and locked away in one room of the echoing house. Ultimately contained by the Musgraves, like everything else. Hannah wondered what the contents of the room were worth altogether. As much as Hillcrest itself, she had no doubt. She shook her head at the irony. Yet again the Musgraves had found another local resource and mined it, profiting from Linton's hidden treasures.

Impulsively, she seized a little study of the cottage, surrounded by laden rosebushes, bathed in late-afternoon light. No one would miss it – how could they, when only she and Mrs Graham-Potter knew that any of this was here? It wasn't much, but it would settle a little injustice. Even if she was a Musgrave herself, Hannah knew where her other loyalties should lie.

She was striding down the hill before she could change her mind. Betty Fisher's number had been in the phone book, the only Fisher listed in the town. The Rookery was on the Etterthwaite Road, out towards the rows of cottages built for the miners working in the Back Pit, sealed up long before Hannah was born. The cottages were now full of supermarket workers and call-centre staff, outside walls studded with pearly satellite dishes.

The Rookery stood on its own: a small, solid house with deep-set windows and a large overrun garden, choked with sea-roses and weeds. Hannah shoved open the gate. It came off one hinge and hung awkwardly, covering her legs with a shower of rust. It felt like a warning, but she strode through the grass to the front door, trying not to notice the mounds of Alsatian shit everywhere. There was no bell so she rapped the large old-fashioned knocker smartly against the peeling paint before she had time to change her mind.

An age passed before a chain clattered on the other side, and Betty Fisher's beady eye appeared in the crack. A dark smell of dogs, sweaty clothes and unemptied bins slipped out, catching Hannah unawares and nearly making her gag.

She swallowed and fixed a smile on her face. 'Hello,' she said brightly. There was no point holding her breath – if she was going to go in she'd have to breathe at some point. 'Could I come in for a moment, Miss Fisher? I have something for you.'

'What is it?'

Hannah wavered. Was it fair to consign this little picture to such a dump? Then she remembered why she was there. Don't be a snob, she told herself. 'Can I come in?' she repeated.

Betty Fisher's face vanished, the chain rattled and the door opened wider.

Hannah peered inside, overwhelmed by a gut reluctance to go any further, then walked in.

'You'd best come through to the parlour.' Betty Fisher stumped down the small hall and into the front room.

Hannah followed gingerly.

'Now,' said Betty Fisher. 'What've you come to say?' She sat down at the table and stared at Hannah over a bowl of dusty wax fruit.

'I've brought you something from the house.' Hannah reached into her satchel and brought out the painting, wrapped in a duster. 'I've been going through the artwork and I think you should have this.' She handed over the sketch of the cottage.

Betty Fisher took it, glanced at it, and a faint expression of pain crossed her face. 'What med you think I'd want this, then?'

Hannah was taken aback by the defiance in her voice. 'Well, it's one of Matthew's. I didn't think it was right that most of his work should be up at Hillcrest when you're his relative . . .' She was about to say 'too' but stopped herself just in time. 'It's worth quite a bit of money,' she added.

'Is it, now?' Betty Fisher's tone was steely. 'And that's summat you'd know all about, isn't it? Money.'

Hannah's chin jutted. 'It's a beautiful painting. Matthew was a talented artist.'

'Well, you'd know best. But why do you imagine I'd want a paintin' of the place where she had him hid away like a pet dog, eh?'

'I'm sorry?'

Betty Fisher glared at Hannah, with a ferocity that made her flesh creep. 'Aye, you've no idea. Just like your mam. You'd think all t' sacrifice was on her side, wouldn't you? Stoopin' to be wid a poor miner from her father's pit? Wouldn't have him in that grand house, though. Even when he couldn't go back to his own home.'

'I don't—'

'Aye, he were no great hero to his marras, once he'd tekken up wid that Faith.' Betty Fisher was almost spitting with bitterness. 'We've long memories here, lady. Long memories. There were plenty round here ready to lynch Matt when they knew. Givin' up a man's job to paint pictures for t' lady of the manor.' She made a guttural noise of disgust.

'You can't say that,' protested Hannah hotly. 'Matthew Fisher's a very important local artist!'

'He were a traitor to his mates. And he could nivver come back here again after. She had him by the balls for the rest of his life.'

Hannah pushed back her chair and stood up. Her legs trembled. 'That's not how it was.'

'How do you know? Were you there?'

'I'm very sorry if that's how you feel, but I was just trying—'

'You were just trying to tell other folk what to do, being the big boss,' snapped Betty Fisher. 'Playing Lady Bountiful. Just like Faith. And that Dora. And your do-gooder mother. You're all the same. Don't tell me how it was. You don't know near enough to start following in their footsteps, young lady. You know nothing at all.'

Hannah could feel hot tears prickling at the back of her eyes, but she set her face, clinging to her dignity as best she could. 'Keep the picture. Sell it. Do what you want with it. But I think you should have it.'

'That'll make you feel better, I suppose? Buying folk off. There's no change in your family.'

Hannah couldn't bear the sneer in Betty Fisher's voice. She didn't think she'd ever felt such powerful dislike from someone and it shook her. But underneath that was her own pain – of realizing that she *had* done the wrong thing, and that most of what Betty Fisher had said was true. That deep down, Hannah was just as patronizing and controlling as Faith had been: she couldn't help it.

Betty Fisher didn't seem mentally unbalanced now. She seemed clear-eyed, sharp and hard.

Hannah grabbed her satchel and made for the door as quickly as she could, bumping into stacked newspapers, dirty bags and coats piled up along the walls like insulation. As she left, she could hear the dog barking furiously in the back garden and, from the corner of her eye, spotted three distinctive little harbour views, tacked to the wall.

Mrs Tyson had returned for her mid-afternoon tea and had brought Hannah a speckled custard tart from the bakery. It was waiting for her on a blue china plate, next to the teapot and the copy of *Now* magazine. She liked to pore over it with her tea and biscuits, in search of celebrities who'd lost too much weight. Any woman under thirteen stone was 'thin' to Mrs Tyson, whose family prided itself on its solidness.

'Is this for me?' asked Hannah, making sure before she tucked into it.

Mrs Tyson nodded and carried on washing up at the big stone sink.

'Is it your birthday?'

'No,' said Mrs Tyson. She shook out the cloth and hung it over the taps to dry. 'I just thought you're looking too thin these days. And,' she added, 'they were reduced at the bakery. Four for the price of three.'

'Thank you,' said Hannah, unaccountably flattered. After the shock of the morning, she felt childishly grateful for any kindness. For a moment she considered telling Mrs Tyson about Betty Fisher, but a voice in her head warned her to forget about that – forget she'd ever been up there.

She sat down at the table. 'Can I pour your tea?'

'Yes,' said Mrs Tyson, stiffly. 'That would be kind. You know how I like it.'

Hannah did. The colour of a house brick, with four sugars and strong enough for any lost dunked digestives to remain on the surface. Before she could think of any anodyne gossip to use as bait for juicier stuff, the back door opened with a gust of cold sea air and Dora strode in, bearing an enormous bunch of flowers from her garden, a copy of the paper and, somewhat tactlessly, in Hannah's opinion, her in-memoriam notebook. Her brain raced to make the connection between the sleeping child of the painting and this regal old lady.

'Ah, hello, Irma,' Dora said, briskly, not seeing Hannah at the table. 'I don't suppose you could clear the fireplaces out in the drawing room and the study, could you? You'll need to check the chimneys for birds' nests, I'd imagine, but there should be plenty of coal in the cellar.'

'Hello, Granny,' said Hannah. 'Planning on burning something?'

'Oh, Hannah!' said Dora, with feigned cocktail-party delight and a smile that didn't quite reach her eyes. 'Of course I'm not burning anything. They're for Louise – she'll need to be kept warm.'

'Nothing like a real fire when you're poorly,' agreed Mrs Tyson.

Hannah thought of the elaborate central-heating system, working perfectly well in the house; the brass pipes that gurgled and clicked in silent rooms. The pagan comfort of a real fire was different, she supposed.

Then her mind slipped to Betty Fisher's house, stacked with papers, junk and resentment. She had to close her eyes and take a mouthful of scalding tea to dispel the image.

'So, how is she?' Dora asked Hannah. 'Your mother said Mrs Jackson had been in and that's always akin to calling for the Last Rites.'

'Um, she seems pretty lucid,' said Hannah, with a quick sideways glance at Mrs Tyson, who knew much better than she did. 'She's asleep now, isn't she, Mrs Tyson?'

Mrs Tyson merely huffed and returned to the sink with her pan scrubber.

'Good,' said Dora. 'I'm pleased she's peaceful.'

She looked at Mrs Tyson, who was vigorously scouring tea-stains off the sink. 'Irma, it would be so helpful if you could make a start on those fires now.'

Mrs Tyson gave Dora a hard look, then grudgingly set down her pan scrubber and picked up her mug of tea.

'Thank you so much,' said Dora, with her winning smile. 'I know it'll make the world of difference to Louise, being able to smell a good roaring fire airing the house.'

Hannah added her own, less certain smile, which Mrs Tyson partially returned before she stomped off down the corridor. She picked up her own tea and looked at the custard tart. She didn't feel like eating it now.

Dora started hunting about the big kitchen cupboards for a vase to put her flowers in, opening and shutting the doors with an unnecessary amount of vigour.

Hannah wondered about coming straight out and telling Dora what she'd found upstairs, but some instinct made her hold back. 'Granny, what did Mrs Graham-Potter say to you last night?' she asked instead, as soon as Mrs Tyson was out of earshot (inasmuch as she ever really was). 'I know she came down to the cottage.'

Dora's back straightened and she put a large crystal vase on the table. It spread little diamonds of light on to the pine as the sun shone through it.

'Well, if you must know, she came to talk to me about Faith,' she said. 'I don't know exactly what brought it all on. She was in a very queer mood, and I did wonder then if she was sickening for something. I thought she was going to confess to poisoning the lot of them.'

'But why on earth didn't she just *phone* you instead of walking through the garden at that time of night?'

'That's what I said to her!' Dora shook her head. 'She insisted that she wanted to talk to me face to face. I have no idea how she got through the orchard – it was pitch black and she can't have been in it for years. Old women, Hannah. Who knows what they're thinking?'

'So what did she want to tell you that was so urgent?' asked Hannah curiously. It *must* have been the paintings she'd gone down to talk about. Before it was too late. Her heart quickened.

Dora turned away slightly, so the light caught the wrinkles and shadows of her profile. 'She asked me if I wanted to know who my parents were. And I said no, I didn't. And that was that. I made her some tea, and we talked about the weekend parties they used to throw, and about the people who'd come up from London and stay in the house. Nice things like that. Happy memories for both of us.'

While she talked, Dora was unrolling the flowers from their newspaper. Although winter was creeping quickly into the air, her walled garden was still mysteriously full of scent and glowing colour. She'd picked musky late roses, some heavy-headed and full-blown, others with little pinched clustering heads, laid on top of spearmint-green eucalyptus and dark green foliage. At the end of each stem there was a neat white circle where her secateurs had cleanly separated it from its living branch.

Slowly, the strands of secrets and motives twisted into a chain in Hannah's mind, as she watched Dora disentangle the flowers and arrange them in the vase. If Louise Graham-Potter had gone to the cottage to offer to tell Dora about her parents, and Dora had refused, then surely that meant more than just the tacit permission she had needed to show the paintings to Hannah? Didn't that confirm who her parents really were? If Dora had wanted to be told that she was the secret child of Faith and Matthew Fisher, it would have been up to her to look at those paintings first, and deal with their complicated legacy.

But Dora hadn't wanted that, so the weight of responsibility for the secret and the paintings had remained on Louise Graham-Potter's shoulders; she knew she could now ignore the former, and pass on the latter to Hannah, so the two old ladies had both been freed, in the middle of the night, in the cottage that had held the secret for years, to talk about dinner dances and the difficulty of getting a decent four-piece jazz band in Linton.

To pretend, just as she had pretended about Hannah's overdose, that none of it had ever happened.

Hannah looked up at her grandmother, and tried to see Faith's burning eyes or Matthew Fisher's strong cheekbones. She could see only Dora's delicately applied rouge. 'Couldn't it have waited until the morning?' she asked, knowing it couldn't.

Dora tweaked a eucalyptus stem. 'Who knows? We all have strange thoughts in the middle of the night, and when you're as old as Louise ... Your being in the house has stirred up a lot of memories, I think.'

'Really?'

'Oh, yes. Seeing you looking through her past, asking questions, making her remember. I think she wanted to go back to happier times in her head, you know. When everyone else has gone it's hard to believe they ever really happened.'

Hannah wondered if Dora saw the irony in that. Once again, Mrs Graham-Potter had offered her a chance to uncover her beginnings and set her own daughter free of confusion, and once again she'd turned it down, in favour of comforting memories of parties and satin shoes. Hannah wished Dora hadn't told her that. She wasn't sure she had the strength not to tell Fran – if, indeed, she was meant to keep this to herself. Whatever mind-games Dora and Mrs Graham-Potter were playing with each other, Hannah didn't know if she had the intelligence to join in. How could she ever have imagined that Linton was some kind of intellectual backwater?

She looked again at the custard tart, and wished Dora hadn't appeared. She could have been enjoying a strong cup of tea and some criticism with Mrs Tyson now. She couldn't even take unalloyed pleasure from the paintings, feeling the responsibility of knowledge that came with them.

'There!' Dora stood back from her arrangement. Her flowers had filled the huge crystal vase, which presumably had once stood in the entrance hall of the London house, resplendent with an elaborate Victorian arrangement. It was too big for normal use now, needed a whole armful of blooms to do it justice.

'Beautiful.'

Dora smiled. 'Do you think your mother would mind if I popped up for dinner tonight?'

'Well . . . I don't know,' said Hannah. 'I'm not in this evening.'

Dora's smile froze. She picked up the vase and took it to the sink. 'Really? Where are you off to?'

'I'm having a pizza in town with Fiammetta.' Hannah could feel the chill almost immediately. 'Then we might go and see a film,' she added recklessly, even though they weren't planning to.

'Again?' There was a loud gush of cold water.

'Yes, again,' said Hannah. 'It's not a *Coronation Street* night, and we're working our way through the new restaurants. I'm thinking of offering my services to the *Gazette* as a food critic.'

'That's not what I meant.'

Hannah knew that, but she didn't think Dora deserved to be humoured, after what she'd just told her. The urge to stir things up was too powerful to resist, especially when Dora was behaving like a member of the Royal Family. 'I don't know what Mum's up to, though,' she added. 'She's very cagy about her movements at the moment. Probably something to do with the amount of time she's spending up at the hospital. She still doesn't know what's causing her funny turns. She's seeing the psychiatric consultant.'

She glanced up to see if this had any effect on Dora, but if so, it didn't show on her face.

Dora wiped the bottom of the crystal vase with a tea-towel. 'Never mind,' she said, brightly. 'I've some fishcakes in the freezer.' Her expression changed as her eye fell on something on the table. She replaced the vase absently on the draining-board and Hannah watched as she picked up the custard tart and lifted the plate into the air.

'Mrs Tyson brought it from the bakery,' she said. 'Have it, if you want.'

'No, no.' Dora dumped the tart on a saucer and turned the plate over in her hands, her eyes sparkling as her fingers ran over the pattern of the faded gilt. 'It's from the dinner service,' she said, 'the smart one from the London house. The one I used to have my dinner sent up on, if I was ill or if Faith was entertaining. Oh, I've often wondered where it was.'

'I think it's just a loose plate,' said Hannah awkwardly. 'Mrs Tyson uses it for her biscuits sometimes.' It was so hard to stay cross with Dora when her moods changed like the wind.

Dora frowned, as other thoughts skimmed across her face. Clearly she didn't intend to share them. She sighed and put down the plate.

'Let me know if Mrs Graham-Potter wants anything,' Hannah offered.

Dora's mouth puckered into a grudging smile. 'You've got quite enough to do running around after other people,' she said, and swept out with her flowers.

Chapter Twenty-three

Hannah spent the rest of the day noting any interesting books in the library under the supercilious gaze of Sir Samuel Musgrave, whose later portrait, as an older, more bilious-looking man, hung above the fireplace. She was unwilling to go back to the sewing room while Dora was in the house; even knowing that the paintings were there made her feel guilty, and she had an inkling of why Constance had found it easier to shut them away.

Sir Samuel's library was much the same as his study downstairs, filled with books she doubted he had ever opened, let alone read. The one item of interest that she found among the *Cumberland Directory* and bound reports from the family mines was a leatherbound book detailing running expenses for the London house, until it was sold in 1960. It made fascinating reading, the lists of provisions for the kitchen and standing orders with farriers and coalmen but, most interesting of all, Hannah could work out when the house had been used for parties or for the season, and when it had been left to tick over with a skeleton staff. Between 1919 and 1922, someone had lived there all the time – someone with a lavish taste for flowers and driving in the park.

At five, Hannah gathered her things together so she could go home to change before she met Fiammetta. As she let herself out, the house was eerily quiet despite the three other people in it. She knew that, in Faith's bedroom, Dora would be scribbling away at her in-memoriam verses, keeping an eye on Mrs Graham-Potter while she slept. Mrs Tyson would be polishing monogrammed silver, bought by Sir Joseph Musgrave, used by his son, and left untouched by anyone other than the cleaner for the last thirty years or more.

No matter how many books she listed, Hannah couldn't ignore the nagging voice telling her that Dora was Faith's daughter and should know the truth; certainty swelled in her mind until there was no room for any other thought. All afternoon, as she'd worked at the desk and averted her gaze from Sir Samuel's smug glare, trying not to feel his hands on the books she was handling, the only tiny whisper that crept around it told her that in this house she was staff and always would be. And that by refusing to give Hannah a proper sense of place, by refusing to address her origins, Dora was shutting the door on her.

Fiammetta was waiting for her at the Coffee Pot Café, their agreed rendezvous before hitting the delights of Linton's haute cuisine. Hannah spotted her straight away. She was sitting in one of the window booths, her brow creased as she chewed a biro and looked at the crossword folded on the table in front of her.

A wave of relief swept over Hannah's heart, like the first rush of bonhomie that coffee brought her, and she crossed the street so that Fiammetta wouldn't see her approaching. That gave her a few moments more to watch her, sitting there as if she were in some Fellini film.

God, it was worth all the misery of coming back just to be friends with Fiammetta again, thought Hannah fervently. Having a proper friend made all the difference. She felt calm and happy to be with Fiammetta after a day of tiptoeing up at the villa. Somehow Fiammetta made her a more interesting version of herself. She never even had to think of how her words might be interpreted, sure that Fiammetta knew what she meant. Hannah felt herself growing like a sunflower when she was in the sunshine of Fiammetta's company, reaching out for things she hadn't dared look for previously.

She pushed open the café door and was pleased to see Fiammetta smile as the bell jangled.

Hannah edged round the tables to get to the window booths. It was reasonably busy for the end of the day. Mrs Woodward and Mrs Bradley were having tea and scones in the far corner, their furry berets sitting on the table like a couple of cats; Mrs Kelly was distributing knickerbocker glories between three face-painted kids in Manchester United kit; three separate but instantly identifiable gangs of teenage girls were crammed into the other booths – the swots with their stacks of library books, the girls who smoked, and the girls who didn't fit in with anyone else. Still reeling with goodwill, Hannah noted happily that there was a place for everyone in the Coffee Pot Café.

She arrived at the table at the same time as a cappuccino and a Hallowe'en spider cake – black sugar paste arachnid on a pumpkin orange fondant web.

'Hello!' said Fiammetta, leaning over the table to kiss Hannah's cheek. Hannah inhaled her aura of hairspray and coffee, and ignored the waitress's loud tut. 'I knew what you'd have, so I ordered it.'

'Thank you,' said Hannah. 'You're the second person to buy me a cake today.' She slipped into the booth. The cake glowed luridly on the plate. When she cut into it, it was orange sponge all the way through, with a walnut-sized blob of white icing on the top, making the tuffet for the spider to sit on outside.

'Oh, that's very good,' said Hannah, delighted. She couldn't tell whether everything was better when she was with Fiammetta because they did interesting things, or whether she was just more positive about life in her company.

'Ah, how touching. You're easily pleased.' Fiammetta sipped her coffee.

Hannah beamed. 'Well. I'm a girl of simple pleasures, really. Good company, good coffee . . .'

Fiammetta smiled, and her cheeks went into round little apples.

They sat and drank their cappuccino, and laughed about the salon and the book group, while the boy racers went past the window in their lowered Golfs and Fiat Unos, circling the limits of the town centre with more noise than speed, peering through their blacked-out windows for signs of female admiration.

At half past six, Hannah and Fiammetta were the last customers in the place and the waitresses had wiped their table twice. This ritual display didn't hurry them: they'd often been the last ones to leave when neither had particularly wanted to go home. Hannah herself had been the snotty waitress and knew all the snotty moves though she was too polite to be good at them; Fiammetta, on the other hand, could have taught even these sullen teenagers a thing or two.

'Fancy a glass of wine?' Fiammetta licked her finger and picked up the last of the cake crumbs.

'I thought we were going to try Pizza the Action.'

'I'll tell you what it's like now and save us the trouble.' Fiammetta rolled her eyes. 'Two waitresses to serve the whole place. A kitchen that will run out of pizzas at half nine and send one of the two waitresses out to Morrisons to get frozen supplies. A bad Italian menu that is based on an intimate knowledge of the Cornetto advert. And, frankly, after the day I've had, I'd prefer to get straight on to the liquid medication.'

'Fine with me,' said Hannah. 'We'll go to the Bond.'

They walked down the high street towards the harbourside, and Hannah tried not to glance at their reflection in the shop windows. There was a definite nip in the air when the sea breeze whipped out from between the buildings, and she hugged her coat tightly round her, feeling the curves and softness of her body. Most of Hannah's teenage years had been spent trying miserably to picture the gentle relief map of flesh that covered the parts of herself she couldn't see (the indentations of flesh round her bra, the broad shelf of her arse), but for once, she didn't mind. A layer of warmth was comforting up here. It made practical sense.

This is age, she thought. Next stop Dannimacs.

'You must be nearly finished up at the house,' said Fiammetta, as they went past the grand building that used to house the town's mining offices. It was now an estate agent, selling Lakeland cottages far out of most Lintonians' price range.

'I suppose so.' Hannah hadn't thought about when she'd finish or, indeed, what she'd do when she did. A forgotten end-of-term shudder ran through her. 'You could do it for ever, though,' she added. 'There's so much *stuff* up there. It's like the rock of Sisyphus but with antiques. As soon as I finish one room, she opens another.'

'Then what are you going to do?' Fiammetta didn't look at Hannah as she asked, but stared straight ahead.

'I don't know,' Hannah admitted. 'Guess I'll have to go back to London.' As she said it, she knew she didn't want to.

'You could do something similar for other people,' suggested Fiammetta. 'You know, going through their houses, valuing the estate, putting it all in order. I bet there's things you've found out that no one's known about for years up there. I'm sure there are plenty of folk who inherit stuff they know nothing about.'

It wasn't a bad idea, Hannah thought. 'I'm not sure I could go through people's history like that. It's a big responsibility, you know, dealing with what you might find.'

'I don't think you know *what* you want,' said Fiammetta, testily. 'I think it's so long since you thought for yourself that you can't even decide what you want out of life.'

Hannah stopped walking. 'That's not true,' she protested. 'I've got everything I want out of life! Had,' she corrected herself. 'I *had* everything I wanted. And now I don't.'

'Really?' Fiammetta stood still and put her hands on her hips.

Hannah couldn't read the expression on her face, or be sure what it was that Fiammetta wanted her to say.

There was an awkward silence.

'Yes,' said Hannah uncertainly. She paused. 'No.'

'Yes, no,' said Fiammetta. 'Yes, no. Yes? Or no, Hannah?'

'No.'

'Sure?'

'Yes.'

A huge seagull swept over their heads, cawing with an ugly screech. Fiammetta didn't flinch. 'Are you sure you don't want to check with your mother?' she asked, sarcastically. 'Or maybe your grandmother?'

'Yes!'

Fiammetta carried on walking, twitching as though she could barely contain herself. 'So, that was all you wanted, was it? The crap boyfriend, the job that freaked you out? And the flat you couldn't afford?' Her voice was thick with contempt.

'You're just looking at this from a typical Linton perspective,' Hannah said. 'My flat was fine! It was more than fine compared with the dumps some of my friends lived in.'

'The flat . . . Oh, well, first things first,' snapped Fiammetta, sardonically. 'And this was going to be *enough* for the rest of your life?'

'No!' said Hannah. 'But I thought it was!'

'Until when?'

Until when?

Not when she'd left her job: that had made her feel sick with panic that she'd never get another.

Not when Toby had dumped her either: there was nothing she wouldn't have done to get him back.

Not even when she'd first come back, because until now, she'd always assumed she could return to London and pick it all up again.

Now, though, Hannah knew she didn't want to do that, because what she really wanted wasn't as simple as the right job or a big flat. Nothing was that simple any more. Maybe it never had been, and she'd ignored it. Hannah looked at Fiammetta, her quick eyes and bright red mouth, and wished there was some easy way she could make everything simple again. 'Until now,' she said, bravely. 'I thought it was what I wanted until now.'

'What is it you wanted that you don't have?' Fiammetta's voice was low, and insistent.

Hannah shook her head. She wasn't going down this rabbit-hole again, not while she was still sober enough to stop herself.

'What is it?' demanded Fiammetta.

'Nothing,' said Hannah. She rubbed her eyes with the back of her hand. 'It's nothing. I want a drink. Come on.'

She strode down the high street towards the Bond, already working out in her head how much she could drink and still get home safely. There were taxi numbers in the bar, if the worst came to the worst, and she had her own keys.

Deal with one thing at a time, she told herself. If you unravel Dora's big secret, maybe everything else will work itself out.

Fiammetta stood for a second, looking down the street after her, then strode on to catch her up.

They stayed in the Bond drinking wine and talking too quickly until it shut. First a bottle of red, then a bottle of white, and then, because Hannah no longer cared what happened to her credit card, two bottles of champagne. No matter what she drank, she didn't feel as drunk as she should have.

When chucking-out time came, Hannah was gripped by a sudden desire to see the harbour and stumbled outside, leaving Fiammetta arguing with the coat-check girl about which leather jacket was hers.

The cold night air made her gasp for breath after the stuffiness of the smoky bar. A few feet below where she stood, the tide was lapping in and the moonlight shone over the oily water, glinting off the new metallic flags the council had hung round the harbour to represent the trade winds that had blown Linton's sailors around the globe and back into their own dour port.

Hannah thought of Constance standing where she was now, then leaping into the freezing darkness, searching in the dirty water for her spaniel, and shuddered. The docks were deep at high tide and hid God knew what beneath the surface – dead seagulls, fish guts chucked overboard from the trawlers, all kinds of detritus. At least one man fell in pissed each year and was taken straight to the infirmary as a precaution – not for drowning but possible poisoning.

'You OK?'

Hannah jumped.

Fiammetta put an arm round her, hugging her from behind. 'Careful! If you're going to be sick there are much safer places to throw up.'

'Not going to be sick,' said Hannah.

'Are we going to get a cab, then?'

Fiammetta's face was close to hers and Hannah could tell she was more drunk than she looked. She had always been able to feign sobriety. But it didn't really matter for Fiammetta – she had a flat of her own, and could collapse in any kind of state, whereas Hannah had to let herself in and discuss her evening with Fran.

Inebriation seemed to come and go in her head, in waves of sound and confusion, followed by calm reason. In a moment of clarity, Hannah remembered that she had promised herself she'd sit down that evening with Fran and pass on her theory about Matthew Fisher, Faith and Dora. Then the wine clouded it again, like the tide washing away sandcastles on the beach.

'Do you want to come back to my house?' suggested Fiammetta, unsteadily.

Hannah was still thinking about Fran. She had to discuss it before it was too late and Mrs Graham-Potter clammed up again. 'No,' she said. 'Should get home tonight. Maybe we should walk a bit, pick up a cab on the main road.'

'OK,' said Fiammetta. ''S a beautiful night.' She wagged a finger. 'You'd better make the most of this if you're going to be leaving us soon. To go back to London. And your lovely flat.'

'Yeah,' said Hannah.

They walked back through the harbour, down the deserted high street and out towards the hill. There was little traffic on the road, other than the occasional taxi, or a pair of Vauxhall Novas racing each other out to the Etterthwaite estate, leaving trails of synthesized bass beats, dope smoke and girls' squeals on the still night air.

They didn't talk, but Hannah felt more settled and companionable than she had at any other time in her life. As the hill steepened, she realized that they were walking home, and even the thought of arriving back drunk with Fiammetta in tow didn't bother her unduly. An unfamiliar fearlessness was spreading over her and she could only think it was the wine.

At the top of the hill, the villa loomed into sight like an ocean liner, white and stark against the inky-blue sky. Hannah's nerve went and she stumbled. 'Stop!' She put her arm across Fiammetta's chest.

It took them both a few steps to come to a standstill.

'Sorry. Pavement's very slippery,' explained Hannah, sternly.

'What?'

'Pavement's slippy. I'm usually fine in heels. Don't think that.'

'No,' said Fiammetta patiently. 'I meant, why've we stopped?'

'Mum,' said Hannah. 'Mum'll be in the kitchen, waiting up for me.' She didn't mean Fran. She meant Dora but knew that mentioning her name would set Fiammetta off again. Dora would be there, waiting on some pretext, knowing where she'd been, and it had been too nice a night to spoil with a row.

'And?'

Hannah sighed. 'Fi, I've had such a nice evening. 'S been a lovely evening. And I'm not going in there to have a big lecture 'bout drinking.'

'Hannah,' said Fiammetta, 'you're nearly thirty. You don't need your mum's permission to go out. This has got to stop. And I don't think she'll care anyway. Not about the drinking.'

Hannah gazed at Fiammetta. Her skin was translucent under the streetlight, all shadows and peachy smoothness. She yearned to touch it, to see if it felt as smooth as it looked. 'Fi, we're both *pissed*,' she said, hoping that would cover her for any inappropriate comments that leaked out.

'I'd hope so after the amount we've got through.'

'Mum'll be all . . .' Hannah struggled for the right word. 'Disappointed.' As she said it, she could feel her heart sinking into her stomach, and in a flash of sobriety, wished she hadn't had the last big glass of champagne. The glasses were so *big* round here. Then the sobriety vanished and the spinning sensation intensified.

'So come back to my house.'

Hannah was concentrating too hard on keeping herself moving to take any notice of the ambiguous expression on Fiammetta's face. She really, really wanted to go back to Fiammetta's. But she had a drunken certainty that she shouldn't.

'No. Need to keep walking. Just need to . . .' Hannah nearly slipped off the pavement and on to the road.

Fiammetta grabbed her arm and hauled her upright.

A sharp gust of cold air swirled between the seafront houses and pushed the seed of an idea into Hannah's head. 'Let's have a walk round the garden,' she said. 'That'll sober us up.'

'Are you sure?' Fiammetta hugged her leather jacket tighter round herself.

'Why not?'

'Well . . . it's a bit creepy.'

Hannah shivered pleasantly. 'I know. We can go in through the secret way.'

With rather more care than was strictly necessary, they sneaked back down the road and took the overgrown side path that led round the back of the gardens, and eventually down on to the coastal track. The two bottles of wine in Hannah's bloodstream was insulating her against the chill in the air better than her thin winter coat – a 'fashion coat', according to Fran – but the elation surging through her would have melted an ice floe.

'Where're we going?' demanded Fiammetta, clattering down the shale path. 'Feet hurt.'

'Sssh!' said Hannah.

'Are we going to get into your house through the back gate? Tell me we're going inside at some point.'

'Can't. It's locked from the inside,' said Hannah. The back garden gate was never opened; Fran had let the rust grow over the lock, making it more secure, she said. 'There's another way in,' she added. 'Secret nuns' hole.'

She and Fiammetta sniggered at the same time, which made them snigger even more.

She wouldn't have been able to find it sober and in the light, but instinct took over and guided her feet straight to the hidden door in the brickwork that she and Dominic used to squeeze through to save walking all the way round to get to the sea path. The wooden door was covered in ivy, but when Hannah found it, the sheet of leaves lifted away like a curtain. Her fingers flicked the secret latch, moving with forgotten deftness, and the door creaked like a distant seagull, and swung back. A dark space appeared in the wall.

'Who built that door?' asked Fiammetta behind her.

Hannah stared at it. The nun story was just too stupid to tell anyone else. 'I don't know.'

'Why is it there?'

'I don't know.'

'It's too small for a person to get through. Is it a cat flap?'

'I don't know.'

'Don't you ever ask any questions at all?'

'Do you think you can get through that?' asked Hannah, squinting critically at the gap. Surely she could get through. People climbed through cat-flaps all the time on television. If she angled her pelvis diagonally, it should fit, shouldn't it?

A black doubt floated over her mind. Weren't those people who climbed through cat-flaps normally caught on *You've Been Framed!*?

But before she could communicate her fears about getting stuck and having to call out the fire brigade, she felt Fiammetta's bag being thrust into her hands.

'Well, let's have a go.' Fiammetta zipped up her jacket and crouched down, slipping her arms and head into the hole as if she were diving through it. With a quick wriggle she vanished up to her waist, leaving her long legs sticking out of the ivy-covered wall, then with another rustle of leaves, she vanished altogether. Only a dull thud on the other side, as she rolled to her feet, indicated where she'd gone.

Through the slow-moving fog of wine inside Hannah's head there was a moment of panic that Fiammetta was inside the garden on her own, and that she might not be able to get through the door before anything happened to her. It was succeeded almost before she could recognize it with a familiar pinch of envy. It always had been really easy for Fiammetta to do things like that. Taking mad risks was much easier when you had hips like a fifteen-year-old lad.

Fiammetta's face reappeared in the hole. Her pale skin was smudged with mud and a couple of stray leaves were sticking to her hair.

'Come on,' she said. Her eyes gleamed in the dark, and Hannah was uncomfortably reminded of Mrs Graham-Potter's cats. 'There's *loads* of room.'

'Even for me?' asked Hannah doubtfully.

'Even for you.'

Hannah was tempted to say no, but some impulse made her shove both their bags and her own coat through the gap. Thus committed, she took a deep breath and crouched down. Maybe she could get through. She shut her eyes, as if it would make her slippier, and put her hands through, holding her breath and leaning forward with blind hope, the way she used to when doing forward rolls onto uncertain gym mats at school.

Her hands made contact with soft earth on the other side; it wasn't cold and feeling it sinking between her fingers had a weird soothing effect. The position was comfortable: no weight on her feet or hands, which eased the spinning in her brain. A warm blanket of peace descended on her. Hannah blamed this on being drunk rather than any sudden pantheistic empathy with the soil, but she savoured the feeling of calm, knowing it wasn't something she'd be able to revisit sober.

Comfortable as it was, being soothed by the earth between her fingers, Hannah couldn't forget her outward appearance for long; she was very conscious of her arse sticking up in the air on the other side, and transferred her weight to her palms, squeezing her upper chest through, then her ribcage.

There was no sound of encouragement from Fiammetta. Hannah didn't mind that. This wasn't something she particularly wanted Fiammetta to see.

She eased her body through the gap, feeling the edges of the door-frame grate against her ribs, then her waist, then, more painfully, her hips. At that point she realized she was stuck. Don't panic, she told herself, her eyes squeezed shut. She knew if she opened them, real panic would set in.

Gradually she rotated her pelvis, trying to find a way her hips could slide through, but it was difficult as her clothes caught on twigs and snagged on splinters. With a superhuman effort, Hannah pushed down the rising tide of childish dread that was swirling in her chest.

Breathing hard, she inched backwards and felt her ribcage jam against the wood. She could hear the distant boom of the tide turning in the harbour, and an image of the mine seams deep under the sea flashed in front of her eyelids. The miners cramming themselves into three-foot tunnels, dust in their mouths and eyes, crawling further and further away from the light, the waves rolling over their heads, carrying the ships in, pressing down on the roof of the tunnel . . .

Hannah heard a yelp of fear. She assumed it had come from her own mouth and opened her eyes to see if anyone had heard her. Then she gasped. She realized she couldn't have made the first noise: it had been Fiammetta.

'Oh, my God!' breathed Hannah.

Fiammetta was standing barefoot in the middle of the apple trees, frozen to the spot with her shoes dangling from her hands. From the way her arms were spread out, like Dancing Daisy's, it looked as if she'd been enjoying the sensation of wet grass on her bare feet before something had caught her. The fear on her face was as clear as if she'd been spotlit on a stage.

Hannah saw the dark varnish glittering on Fiammetta's toenails and the blades of wet grass pushing up between her white toes. She saw her chest rising and falling quickly with shallow breaths. But she couldn't see what was frightening her.

Hannah didn't know how she freed herself from the door – the alcohol seemed to be compressing time as well as numbing pain – but the next thing she knew she was hurtling over the garden, her feet slipping on the damp grass.

It took her only a moment to reach Fiammetta. She threw her arms round the slight frame, nearly knocking her to the ground. 'What is it?' She could smell the almond hair wax from the salon. 'What's the matter?'

Fiammetta was still breathing quickly, like a frightened animal. 'I could hear laughing,' she whispered. 'under my feet or in the trees. I couldn't tell. Someone was laughing.'

Hannah's blood chilled. 'A woman's voice?'

She felt Fiammetta's head nodding against her shoulder, then her friend's hands pushed her away.

'What?' Hannah was confused.

'I want to *see*, Hannah,' Fiammetta hissed. 'I want to see where it's coming from. I don't want to hide from it. What's the worst thing it could be? A ghost? Don't you want to see it, too?'

The slurring had gone, but Hannah could only think that, from the mad excitement in her voice, she was still drunk.

'What do you mean?'

A fresh breeze scuttered through the branches of the trees above them, sending drops of old rain on to their heads. Fiammetta's breathing was still quick and shallow, but defiance gleamed in her eyes, and her pointy chin jutted. 'If I'm going to be shit scared, I want to *see* where it's coming from.'

'It's the water in the ventilation tunnels under the house.'

'Oh, come on. Don't you want it to be something more exciting than that?'

'No, I don't.'

'Yes, you do.'

Half-way up the garden, there was a bloodcurdling yowl.

Hannah jumped.

'Just a cat,' said Fiammetta. 'On heat. They sound horrible, don't they? All desperate. Like they don't care who hears them.'

'It's one of the cats from the villa,' said Hannah, with distaste. But it was impossible to imagine one of these slinking, superior cats turning feral like that. 'Didn't think they'd go in for that sort of thing.'

The lonely yowling stopped, leaving only the distant sea and the rustling leaves to fill the darkness.

Then, just as Hannah had recovered herself, another ear-splitting yowl, louder than the first, shattered the silence, and then a different one, like fabric ripping, from the other side of the orchard, and another, from up near the house. It sounded as if the garden was full of predatory toms, closing in on a howling female.

Fiammetta laughed. ''S like Linton on a Friday night.'

'Don't say that.' Hannah was sobering up.

Fiammetta pushed her again, gently this time. 'Oh, Hannah! Come on, it's just like outside Cinderella's! You haven't been out in town, that's your problem. You're spending too much time with old women . . .'

Hannah realized that they were breathing in time with each other. Fiammetta was swaying slightly, as if her centre of balance was moving with the tide. She suddenly leaned forward, stretching up on tip-toes, and touched her lips to Hannah's forehead. They were soft, dry and warm against the damp sweat that covered her brow.

Hannah's heart stopped and all the breath rushed out of her as if she'd been punched. She looked up – and felt she could have gazed at Fiammetta for ever.

Fiammetta's gaze, moving all over Hannah's face, from her eyes to her mouth, then up to her eyes again, looking for a sign.

Then Hannah leaned forward, tilted her head as boys had at school discos to make their intentions unmistakable during slow dances, and held her breath.

Fiammetta didn't move away.

Instead she carried on swaying gently, angled her head in the opposite direction and closed her eyes, letting the rocking motion of her body lead her into the reach of Hannah's kiss.

Hannah could smell the almond hair wax again, the flowery perfume, the spiciness of Fiammetta's skin before her lips touched her cheek. She paused for a second, then kissed her again, fractionally nearer her mouth, lingering longer to feel the softness of Fiammetta's downy cheek on her lips.

Hannah didn't think about what she was doing any more. All she could think of was how cold Fiammetta's skin was, and how warm her lips were.

While Hannah was marvelling at what was happening, Fiammetta moved her head and Hannah's next kiss landed on the corner of her mouth. Hannah would have started back, afraid that she'd gone too far, but Fiammetta's slim, strong fingers moved up and cradled the side of her face while the kiss slid gently on to her lips. Her other hand was tangled in Hannah's hair, the hair that she'd cut into its new shape and treated with conditioners to stop it falling out.

Hannah felt trapped in Fiammetta's hands and ecstatically happy. She let her mouth open slightly so she could taste her too.

They kissed in the shifting darkness of the garden, their mouths a tiny oasis of heat, until Fiammetta pulled away. 'Are you OK?' she whispered.

Hannah felt her breath on her face. 'Mm,' she said, her eyes still shut. She didn't dare say any more.

This was what she had wanted all along, she was certain of it. And *not* having it was the black hole that nothing else had been able to fill. Everything she had thought she knew about herself – her flat, her job, Toby – seemed oddly detached from her. None of it felt real, even the things that she thought had upset her: they hadn't made a true mark in her memory. Thinking of that now felt like recalling conversations about friends of a friend.

She opened her eyes, very deliberately, to look at Fiammetta, in case it was a vivid dream or some drunken hallucination. Their faces were so close she had to blink before Fiammetta's dark-lashed eyes came into focus. Even though the moonlight was turning the garden monochrome, in Hannah's imagination everything was too-bright Technicolor.

She blinked.

Fiammetta smiled, snaked an arm round her waist, pulled her close and kissed her again, more definitely this time, but as slowly as before. The strangeness of it heightened all the sensations exploding like flowers in her head: another woman's curves pressed against her own, yielding in the places where she was used to feeling hardness, everything at the same level as her own body, and thin enough to wrap her arms round completely. Even the smells – of moisturizer, perfume, the wine on her breath – were disorientatingly familiar.

'So,' said Hannah, when they paused to breathe. She could barely form the word for the smile breaking across her face.

'So what?' asked Fiammetta. They were both whispering.

'So, no lightning strikes come down from heaven to sizzle me.'

'Did you expect it to?'

'Yes.' Hannah turned and nervously scanned the garden. 'I expected at least one member of my family to pop up and tell me I was dragging the family name into disrepute.'

'Wait,' said Fiammetta. She put a finger on Hannah's lips. Her face was serious. 'I have to tell you something.'

Hannah giggled. The wine, the kisses and the protracted periods of standing up with her eyes shut were making her feel light-headed.

'No, really,' said Fiammetta. 'Don't laugh. It's about Dominic.'

Hannah's eyes snapped open. 'What about Dominic?' So this was the price of being happy. Please don't tell me you were in love with him, she begged silently.

'He . . . I know you loved him very much. And I know you were miserable that he never came back home,' said Fiammetta. 'Well, it was my fault.'

'No,' said Hannah. 'How could it have been? He hated it here. He felt hemmed in. He was always telling me to get out and have a life – that I couldn't live here in the past.'

Fiammetta shut her eyes and rested her forehead on Hannah's shoulder. Then she looked up, and said, 'When we were doing our A levels, before – before your overdose, he had that year out, remember? Well, he wanted to see me. Wanted to . . . you know. Take me out. I said no, and we had a row and . . .'

'Did you tell him . . . why?'

'I told him I loved you, but you didn't know and I didn't want to make things even more difficult for you. And he said no one could love you as much as he did. I think he was a bit, um, hurt.' Fiammetta looked up with a glitter in her eye. 'He was a very handsome man.'

Hannah's heart was pumping as hard as if she'd drunk ten espressos in a row. 'He is.'

'But not my type.'

'You must have thought about this a lot, then,' said Hannah.

'I have,' Fiammetta said. 'I've thought about it for years.'

'Really?' said Hannah. A warm flush ran through her, warmer than the wine.

Fiammetta nodded. 'And every time you said you didn't remember what happened the night you overdosed, it was like you didn't want to remember me.'

'But nothing happened,' said Hannah. 'I didn't . . .'

'No, you didn't,' said Fiammetta. 'But it was there, wasn't it?' She looked straight into Hannah's eyes and Hannah felt something inside her want to loop round Fiammetta's heart and tie them together.

'Yes,' she said. 'Of course it was there. It was always there.' There was a tiny pause, full of possibilities. 'I feel more drunk now than I did in the bar,' she admitted, and smiled.

'Good,' said Fiammetta. She traced her finger along the arch of Hannah's browbone, leaving a tingly trail on Hannah's skin.

'I think you should come inside for a drink,' said Hannah. Her voice sounded thick to her, her words all jumbling in a rush to come out.

'Is that a good idea?'

'Why not? It's my house too. I don't need permission. I'm a grown woman, with my own job. My own life. My own ideas.'

'Yeeesss,' said Fiammetta. Her fingers moved down Hannah's nose, round her cheek and down to her mouth again, tracing the fullness of her lips, as if she were trying to read her face the way she could read her hair.

'Please?' said Hannah, kissing her fingertips. 'I want you to.' She smiled, making Fiammetta's fingers slip past her lips, and touch her teeth. 'It would mean a lot.'

'Well . . . OK,' said Fiammetta. 'Just very quickly.'

Hannah reached out for her hand, and led her through the shadowy garden. Only a vague sense of *déjà vu* bothered her.

Chapter Twenty-four

Hannah handed in her final exam paper at three thirty exactly. She knew she'd done well, answering both questions she'd prepared for and throwing in a little extra reading to boot. And with that she felt she had discharged her duty to the school, her mother and herself.

She had walked home on the shady side of the road, already in a semi-trance but soothed with the knowledge that she'd decided what to do to settle all the whirling in her head. Hannah liked following plans.

Now, some hours later, from somewhere near the moulded cornices in Rose View's bathroom, Hannah gazed down at her own naked body lying in the bath. For once she didn't cringe with revulsion. Instead, she was surprised at how magnificent she looked. The roll-top bath, installed at great expense by Faith Musgrave's designer, was huge and its majestic dimensions made hers seem delicate in comparison. One long white arm dangled over the edge with an elegant languor. She had washed and combed her hair before she had taken the pills, and now it was drying, in steamy damp curls. Under the water, her skin looked like marble. A creamy Greek statue reclining in a pool.

There was enough bath oil to stop her going wrinkly for at least a couple of hours.

The only thing that spoiled the scene, thought Hannah objectively, was the empty bottle on the window-sill: the sleeping pills with Fran's name on. She hadn't meant to leave it there. It looked tacky. Melodramatic. It also looked rather cowardly, as if she was leaving a little loophole for them to save her. 'Typical Hannah', they'd say, 'so neat and tidy'.

It dawned on her belatedly that Fran would seize on that as her cue to blame herself and, really, Hannah didn't want anyone blaming anybody. Too late for that now.

'Hannah! Hannah?'

The voice was coming from downstairs. Unsurprisingly, the Hannah in the bath didn't react.

Hannah noticed her long lashes and wondered why she had wasted so much time trying to dye them as black as Fiammetta's. They were gorgeous as they were. And the rosy blush on her cheeks.

What a waste, she thought sadly. If only I'd been able to see myself sleeping I'd never have bothered with all those face masks.

'Hannah! Where the hell are you? I need to talk to you!'

The voice was getting nearer.

Someone was shoving at the bathroom door. Hannah hadn't bothered to lock it since everyone was out. The damp in the air was making it stick and whoever was behind it had to shove hard before it would budge.

'Listen, I'm coming in. I need to talk to you!'

The door burst open and swung back, cracking the plasterwork.

Fiammetta staggered into the bathroom. She had a bottle of red wine under one arm and some textbooks in the other.

'Hannah, where did you get to after— oh, my God,' she said. Her little white hands flew to her mouth. 'Oh, my God, oh, my God, oh, my God!'

Hannah watched with interest as the bottle slid from Fiammetta's grip and shattered on the corner of the bath, sending a dramatic fountain of red wine over her marble body and little pieces of green glass all over the tiled floor.

'Shit! Shit! No,' said Fiammetta, gripping her own face in her hands. 'Stay calm.' Her head jerked from the broken glass to Hannah in the bath to the wine soaking into the white towels on the rail.

Which would I choose first? wondered Hannah. The floating sensation seemed to be making her much more objective than normal. Broken glass, so the ambulancemen wouldn't slip and injure themselves, or the towels, before they stain?

Or, in fact, the body in the bath?

Fiammetta grabbed the towels and began sweeping the glass towards the basin, pushing little crimson tides over the black and white tiles. She half muttered, half sobbed to herself the whole time, in a mixture of Italian and phrases from television hospital dramas. When she'd cleared a space, she knelt carefully by the bath, took a deep breath, pushed back the sleeves of her white school shirt and thrust an arm under Hannah's shoulders, pulling her out of the water.

Hannah's head rolled back, exposing the whole arch of her bare throat. She reminded herself of one of Ovid's swan-women, turning into a huge white swan to avoid Zeus's marauding desires.

Fiammetta's garbled Italian turned into panic. For a moment, she hesitated with the limp statue body in her arms.

From her vantage point high in the corner of the room, Hannah wished violently that she could be in that hated body now, feeling Fiammetta's arms round her neck. She half expected to feel a great tug, as if a desire that strong could somehow drag her back to life. But she didn't, and only then did she feel the bitter pang of regret.

'Hannah! Hannah! It's me!' Another voice downstairs.

Hannah didn't remember people announcing themselves to her like this normally. It seemed unusually formal in a house where slamming doors announced people's entrances and exits. But, then, she had got into the habit of revising with her Walkman on some time ago to shut out the rows so maybe she'd never noticed.

Fiammetta didn't seem to have heard the voice either, or the sound of sensible shoes making their way up the staircase. She looked hard at the unconscious body in her arms, then pinched Hannah's nose and pulled back her head. She launched into the artificial-respiration technique they'd learned at school and promptly forgotten.

Oh, my God! thought Hannah. Fiammetta's giving me the kiss of life!

'Are you in the bath, Hannah?' Dora sounded as if she was hallooing at a hunt meeting. 'Hannah? Is there something wrong, darling?'

The bathroom door inched open and Dora's hand waved round it, followed almost immediately by her head and the rest of her.

'Can I smell— Good God! What the hell's going on?'

It was to their credit that neither Dora nor Fiammetta screamed, although the scene when Dora arrived was gory – the bathroom was splattered with what appeared to be blood and broken glass – and, far more salacious, the naked girl in the bath was apparently being seduced by another.

Dora's expression was a mixture of shock and outrage. 'Didn't you listen to a word I said?' she demanded cryptically.

'I've just found her,' wailed Fiammetta. Hannah's head slumped back and Dora let out a moan of horror. 'I think she must have taken some tablets. Oh, my God, I knew she was unhappy about something but I never dreamed she'd do something like this! She's unconscious!'

'And she just *happens* to be naked!' hissed Dora. 'And in the bath! And I see you'd made yourselves comfortable with a glass of wine! What, in God's name, have you been doing to my granddaughter?'

Fiammetta was rendered speechless by this imaginative interpretation of the evidence. For a moment, neither of them noticed Hannah's body slipping back into the water.

'You've been nothing but trouble ever since you met her!' yelled Dora. 'Are you happy now you've spoiled her whole life? Just because you're going to live and die in this godforsaken backwater, doesn't mean that she has to!'

'Shut up!' yelled Fiammetta. 'Shut up!'

'No, I will not,' hissed Dora. 'This is my house!'

'I adore her!' Fiammetta looked as if she was about to throw up. 'How can you think I'd want this to happen?'

Hannah felt a little piqued that they weren't paying her the attention she deserved. Surely they could be having this argument in the ambulance?

'Mrs Marshall,' Fiammetta pleaded, 'come on! We have to do something! Quickly!'

'Why is my bathroom covered in glass?' demanded Dora. 'Were you fighting? Were you trying to drown her in the bath – was that it? Didn't I tell you to leave her alone? Didn't I?' Her voice was rising as her hands flew in hysterical arcs.

It isn't your bathroom, thought Hannah. It's mine and Mum's. She noticed that Dora was averting her eyes from the bath, as if she was too embarrassed to look at her naked body, dead or not. She was taken aback by how badly her grandmother was dealing with this.

Clearly Fiammetta thought so too, because she turned away from Dora's windmilling arms and started to drag Hannah out of the bath.

'Help me,' she snapped at Dora. 'Get a towel or something to put her on.'

'You're all the same! This kind of carry-on might be acceptable in Italy, but it certainly isn't here.' Dora's voice was getting shriller.

Fiammetta pushed past her and grabbed a couple of thick white towels from the towel rail. They were Fran's best towels, only there for show. Fran would go mad when she found them ruined. Hannah conceded that Fiammetta wouldn't know she should have gone into the airing cupboard for old family-use ones.

Dora was suddenly silent as the enormity of the situation dawned on her. Hannah could see consternation, then fear freeze her face. One hand went slowly to her mouth.

Meanwhile, Fiammetta had somehow manhandled Hannah out of the bath and was dragging her round the bathroom.

'Wake up, Hannah,' she yelled through the veil of hair now covering Hannah's face. 'Mrs Marshall, slap her. Come on, slap her! We need to wake her up.'

'Don't be so revolting!'

'Oh, for God's sake!' Fiammetta was near to tears.

Hannah wondered where Fiammetta had got the strength to haul her around like that. Her feet were trailing on the ground like seal's flippers.

'For fuck's sake! Call an ambulance. We need to get her into hospital, as quickly as possible. She could go into a coma.' Fiammetta staggered backwards, and rested Hannah on the bathroom chair. She pulled back the hair from her forehead with an incongruous tenderness, then gave her a ringing slap in the face.

Dora winced.

No response.

Fiammetta stood up and looked as if she was about to slap Dora next. Hannah had never seen her look so fierce or so scared. 'Phone for an ambulance,' she yelled. 'Phone for a fucking ambulance!'

Dora wavered, then walked slowly out of the room.

Fiammetta peeled back one of Hannah's eyelids. Only the white of her eyeball was visible.

'Oh, God,' she moaned, grabbing Hannah's limp arm and levering her to her feet again. 'I'm so sorry,' she murmured. 'I'm so sorry.' Over and over again. 'I'm so sorry. So sorry.'

For what? Hannah wondered.

The door opened again and Dora reappeared. This time she looked more like her old self. Fresh red lipstick gleamed on her mouth, which was set in a straight line, and she was fidgeting with her diamond eternity ring. 'All right,' she said briskly. 'Everything is going to be fine.'

'Have you called the ambulance?' Fiammetta struggled to hold back her tears. 'Please tell me they're on the way.'

'I don't think there's any need for that.'

'*What?*'

What? echoed Hannah's mind.

'I don't think there's any need to have an ambulance blaring its way up here, attracting all kinds of gossip and attention. There's no need. I will take Hannah to the hospital myself. In my car.'

Fiammetta stopped dragging Hannah around and gaped openly at Dora. With red wine stains all over her school shirt, not to mention the blood trailing from Hannah's legs where shards of glass had nicked her wet skin, they looked like the survivors of an air raid. 'Have you gone insane?' she demanded. 'Hannah needs medical attention *right now!* This isn't the time to be worrying about what the neighbours will think!'

Dora shook her head, as if she had mild tinnitus. 'I don't expect you to understand. We need to be quick about it. Please leave.

Hannah needs to . . .' She flapped her hands in the direction of the naked body, and averted her eyes again.

'Hannah doesn't need anything except a stomach pump and a life of her own!' yelled Fiammetta. 'There's no way I'm leaving. And I hope you realize that this is your fault! If you'd just listened to me . . .'

'This is not the moment to apportion blame,' said Dora, primly. 'And if anyone is going to be blamed, then I think you'll find that the responsibility lies much closer to your door.'

'You're a selfish crazy old bitch!' spat Fiammetta, still clinging onto Hannah's body. 'I'm not leaving her here with you. You'd rather let her die, wouldn't you, than embarrass your family? You'd rather put her life at risk! Can you hear me? She. Is. Dying!'

A dark cloud swept across Dora's face. 'Leave now.'

'No,' said Fiammetta, very quietly. She wiped her hand across her mouth, and squeezed her eyes tight shut, desperately trying to control her emotions. When she opened them again, her eyes were as steely as Dora's.

'I might be a selfish old bitch,' said Dora, 'but when Hannah comes round she won't want the entire town talking about her, will she? Now we're going to put her in some clothes, I'm going to take her to hospital, and you're going to clean up this bathroom until it's spotless. Then if anyone asks, you were at home all afternoon and you never came near here.'

Fiammetta stared mutely at her.

'Then,' Dora went on, 'when Hannah is better, I'm going to tell her that she accidentally took one tablet too many, trying to get to sleep with one of her migraines, and that I took her to the hospital to make sure she was OK, and that we never need to talk about it again. And you will never, ever come round here. Or discuss this with anyone. In a month or two she's going to get her results, go to Oxford, and start a life away from here. Away from you and away from us, as well.' She looked directly into Fiammetta's glowering eyes. 'I'm not as selfish as you think.'

Fiammetta snorted. 'She'll ask questions. She'll know what she did, why she did it . . .'

Dora shook her head sadly. 'I think you'll find that she won't. Now, I've got some clothes out of the washing basket. We need to get her covered up.'

'Give them to me,' said Fiammetta fiercely, holding out her hand. Dora looked as if she was about to snatch the T-shirt from her. But something in Fiammetta's manner made her stand back and hand over the clothes.

High up near the moulded cornice, floating like the warm air still rising from the bath, Hannah watched as Fiammetta carefully slipped a pair of white cotton knickers over her feet and up her thighs. Her hands were hairdresser-steady, easing the knickers over damp patches on her legs where the bathwater made the cotton stick. Hannah was glad that she'd shaved her legs, so her shins were smooth and her bikini line was neat. This was the way she wanted Fiammetta to remember her, the one and only time she would see her naked.

'Hurry up,' said Dora.

Hannah was pleased that the bra matched the pants: the daisy set from M&S that she'd bought on a shopping trip with Fiammetta before their mocks. Fiammetta's little hands didn't hesitate; she fastened the hooks behind Hannah's back, pulling the straps over her shoulders, gently untwisting the left strap when it caught. Then she pulled a T-shirt over Hannah's head, and stepped back.

She was crying.

Dora held out the jeans.

'No,' said Fiammetta, wiping the tears away with her hands. 'We'll never get them on. She always buys them too small. Get her tracksuit bottoms, the ones she wears for games.'

Dora marched out and returned with a pair of navy sweatpants. Hannah had bought them when she swore she was going to take up jogging along the Ramble Way. Fiammetta yanked them on to her legs, leaving trails of blue fluff on the newly shaved shins.

'There,' said Fiammetta. Hannah lay in front of them, slumped on the chair as if she'd dozed off in front of *Coronation Street*.

'Right, I'll get her down to the car,' said Dora. 'Mrs Tyson keeps all the cleaning equipment under the kitchen sink. Wash everything, and make sure you open the windows. It smells like a public house in here.'

'You'll phone and let me know how she is?'

'Of course.'

With her new omniscience, Hannah knew her grandmother was lying, and it looked as though Fiammetta thought so too.

'Do you want some help?'

'No, I can manage.'

Hannah looked on with surprise, as Dora effortlessly humped her over one shoulder, as if she were a bag of coal, and walked carefully out of the room.

The sensation of being nothing more than atoms of light increased but before the room fractured into tiny crystals, Hannah saw Fiammetta bend down and pick up the note she had left, tucked under her clothes. She opened it, and started crying again.

Then Hannah felt herself flying up and up, as if she were on the end of a piece of retracting elastic, with nothing around her except seas of light, until her mind seemed to dissolve in her surroundings and everything around her was pure white, like the untouched snow on the fells in winter or the solid chest of a seagull flying over the harbour.

Chapter Twenty-five

Hannah held Fiammetta's hand as they walked through Rose
View's chilly cellar, but she didn't switch on the lights to chase
the shadows out of the corners as she normally did, even now
she was grown-up and not scared of what might be hiding there.
She didn't let go of Fiammetta's hand as they walked up the stairs,
in case she never got to feel the soft warmth of the delicate fingers
in her own again. Her head was filled with a bright light and a deep,
fulfilling warmth spread through her; she could only imagine that
morphine was like this.

At the top of the stairs, at the door that led into the house,
Hannah reluctantly dropped Fiammetta's hand. She thought about
concocting a cunning reason for coming in to this back way for the
benefit of Fran the watchdog, who would be tapping her fingers on
the kitchen table and checking the clock, but she was too dazed to
form ideas that didn't involve Fiammetta. She hardly dared open
her mouth for fear of blurting out all the fabulous, somersaulting
thoughts exploding in her head.

Instead, Hannah opted for a studied casualness to cover her

drunkenness, despite knowing already that if the wine caught up with her again she'd be unable to pull it off.

Still, she reminded herself, I'm a grown-up. I can do what I want. I *have* to do what I want.

'Hi, Mum, we're back,' she said, pushing open the kitchen door and speaking quickly to hide any slurring. 'OK if Fiammetta has a quick coffee?'

'No.'

Hannah froze. As she'd guessed in her worst-case scenario, it wasn't Fran sitting in the kitchen chair. It was Dora.

Fran wasn't there and, instinctively, Hannah knew something terrible had happened.

She moved to hide Fiammetta behind her, but then decided not to. What was the point? 'Hello, Granny,' she said, suddenly feeling more sober. 'Fiammetta's come in for a drink.'

'Hello, Mrs Marshall,' said Fiammetta.

'I'm surprised you dare show your face in this house,' said Dora icily.

'Oh, please.'

Hannah looked from one to the other, and felt the delicious warmth slide out of her veins, leaving a deep chill round her heart. Sickness crept up in her throat and she cursed her own stupidity in having allowed this conversation, this subtle, complicated explanation of her own plaited loyalties, to take place when she was drunk.

'Please don't start,' she implored. 'Not now. Please don't. Where's Mum?'

'Hannah?' Dora was glaring at her.

She felt something warm in her hand. It was Fiammetta's fingers, searching out hers behind her back.

Dora saw.

'Where's Mum?' demanded Hannah again, but Dora's attention was fixed behind her.

'You should go, madam,' she said. 'You've done quite enough damage to this family.'

'Me?' said Fiammetta. She sounded surprised. 'Me?'

'You. Hannah was perfectly happy until she met you. You were a distraction.' The words were snipping out of Dora's mouth like hailstones – hard and cold. Hannah noticed that the bottle of Christmas brandy her mother used for emergencies was open on the table.

'I don't know how you can say that,' said Fiammetta. 'I've never lied to Hannah, I've never forced her to be something she's not. I've never hidden anything from her.'

'And I have, I suppose?'

'Oh, you *know* you have!' pleaded Hannah, leaping in before Fiammetta could say it. At least coming from her it was the painful truth, rather than an insult from a stranger. 'You *know* you have.'

'What are you talking about?' said Dora, impatiently, but Hannah could tell she was rattled.

'Everything. There's so much we don't know and we'll never know it when you tell us. Your parents. Mum's childhood.' Hannah swallowed. She felt as though the words were being ripped out of her. These weren't things she wanted to say in front of Fiammetta, yet only her presence made it possible. 'My overdose.'

Dora flinched visibly. 'I've always told you everything you needed to know. It's a *mistake* to want to know everything, it's a responsibility. You wanted to force your mother to deal with your overdose, on top of her divorce and Constance's death? You wanted that?'

'That's not what I said,' protested Hannah, but she was drowned by a wave of anger coming from Fiammetta.

'But that's *Hannah*'s right, not yours!' snarled Fiammetta. 'It's up to *her* to deal with it. All you've done by protecting her from the truth is to turn her into a zombie who can't make up her mind about anything. She's a child! She's never had to face anything she didn't want to!'

'And Mum,' said Hannah softly. 'She's going mad with worry.'

'You should go,' said Dora to Fiammetta. The tendons on her neck were rigid with anger. 'This is a very bad time. There are things Hannah and I need to talk about on our own. Private family matters.'

Hannah's blood ran cold.

Fiammetta raised an eyebrow. 'As long as you talk about something.'

She kissed Hannah's cheek. 'I'll give you a ring tomorrow. OK?'

'OK.' This wasn't the way she had wanted it to be. But she'd never been able to imagine how it *could* be, never been able to put the amorphous longings that tormented her into a proper fantasy. Now it was in front of her, a fabulous, dangerous reality, glittering with possibilities and problems – she knew she'd have been too scared to dream it anyway.

Knowing that Dora was trembling with tension, Hannah didn't turn to watch Fiammetta leave. She sat down at the table opposite her, and waited.

'What's happened? Or should I not ask?' Dora's voice was icy.

Hannah shrugged. A petty little revenge, but she couldn't help herself. She wasn't sure, either, that she could speak.

'Are you . . . ? Hannah, I really don't . . .' Dora scrambled for words and pursed her lips in frustration.

'Where's Mum?' asked Hannah.

'I have some bad news,' said Dora. 'Louise has died.'

'Died?' Hannah's stomach jolted – with relief that Fran was OK and with sick frustration that the last link with Faith, Constance, and Matthew Fisher had gone. The precarious bridge to the past had swung down into the abyss, leaving her on the other side, wondering at all the secrets that had disappeared with Mrs Graham-Potter's snobbish discretion.

'Oh, God,' whispered Hannah, longing for her own vanished past. 'Oh, no!'

'Your mother's over there now,' said Dora. She poured a glass of brandy for Hannah and pushed it over the table towards her. 'She's going to lay her out.'

'She's what?' Hannah put the glass to her lips and nearly choked on the fumes.

'She's laying her out. Louise asked. Quite right too, in my opinion. She didn't want someone from the town coming to nose around the place, poking in her drawers.' Dora helped herself to more brandy and sipped it quickly. 'Frances is so good at things like that. She even puts the little pieces of cotton wool in the nose. Stops it collapsing. Louise would appreciate that.'

'When?' Hannah racked her brains. 'I only saw her this morning. I sat with her for a while, and she seemed fine. Weak, but . . . fine.' Hannah's voice trailed off, thinking about the look on the old lady's face as she slept, the eyes moving rapidly under the paper-thin eyelids as she dreamed. Had she known she was dying?

'She took a turn for the worse this afternoon,' said Dora. 'It can happen very quickly at her age, you know. Mrs Tyson called your mother, and we went up this afternoon. She insisted that the doctor wasn't sent for because he'd have packed her off to the infirmary and she didn't want that.'

'No,' said Hannah, thinking of Mrs Graham-Potter sitting bolt upright in a ward full of senile old women, gobbling like turkeys – men too, all jumbled in together. She would have hated the lack of order and being lumped in with no one to lord it over. No Mrs Tyson, or Fran or Dora.

Hannah remembered too late that Dora, too, had lost the last link with her childhood and was ashamed of her selfishness. 'Oh, God. I'm so sorry,' she said quickly, putting her hand on Dora's. 'I'm sorry. You must be . . . um . . .'

'Oh, I'm not that sorry,' said Dora. 'She was very old. I preferred her old too.'

'How do you mean?'

'Well,' Dora made a sweeping gesture with her hand, 'Louise wasn't very nice when we were all young. Not family. Oh dear.' She lifted the brandy bottle to pour herself some more, then put it down. 'Now isn't the time to speak ill of the dead, is it?'

'Probably the only time, I'd say.'

Dora smiled, but there wasn't any warmth in her face. 'That's very true, darling. A few minutes before the general pardon of death sweeps all the living difficulties under the carpet and all is forgiven, and what can't be forgiven is conveniently forgotten.'

'That's a bit rich, coming from you,' objected Hannah.

'I know.' Dora picked up the bottle again and poured herself another hefty slug of brandy. 'I've forgotten a lot on behalf of my family.'

'She showed me a room full of Matthew Fishers,' said Hannah. 'I think you should see them. They're of . . . well, they're portraits of Faith.'

Dora's eyes widened, then she sighed. 'Maybe I should have a look.'

Hannah wanted to say, 'Maybe you should go up to the house and see what's rightfully yours,' but it seemed far too grim. Instead, she said, 'Shouldn't we go up to help Mum? Don't you want to, you know, see that Mrs Graham-Potter is as she'd want to be?'

Dora swirled the brandy round her glass. 'No.'

'I think we should.'

'Frances is perfectly capable of dealing with everything. She laid out Constance when she passed away. She's always been much better at those matters than I have. Let's leave her to it.' She set her jaw with the saccharine-sweet smile that barely concealed her iron determination, and Hannah saw a glimpse of the wilful princess her mother talked about. Suddenly she understood how frustrating it must have been for Fran to grow up full of questions that were never answered and deal with a mother who refused to look at anything she didn't like. A mother who didn't, in fact, behave like a mother at all. No wonder she'd been so angry with her. No wonder she'd been jealous of the Musgraves, having something she needed.

'Well, I think we *should* go up there,' she said.

'Why?' Dora's mood tipped. She glared at Hannah, eyes sparkling with ferocity. 'Why should we run up there? After a woman who had everyone running around for her entire life? She's dead!'

'Because she's your family!'

'She's *not* my family! Never in a million years is she my family!' exploded Dora. 'I don't ever want to hear you say that again.'

'Why?' demanded Hannah.

'Because I say so!'

'But why?'

'Hannah . . .' said Dora, warningly.

'You can't just come out with things like that and expect me to ignore it.' Hannah slapped her hand on the table. 'You visited that old woman nearly every day for fifty years! You had me going through the house and its contents for her like a bailiff! Or was that some other plan you didn't bother to tell me about?'

'I don't know what you mean.'

Hannah glared at Dora, who had slugged back her drink in one. 'You have to tell me. I won't stop asking.'

'Louise Graham-Potter was a leech,' said Dora, talking to her empty glass but making each word crystal clear. 'She hung around Constance, never letting anyone else near her, dragged her name into gossip, spent her money on clothes and shoes. She was a taker, and she knew it. No better than those tarty little pieces you see on the high street, but with enough brains to disguise herself as the lady she wasn't. And when I look at Fiammetta Rissini I see exactly the same thing.'

Hannah stared in astonishment at her grandmother, and marvelled at the tenacity of her Victorian self-control, that it had lasted so long against the force of this fury. Dora's cheeks were flushed with it. This was passion built up over years and years, simmered down into pure loathing, thick as oil. How on earth had she bottled it up? How had she maintained enough civility to carry on going up to the villa for coffee and cake?

'You're wrong,' she said, but Dora wasn't listening.

'It isn't her house. It's Constance's. Faith wouldn't have put up with . . . what went on.' Dora bit her lip, and fell silent.

'Constance and Louise . . .' Hannah began, unsure of the instinctive picture that was unfolding in her mind. Was there *another* reason why she'd been so violently opposed to the friendship with Fiammetta? Did that adjoining bathroom suggest something more than genteel companionship? She looked at her grandmother, but Dora's head was bent. 'Constance and Louise weren't . . . ?'

'It wasn't right,' said Dora, into her brandy glass. 'It wasn't fair.'

They sat in silence and listened to the clock striking the half-hour in the hall.

Hannah thought of Faith's shadowy bed, now with a dead body lying under the heavy coverlet. She thought of her mother tidying up in the ticking semi-silence of the house, moving around the room with her precise motions, not stopping to allow herself to be spooked, as Hannah would be, but making a list of people to call and matters that would need to be tackled. Reducing all the problems and worries to a list of jobs, while Dora sat seething in the house that Faith and Constance had built for her family to grow up in. A family neither of them had had for themselves. Like a doll's house at the end of their garden, but with real people inside it.

Dora poured another inch of brandy into her glass.

'I think I should go up to the villa,' said Hannah. She pushed back her chair, scraping it on the stone flags. 'And I think you should too.'

Dora gave her one last mutinous glance, then tossed back her drink and stood up. She didn't waver.

Chapter Twenty-six

Hannah's penultimate exam (the Shakespeare paper: *Twelfth Night* and *Othello*) had finished at three and since then she'd been walking and walking. Now she seemed to be walking through the orchard without knowing how she'd got there. She didn't know how it had got so dark either, but she guessed from the distant chimes of the town hall clock that it must be past ten. When everyone else had stormed out of the exam to go to the pub, she'd picked up her satchel and stumbled out in a daze, her head ringing and her heart thumping with an ache that couldn't be soothed or ignored.

She walked because there was nowhere she wanted to go. She didn't want to stay at school, she didn't want to go home, she didn't want to go to the Coffee Pot and drink cappuccino and watch the boy racers drive round the grid pattern in their Escorts, because all those places reminded her of either Fiammetta or her family, and since she couldn't think of one without ricocheting into guilty thoughts of the other the whole town was one big torment.

Instead she walked down the hill and on to the Ramble Way that ran up to the old mineworks. She sat for a while at the ventilation chimney and looked out on to the sea, enjoying the pleasant numbness that came over her when she made all the thoughts drain out of her mind. Unlike the rest of her class, Hannah had actively enjoyed doing five A levels because sitting in silence for three hours at a time, regurgitating facts she knew that could be arranged into the right answer, was positively soothing compared to the deafening chorus of self-reproach that filled her head when she wasn't concentrating on her set texts.

Now, however, the A levels were virtually over, and in the brief summer before she went away to Oxford (Hannah had no doubt that she would go: Fran's violent willing of it couldn't fail) she would have to settle the real-life problems mounting up just out of her field of vision – not the artificial 'compare and contrast' puzzles about girls disguised as boys and boys pretending to be girls.

Dominic would have understood, she thought. But Dominic had gone, left her all on her own.

Now only Fiammetta would understand, and she was the only person Hannah could never talk to about this.

Hannah pushed her hair out of her eyes and sat down on one of the benches under the apple trees. Now she'd stopped walking, her thighs ached. It was a hot night and she smelt of sweat, worked up from striding up the Ramble Way, ozone and White Musk from the Body Shop, a birthday present from Fiammetta.

There were many voices in her self-reproach and they blended into a seamless wall of sound: her mother's bitterness about Keith's new wife and baby (how could she imagine she was hiding it from her?), Dominic's withdrawal into his own world, the fear that she might not do as well as her mother hoped, the shame that she was disappointing Dora, and beneath it all, humming wordlessly, her confusing, embarrassing feelings for her best friend.

Hannah knew what they were, even if she couldn't make herself put a name to it. Her English A level had been one tormented, unstable love affair after another: *Twelfth Night, The Changeling, The Bell Jar*. She'd read enough seething poetry and anguished sonnets to recognize love – or, rather, unhealthy, Byzantine love – when it sat in the back of her mind all the time, like a goblin.

Fiammetta was the person she wanted to be, and if she couldn't be her, Hannah desperately wanted to be near her. All through the stifling summer of gorging, then reproducing information, she had hoarded fragments of intimacy to bring out and roll around in her mind when an exam was done and she could luxuriate in the quiet final minutes ticking by: the minuscule pearls of sweat forming on Fiammetta's downy upper lip as she scrawled through her papers; the musky heat of her skin when they sat squashed up to drink frappés in the window booth of the Coffee Pot; the slightly aspirated foreign way she said Hannah's name, giving it a secret smile at the end.

Hannah felt a closeness to Fiammetta that bordered on a sixth sense; when she spoke, there was a tiny frisson of *déjà vu*, as if Hannah already knew what she'd say, how she'd turn her head. Sometimes, Hannah thought, they were so tuned into each other's way of thinking that they were like Donne's lovers, joined by a thread running through their eyes; other times Fiammetta's Bohemian differences and unpredictable temper made Hannah shudder with fear that she had got everything wrong, and her solid Linton frame was no match for something so exotic.

Hannah sighed. Her own temper, once predictably placid, had fluctuated wildly all summer, throwing her moods around like a fairground waltzer. She tried to tell herself it was nerves about the exams, or the late onset of adolescent sulkiness – Hannah had never had much of a teenage rebellion, outside reading *Kerrang!* for a while, so maybe this was it.

She knew it wasn't, though. It was far darker, far more serious, than that. For weeks Hannah had woken herself up crying, convinced that she was going mad, her legs knotted in the sheets, her head ringing with voices telling her what to do. There was always someone hovering in the shadows of her bedroom now, but instead of willing them away, Hannah longed to ask them what the hell she should do. In the shifting greyness before dawn, she saw the grim certainty lingering behind the busy to-do lists: she would have to choose. She would have to lose one thing she loved to keep another. And that time was getting closer and closer.

With all her heart, she wished the choice wasn't up to her, and buried her head in another day's revision.

Hannah's wanderings along the Ramble Way had turned towards home as dusk had begun to fall, and had led her into the orchard behind the house. Normally she would have been pleasantly jumpy with nerves, but tonight she had no time for rustling leaves and ghosts. In fact, this was as close as she wanted to come to her family right now, and in the familiar paths of her childhood haunts she felt quite peaceful.

The moon was extraordinarily bright above her, and seemed too large to be real. Hannah knew this was a trick of perspective, but it fitted her mood: all the emotions and problems felt too large for her head.

She walked into the deeper area of trees between the villa and Dora's cottage, where she couldn't be seen from Rose View, and dropped her bag on to one of the wooden love-seats. It wasn't a part she normally went in to, but her attention was drawn by something she hadn't noticed before; the moonlight glinting off little metallic plaques, fixed to the apple trees.

Dreamily, she walked towards them and ran her hands along the rough bark, overgrown with moss, then on to the cold metal drilled into the trunks. Samuel. Merlin. William. Derwent. Just names in italic script: no dates or explanations. Like Ovid, thought Hannah. People turned into trees, fixed to the ground, rooted in this soil. How odd.

She felt hot, then cold, and wondered if she'd caught something. Dora was for ever warning about the danger of summer chills.

Hannah sat on the bench with a thud and put her hands over her eyes. Her forehead felt hot and her palms were damply cold. Behind her eyelids, the huge moon glowed white. Fiammetta's name floated automatically into her mind.

In the distance, Hannah listened to the sea rolling in and slapping against the harbour walls. The sound carried quickly on the night air, deceptively loud. Maybe if she and Fiammetta went away, as far away as some of the Linton sailing ships had gone, to the Americas and to Africa, it would be all right.

Hannah tried to imagine herself settling down somewhere other than Linton, far enough away from her mother and grandmother that they'd never know she wasn't what they'd hoped, and fierce panic gripped her.

The sound of the sea faded and a cool breeze brushed past her face. With her eyes closed, Hannah had the strong impression that something was moving in front of her. She took her palms off her face, and opened her eyes slowly.

She wasn't scared by what she saw. Instead, a deep sensation of familiarity spread through her. Hannah recognized the shape even before she saw it: a woman's figure, moving between the trees, then emerging like a low, dense cloud and vanishing again behind the thick bushes, sometimes solid enough for her to make out the print sprigs on the long skirt, sometimes transparent enough for her to see the dark leaves of the rhododendrons gleaming through.

A White Lady.

This is it, thought Hannah, calmly, one hand on her forehead. I'm going mad.

But she wasn't frightened, only curious. The figure wasn't coming near her. It seemed to be moving in a definite line, from the villa to Dora's cottage. Hannah knew instinctively that it wasn't a real person, or a trick of the moonlight: somehow she felt the woman's impatience to get to the cottage, as if the need had been so strong it had left a trace in the air like perfume.

So the White Lady was real, she thought. She felt pleased. Dominic's stories hadn't just been stories after all. Hannah wondered what else might be true.

She watched the figure moving nearer the cottage. She couldn't make out a face, but there was a long plait swinging down the lady's back, reaching almost to her waist. That's Faith Musgrave, she thought, and wondered how she knew.

Maybe I should go to see Granny, talk to her. Perhaps that was what the apparition was telling her to do.

The ease between them had been strained recently, due to Dora's irrational dislike of Fiammetta, which only made Hannah's dilemma more painful, but Dora was still the only person she could talk to. And she had to talk to someone, or she really would go mad with the pressure in her head.

Slowly Hannah got to her feet, not wanting to follow the ghost too closely. She followed it for maybe half a minute, towards the back of the cottage garden then came across a figure that startled her even more.

Standing in the pale light filtering out through the kitchen nets, Dora looked exactly like a more *outré* photoshoot in *Vogue*. The moonlight caught the silveriness of her hair running down her back out of its daytime pins, and her lipstick-pink wellingtons were a splash of faint colour beneath her white silk pyjamas, which she was accessorizing with a full-length mackintosh. She had forgotten to remove her diamanté earrings, which made the whole ensemble rather festive.

She seemed to be planting a rosebush.

That can't be right, thought Hannah.

'Oh, hello, darling!' said Dora, as if it were the most normal thing in the whole world to be found planting rosebushes at night.

'What are you doing?'

Dora looked slightly disarranged, as if she'd been drinking. 'Gardening.'

'At this time?'

'The plants like it. Can't you smell how much more fragrant they are in the evening?'

Hannah took a deep breath, and her head filled with roses, sea-salt and honeysuckle.

'Most plants bloom best in the dark,' said Dora. She laughed at some joke of her own.

'Granny, are you all right?' asked Hannah.

'Are *you* all right?' Dora stared closely at her.

'Yes,' lied Hannah.

'Is it that Italian girl?'

'No. Why are you out here?'

'I told you, I'm gardening.'

Hannah looked down at what Dora was planting. She had a trug full of small rosebushes and a trowel, and when she looked closer, she could see that the hole Dora had been digging was next to a little stone cross.

Hannah laughed. Mousy. It was nice to see Dora being sentimental once in a while. She'd told Dominic and Hannah that Mousy, her old cat, had died and gone to heaven. Then, when she thought they weren't listening, she'd told Fran she'd chucked his corpse on to the bonfire. ('Cremation, darling. It's what he would have wanted.')

Hannah was pleased. She had loved Mousy when she was a little girl. 'Granny, is this where you buried Mousy?'

'Mousy?' Dora gave her a funny look. 'Darling, Mousy went to the cat crem. Griddled, darling, on Mr Tyson's bonfire.'

'Then . . .' Hannah faltered and pointed at the stone.

Dora pursed her lips, then cackled. 'Oh, you've caught me out, Hannah. You've caught me out in a fit of uncharacteristic sentimentality and superstition.'

'What do you mean?' Hannah shivered. There was something not quite right about Dora's voice, the way she wouldn't stop moving. There was a faint smell of spirits about her, and her eyes were shiny.

'I mean,' said Dora, 'that shame is a terrible, terrible thing. It can make people do awful things, cruel things, to one another, just to avoid shame.'

'Is that . . . a pet?' asked Hannah, with one last shred of hope.

'No, darling, it's a baby.'

Hannah wanted to scream, but her throat was dry. She put one hand to her face in case the scream slipped out. 'Why . . .' She swallowed. 'Why is there a baby buried in our garden?'

'Because what does the baby know about where it's buried?' Dora looked at her seriously. 'Does it know if it's in St Peter's churchyard with all the other little babies and their hideous stone cherubs, or in our garden with all the beautiful flowers? Does it matter? Is there only one way to heaven? I don't think so.'

'But . . .'

'Just you remember, Hannah,' Dora jabbed her trowel towards her with a definite gust of brandy, 'in life, you only have one chance at a reputation. Once it's gone, you'll never get it back. You'll always be the girl who shamed her family, the girl who slipped up, the girl who squandered her chances. Always the girl, you see. Not the woman you might grow into. Trapped!'

'Whose baby was it?' stammered Hannah.

'Does it matter?' asked Dora lightly. She took the first rosebush from the trug, humming to herself.

'Of course it matters!'

'Why?'

'Because . . .' Hannah's head throbbed, too many black thoughts cramming in on her all at once. She knew Dora was right. If anyone found out about Fiammetta, that would be it: her reputation fixed in stone here for ever, not as the golden girl but as the family embarrassment. Fran would blame herself, blame her and Keith's savage bickering for turning Hannah away from her charmed path; she'd martyr herself on it and everything would be her fault.

To her horror, Hannah realized that Dora was humming a lullaby.

'Whose baby was it?' she demanded. 'Just tell me it's some baby from the village! Some baby Faith looked after for a sick miner!'

'I'm not going to tell you, darling,' said Dora, calmly. Too calmly. 'It's one thing fewer for you to worry about, and it wouldn't make any difference even if you did. Just remember what I said. Momentary lapses of judgement may come and go, but the consequences stay with you for ever. Don't do what I did and be trapped, just for the sake of some little nothing that was as sick as I felt.'

Hannah put one hand to her mouth to stop the bile that surged up her throat, then turned on her heel and ran as fast as she could up to the house.

There was no doubt now in her head. She couldn't stay here and not tell Fiammetta how she felt, and clearly there was no way she could stay and tell her. At the same time she couldn't bear the thought of being separated from her, as she surely would be if anyone found out, and as she would be anyway when the results came through and she was carried off to Oxford on a tide of Fran's determination.

The only certainty in Hannah's mind was that she couldn't stay and she couldn't leave. And that left only one option.

Chapter Twenty-seven

Hannah and Dora made slow progress through the garden up to the villa. Hannah's feet kept stumbling over roots and sliding on wet grass as flashes of memory came back to her, incomplete but vivid, like shards of broken patterned plates. She didn't know if she was drunk any more, but her mind seemed to slip from one horrible image to another – Dora in the garden with the little gravestone, a line of sleeping pills laid out along the bathroom window-sill – and she didn't know if they were just bits of dreams coming back to her or real memories.

Hannah wasn't sure what was real any more. The whole evening had been too far outside the limits of her imagination for her to rely on automatic responses to any of it, and she berated herself for being drunk and vulnerable. She didn't *feel* drunk now, but she knew there was too much alcohol in her blood for her to react normally, which put her at a dangerous disadvantage – everything seemed to be moving just out of reach of her fingertips.

'Hurry up,' she snapped at Dora, who was dragging her feet like a child.

Dora glared at her, and Hannah glared back. The familiar roles were dissolving in the light of the strange new developments: Dora wasn't being strong or coping, but neither was she incapacitated with grief. She just looked sulky and cross. Hannah, though, was no longer scared of what she might have to say about Fiammetta, or whether she'd tell Fran and make a big scene. Suddenly she didn't care any longer.

'I'm going as fast as I can,' Dora said haughtily.

The truth was that neither of them was in any hurry to get up to the villa, where Fran would be coping as she always did in any emergency that required a cool head.

Hannah wanted Dora to stride on in front, taking the lead, marshalling the situation the way she marshalled the book group. But she seemed to be regressing into childish truculence, as if Louise Graham-Potter's death was the most selfish, inconvenient act of her selfish inconvenient life.

Hannah thought of Mrs Graham-Potter's mortal shell lying on Faith's bed, holding all the answers to her and Fran's questions inside it. They were locked away for ever now and would go with her into the silence of the stone tomb in St Peter's churchyard, which was how she'd always wanted it. She had left only the in-memoriam version of her memories, the version she was happy for the world to know.

Next to the stone tomb, Hannah corrected herself. Heaven forfend that she should be mistaken for family.

And meanwhile Fran, who'd never been offered the courtesy of owning her past, was laying her out, saving her from the embarrassment of a stranger washing her dead body, dressing her up and making her ready for the undertakers in the morning, so she'd look as smart and neat in death as she had in life.

Hannah's heart burned with the unfairness of it.

She looked over her shoulder. 'Granny, are you all right?' she demanded irritably, a Keith question that wasn't solicitous at all, and only meant 'Get a move on' in polite clothes.

'I'm fine,' said Dora, with an air of wounded patience.

'Then hurry up.'

They stalked to the villa in silence, Hannah swatting away the lurid shards of memory that were swarming in her head like wasps.

The back door was unlocked. Hannah pushed it open, creeping through the kitchen without knowing why she was being so quiet. A lamp was on somewhere deep inside the house, casting enough light for them to see where they were going. She didn't want to flick the switch and flood the place with fluorescent brightness. It seemed disrespectful.

Hannah had almost crossed the kitchen before she realized that Dora was not with her. She turned and saw her tall frame, which almost filled the doorway, silhouetted against the moonlit garden.

'Granny, please.' Hannah held out her hand. It was shaking.

Dora said nothing.

'What?' said Hannah. 'What are you thinking?'

'I never really imagined what it would be like when they were all gone,' said Dora, quietly, 'and I was the only one left.'

Hannah pushed down the nerves that were beginning to unsettle her.

Dora let out a long, shuddering sigh.

She's just winding herself up, Hannah thought suddenly. This is all acting. She's trying to goad herself into feeling something she doesn't.

She chided herself at once for being so cruel. Louise had been Dora's last link with her childhood, and the women who'd brought her up. People reacted in odd ways to death.

'You don't have to come upstairs if you don't want to,' she said.

'You can sit in the drawing room, and I'll make you a cup of tea once I've seen Mum.'

Dora hesitated. 'I might do that,' she said.

Fran met Hannah on the landing. She was looking tired but energized by efficiency. The sleeves of her maroon polo-neck were rolled up to the elbows and her hair was sticking out at odd angles, but she seemed more vivid than Hannah had seen her in ages.

'Are you OK, love?' she asked, and gave her a quick bony hug. She smelt of Dettol.

'Fine, yes.'

Fran peered at her. 'Have you been dri—' She stopped. 'Sorry, that's mean of me. I suppose Mum opened the cooking brandy – to help with the shock?'

'Well . . .' Hannah surprised herself by not telling an outright lie. Normally one would have slipped out without her having to think about it, but she didn't want to cover up any more truths. 'I'd had a few this evening already, actually, but when I got home, Granny had opened the brandy, yeah. I had one with her.' She was surprised by how normal she sounded, how matter-of-fact.

Fran sighed. 'It's not the answer, you know, but if it's what she needs . . . Is she downstairs?'

'Yes. Mum, listen, before you see her, she's behaving really strangely.' Hannah lowered her voice.

'How do you mean?'

'Well, she's . . .' Hannah searched for the right words to describe Dora's mood. 'She's . . . all detached. Not crying – she seems more angry than anything else, but in a sort of random way.'

'Can you be more specific?'

'This isn't court, Mum, I didn't interview her!'

'Ssh!' Fran motioned for Hannah to step back into the alcove, so their voices wouldn't carry down the stairs. She perched on the big oak blanket box, nudging the brass dish of pot pourri to one side. The stained-glass window behind them was dull, and little cracks showed in the leading. 'Don't talk so loud.'

Hannah stepped into the alcove. She wasn't sure she wanted to be upstairs now, surrounded by the photographs and mirrors, with Louise's body in Faith's room.

She shivered. The house felt even colder than normal. 'Mum, I don't mean to seem disrespectful or anything but I've been thinking about what you were saying about Dora's parents,' she said. 'I think I've, um, worked out who they might have been, and I think we need to sort it out tonight, once and for all.'

Fran let out a long-suffering sigh. 'Do you think it's the right time and place for this, Hannah?'

'Yes, I do, actually, Mum!' Hannah marvelled at her assertive tone: she'd sounded more like Fran than Fran did. 'In fact, I think this is the *only* time and place. There must be things in this house that would settle it. It's time we knew. It's time you had some proper information, in case it's relevant to – to your symptoms. And how much more upset can Granny be, for God's sake? Give her a few days and she'll never discuss it again. She's already acting like she's on the way out too.'

'Hannah, I don't think we should—'

'Mum!'

Fran wasn't meeting her eye.

'Mum, don't you want to know? I thought you of all people would have wanted some truth.'

Fran snapped. 'Of course I wanted to know! But it's not always as simple as that, Hannah.'

'Why not?'

'Oh, when you're grown-up you'll realize that—'

'Mum!' hissed Hannah. 'I *am* grown-up! I'm nearly thirty years old!'

'Oh, I'm sorry, love.' Fran deflated. The air rushed out of her in a long sigh. 'I'm sorry. I'm being . . .' She straightened her spine and sat upright on the edge of the blanket box. 'You're right, we have to find out. You have a right to know too. There's no one left to protect now, is there? Whatever it was they were hiding.'

'You think they were hiding something, then?' said Hannah, eagerly.

'Why else would they bother to be so secretive? It must have been something they were ashamed of, something they wouldn't want folk to know about. And Dora must have thought so too, or she'd have found out for herself. She's not backward in coming forward when there's something she wants to know.'

Hannah's heart beat faster. 'I know. That's what I thought.' She could feel her heart racing. 'I've been putting two and two together, you know, while I've been here, and I think there's something you should see. Maybe I've got it wrong, but I think it's . . . well, I don't know.'

'What?'

'Come with me.' Hannah took a deep breath. If Fran hadn't been there, she wasn't sure how much courage she'd have needed to go into the sewing room tonight. She knew it was childish, but even though Mrs Graham-Potter was hardly in a position to stop her, the disapproval emanating from the house was stronger than ever. All those locked doors to walk past, rooms she'd never been into, rooms no one had wanted her to see.

She couldn't put the image of all three old ladies, now reunited, out of her mind: would they still be old ladies? Or if they were roaming their house in spirit form, would they be in the shape of the three smart young women who had thrown parties, entertained London men and not cared about the gossip? Would they be free to move on now or would they hang around still, waiting for Dora, the last contact with the shame they had had to hide from future generations?

Hannah shivered.

'Come with you where?' Fran asked.

'The sewing room.'

'Where?'

'It's always been locked. Have you got the keys?'

Fran held up Mrs Graham-Potter's bunch.

Hannah swallowed. 'OK, I'll show you.'

Fran seemed galvanized again by the need to be practical. She led the way down the corridor, not caring how loud her steps were on the worn carpet, whereas Hannah, out of habit, still trod on the areas she knew wouldn't creak.

The unused corridor was pitch black and when Hannah tried the light switch, the bulb flickered and burned out.

'Typical,' she said. She'd tried to sound jokey but her voice had cracked.

'Not to worry,' said Fran stoutly. She found the key, turned the lock and swung open the door. 'Now, then, what is it we're looking at?'

Hannah followed her in. The room smelt of roses, which she knew must be a trick of the imagination since it hadn't smelt of anything but mothballs previously. She wondered if it was coming from the garden, from the rosebushes letting out their scent into the night air, but the windows were shut and the room faced on to the street. Orange lights shone through the net curtains, giving the room a dull sheen of illumination.

'So?' said Fran, briskly. Her voice echoed in the emptiness.

Hannah went slowly to the first stack of paintings and turned over the first.

Faith sprawled on her bed, soft white arms and legs curving like marble sculpture.

She turned over the next.

Faith glaring out to sea as if she owned it.

And the next.

Faith as a bare-breasted Greek goddess of war in white draped robes and helmet, challenging and proud.

And the next.

Faith lying on her stomach on the four-poster bed, her legs, buttocks and back making a line of rolling curves like sand dunes.

'I think that's enough,' said Fran faintly.

'I found a letter in Constance's room,' Hannah went on quickly. 'Only two of them went to Cambridge, not all three. And the housekeeping book from the London house shows there were running costs, keeping it open all the time they were there. I thought at first that it was Mrs Graham-Potter who didn't go, just pretended she was there with them, but now I think Faith was pregnant with Granny before she left and didn't go at all. She had Granny there.'

'And Matthew Fisher . . .'

'. . . her father.'

'My God,' said Fran. She couldn't take her eyes off the paintings.

'She ought to know,' said Hannah. 'We all should. Betty Fisher's, well . . . she's not mentally stable, is she? And if it's a hereditary problem . . .' The implications for herself, as well as her mother, hit her.

Maybe it wasn't just Fran who had symptoms of something worrying. The blackness she'd felt smothering her before she took her overdose; the simplicity with which she'd found the pills and taken them so methodically; the easy way she'd blanked it from her mind . . . Was that her Fisher legacy? Madness, with art appreciation?

'No. That's not true,' said a quiet voice.

Hannah and Fran spun round in shock.

Dora was standing in the doorway, white as a ghost. She paused, then said, with calm certainty, 'Faith wasn't my mother.'

They stared at each other for a few seconds, as a solitary car drove up the hill and out to Etterthwaite, casting another wave of artificial light over Faith's naked body.

'But, Mum,' said Fran, recovering herself, 'Hannah's right, it all adds up. It makes perfect sense when you think about it. They weren't married, he wasn't of the same class, but she still wanted you to be brought up in her care, have you near her. I know it's terrible, but it's nothing to be ashamed of. Matthew Fisher was an extraordinarily talented artist, and—'

'Is that meant to make me feel better, Frances?' demanded Dora. 'That my mother was such a hypocrite that she couldn't marry my father, because she was mortified by his poor background, yet caring enough to want to bring me up as her own?'

'Well, if you put it like that . . .'

Hannah could see that Fran was trying hard to process all this new information. Where did it leave her, the famous anti-Musgrave critic, now that she was one by birth?

'And I should be happy with that, should I?' said Dora.

Fran decided on her line and set her jaw. 'Oh, well, they were of their time, weren't they? That kind of snobbery was just the way they were brought up. It's disgusting now, of course, but you can't judge people in the context of a different era. We don't know – maybe he was as much against it as she was. Maybe he didn't want to be patronized into marriage.'

Hannah stared at her mother in astonishment at this wholesale abandonment of her socialist credentials. So this was the price of her birthright: she was willing to excuse Faith's breathtaking upper-class hypocrisy because it came with a trade-off of genuine working-class genius.

Too much was shifting tonight, thought Hannah. Nothing seemed reliable any more.

Dora walked across the room and sat down in the chair by the window. She looked very old, and very tired.

No one spoke.

Hannah's feet moved without thinking, to the other chair, facing away from the window, and looking straight at the door and the canvases stacked by the wall. She sank into it.

Only Fran was left standing, staring uncomprehending at the paintings.

'Mum,' whispered Hannah.

Fran turned, as if she didn't recognize the voice.

'Sit down,' said Hannah, and indicated the last chair.

After a moment's hesitation, Fran walked to the chair and lowered herself into it.

All three stared into the unlit grate of the huge tiled fireplace.

Hannah wondered how many times Faith, Constance and Mrs Graham-Potter had sat there with the same jostling silences between them.

Then Dora put a hand to her head and started to smooth down the wisps of hair that had frizzed up while she walked through the damp garden. 'Frances, dear, did Faith ever feel like a grandmother to you?' she asked.

Fran suppressed a snort. 'No. None of them did. I don't think I was the kind of little girl they liked. But that doesn't mean she wasn't.'

Dora sighed. 'No,' she said, simply. 'No, it's very clever of you, and I can see why you want it to be true. You'd like to have Matthew Fisher as a close relative, wouldn't you? Maybe not Betty Fisher, though. But, darling, I was *there*. I knew Faith, Constance and Louise better than you know me, questions or no questions.

'Oh!' She raised a hand as Fran opened her mouth to protest. 'They didn't *tell* me who my mother was but, you see, they didn't need to. I didn't ask questions, or go nosing around the records office, investigating their family tree, the way everyone does, these days. I didn't demand to go into counselling because I didn't know where I came from. But I still knew.'

Fran flushed beetroot red, though whether from anger or shame, Hannah couldn't tell.

'I *listened*, Fran. I listened to them, I listened to the servants, I listened to the house. I listened to the things they didn't tell me, I thought about all the things they wanted me to do differently.'

Dora looked at her daughter, and her eyes were sad. 'Faith wasn't my mother, Frances, but that doesn't mean she didn't look after me like a mother. She wanted to make sure that I had things she hadn't had herself, things that—'

'Oh, please!' Fran interrupted. 'Stop that now! What things did Faith Musgrave ever lack? That woman never had to do a hand's turn! The only thing she ever did was build you a house and make sure you were married off to some uncomplaining middle manager so you never had to either!'

'She wanted me to have a good reputation,' snapped Dora.

'Surely that was up to you, not her.'

'Life is not that simple, Frances. Not in little communities like this.'

'I don't want to start this circular argument again,' said Fran. Her voice shook with frustration. 'I just want you to tell me who your parents were.'

'I'm trying to explain to you, darling, that it's not so simple. There's so much attached to it.'

'Stop dramatizing yourself. It's very childish.'

'There's no need to take that tone with me. This has been a very emotional evening, all round.'

'So who *was* your mother?' demanded Hannah, before Dora could move on to her.

Fran and Dora turned to look at her.

'Come on,' said Hannah, more gently. 'Who was it? You obviously knew all along. Don't you think you've got a moral obligation to tell us?'

'You knew all along,' echoed Fran, in a hoarse whisper.

Dora laughed mirthlessly. 'An obligation? You think I've kept this to myself for all these years out of a sense of . . . spite? Just to be difficult?'

'It's felt like that,' said Fran.

'Well, I haven't.' Dora's voice cracked. 'I know you don't think I've been a very good mother to you . . .'

Fran pointedly didn't interrupt or protest.

Dora sighed, and went on, 'But I tried to protect you as best I could. I made you independent, didn't I? I made you intellectually curious?'

'Only because you were so bloody mysterious about everything!' Fran's face was white with anger.

Dora tightened her lips. 'You think that knowledge is some kind of right, Frances. It isn't. It's a huge, demanding *responsibility*. I never knew for certain where I'd come from, because for Faith to have told me would have been to load the responsibility on to my shoulders. She didn't think I needed that, or didn't think I could take it. She let me work it out for myself.'

'Just tell us, please!' howled Hannah.

'She didn't let you work it out!' Fran jabbed her finger at Dora, the way she did in court when the truth was escaping her. 'She was going to tell you, and you threw the papers on the fire! Why?'

'No.'

Fran threw back her head in frustration and shook it from side to side, as if searching for some reason in what she hearing. Then she glared at Dora. 'Did you think it would spoil your cosy little relationship to know the truth? Did you think that, once you knew, you might have to admit you were an adult, with a duty to the family you had at home, instead of sitting up at the villa with those three dried-up old spinsters, drinking tea, happy to be their middle-class charity case?'

'Mum!' said Hannah in shock.

'Oh, it's all about *you*, isn't it, Frances?' Dora's tone was icy. 'You, you, you. Me, me, me. Did it ever cross your tidy mind that the truth isn't ever about just one person? That maybe it might *temporarily* make you feel better, telling the truth, but it can hurt others even more?'

'So your refusal to face up to your past was a sacrifice, was it? An act of maternal selflessness? Never mind how it might affect us.'

Dora smoothed her skirt and took a few deep breaths. 'I'll tell you who your grandparents were,' she said quietly. 'But I don't want to discuss the matter ever again. And I want you both to know that I was willing to swallow all this, for you, so you'd never have to have this knowledge on your shoulders.'

'It's already inside me,' hissed Fran, 'like some kind of parasite, eating me up, but *I don't know what it is.*'

Hannah hardly dared breathe. She was shivering with tension. She fixed her eyes on Dora.

'I never asked Faith or Constance where I'd come from,' said Dora calmly. 'I had an instinct that it would be inappropriate somehow. That it would hurt them, when they'd been so kind to me. Obviously none of the servants ever made any reference to it, and they treated me as if I was just a younger sister. I don't remember much about Faith's parents – her father died after the war and her mother spent a lot of time going back and forth from one spa to another. She didn't want to spend much time here.'

Fran snorted.

'I didn't want to know, so I didn't ask,' Dora admitted. 'I smoothed it over in my mind. People did that a lot more then, to save the pain of things they couldn't change. Men lost in the wars, or down the mines. One just moved on, always looking ahead. And, really, I suppose I might never have known, but one night I heard Constance and Louise arguing about it in her room. I don't think I'd have minded too much if I'd *never* known. It might have been easier.'

She examined her hands sadly, turning her seed-pearl ring round on her thin fingers. 'I always used to tell you that little piggies had big ears, Hannah. They do, don't they? I heard Louise nagging at Constance – terrible common voice she had when she was angry, telling her that I should be told. That there might be *implications*.'

'For what?' muttered Hannah.

'She was a selfish bitch.' Dora sounded almost matter-of-fact as the memories floated up in her mind, fresh from lack of re-examination. 'What she *meant* was, "How will it affect my own position in the house?" As if she wasn't leading Constance around by the nose already!'

Fran gave Hannah a look that said clearly, 'How much brandy did you let her have?'

'Constance didn't think that, of course,' Dora went on. 'She never did. She thought Louise meant about the medical implications.'

'Finally,' said Fran, under her breath, 'we get to the point.'

'Granny,' said Hannah, deciding to take a different tack to prompt Dora into specifics, 'who was your father?'

Dora looked at her for a few long moments. Her skin was so pale that the tiny thread veins in her cheeks were scarlet in the street-light.

Hannah felt her breath go in and out, counting away the seconds.

Finally, Dora parted her dry lips and said, 'My father was Samuel Musgrave. Faith's father.'

Fran turned ashen.

'It turned out that I was one of their sisters, after all.' Dora's eyes darkened. 'But I was taken in, and brought up as if I wasn't. Funny sort of compromise, wasn't it? Mind you, at least I was taken in,' she added. 'Plenty around the town weren't. Samuel had a habit of impregnating his servants, I hear.'

'Betty Fisher's grandmother,' said Hannah, without thinking. That was what the message had been at the spiritualist meeting – Bert Fisher's daughter Molly had been raped while he was on his shift. And, as a relative of Samuel Musgrave, she was the link. He had been her great-grandfather. Hannah put a hand to her mouth. 'Cath Fisher. She was Musgrave's daughter, too.'

Dora nodded. 'Yes. But I don't know if Betty knows. Molly refused point blank to talk about it, then died of diphtheria when Matthew's wife and children caught it. Such small houses, you know, no proper sanitation. Faith knew that Molly fell pregnant and was dismissed, but she didn't know who the father was until Matthew told her – it was one of the reasons Faith took such an interest in their family, you know. They were so ashamed, especially Constance. They wanted to do what they could, but people are very proud. It's not easy to help folk round here sometimes.'

Hannah felt Fran stiffen next to her and noted, with a stab of wryness, how much easier Fran and Dora found it to turn the topic away from their own history, even now, in the middle of a near century-old secret.

'Why would they want dirty Musgrave guilt money anyway?' demanded Fran, recovering some of her familiar ferocity. 'If they'd paid for proper sanitation in the first place, diphtheria wouldn't have killed so many poor kids! I wouldn't touch his money! I wouldn't . . .' Her voice trailed off as it dawned on her that a lot of dirty Musgrave money would be coming her way, whether she liked it or not.

'And your mother?' asked Hannah. 'Was she a housemaid too?'

Dora sighed deeply. 'No.'

'Maybe Faith didn't know,' suggested Hannah, wanting to give her grandmother a way out. The atmosphere around them was thick with tension. 'Were you left on the doorstep?'

'No,' said Dora. She twisted her ring again, round and round her finger.

Hannah leaned forward and touched her grandmother's hand, but Dora shrank away. 'Just tell us,' said Hannah, softly. 'We're hardly going to judge *you*.' You're one of us, she wanted to say, not one of them.

Dora looked up and smiled with heartbreaking sadness in her eyes. 'You will,' she said. 'My mother was Constance.'

There was a terrible silence, then Fran let out a low moan of horror.

'Louise told me, in a moment of pure fishwifery,' Dora went on. 'I was fourteen. I forget what I'd done, but I'd enraged her in some way, cheeked her probably. She never liked me. Jealous of my relationship with Constance, I suppose. But she was scared of being kicked out, left on her own, and when it comes to it that sort of person will do anything they can to cling some kind of control. But I think I knew all along.'

'No,' said Fran. 'You're just . . . making it up . . .'

Hannah knew she wasn't.

'I didn't believe her, but she showed me a birth certificate. No father named of course. And told me how my mother had tried to drown herself in the harbour rather than let both of us live.'

'I know,' said Hannah. She could barely move her lips for shock. Shock that she, too, had always known, somewhere deep in her brain. 'I saw the clipping.'

'Oh.' Dora gave her a rueful smile. 'You found it?'

Hannah nodded.

'I found it in the family Bible,' said Dora. 'I don't know who kept it – Faith or Constance. Maybe even Louise. But I put it behind the photograph because I didn't want to lose it. I didn't know what else to do.' She grimaced. 'Maybe I was leaving it as a clue, against the chance of my not ever telling you myself. The dates, you see. What did you think when you found it?'

'I thought there was something odd,' Hannah said slowly. 'But, then, the whole study made me feel uneasy, like something incredibly sad was waiting for me to find it.' The thought of Samuel Musgrave's hand resting on the Dalmatian's fragile skull made her shudder. 'But I didn't know what.'

'It didn't take a genius to work out the dates.' Dora sounded resigned now. 'Constance couldn't swim, I knew that. Whenever we went out on the pleasure boats on Windermere, she'd always make such a fuss about having a lifejacket. She wouldn't have dived into the harbour, even for her dog.'

Fran, forgotten in her chair, put her fingers over her eyes.

'Faith would have,' said Dora, as if considering it, 'but then Faith always had more go than Constance. Constance would rather have slipped away, not made a fuss. Not have had to tell anyone what happened. Louise, of course, said it would have been better all round if the shock had brought on a miscarriage.'

Hannah gulped.

'Well, how can I blame her?' Dora spread her hands on her knees. 'Constance didn't know what else to do, I expect. But, then, that's the family way, isn't it? Do away with yourself instead of facing up to your troubles.'

'I thought it was something to do with Matthew,' said Hannah. 'I thought maybe she was in love with him.'

Dora smiled ruefully. 'She might have been. He was a very good-looking man. So kind and gentle. Not something either of them were used to.'

'But how did . . . how did it happen?' asked Hannah. Lurid possibilities flashed before her eyes. 'Did Louise tell you that too?'

Dora nodded. 'She told me. She didn't want me to think that it was a regular habit of Musgraves, I think. Such a snob.' She shook her head. 'Such a twisted sense of snobbery. I worked the rest out from gossip. It happened during the flu outbreak after the war. There was always something going round. The girls used to visit certain families they knew, old parlourmaids or acquaintances from their literacy classes. They used to go round and check they had enough bread, enough coal for their fires – you know, charitable works, taking care of people. They went while the cage was down in the pit, so the men wouldn't send them packing. Pride, you see.'

Dora licked her lips. 'They'd gone round to check on the Fishers. You were right to guess that Matthew and Faith had got friendly before she went away. They were thick as thieves, but very secretive about it while Samuel was still around. He'd have gone *berserk*. Matthew's family were all living in that tiny house, with quite a few little ones there, all borderline starving.'

She sighed. 'I don't want to dwell on the details, but from what Louise could drag out of Constance later, it seems that Faith and Matthew had gone out to look at something he'd been sketching, and left Constance seeing to Molly, who was upstairs with the baby. Samuel came in. It was winter, getting dark, and none of those cottages had electricity until much later. He was blind drunk.'

Dora paused.

'He drank constantly after his sons were killed, Faith told me. He would get staggering drunk, and smash things to bits in the cellar. That's why there's that big lock on the cellar door. Faith had it put on. She and Constance never wanted to go down there again, always sent servants to fetch up the wine for parties. It was one of the reasons Ellen refused to stay in the house after the war. She thought he'd break her too, if he got near enough. So he was blind drunk, roaming around, looking for something to break.'

Hannah thought of the cellars under the villa. Row upon row of wine bottles, and dozens of empty racks. The wine that Faith had been determined to work her way through once the house belonged to her and Constance, pouring it down the throats of endless party guests she knew her father would have hated.

'Poor Constance.' Dora looked unbearably sad. 'You know, it was her thoughtfulness that made this happen. She was wearing some horrible old coat. She always did that when they were going out. She didn't want the women to think she was being Lady Bountiful, coming up to their houses in a posh frock to hand out charity. Faith, now, she always said they expected a show. She wore her best clothes, but Constance wouldn't have dreamed of it.

'Anyhow, who knows what he thought? Barged straight in, like he owned the place, which I suppose he did, saw a girl who looked like Molly from behind, probably thought he was entitled to have another go.'

Hannah was silent. The pictures of Constance slipped one by one into her head. Pretty, soft, appealing Constance, the secretary, the needleworker, the giver of Sunday School prizes. She couldn't think of a single image where her eyes weren't haunted by that deep, silent sadness. Constance was so small and slight – how could she have fought off a man of her father's size, fuelled with drink and rage?

And the shock. Hannah couldn't begin to imagine how paralysing that must have been, recognizing his smell, his clothes. Unless, of course, it wasn't a shock . . .

'Did he know?' she asked.

Dora shook her head. 'I couldn't tell you. He died a few months later.'

'How?'

'Heart-attack, brought on by drinking and the terrible mental stress of his sons' deaths, the doctor said. But I wouldn't have put it past Faith to have smothered him while he was drunk. She hated him. They all did. They hated him before any of this happened. Only Louise was taken in by the title and the money.'

'And you . . .' Hannah wasn't sure how to go on. It felt wrong to associate the fragile, familiar old woman in front of her with the terrors of what she had just told her. But Dora was the result of that violation, the undeniable proof that it had happened.

And I am too! she thought. *And Mum and Dominic – and nothing can ever change it or make it go away. His blood is running through my veins, and his genes are mine.*

Her skin crawled for a second as Dora's bare words revealed a flash of the real horror, the inescapability of that legacy. Instinctively Hannah shoved the thought away and her mind closed against it, blanking it with whiteness.

'And you were born . . . where? In Cambridge?' she asked. Her voice wobbled.

'No, not exactly. The other two went, as planned, and all three left Linton with great ceremony on the train, letting everyone think that was where Constance was going too. Faith and Louise went up to Newnham, took the exams women were allowed to take in those days. Had a wonderful time. Constance went to live in the house in Knightsbridge, where I was born, very discreetly, of course. When they came back, a veil was drawn over my origins, and when the gossips started up, Faith let everyone think I was hers to spare Constance any more pain.'

'That was noble of her,' said Hannah.

'Oh, people said a lot worse,' said Dora. 'We were all loose women, we had German income during the war, we were Communists. There used to be a rumour that they were running some kind of upmarket brothel here, that they entertained whole parties of men. Faith didn't care. She didn't mind using people's imaginations when it suited her. Like that old story about the White Lady in the garden?'

Hannah nodded.

'She told one servant, who told another, who told another, who eventually told me, and if any one of us had seen a woman in a white nightgown slipping through the garden to the gardener's cottage . . .' Dora smiled sadly as the cleverness dawned on Hannah.

'At least Faith made her own myths work for her,' she said. 'She must have gone mad round here, letting all the gossip hem her in.'

'She was too bright for a small life, I know. I think she'd have been happy to stay in London, if Constance hadn't needed her. She'd have been a wonderful politician or journalist. But she came back to Linton.' Dora patted Hannah's knee. 'Like we all do, for one reason or another. And she had her reward, you know. She and Matthew were happy. Something good came out of it.'

Hannah thought it so sad that Dora didn't think of herself as the good that had come out of it. She put her hand over her grandmother's cold fingers and squeezed them. 'You seem very calm about this,' she said.

'I'm not really. It makes me feel sick. But it's done. It's fact. I can't change it by getting angry. What makes me *angry* is the way Louise used Constance's shame as a means to an end. She knew Constance would never want to tell me, but only she and Faith knew the truth, could understand her pain, and that kept Louise nice and cosy in her nest.'

'So,' said Hannah, thinking slowly, 'does this mean the house is yours now?'

Yours, she wanted to say. *Not ours.*

'I don't know,' admitted Dora. 'I never saw the will. Everything was left to Louise, as far as I knew. She was always highly secretive, even when she had nothing to be secretive about. Quite a legacy, though, isn't it? I mean, for whoever gets it now.'

'Yes,' said Hannah. She didn't mean the house and the paintings and the silver dinner services, but thought of all the other legacies left for the three of them to sift through: the swallowed secrets, the grains of fact behind the rumours, the seams of truth buried deep in local gossip. She didn't know where to start when it came to valuing those.

A low moan jerked her back into the moment.

Fran's head was in her hands.

'Mum?' Hannah leaned forward.

'What's the point?' Fran sounded as if her heart was breaking, and her face was young with despair. 'Everything I've ever tried to do, there was no point in any of it.'

'What do you mean by that?' Dora sounded brisk.

'I mean,' Fran spread her hands in dumb surrender, 'I wanted to give something *back* to this community, to make up for the way the Musgraves had stripped it bare. I wanted to do the right thing. I wanted to make a difference! And all along I've been one of them.'

'It doesn't make a blind bit of difference who your parents were,' said Dora. 'You did everything yourself.'

'It makes *all the difference*!' yelled Fran. The bitterness in her voice was horrible to Hannah's ears – grating and out of control. 'And it's your fault! Everything, eventually, is all your fault!'

'Your life is what you've made of it, Frances,' retorted Dora. 'I didn't make you marry that foolish man. I didn't make you move back here so you could let your life slip away.'

Fran's face lengthened as her mouth made an O of amazement. 'You were the worst mother anyone could imagine,' she said. 'Your own marriage was a horrible sham, and you treated me like an inconvenience until I was old enough to leave. And you honestly believe you did the best you could. What sort of delusional coward are you?'

Hannah rose to her feet before she could hear any more but Dora and Fran were too busy shouting at each other to notice. She could feel years and years of tension and resentment building to a peak in front of her, and she didn't want to hear it. It didn't matter what they said, how much truth or fairness there was in it, it just needed to be let out, like a boil being lanced. And they would fight it out better without her.

And there were some things she still didn't want to know, no matter what.

Hannah's heart ached when she imagined the loneliness Dora must have felt, growing up afraid to acknowledge any mother for fear of opening old wounds, and jealous of Constance's easy affection for Louise; she could also see how she'd repeated the pattern with her own cross, lonely daughter, letting the villa come before poor Fran, who had tried so hard to be worthy of her attention and who had devoted much of her professional life to hounding and discrediting the Musgrave family.

Hannah didn't know how long it would take them to see the other side of their own pain, but she didn't think she was the one to point it out to them.

Her footsteps were soft as she walked through the house, which no longer felt shadowy or threatening. It seemed to breathe in time with her. She walked down the corridor to the main landing where the moonlight filtered through the diamond panes of coloured glass, then down the stairs to the hall, breathing slowly and deliberately, taking in the night-time smells of beeswax, old coats and faded pot-pourri as peace spread through her.

She walked out through the kitchen, which had once rung with the clatter and chat of a cook and four kitchenmaids, and into the garden, the silent receptacle of a family's secrets.

She stood for a moment in the dark, drawing in deep lungfuls of sea air, fresh with green leaves and rain. Then she took out her mobile phone and started back towards Rose View, towards the road, towards the centre of town, towards Fiammetta's own small flat, towards her own future.

Chapter Twenty-eight

Constance Musgrave's solicitors were as reassuringly expensive as everything else the family had chosen to represent it. Wilson, Perry & Curwen, who had taken over the Musgraves' affairs from their London solicitors in 1958, was the oldest law practice in Linton. Their offices were in a tall white townhouse behind the library, and had been there since James Wilson had joined forces with Abraham Perry in 1807, and co-opted his brother-in-law, the shipping and tax commissioner, in to the firm in 1871.

Wilson, Perry & Curwen did not, Fran observed acidly, take legal aid cases.

To the eyes of the world, Hannah, Fran and Dora arrived at the offices for the will reading together, a supportive family unit at this time of sadness, as the death announcements had it. To the eagle eyes of Mrs Tyson, however, they had met at the door of Rose View, having set off from separate starting points, and greeted each other with stiff Royal Family-type kisses on the cheek. There was no sniping, though, and Fran had driven them slowly into town without a single criticism from Dora or Hannah. That was more a mark of tension than an all-out screaming match would have been.

The receptionist at Wilson, Perry & Curwen wore a spotless white blouse, without a name badge, and said, 'Good morning,' instead of 'Hiya!' when they arrived. She welcomed them into the waiting room in polite, hushed tones and brought a tray of filter coffee and individually wrapped shortbread biscuits, which now sat untouched on the occasional table in front of them, along with the current edition of *Cumbria Life* and, appropriately enough, a fan of leaflets about making a will.

'How kind,' said Dora, as the girl put the tray down. 'Thank you so much.'

Fran muttered something to herself about ladies of the manor and pulled irritably at her collar.

Each wore their own interpretation of a sober reading-of-the-will outfit: Dora had dressed in her best tweed suit and three-strand pearl necklace, Fran wore her Crown Court Windsmoor trouser suit with an uneasy splash of plum lipstick, and Hannah, who had been staying at Fiammetta's for the past two days, had borrowed a silk jumper and a pair of black bootcut trousers; Fiammetta had blow-dried her hair so it swung round her face, a convenient shield.

Dora raised an eyebrow at Fran's chuntering, but said only, 'Frances, please don't.'

In the calm of a sunny winter morning, Hannah wondered exactly what had been discussed after she had left Fran and Dora yelling at each other in the shadowy sewing room. They must have had a soap-opera list of grievances to hurl. She got the feeling now, though, that the storm had blown out, and they were left with the wreckage of their anger, trying to piece together their relationship from what was left, testing which old patterns no longer fitted. Most of their snapping was habitual and, Hannah supposed, comforting.

She hadn't been home since she had arrived on Fiammetta's doorstep that night. Fiammetta had phoned in sick the next morning, and they'd spent a day and a night just talking and talking, touching each other's faces and smiling crazily at nothing. It felt like waking up on holiday. Hannah smiled now, thinking about it.

'Coffee, darling?' said Dora, lifting the jug. 'I assume you've had some breakfast?'

Hannah didn't take the 'darling' to mean anything had changed in Dora's attitude to her relationship with Fiammetta. But that didn't matter so much to her now. In fact, it barely mattered at all.

Before she could reply, Mr Curwen, the senior partner, appeared at the door of his office. He seemed to recognize Fran straight away, and smiled at her. 'Hello, Mrs Marshall,' he said, and got a wintry smile from both Fran and Dora for his trouble.

It was entirely appropriate, thought Hannah, that Constance and Louise's solicitor should look as if he came straight from country-lawyer Central Casting; anyone less than Robert Hardy would not have done justice to the occasion. Mr Curwen was stout and wore a dark three-piece suit with a green-spotted handkerchief in the breast pocket. Hannah hoped he would mop his brow with it at some point or use it to polish his spectacles.

'Would you like to come through?' he asked. 'Caroline, be so kind as to take my calls.'

Dora, Fran and Hannah trooped into the book-lined office and sat in a line with their knees together opposite his desk.

'Now, I have here Mrs Graham-Potter's will,' said Mr Curwen. He sat down and smoothed his pile of legal papers portentously. 'And also the will of Miss Constance Musgrave, as the two are somewhat interlinked.' He paused, to give this revelation due weight.

Hannah raised her eyebrows. She felt it might be expected at this juncture. Dora and Fran made no outward sign. If Fran had realized how much her own expression resembled Dora's imperious patience, she would have been horrified.

'It is . . . somewhat irregular,' he went on, as if trying to absolve his firm for any later accusations of chicanery. 'Well, anyway, I should perhaps start with Miss Musgrave's will,' he said. 'When she died in 1991, she left her entire estate to Mrs Graham-Potter, but to enjoy for her lifetime only and with the provisos that nothing belonging to the Musgrave family should be sold, given away or removed from Hillcrest Villa. After Mrs Graham-Potter's death, we were instructed to open a letter she lodged with us, which would cover the further disposal of her estate, in a secret trust.'

He handed Dora a silver letter-opener and a small crested envelope, sealed on the back with red wax.

'Goodness me,' said Dora mildly. 'How mysterious. I feel as though Miss Marple should burst in now and announce that everything has been left to Mrs Tyson.'

'I must say it's not entirely agreed procedure, keeping information back like this,' said Mr Curwen, as Dora slit the envelope, 'but Miss Musgrave was most specific about her affairs. As long as the trustee is aware of the subsequent beneficiaries, it's perfectly legal.'

'She did read a lot of Agatha Christie novels,' observed Fran.

Mr Curwen leaned back a little in his chair and smiled benevolently at her. 'Of course, you're much too young to remember, but my father often used to talk about the wonderful parties the Misses Musgrave held up at Hillcrest, all the marvellous wine they served, and the most interesting guests—'

He was interrupted by a cackle of laughter from Dora.

'What?' said Fran impatiently.

Dora waved her away. 'I'm reading.'

'Well, can't you read it aloud?'

'Certainly not. This isn't a playgroup.'

Fran, Hannah and Mr Curwen sat and waited while Dora's eyes skimmed across the lines of cursive script, occasionally pausing to blink with surprise.

The large ormolu clock on the fireplace ticked, then chimed the half-hour.

'Well,' said Dora, eventually. 'Fancy that.' She handed the two pages back across the desk. 'Perhaps you ought to read it aloud, Mr Curwen. I don't think Frances will believe that I'm not making it all up.'

'As you wish.' Mr Curwen coughed discreetly. 'Unless Ms Marshall would like to?'

Fran shook her head. 'Well, unless she *has* left everything to Mrs Tyson.'

'Don't worry, darling,' said Dora. 'Although that would have been a splendid test of your social sensibilities, wouldn't it?'

Ouch, thought Hannah, then wondered if Constance might not have done something like that. It was quite possible that the whole lot had been left to charity, and that they would get nothing at all.

Mr Curwen adjusted his glasses. '"To whom it may concern."'

'Personal as ever,' said Fran.

'Do be quiet, Frances,' said Dora, in her most charming tone.

Mr Curwen looked briefly discomfited, then continued, '"I am writing this letter and placing it in the care of my solicitors, who are also the executors of my estate, in order to ensure certain information will be passed on after my death,"' he read. '"While I have always appreciated the delicacy of Dora's refusal to hear certain facts about her origins in my lifetime, I do not think that such delicacy should apply after Faith and I are both long gone, and it should certainly not stand in the way of her enjoyment of what is rightfully hers."'

Fran looked at Dora pointedly.

'Well, the certain facts have been passed on,' said Dora. 'So I think you can put that bee out of your bonnet once and for all.' She turned back to the solicitor. 'Mr Curwen's discretion goes without saying, does it not? Please do carry on.'

'I am a solicitor, Mum,' said Fran, through gritted teeth.

'I know, darling,' said Dora, and patted her knee.

Fran looked as if she was about to say something, but reined herself in with a visible effort.

Mr Curwen picked up his place in the letter and cleared his throat again.

Hannah wondered if coughing was the little-heard male equivalent of the critical Linton sniff so beloved of the book group.

'"I trust that Louise Graham-Potter has enjoyed long and happy years in the villa where, latterly, we were all most content. It may have seemed unfair that she should appear to be my sole beneficiary, and I expect there were many unkind comments made about her right to be there, but those who knew her and who knew me would understand that Louise's companionship and devoted friendship deserved proper acknowledgement, and this seemed to me an appropriate measure of the great regard and fondness I had for her.'"

As Mr Curwen read Constance's words aloud in his brisk Linton accent, Hannah could hear the kindness in them: leaving Louise the villa for her lifetime was a gentle courtesy, Constance's way of showing that she valued Louise as family after the years they had spent together. It also revealed, rather airily, that Louise had little of her own, beyond what the Musgraves had lent her by association – good or bad. Where would she have gone if she hadn't been allowed to live there? Regardless of what their true relationship had been, Louise Graham-Potter had spent her whole life surrounded by Constance's family, in reality and in shadows; she had shared the burden of Constance's secrets and nightmares, all the time knowing that the price was that she'd always be judged a hanger-on.

Hannah wished that Constance's sloping handwriting would reveal what Louise's real reward for this had been, what secrets they had shared, but she knew it wouldn't. Now they would never know exactly what kind of love had run through their relationship for fifty years. Maybe that had been the point of leaving Louise secure in the house for her lifetime: how would anyone else know to be kind to Louise if they had no idea what they were to be kind *for*?

"'I wish to bequeath the financial part of my estate – the stocks and shares, bank accounts and so on, as detailed in the attached notes – to my daughter, Dora Marshall, and I pray she is still able to enjoy her legacy on the occasion of this will reading. With her grip on life, I cannot imagine that she will not be. Should Dora predecease Louise however, then her daughter, Frances Marshall Kirk is to inherit in full.'"

Mr Curwen looked up. 'We're still establishing the extent of Miss Musgrave's estate, since she had a significant portfolio of investments and trusts, here and overseas, but I can tell you it runs into quite substantial figures. She was shrewd enough to make offshore provision to cover death duties and seems to have had excellent financial guidance. There's a sizeable yearly income alone, without taking the value of the investments into consideration.'

Hannah wasn't surprised by that. There must have been a fortune running through the family over the generations, and parties and shoes aside, the sisters had lived a frugal life, considering. She could quite imagine Samuel Musgrave protecting his money – with a consideration he hadn't shown his children.

Mr Curwen was rushing through the list, now he was safely out of any emotional outpourings and into the safer waters of specific bequests. "'I bequeath the gardener's cottage to Dora, since it is the house in which I think she was most happy, and –'"

Fran drew in a surprised breath. 'But what about the villa?'

Dora held up a hand. 'Wait.'

"'– I also leave her my jewellery, which is held in a strong room specified in the documents attached, and the collection of Matthew Fisher paintings, currently stored in the sewing room at Hillcrest. Legacy is not merely a matter of apportioning money and jewellery, and therefore my intention is to leave her only happy and fortunate items.'"

'So who has to deal with all the unhappy and unfortunate ones?' demanded Fran. 'Me, I suppose.'

'I bequeath thirty-six Eagle Wharf Street, London E1, to Frances Marshall Kirk . . .'

Eagle Wharf Street, thought Hannah. Where had she heard that?

Fran's piqued expression slipped to one of confusion. 'What?' she said. 'Hang on a minute, I don't think that's right.'

'That's what it says here.'

'But their house in London was in Knightsbridge,' said Fran. 'Wasn't it?'

She turned to Hannah, who nodded, then shook her head. 'Well, it was,' she said. 'But I thought it was sold.'

'It *was* sold, in 1960,' agreed Dora.

'So what's this one? Don't tell me they were slum landlords too.'

'Darling,' said Dora, 'normally we wait until the will is read before contesting it. Are you going to let the nice man read this letter or not?'

'Please don't talk to me like that, Mother.'

Eagle Wharf Street, thought Hannah. It was one of the things Mavis Todhunter had pulled out of the air at the spiritualist meeting.

Mr Curwen cut in. 'It would seem,' he said, 'from various documents passed to us from Miss Musgrave's London lawyers,

that thirty-six Eagle Wharf Street has been in the possession of the
family since 1880. It formed part of the dowry of Ellen, Lady
Musgrave, and was, er . . .' He searched delicately for words.
'. . . involved in the production of cotton garments.'

'So it was a sweatshop,' said Fran, flatly. 'I might have guessed.
I don't want it.'

'Now, wait . . .' said Dora, a smile playing at the corner of her
mouth.

Mr Curwen slid an A4 file over the desk to Fran. 'It hasn't been
used for manufacturing purposes for many years. Since 1968, at the
initial instigation of Faith Musgrave, the house has been run as a
private charity for, er, victims of domestic violence.' He consulted
his notes. 'There is a sizeable income from investments following
the sale of the Knightsbridge house, and a portion of that has been
used to finance the day-to-day costs of the refuge. As I understand
it, the venture has been running itself for the past decade, with no
intervention from Mrs Graham-Potter.'

Cautiously, Fran opened the file and began to read the
correspondence. Hannah could see legal letterheads, reports, some
handwritten notes, the occasional photograph and report.

'I understand several members of staff are housed within the
building, and an average of ten or so residents at any time. Miss
Musgrave was the patron, and, until a few years before her death,
quite active in its administration. The money held in trust runs into
several hundreds of thousands.'

He looked up. 'The house alone is worth a great deal in today's
market. Very generous, don't you think, to allow someone else to
have the use of it for nothing?'

'Very.' Fran looked stunned. 'And why this has been left to me?'

'If I may . . .' Mr Curwen coughed discreetly and returned to
Constance's letter. '"I bequeath thirty-six Eagle Wharf Street to
Frances Marshall Kirk, to carry on the administration of the charity

or to sell as she wishes. Faith and I always held that true charity is that which goes on unseen, and offers aid to the very suffering that one best understands oneself. Eagle Wharf Street has helped many unfortunate women escape abusive situations and start afresh, and I hope will continue to do so, at least for the remainder of the lease agreed to the charity committee. I am sure Frances could put her considerable talents to good use in assisting these women; however, she is perfectly free to sell it when the lease expires at the end of 2020.'"

'No pressure there, then,' said Hannah lightly.

'They built a women's refuge and never even mentioned it to anyone?' Fran murmured. 'That's . . .'

Hannah hadn't seen her mother so taken aback. It suited her. But what about the villa? she wondered. Was that to be handed over to charity too? Maybe the point of her going though everything in it was so that what was there could be sold and the villa turned into a residential home for retired painters, or miners, or something. Constance seemed to have been determined to make amends for her family as dramatically as she could.

Mr Curwen peered at her over his glasses. 'Finally, I bequeath Hillcrest equally to Hannah and Dominic Marshall.'

Hannah's jaw dropped. 'No . . .'

Dora smiled and patted Hannah's knee.

'"The house holds too many memories for both Dora and Frances for such a bequest to be welcome to either. Hannah and Dominic, however, will make something fresh of it. Watching them playing in the garden as children was one of my great joys – whatever they decide to do with Hillcrest is entirely their decision. It is, after all, their family home. However, as with Eagle Wharf Street, I would not be unhappy if they should decide that selling the house would be the family's best gift to their future. I have attached a list concerning the disposal of specific items of furniture. I should like Dominic to have the first editions in Faith's library, as I am sure he will appreciate them. I should like Hannah to have Matthew Fisher's sketches of Dora as a child, for the same reason.'"

I own the villa, thought Hannah, in shock. It's mine. It's been mine as long as that envelope's been waiting in the vault. And Louise Graham-Potter must have known that. She must have known all the time I was giving her those lists of auction prices, all the time Dora was sitting taking tea with her in the drawing room. And *still* she had tried to make Hannah sell the paintings to protect her friend's reputation . . .

'Granny,' she said suddenly, turning to Dora, 'that's not right, it shouldn't be me.'

'No,' said Dora. 'It is right. Constance was right – there are too many memories there for me and for your mother. You can do something fresh with the place. The money's there to maintain it – it's not such a white elephant. You can paint again, or set up some kind of archiving business.'

'If she wants to stay here,' added Fran, darkly.

If I stay. Hannah bit her lip. *If I stay*. She could travel a long way, and for a long time, just on the proceeds of one or two discreet picture sales.

'There are some smaller individual bequests,' added Mr Curwen. 'Ten thousand pounds and the silver tea service to Mrs Irma Tyson. Ten thousand pounds and the deeds to the Rookery, Etterthwaite Road to Miss Betty Fisher. Three fur coats to the Linton Amateur Dramatic Society, care of Mrs Judy Hind. Three thousand pounds to Linton Municipal Library to be spent on . . .' He peered closely at the paper. '. . . talking books for the blind. And three thousand pounds to Linton Town Council to have some cherry trees planted in the churchyard.'

There was another pause.

'With commemorative plaques attached?' asked Hannah.

'Er, yes, now you mention it, there is that proviso.'

Fran leaned forward and brought the conversation round to various legal niceties. Hannah leaned back in her chair and tried to understand what this meant. All she could think was that she needn't feel guilty any more about wanting to be in Linton. She owned a house here. She was a resident.

And Dominic. It was almost strange hearing his name caught up in this string of mothers and daughters. Of course Constance would split any inheritance between them: she and Dominic were her great-grandchildren. Hannah's heart softened as she imagined Constance watching them from her wing chair, swinging off the trees, running around her garden, maybe with a freedom she had never enjoyed with her own brothers. She felt guilty now for the times they had joked about the spooky old women in the house, and not gone in with Fran when she had called for tea. Perhaps this was Constance's way of bringing back the splinters of her family – offering a future for Dominic in Linton. Whether he'd leave New York or not, Hannah didn't know.

Dominic and Fiammetta. The two influences on the shaping of her childhood and adolescence, pulling and twisting her like molten glass into the woman she was now. Perhaps she had to lose one in order to love the other. Maybe, now she was strong enough, she could have them both again.

A little thrill ran up her spine at the novelty of thinking about Fiammetta without the dulling layer of guilt, and she felt impatient to be out of the office and into her new life.

'It's signed and witnessed by both Mrs Musgrave and Mrs Graham-Potter.' He held up the page. 'It's somewhat unusual – Miss Musgrave had only Mrs Graham-Potter's word that she would protect the estate in her lifetime. You might call it an act of real trust, as much as a legal trust.'

Very Constance, thought Hannah. But with a touch of Faith, in the hidden test.

'Is that everything?' she whispered to Dora. 'Do we have to sign anything?'

'Your mother is dealing with that, darling,' said Dora. She also looked eager to leave. 'I'm sure we don't have to sit and supervise her. Perhaps we should leave her to it?'

Dora rose, but Mr Curwen coughed.

'There is also the matter of Mrs Graham-Potter's will,' he said apologetically.

Dora lowered herself back to the chair. 'But surely that's covered by Constance's letter?'

'She would have had some property of her own,' said Hannah, with a mild look of reproach.

Dora crossed her legs.

'It won't take a moment – her bequests are really very straightforward,' said Mr Curwen. 'She leaves five hundred pounds to Sophia Rissini, her hairdresser, a hundred pounds to Mrs Irma Tyson, and a thousand pounds care of Mrs Jackson to provide magazine subscriptions to the residential home.' He looked up. 'She has specified *Vogue*, *Tatler* and *Harpers & Queen*, but that may not be legally binding.'

A wicked smile touched the corner of Dora's mouth.

'She asks that you look after the cats between you,' he added. 'How you want to arrange that is really up to you.'

'You can have them,' said Fran shortly. 'I'm allergic to cats.'

'There is a specific photograph in a frame on her dressing-table, which is to be given to Frances Marshall Kirk, and her own personal photograph albums are to be given to Hannah Marshall Kirk. The remainder of the money in her accounts is to go to set up a scholarship fund for students of Linton School wishing to attend Cambridge University, "so that they can be encouraged to broaden their horizons as she did and not feel obliged to aim low in their academic standards." I'm quoting there,' he added quickly. 'It's not a personal comment. I don't think we're talking about a massive bequest.'

'Very good,' said Dora. 'And how *generous* of her! I can't wait to tell Mrs Tyson.'

Hannah thought it was sad, how little Louise had of her own to bequeath. Still, she'd organized what little she had to maximum effect, and, best of all, she had managed to take her own secrets with her. There was nothing in there for gossips to pull apart and judge over tea and scones in the café, which was a little triumph in itself, she supposed. Even Faith and Constance had had to let their secrets slip out, their hands forced by Matthew Fisher's paintings, and the house, all of which demanded their privacy come second to settling their inheritances.

They left the oak-panelled solicitors' offices and stepped into the bright sunshine that flooded Corsica Street.

'Stay there and I'll get the car,' said Fran. Her mood had subtly transformed from the earlier snappishness. She seemed lighter and more positive, her mind working on a different level.

'Do you think she'll go to London,' asked Hannah, when Fran was out of earshot, 'and work for this charity?'

'I don't see why not,' said Dora. She took out her gold compact and discreetly powdered her nose. 'She wouldn't have to do it full-time. And she needs something new in her life – I've said so for years. She'll go through that place like a dose of salts. I'd lay money that's what she was sickening for, something new to do.'

If only it were that easy. Hannah thought of her mother's miserable round of tests and examinations. Maybe now that she knew where she'd come from she'd settle for the mundane explanations the doctors had offered. Work stress. The menopause. General weariness.

Although Ellen's 'delicacy' and serial spa visits didn't seem to bode well for her, while Betty Fisher's wanderings . . . And that was without even thinking about Dora's blend of genes . . .

'*Were* you most happy in the cottage, Granny?' she asked, to stop herself thinking about the possibilities trickling through her own veins.

'Yes, I was,' said Dora. 'I loved the cottage when Matthew was there and I was little, and I love it now. I never liked Rose View – it was too big, too critical of all the things I hadn't lived up to. Those endless bedrooms I couldn't fill with children. I certainly never wanted to tackle the villa, if that's what you're getting at. Oooh, no.'

She shuddered as a stiff breeze lifted the trailing fronds of her scarf into her pale face. She brushed them away. 'No, my happiest memories are of being a little girl in Matthew's cottage. Falling asleep in Faith's arms on the big bed, listening to Matthew reading to me.' She smiled. 'He read beautifully, that big man. He'd do all the voices. I felt so safe there. Like I had a proper family, even though, of course, it wasn't.'

'You *knew* that sketch in your loo was of Faith, didn't you?'

Dora smiled. 'Of course I did, but one has to be discreet. Matthew was the most discreet of all of us.'

Poor Constance, thought Hannah. Was Faith compensating for a mother-love Constance couldn't dredge up, or did Faith annex Dora, as she did everything else, to finish off her own secret family? Hannah looked at her grandmother, and knew she would never know the labyrinthine twists of her mind, and the shades and secrets she held in there. It didn't matter, as long as she had unknowable twists of her own.

Dora squeezed Hannah's arm. 'I agree with Constance. It's right that you have the villa. You have no expectations of it, no fears. What will you do with it?'

'I don't know,' admitted Hannah. 'It's too big to live in. Maybe turn it into a civic museum for all those Matthew Fisher paintings? The industrial ones,' she added quickly. 'Not the nudes. I'd like to keep them all together, and maybe set them in a historical context. I don't know. I'll have to talk to Dom.'

'You don't plan on filling it with children?' Dora gave her a hopeful look. 'Lots of bedrooms for nurseries.'

'No,' said Hannah firmly. 'I don't think that's going to happen.'

There was a pause.

'Not yet, maybe?' suggested Dora.

'Granny, not ever.'

With uncharacteristically deft timing, Fran drew up next to them before either could speak again, and Hannah opened the car door for her grandmother.

From the moment they walked through the back door Hannah sensed a change in the villa. It felt empty. 'Who would like a cup of tea?' she asked.

She wasn't sure why they'd come to Hillcrest rather than Rose View, but they were here now, in the kitchen where the cats were circling their empty china dishes and making aggrieved mewing noises.

'Those poor cats,' said Dora absently. 'They'll be half starved.'

'I imagine they're supplementing their diet with takeaways from the garden,' said Fran drily. 'I'd love a cup of tea, thank you, Hannah.'

'Fine. Go and sit down and I'll bring it.'

Fran looked as if she was about to say something, then closed her mouth and walked out of the room. Dora chucked one of the cats under the chin, and followed Fran.

Hannah found the teapot and some cups, not the mugs she and Mrs Tyson used. As she moved from cupboard to kitchen table across the stone flags, she tried to stop the fluttering in her stomach. This was hers. Her pine table, her cups, her view from the window down into the wild garden.

Her garden, in fact. And everything in it – trees, roses, honeysuckle bowers, ghosts, voices . . .

The kettle boiled and she made the tea, then loaded the tray.

As Hannah walked past the huddle of dusty astrakhan coats hanging on the hooks in the hall, she hesitated for a moment. Then she put down the tray on the sideboard, returned to the kitchen for bin bags, and bundled the coats into them. They filled three bags.

Immediately the hall seemed lighter and brighter, and the sun glimmered in the speckled mirror.

Hannah smiled, picked up the tea-things and went into the drawing room.

She paused at the door. Dora and Fran were sitting in the wing chairs, having an animated conversation about Dominic's return from America. She had called him the day after Mrs Graham-Porter died, and he had agreed to come over just as soon as he filed his latest overdue copy. The wide leather arms were perfectly designed for Fran's drumming fingers and Dora's languid elbows. They two looked as if they'd always sat there.

'There's no reason why he can't write from here,' said Dora. 'I am aware of the Internet. You don't have to be in one place, these days. He could work from home again.'

'But, Mum, why would he want to? It's so typical of the Musgraves,' said Fran, albeit with half as much of her usual bile. 'They give with one hand and take away with the other. Why would two young people want to be saddled with a place like this? At their ages?'

'You can't ramble around without responsibility for ever,' said Dora, and saw Hannah at the door. 'Ah, darling, come in.'

Hannah settled the tray and took the final chair at the empty fireplace. Faith's chair. 'Is that the picture?' she asked, seeing a silver frame on Fran's knee.

Fran gave her a twisted smile and passed it to her.

It was a small black-and-white photograph, hand-coloured in supernatural pastel shades, taken in the garden by the honeysuckle arch. Constance sat on the garden seat in a chic tailored two-piece, her blonde hair tucked into a turban, white-gloved hands folded on her lap. Dora sat next to her, slim and beautiful in a flowery tea-dress, holding a round-faced baby swaddled in a frothy lace dress and sun-hat. Her long legs stretched out lazily across the grass, in contrast to Constance's knees-together pose. But their eyes were trained on someone to the right of the camera – something had made them both laugh. The family resemblance was striking, not in the eyes but in the wide, unselfconscious smiles lighting up their faces.

Hannah wondered who the other people were, the one taking the picture and the one making Dora and Constance laugh. There was always someone else in the background, someone almost invisible, but not quite.

'It's lovely,' she said. 'This is you, isn't it?' she added, looking up at Fran.

'It is. Your grandmother burned the official version.'

Dora tutted. 'This one was nicer, anyway. I didn't know Constance had kept it – a proper photographer came, you see, to do a christening photo. This was just one Faith took while he was changing his film. I didn't know Constance had it. Matthew was in the background, you see, making Constance laugh. He was very good at that. He was about the only person who could.'

Hannah looked up from the baby Fran to the woman sitting opposite her, fiddling with her cufflinks. 'And she kept it on her dressing table all those years.'

'Evidently.' Fran took it back. Her face was saying nothing, but her eyes were glistening with tears.

The three sat and drank their tea in the silence of their own thoughts, while the birds twittered in the garden and the town rushed and bustled in the distance. It was a very companionable silence.

Chapter Twenty-nine

Hannah looked out of the window of the Coffee Pot Café at the street of tall houses opposite, four storeys of high-ceilinged rooms, the exteriors painted almond green and cream, and felt a deep calm. She couldn't say exactly why she loved the high street so much: it wasn't especially exciting or beautiful, particularly after the ever-shifting kaleidoscope of news and ideas and people she'd grown used to in London. Linton might have had an Internet café where the old shipping office used to be, but it was used mainly for booking holidays to Menorca or sourcing cheap booze.

But when the town had been in its prime, when all the world docked its goods in the Sugar Tongue, and the ships carried the name of Linton into spicy, noisy foreign harbours, the view out of the Coffee Pot window had been the same. Then, as now, Corsica Street had been at the heart of the town, as big and busy a main road as there was in the county. The green- and cream-fronted houses had been prized by successful merchants, decorated by ambitious ladies who were proud to entertain in their elegant drawing rooms, paid for by tea and tobacco. The church gardens opposite would have bloomed with the same vivid colours, and the market would have brought the same flock of gossips and housewives who came now to haggle over cheap shoes and fruit.

The dates and stone-carved wreaths on the fronts of the high-street houses had seen the town decline and fade while the rest of England grew, but the street saw the same traffic of people and business, rumour and life. The houses hadn't changed and, deep down, neither had the people who lived in them.

Maybe that's why I feel so whole here, thought Hannah. Maybe there's a tiny thread of that pride left, passed down from generation to generation. A blood memory of the dignity and dynamism that was once here, before everyone overtook us.

She looked out of the window and sipped her coffee. If she was honest, nothing struck her soul in the same way that the rows of Linton roofs did; not churches, or sad news, or beautiful paintings. When she looked out over the harbour, her heart rang like a bell until she vibrated with a sense of belonging and pride, near to tears for a loyalty she couldn't define. All the muted colours of Linton's history – the miners, sailors and iron-workers, the bustling ambitions of the port, the contradictory dignity and narrowness of the people, the resignation with which Linton had allowed its fortune to slip away – were woven into the tapestry of her past.

Hannah finished her coffee, squashed up the last few crumbs of her Kermit the Frog fondant, and walked to the harbour, where she'd arranged to meet Fiammetta. The weather had turned cold now, and she hugged her old duffel coat tightly round her.

The fishing-boats were coming in to tie up, and Hannah sat on one of the new wrought-iron benches and watched them. A large black snail was inching slowly along the metal, its silvery trail leaving a surprisingly curly track. Hannah left it to wander wherever it was going.

'That'll be a nice lunch for some seagull,' said Fiammetta, into her left ear.

Hannah jumped, then smiled as Fiammetta sat down next to her and offered her a paper cup of coffee. Hannah took it gratefully. Linton was building up her coffee addiction again nicely.

They sat close together on the bench.

'Have you decided yet?' Fiammetta asked.

'Yes,' said Hannah. She sipped her coffee. It was very hot on her tongue, and very good. Better than Starbucks. 'I talked it over with Dom and we're going to turn half the house into a museum of Matthew Fisher's paintings, and make some kind of contextual display, about miners' work and local art, that sort of thing. We don't want to sell them, but it's selfish to keep them to ourselves.' She added, diffidently, 'And I might start a business of my own, freelance estate valuations, with some family research thrown in.'

'Wonderful. And Dom's happy with that?'

Hannah nodded. 'He's coming back for a while. It's ironic, really. Mum's gone to London, to look at this refuge, Dom's coming to stay in Rose View, Dora's talking about going on a *cruise*, and I'm the one worrying about whether we'll have enough food in.'

'I hope Fran's given you a long list of things to do,' said Fiammetta, seriously.

Hannah rolled her eyes. 'And the rest.'

Fi slipped her hand under Hannah's crossed leg for warmth. 'What about you?'

'What about me?'

'Are you happy?'

Hannah leaned over and kissed Fiammetta's forehead. It was easy to be affectionate now that she didn't have to hoard every tiny touch in her memory. 'I am. Tired, but happy.'

She had spent the last few days going through all the rooms in the villa, even the ones that had been locked. She'd found Dora's old nursery, just as it had been left, with rows of little shoes and expensive old teddy bears ranged eerily along the scaled-down sleigh bed. Most rooms had little in them, apart from beds, wardrobes and empty trunks – the boys' bedrooms, she guessed.

She had left the locked bedrooms by the painting of the house until last, and fortified herself with a brandy before she took the bunch of keys up there. She had worked out that they were Samuel and Ellen's interlinked rooms, where Samuel had died and Ellen had wept, night after night, as she dissolved into her own fractured world.

Hannah had taken a deep breath before she turned the key in the lock and pushed open the first door before she could change her mind.

Both rooms had been stripped bare. No curtains, no furniture, no wallpaper, no carpets. Everything had been removed. She walked from one room to the other, her feet echoing on the bare boards, and threw open the windows to let in the sea air. The view of the harbour and the sea was magnificent, but not magnificent enough for Faith and Constance to bring themselves to sleep where their hated father had woken every morning.

I can, though, she had thought. And I will.

Fiammetta's tickling hand drew her back to the present. 'I want to go away for a while,' said Hannah. 'I'd like you to come with me, if you want to.'

Fiammetta pretended to think, then grinned. 'OK. Where?'

'I don't know. I'd like to travel for a bit. I found an old itinerary in the library of the tour that old Joseph Musgrave made with Isabella when they got married. Massachusetts, New York, then down to Carolina, Virginia – Linton had trade links or cotton interests there, I suppose.'

'Nice working honeymoon. Did he make her take notes?'

Hannah pulled a face. 'Don't. Anyway, we can stay in Dom's flat for a while, then just drive. Sleep in motels, eat pancakes.'

'Sounds fabulous,' said Fiammetta. 'Then what – when we have to come back to Linton?'

'Who knows?' Hannah leaned her head into the hollow of Fiammetta's neck, and breathed in happily. She smelt of shampoo. 'Let's just leave it and see what happens.'

She looked out to sea, at the gulls swooping and diving after the fishing boats, solid white against the shimmering blue of the sky. Hannah knew she didn't have to leave or stay to find what she was looking for. Linton would always be the same, and, deep in her heart, deeper than the mines that ran below the waves, so would she.

Acknowledgements

Linton is inspired by, but not based on, the ports of Whitehaven and Workington, on the west coast of Cumbria. Like Linton, Whitehaven made its money from coal and foreign trade, and boasts spectacular floral displays; unlike Linton, regeneration is slowly returning the town centre and harbour to an area of Georgian elegance, as the town reclaims its history. The mine seams snaking out for miles under the sea are real, but all other details, places and especially people, are fictitious.

I'd like to thank Julien Allen for his patient legal guidance (any errors are mine, not his), and the Westminster Café on Lowther Street, Whitehaven, for letting me sit and work for hours with cappuccinos and toast. Their waitresses are charm personified. I'd also like to thank Liz Farrer Hair Shop for many entertaining hours of hairdressing; my hair is no longer falling out, thank you, Liz.

Finally, I'd like to thank my own mother, in whom there is *no* trace of Fran or Dora, for her wit, her insights and wonderful company; and my father, for sharing his love of the fells, the mines, the sea, the lakes. Wild horses couldn't keep me from going home.

POCKET
BOOKS

Also by Victoria Routledge
. . . And for Starters

Iona knows her friends very well. A little too well.
There isn't a single crush, grudge or secret she doesn't
know about. And given a free hand, she would like to
slap the lot of them.

There's Tamara, who's spent more time on the single's
chart than 'Mull of Kintyre'; Ned, brilliant chef,
professional time-waster; Angus, Iona's workaholic
boyfriend; and Jim, the only property developer in
London who still does the office coffee run.

And Iona? Living with Angus, with their own luxury
sofa and a subscription to Private Eye, the only
qualification she doesn't have is a driving licence. But
maybe that's the problem.

Perhaps learning to drive and running a restaurant –
team efforts both – will provide excitement, that great
Elastoplast for problems. But as Iona's finding out,
you can't make an omelette without breaking eggs . . .

ISBN 0 7434 1518 3
PRICE £5.99

POCKET
BOOKS

Also by Victoria Routledge
Swansong

Patrick, Robert, Greg and Barney Mulligan have little
in common apart from their mother Rosetta's dark
brown eyes, a certain bloody-mindedness, and the
kind of mutual suspicion which only flourishes
successfully in larger families. In fact, the sole thing
they agree on is that mild-mannered Brian, logistics
manager turned global tour co-ordinator, cannot
possibly be their father. And that there is nothing
glamorous about a tour-bus toilet.

Rosetta was not a conventional mother – 'Mum' being
a banned word, for a start – and for twenty years, she
has resisted tempting offers to write about her life on
the road. But with Barney, her adored last chick, about
to be shoved from the nest, and newly married Brian
on the verge of mid-life fatherhood with his Swiss
masseuse wife, the time seems right to parcel up her
past and move on. The trouble is, how much of it will
be news to her boys?

ISBN 0 7434 1519 1
PRICE £6.99

**POCKET
BOOKS**

This book and other **Pocket** titles are available from your bookshop or can be
ordered direct from the publisher.

0 7434 1520 5	**Constance & Faith**	**Victoria Routledge**	£6.99
0 7434 1519 1	**Swansong**	**Victoria Routledge**	£6.99
0 7434 1518 3	**. . . And for Starters**	**Victoria Routledge**	£5.99
0 7434 9221 8	**Skin Deep**	**Catherine Barry**	£6.99
0 7434 8950 0	**The Dog Walker**	**Leslie Schnur**	£6.99
0 7434 6884 8	**Red Letter Day**	**Colette Caddle**	£6.99

Please send cheque or postal order for the value of the book, **free postage and
packing within the UK**.

OR: Please debit this amount from my VISA/ACCESS/MASTERCARD:

CARD NO: . . . .

EXPIRY DATE: . . . .

AMOUNT: £ . . . .

NAME: . . . .

ADDRESS: . . . .

. . . .

SIGNATURE: . . . .

Send orders to SIMON & SCHUSTER CASH SALES
PO Box 29, Douglas Isle of Man, IM99 1BQ
Tel: 01624 677237, Fax: 01624 670923
Email: bookshop@enterprise.net
www.bookpost.co.uk

Please allow 14 days for delivery. Prices and availability subject to change
without notice